About the Author

S M Rush was born and raised in Lincolnshire where she lives with her partner and her second love – motorcycles.

As a journalist, she wrote her first feature in 1997, best known for writing features for women's glossies, also for her profiles on sports personalities and celebrities from stage, screen and television.

Blast from the Past is her first action-packed military fiction novel.

S M Rush

Blast from the Past

Olympia Publishers
London

www.olympiapublishers.com

OLYMPIA PAPERBACK EDITION

A CIP catalogue record for this title is
available from the British Library.

ISBN: 978-1-78830-508-2

This is a work of fiction.
Names, characters, places and incidents originate from the writer's imagination.
Any resemblance to actual persons, living or dead,
is purely coincidental.

First Published in 2020

Olympia Publishers
Tallis House
2 Tallis Street
London
EC4Y 0AB

Printed in Great Britain

Dedication

Special thank you to all the military personnel, veterans and families who found their voices to share their memories, experiences and humorous antics.
This book would not have been possible without you.

Acknowledgements

In support of the work of, and in dedication to our armed forces, I will be donating a gift from the sales of the book to each of the charities mentioned below

COMBAT STRESS

(ABF) THE SOLDIER'S CHARITY

I hope this donation will go towards the continued support and well-being of our veterans and serving personnel.

***

*Since 2001, the British Forces' death toll in Afghanistan exceeds that of the Falklands War (April–June 1982) that claimed the lives of the **255 British servicemen** during the ten weeks of fighting.*

***

*In recognition of the **456 members** (known to date) **of British Army, Territorial Army (TA), Navy, RAF, Marines, and Special Forces** service personnel who have lost their lives in the fight against the Taliban since the Afghanistan conflict began.*

*And the thousands of British Forces men and women **Wounded in Action**. And to the many who continue to battle with Post-Traumatic Stress Disorder **(PTSD)**.*

Preface

Words from the author

Blast from the Past — first came to me when talking with forces' wives and veterans about life in the military and how it has changed over the years. I was fascinated by their stories and experiences. When I heard of some of the selfless acts of courage, bravery and honour in the most adverse conditions, this showed me that these groups of soldiers are a credit to this country.

As an idea for a book formed in my head, I began to seek information on what Afghanistan was actually like for the troops deployed there. Some were reluctant to discuss anything about what happened to them, at first guarded by traumatic events. Others were a little more forthcoming and had some astonishing stories to tell, and shared their experiences, and sometimes humorous escapades. For the first time, I heard of life-changing mental health problems that became agonisingly real.

I want to show that not only does deployment affect the service personnel, but it also has a significant impact on the family and friends they leave behind. Also, the trauma of those who have mental health issues can be life-shattering. Rebuilding lives from being wounded, or as an amputee, and those who have PTSD, takes great strength. Some of the severe cases of mental health issues can often result in death, self-harming or committing a serious crime, and this story shows what can happen when mental health is ignored.

The journey of this book led me on a road of self-discovery and understanding. While talking to the families, the courageous acts of selflessness in them touched me greatly, particularly those who came through the bitter heartbreak of losing someone, either serving overseas or suffering from mental health issues that have resulted in veteran suicides. For the first time, I got a sense of what a close family bond military personnel share, and the difficulty of the transition when becoming a civilian and the feeling of abandonment by the country they served during a crisis.

From the beginning, this book has been painstaking, intensive and extensively researched for four years. It has taken not just considerable time and effort, but also a great deal of patience. Including a willingness to listen to the veterans and families as they were instrumental in the writing of the book. It was listening to these unique stories, experiences and funny antics that revealed the actual characters that made this story so necessary to be told. I feel humbled by the fact that the characters in the book trusted me to portray the events in a real and transparent manner. Why did I write this book? I wanted to give an insight as to what it was actually like for the British troops and families in a war zone, without judgement and prejudice.

Blast from the Past is a fictional book inspired by actual events as told by some of those who served in Afghanistan and have a story to tell. **Disclosure**: *Names, dates, locations and sequence of events included has no bearing on any of the characters mentioned.*

S M Rush (2019)

Prologue

The continual ringing had woken him with a start, grabbing the mobile phone he always kept close by.

Still half-asleep, Kieran groaned at the sound waking him. The clock on his nightstand showed one-thirty in the morning. Also, judging by the persistent ring-tone, the caller wasn't giving up easily. With a groan, he flicked on the phone before saying, "Hello?"

"O'Neill? We've located her — Sophie Tyson."

He couldn't help it; he sucked in a deep breath at the very sound of that name which sent a spontaneous response as he felt the blood drain from every part of his being, leaving him feeling icy cold and shaken to the core.

Disoriented and unable to see through the darkness in his bedroom, he bolted upright and fumbled to lighten the darkened room. Too shocked to respond, he exhaled slowly and waited.

"Did you hear me? It's Captain Henry Rawlins."

Captain Henry Rawlins — his commanding officer? He cleared his painfully dry throat and said the only thing that made sense. "How did you find her?"

"You would be surprised how resourceful the MOD can be when we put our minds to it." His attempt to make light of the situation did nothing to relieve his overstretched nerves, especially considering the lateness of the call.

It had been a decade since he had heard of *Sophie Tyson*. His instant response was that of gut-wrenching pain as he felt his fingernails dig into the fabric of his quilt. His jaw tightened, and he felt as if he might fall apart at the very sound of this woman's name. The one thing he wanted to know right now was — "Where is she?"

"I have people looking into the details. Intel has revealed she's been living low key under another name but —" he heaved a heavy sigh, "right now — we have bigger problems." Sucking in his breath, he continued,

"A group of terrorists has infiltrated a guarded compound that housed a significant number of high-ranking Taliban leaders. They were being held in detention awaiting prosecution for committing acts of terrorism. Mohammad Yasin was among those that escaped, and he's put a price on our key witness's head."

"What am I supposed to do about that?"

"You're going to have to cancel whatever plans you have. I need you."

"Why?" This two-bedroom house had been his sanctuary for years. He'd spent much of his life living on bases between missions; when he'd bought that house, it was his way of escaping a hectic military lifestyle, and he wasn't about to just give up his well-earned leave on one of Rawlins' whims. "There are other units as capable."

"Not without major upheaval."

"Been done before."

"Come on — all I need from you is a few days of your time."

"Heard that before."

"Don't worry — we have a plan of action. Our witness has agreed to assist us if we agree to the anonymity terms. Trust me — this witness knows how Yasin works and how he thinks. What do you say?"

There was a silence that spoke volumes.

"The sooner this terrorist is brought to justice, the sooner you can return home and enjoy your leave. We need your help to flush this terrorist out."

He pulled at his earlobe. Rawlins made it all sound so simple of course. "You want this person to act as bait, don't you?"

"Someone on my team found out where our witness lives, they have a family and a child, located what school he attends. If the MOD found them so can the terrorists. We received photos of the family a few days ago issuing a death threat from Yasin's group. We cannot afford to think the threat is idle."

As much as he didn't want to admit it — Rawlins was right. "You said you had a plan? What is it? Will our men be safe?" He needed to know what he was heading into, and above all be prepared for the unexpected. It didn't matter how good the plan was or how prepared for the mission the men were, once the boots hit the ground things could change quickly during active duty.

"My plan — to sniff him out and catch Yasin in the act. The assigned men can protect the witness. The security would be so tight; no one would be able to get to the family without us knowing. But it isn't without risk."

"That's your plan?" O'Neill was concerned, to say the least. "It sounds more like we would be putting our guys in a dangerous situation to me."

"Desperate times call for desperate measures," he paused, "what do you say?"

"If you think we'll be safe —" he responded hesitantly.

"I give you my word," Rawlins replied earnestly.

"All right, if you think —" Taking a deep breath and conceded. "Where would I have to go?"

He heard Rawlins take a deep breath of relief. "The only way to capture this man is for him to feel untouchable on his own turf — Kabul."

Kieran almost dropped the mobile. "I feel like we'd be stepping into the lion's den and about to be served up as breakfast."

As if he sensed O'Neill's doubts he said, "Please understand, this problem is not going to be resolved easily — we have no way of protecting the witness or family 24/7 if we let things continue as they are. They need to be where we can protect them. Also, where Yasin feels he's free to make his move without suffering the consequences."

"OK." He relented. "What would I need to do?"

Triumphant in his quest. "Pack your bags. You fly to Kandahar tomorrow."

As the phone went dead, Kieran dropped his mobile on the bed.

His body grew rigid as the nervous anxiety of returning to Afghanistan engulfed him. But not for the reasons Rawlins gave him. Sure, Mohammad Yasin was a cruel and vicious monster — but he had known monsters like him before. He had been deployed to Iraq and Afghanistan more than once and seen the aftermath.

Kieran still had nightmares at some of the things he had seen and been through. With all his heart he wished he could erase those memories forever. But not all those memories were terrible or as easily forgettable.

Others — who had different memories of their time spent in Afghanistan — would strongly disagree.

15

Chapter One

April 2007

0400 hours local time, 3,554 miles from England to the northern outskirts of Helmand Province, *Naw Zad*, southern Afghanistan.

"Fuck me! It's hot here." His thoughts were confirming what he already knew as he wiped the beads of sweat from his forehead and dust from his eyes for the umpteenth time. "Even the fucking wind blowing is roasting my fucking bollocks off!"

Although it was early spring, there was no mistaking the feel of the first winds of the April morning to intensify the heat despite the hour. Another blistering hot day was about to beat down on them.

"Join the army. See the world." The recruiter had told him. He looked up with a half-grin. *"Live the adventure!"* Yep, he remembered those words well.

Through the dust and heat Private Kieran O'Neill focused on his surroundings directly ahead as he patrolled the area. The wind was lashing at his skin as if a thousand tiny needles were pricking at his already heated flesh of his tired forearms. *If the heat and sand did not get to you — the wind would.*

Based outside the DC (District Centre) of *Now Zad* (as it was known as), was a remote desert outpost, located 65 kilometres from Camp Bastion. Once a thriving, bustling town, it was now derelict and virtually abandoned. At first sight, it was like something out of an old western movie: an inhospitable ghost town filled with tumbleweed, debris and nothing but an eerie silence and the wayward wind.

On their arrival, it became an apparent concern that if the platoon came under a severe attack, or suffered any heavy surprise attacks, then the remoteness of the area made it impossible for reinforcements to get to the men – taking at least 20 minutes.

The platoon was 30 strong in total, apart from three, and they were one of the youngest to be deployed to a fully combatant area. None but the platoon sergeant and Captain Dan had previously been involved in combat. Despite this, it didn't mean they were unprepared for action.

Each of the light infantry platoons had at least three sections, A, B and C Company. Consisting of around ten men, split into three units depending on the plan of engagement, each man armed with an LSW (Light Support Weapon), two men with SA80s, two riflemen with Minimis, two rifles with UGL (Underslung Grenade Launcher), and two riflemen with SA80 5.56 mm and a 51 mm LMG (Mortar and Light Machine Gun).

Patrolling the deserted war-torn buildings and harsh, dry desert terrain of the province was Kieran's first experience of combat soldiering in the ever-present danger of Taliban or other militant attacks. Deployment in Afghanistan was a harsh contrast to the *peacekeeping* endurance training the men completed in Kenya and Canada.

Kieran felt the intense heat on his skin, he wiped the beads of sweat from his forehead that were caused by his helmet band. A mark that showed the men had been continuously walking for a couple of hours now, and without the threat of enemy engagement, but it didn't mean the enemy wasn't watching.

Being part of the timed routine *peacekeeping* foot patrols over some rough, inhospitable terrain along with the surrounding outskirts of the city and remote dry, dusty desert was part of the job. The remainder of the platoon kept a tight visual from the outpost. Their position was to keep guard and watch for any unauthorised intrusions or surprise attacks from the insurgents. Surveying the area was part of an everyday task for the men. Each patrol consisted of endless hours of walking while on patrol, often in sweltering heat, at 20 feet apart, searching bombed-out decimated buildings and hours spent minesweeping.

Two front men with military *Vallon* metal detectors (when working correctly), checking for hidden IEDs (Improvised Explosive Devices), inch by inch, walked ahead. All the while checking, searching and listening for every eerie sound and noise, and examining the uncountable remnants of looted businesses, crumbling homes and torched vehicles left wayside of the crater-marked road.

It became evident to the men that the deserted, barren town was as a result of intense fighting and bombing raids; the evidence was visible far beyond the horizon.

Unfortunately for the platoon, their location, Now Zad, sat in a bowl at the base of the mountains. The Hindu Kush mountains dominated the area; some peaked at over 7,000 metres, stretching from the south-west into the east reaching over 600 kilometres. Joined by a cluster of smaller mountains, the mountain landscape measured 960 kilometres in total, making observation difficult without a panoramic view, to say the least.

Further, the concern, on the other side of the scale, within the *Green Zone* and the opium poppy fields, were villages confirmed by intel as occupied by the Taliban and under tight control. Taliban leaders sent a warning to the government and the allied forces — making it clear — the Taliban were prepared to fight to maintain that power.

The British troops now became their prime targets. They were continuously attacked while out on patrol leaving the men exposed and vulnerable. While other insurgents would try to gain an advantage, as they would lie in wait for an opportunity to spring a surprise attack on an unsuspecting platoon.

Abandoned businesses and homes were all that remained of this once busy, thriving bazaar that had lined the entire main stretch of road through the town. A maze of mud-brick houses and compounds, and a labyrinth of narrow alleyways were now riddled with mouseholes, devastation and devoid of human life.

As the US and British governments forged a new *war on terror* and switched attention, and troops, to the threat in Iraq, the interest in Afghanistan lapsed. The Taliban quietly seized the opportunity, and increased attacks and reclaimed some areas.

Between the combined conflict of Iraq and Afghanistan, it was apparent that the British infantry troops and equipment were now spread thin on the ground.

British intel reported that the Taliban held a strict tyrannical rule over the occupied towns and the people. Between 2001 and 2006, Western-funded agencies sent staff to Now Zad to build wells and health clinics. With the destruction of terror and war — everything was now gone. A troubling change was marked throughout 2006, as the increased actions of the Taliban began to escalate and take a terrifying hold.

Distressing reports came as medics and doctors were left beaten and driven out by the insurgents. Others, such as engineers and many civilian aid workers, were claimed to have been killed by the Taliban as an example to oppose the government. The seriousness of these acts led governor Mohammad Daoud to request that the British Army send vital support aid. Military observation intel reported violent attacks had increased in the south, and numbers grew as more joined the Taliban.

A group of Taliban leaders opposed fiercely to government rule set up a tribunal to enforce their own line of punishment to show they were above government law.

Hangings and amputations were harsh punishment for those they considered enemies of the Taliban or those that dared to oppose the insurgents' rule. Taliban leaders implemented heavy taxes, men were openly attacked and beaten, and men of fighting age forced to join their forces; refusing would result in family members beaten and risking death.

Schools forced to close; teachers were beaten, driven out or killed; illiterate children roamed the streets in packs like wild dogs searching for scraps of food. Disturbing reports of people slain openly on the streets happened frequently. Brutal, senseless punishments and unmerciful unjust killings by the insurgents were at a record high.

Four men were hanged for being spies just days before the arrival of the NATO coalition forces. A mother accused of spying for the coalition forces was forced to watch her young son be killed in front of her and then she was hanged as punishment. Men were frequently attacked and stoned for not wearing beards, and women were publicly beaten for not wearing burqas. Mobile phones were banned and television sets were destroyed — punishment by death if anyone was found possessing one.

Things deteriorated further in May, when an ANP (Afghan National Police) force was attacked in Musa Qala by Taliban fighters leaving 20 police officers dead in the attack.

An American patrol was attacked close to the *Green Zone* in June, when three men out of the four-man team of Navy Seals were killed in an ambush in the mountains of Kunar province. The fourth man was rescued after missing in action for four days. The men instantly called for reinforcements at the location. As the helicopter located the ambush site, the insurgents opened fire, hitting the aircraft with an RPG (Rocket-Propelled Grenade), taking it down and destroying the MH-47 Chinook helicopter on impact. All 16 on board were killed. Eight of them were Navy Seals and the other eight were Night Stalkers Regiment US Army, 160th Special Operations Aviation Regiment (aka SOAR). The American forces responded with massive firepower by AH-64 Apache helicopter and B1-bomber.

In July, an airstrike mistakenly destroyed a mosque adjoining the base compound, which suffered profoundly, and became severely damaged, along with a large number of Taliban deaths. During an attack on the compound, fierce firefighting erupted; the insurgents had taken refuge inside, and the mosque was unidentified until it was too late.

This destructive action angered the insurgents as they raised followers to increase their attacks on the military. Taliban radio was intercepted and translated; many insurgents and other militant groups had banded together from neighbouring villages to join the fighting, confident they would drive out the troops from Sangin and would kill any captured coalition forces by sundown. Worse, anyone caught would be beheaded, videoed and the recording released on YouTube.

Although the troops were informed it was no more than propaganda, it was taken seriously all the same.

Some reluctance was met by the MOD to send additional assistance. The safety of implementing a small band of soldiers to fixed locations in such isolated terrain was a huge concern for the British military over the safety and wellbeing of the men. Eventually, the military relented and along with the 1st Battalion Grenadier Guards, C Company — a small platoon of about 30 men — was deployed. It was up to another small band of soldiers of A and B Company of 1st Royal Anglian Regiment to find out how much control the Taliban had regained and at what civilian cost.

Now, in April 2007, those soldiers had arrived. Their orders were simple. Defend and clear surrounding areas of Now Zad, Helmand province, southern Afghanistan of Taliban.

The troops were often on the move between garrisons. Keeping the patrols a secret from the Taliban, some of the infantry soldiers would need to march long distances, sometimes covering more than ten miles a day — some carrying heavy loads, up to their own body weight in equipment, supplies and emergency food rations to last each man 24 hours — in the aim to spring surprise attacks on Taliban fighters in some of the isolated parts of Afghanistan and disarm the enemy — one way or another.

Lifting his head, Kieran glanced at the sergeant to his rear.

The platoon sergeant wasn't hard to spot. Each man wears the standard combat body armour and lightweight helmet. Although Sergeant Andy Jones was wearing his protective headgear, the back of his covered shaved head with a grey bandana tied around his neck was easily visible above the rest of the men following behind.

"Fuck! Eyes alert men!" Corporal Steve *Drews* Andrews called out.

Captain Dan Hale cursed. "Wait!"

An uneasy silence settled over the men. All eyes were on the land around them.

Although Kieran couldn't spot anything, the warning sent the hairs on the back of his neck on edge. His eyes searched the area on full alert while his ears strained for every sound, trying to detect something out of the ordinary.

The British Army had trained him well, always attuned to his environment and landscapes around him; this self-built-in alarm mainly happened when he sensed a challenging assignment that would prove particularly dangerous.

"What the fuck is happening, Drews?" He called out to the front men.

"Thought I heard insurgent chatter on the radio, Jonesy." Signaller, Lance Corporal Daniel *Smithie* Smith responded from his position.

A heavily tattooed arm raised, Andy called over his headset. "Radio fucking silence!"

It was very quiet, maybe a little too quiet. And he was sure he could hear the heartbeat of the man next to him.

In two weeks of Kieran being in Helmand province, it wasn't the first time the troop had patrolled this far out from the base. But it was his. Not that he was green, after all, he'd survived 14 gruelling weeks of hard physical basic training, hadn't he. Although it was training — everything he went through was real. As a learning experience it taught him well — things happen that you don't expect.

Kieran had been 12 years old and at school when he first saw on television, and watched in horror, the Taliban attack on the World Trade Center, New York, and Military Headquarters, the Pentagon, in

Washington DC, America on September 11, 2001.

Within a month, Great Britain was called upon to support the US in the *global war on terrorism* and the fight against the Taliban in Afghanistan, along with France, Canada and a coalition of 40 other NATO countries. *Operation Herrick* was launched in 2002.

Joining the British Army, especially when he joined his father's former '*Viking*' regiment, fresh out of college, he'd felt sure he was going to *make a difference* — the recruiter had told him so. Besides that, it had been his dream to follow in his father's footsteps and be part of something bigger. Kieran believed in himself; nothing was left unchallenged or unachievable.

As a boy he'd always been impetuous when it came to his goals, and would even go so far as to say he thrived on the excitement. So it came as no surprise to his family when at 18, filled with eager anticipation at facing the unknown, he joined the army. After months of intensive training, he'd found something in Afghanistan that hadn't been evident in the beginning — that something bigger, he knew now. Family. Strength of others. Helping each of his band of brothers. Trusting the soldiers around him. Feeling protected before going into any dangerous situation.

Like so many others, he had left RAF Brize Norton on an eight-hour flight on a crowded Lockheed C-130 Hercules aircraft amongst a hundred other deployed soldiers from the Royal Anglian Regiment and Grenadier Guards. Ordered to wear full-body armour and helmet on a packed-out plane didn't make the flight any more comfortable either. The men departed on a tiring journey, that was to take a total of two weeks to reach the frontline, to get to the southern part of Afghanistan. Kandahar, (first stop) one of the 34 provinces in Afghanistan, next to Pakistan, and one of the poorest.

Three days later, one of the newest recruits in the platoon continued their next leg of the journey to Helmand Province and the working metropolis of British base — Camp Bastion, in Lashkar Gah. Built far into the desert in 2006 by 39 Engineer Regiment of the Royal Engineers to house 2,000 troops. Divided into three sections, first being for the British, followed by Camp Barber (US) and Camp Viking for Denmark troops. The isolated location chosen was to enable the military to have clear observation points of any would-be attackers and reduce risk to civilian lives.

From the moment Kieran sat crammed on the crowded helicopter, wearing his helmet and combat body armour, he became filled with the nervous excitement of the unknown as his heart began racing 100 times a minute. A sudden jolt, Kieran felt the pull of restraining chains of the Chinook helicopter as it landed; the two giant twin rotors vibrated, screamed in protest, and finally came to a grinding, whirring halt, sending up cyclones of machine-made dust clouds as the craft came slowly to a standstill on the landing strip in the Helmand District.

The American-built Chinook was known for being the primary form of shipping aircraft used by the RAF 27 Squadron helicopter fleet. Commonly known as the workhorse and most versatile aircraft of the RAF, they moved everything from service personnel and equipment to mail, the Chinook was the aircraft most able to land on makeshift landing pads of the airfield and didn't require long runways for landing. The only thing that stopped these machines flying was adverse weather such as sand storms.

During the flight it became achingly obvious that the aircraft was built for efficiency rather than comfort. Onboard comforts were lacking; there was no seating plan or comfy chairs. Whether general or private, sat shoulder to shoulder, it didn't matter; it was a case of pile onboard, find floor space, and settle in for a very cramped and one of the most uncomfortable flights Kieran had ever encountered. Kieran hoped, if he was lucky, it would be a short flight, and he didn't need to take a piss.

Finally, the slackening of the chains told him he had arrived at Camp Bastion, and nothing seemed real at that point. The thud hit the hard, compressed ground, momentarily causing a cloud of dust that circled his feet and evaporated into the air as he stepped from the aircraft. Once on the ground Kieran, taking a deep breath and immediately wishing he hadn't, dropped his 80 lb packed kitbag, crammed tight with every item necessary for his time in Afghanistan.

The first thing that was evident, and stuck to his nostrils, was the foul stench of stagnant water and human excrement. It was hard to imagine such a putrid, disgusting odour coming from such a well-trained, working military metropolis. This sickening smell caused by mixed urine and putrid water hung like a poisonous mist in the air that seemed to cling

23

to the lungs as each breath was inhaled, making it clear the smell was coming from the direction of the open cesspit of raw sewage that resembled a small lake situated at the end of the airfield.

Kieran could only assume it was likely to be waiting to be treated and dumped, most probably somewhere in the Kabul River. Mixing this with the intense heat, noise and engine fumes from the helicopters, tanks and heavy machinery, and the smell of diesel and petrol hanging heavily in the heat was enough to make the strongest stomachs retch. And just like every person on their arrival, it was the foulest stench he'd probably never forget.

But he was here now. Standing poised and ready to make his mark on the map, and eager to join his platoon. OK, a little bit cocky, but at 18 and fresh out of training, who wouldn't be? After ITC (Infantry Training Centre) the combat training at Catterick, where he did exercises dealing with amputees and severely wounded (ex-soldiers and veterans were used to simulate the casualties, locals and Afghan Army). After platoon training in Kenya, here he stood in the Helmand Province, Afghanistan. As a platoon, Kenya meant a survival course, which handled hostage situations, militant attacks, weaponry used in Afghanistan, dealing with sickness and malaria, and helping with the locals.

On the return to the UK, his orders came through, and within 24 hours, he was shipped out and deployed to southern Afghanistan, where he'd joined his platoon part of the NATO ISAF (International Security Assistance Force) to form as a headquarters and combat unit, part of the Task Force Helmand (TFH).

Operation Herrick VI was part of a plan to inject a large infusion of British infantry troops on a peacekeeping mission to occupied areas. Conducting an ongoing joint British-led forces operation with Afghan National Army troops to assist and fight for control against the Taliban in the regions dominated that posed as a serious and dangerous threat to British forces and to the local people of Afghanistan.

Kieran had been training on the firing range when his section commander called him in for a meeting and asked him if was ready to go to Afghanistan. *"Fucking hell, yes!"* was his instant thought, and was packed and ready for deployment in 24 hours. By the time the details were cleared Kieran barely had time to call his parents and tell them not to worry, and he would be in touch when he got settled.

He'd brushed the dust-covered pack, gathered his belongings, threw them into the waiting *Snatch* Land Rover and made his way to the waiting Chinook ready to transport the men to the FOB (Forward Operating Base), Now Zad. It was known to be a Taliban stronghold.

Kieran had boarded the aircraft the next morning for his final destination to the FOP (First Outpost) in the west by Chinook helicopter. Leaving the aircraft, within minutes of Kieran's arrival, he was already feeling the reaction from the intense sun on his skin as he stepped out of the helicopter and onto the ground. Taking in his surroundings, he observed the isolated location, making him feel as if he was in a giant fishbowl with all eyes on him.

"So, this was Afghanistan — home for the next six months."

Their FOP *home* was a dilapidated, fortified compound situated on the outskirts of the town, housing a single-storey brick and mud building with missing windows, sprayed with machine gun bullet holes, which resembled a poorly shaped crumpet. The sandbags and wooden frames in the *sangers* (fortified lookout posts) plugged with a large number of bullet holes only left him wondering how the sanger was still erect. Evident from the amount of debris spewed throughout, the building had suffered from an arsenal of firepower, from AK-47s to RPGs, and heavy machine guns to a crater where a mortar round had landed outside the main building blowing the windows and doors on impact.

Looking closely, there was a flicker of the original sand-coloured paint lying beneath a small bullet-riddled rabbit-warren building made of mud, straw and brick. There were some blood stains and bullet holes in interior walls too, and the building had suffered intense damage in places. The smaller rooms revealed they had formerly been used as living accommodation and animal shelter for a large family.

The first room (largest), and no doubt because it was the only room with its roof intact, became the platoon's main Ops (Operations) room and HQ (Headquarters) fitted and equipped with all the latest technology to assist the platoon with their duties. And keeping within the military rule of officers housed separately from the regular troops — it also housed their OC (Officer in Command) Major Tyler Morgan-Davies, who operated the VHF radio while patrols were carried out, and Captain

Daniel Hale who joined the men on patrol.

The two remaining outbuildings — with gaping holes in the roof and crumbling walls — were declared unfit for use. Kieran's first thought on leaving the bustling, hectic living quarters of Camp Bastion was that it was beginning to look like the Ritz Hotel. Inspection of the interior was followed by a quick guided tour of the town perimeter by *Ty* (as he preferred) on meeting the platoon, "None of that 'Sir' bullshit for me," followed by his words of wisdom, "Stay hydrated, this heat will kill you."

Once the men had inspected the run-down isolated OP (Outpost) compound, two men located a fortified building, formerly a government building, that could be used as their base. Secured only by a barbed-wire perimeter and mud walls, the men erected barricades and reinforced the walls with sandbags on rooftops. The soldiers based there had painted a wall of the compound — it had in big letters 'Welcome to Apocalypse Now Zad' as a mark of reference to the Vietnam War film *Apocalypse Now* that marked the heavy fighting the troops had suffered from 2006.

This derelict building, now in disintegration, was occupied as a base for the platoon and a prime location that was virtually riddled with firing points and tunnels, making the men aware the Taliban could spy on the soldiers or attack close to the compound wall at any time. The compound (perimeter wall) was filled with mouseholes and tunnels, mud huts, crumbling buildings with gaping mortar holes and collapsed roofs — nothing was left untouched.

Looking around, Kieran didn't want to underestimate how smart the enemy was. He spotted blood-splattered walls left as a reminder of the living hell and battles soldiers had gone through before them, taking a moment to observe his surroundings and dusty dryness on the compressed ground that cracked beneath his boots as he walked. The living quarters of a dirty, dusty cave were primitive. With no hospital and limited medical facilities, bathroom and toilet amenities were basic, campfires for cooking the same daily rations and bottled water to drink. Overall, this could only be described as hot and sweaty, and cramped at best. It was like no place he'd ever seen. And on the first impression — not for the better. A few days later, it was made all too clear to the men that the Taliban were watching the platoon just as they were observing the insurgents' activity.

Kieran was searching the landscape through binoculars on the flat rooftop and, to his amazement, a Taliban spy known as *dickers* popped his head up from the roof of a nearby hut, bobbing up and down like a wilderness meerkat, watching him in return with the same type of military issue binoculars. As if confirming what Kieran suspected, not only did the Taliban know they were there but how many too.

Judging by the short random periods of small arms' gunfire the men incurred, the insurgents could take out the men at any time. Making the feeling of being trapped in a goldfish bowl a whole lot smaller in a confined space.

Luckily, so far no one was hurt.

Buildings situated in the middle of the town — the DC — were a cluster of low houses with flat roofs and walls made up of cement, mud and straw surrounded by a compound perimeter boundary that was less than six feet, which provided less than adequate protection.

The intention was to win over the local people by promising to supply an overwhelming amount of military personnel of over 2,500 men to protect the people. This action appeared to have the opposite effect, and people left the most populated areas of the district centre in droves, estimated at 35,000. This caused most of the inhabitants of the town to flee as the fighting increased leaving the town virtually deserted.

It didn't help when British forces' intelligence observed that the Taliban *dickers* had begun to circle along the outskirts of the compound. Each evening the insurgents would return to make several attacks with small arms' fire and RPGs trying to catch the men off guard. Despite being trained for every eventuality, other threats to the British light infantry foot soldiers were increasing by the minute. The troops clashed daily with the Taliban and other militant groups, leading to casualties that came from open attacks caused by indirect fire and sniper fire.

No longer content to be sitting targets for the insurgents to take pot-shots at, the soldiers made plans to settle in. Orders came to extend the patrols in the area in preparation for defence. Plans were carried out for the compound perimeter to be made secure by blowing up 100 ambush points, letting everyone know for miles around — the British Army was here to stay. Walls and bombs were planted to secure the base which took a week to clear. For such a small garrison, the men accomplished more than possible within a short space of time.

With the perimeter secured, Kieran, along with the rest of the men, was able to find settling in a little more comfortable, which became more routine. And the platoon was able to patrol areas of the northern part of the old town, although now deserted as a result of intense fighting and bombing raids, it still held an element of danger. Sealing the many tunnels, mouseholes and reinforcing the bunkers and watchtowers didn't stop Kieran being nervous. For the first few days, every little noise and bang made Kieran jump to see what it was.

Fearing the insurgents would climb over the wall or through one of the many mouseholes close to the perimeter wall, Kieran kept his hand weapon close, but hearing the whispering, scraping and scurrying of the insurgents beyond the perimeter wall during the night didn't help. With an uneasy feeling, Kieran felt more secure sleeping with his gun on his bed every night, at least for the first couple of weeks. If someone was coming for him while he slept, he was going to be ready for them and shoot the bastards if he had to.

Looking at himself now, he'd matured. Kieran could hardly believe it was just a few short weeks ago. He no longer felt a fresh-faced kid with the illusion he was going to change the world.

Chapter Two

"Fuck! Hold up!" the point man, Corporal Steve *Drews* Andrews, called out over his radio headset.

The Afghan interpreter, the platoon called him *Abe*, ICOM (Intercepting Communication) relayed he'd overheard Taliban chatter picked up on the radio. Abe said the insurgents were in the area and knew the location of the soldiers.

"What is it?" Kieran's hushed voice responded.

"Fucking hell! Those fucking bastards are out there!" Lance Corporal Jordan *Kenny* Kennedy reported back.

Lead Captain Dan Hale responded, "Let's get moving, ladies; they could be closer than we think." Taking a moment to scan the area before raising his arm to signal clear, as he knew the information could be fake, but he was taking no chances.

"Location — two kilometres left of the wadi," Abe informed Jonesy, following up the rear as *tail-end Charlie*.

For some reason, this didn't appease Kieran's raised senses. He glanced at the men, and just like him, he could see the nervous apprehension of the unknown clearly on their faces.

"Let's keep the chatter to a low. If we can hear the fuckers — it means they can hear us too," Captain Dan Hale confirmed.

Each man lost in his thoughts, Kieran swore under his breath at Dan's warning.

"Keep your fucking eyes peeled, men!" Jonesy ordered, and gave the signal for everyone to move forward once more in radio silence.

The first thing Kieran noticed about Sergeant Andy Jones — *Jonesy* to his men — was his constant use of the word *fuck* and how he managed to use the word in almost every other word spoken. But Kieran admired his physical strength and his dedication to his job, along with his extensive collection of colourful tattoos on his arms and shoulders. Around six feet six inches and looked as broad as he was tall, he was a heavily tanned muscle man that carried his weight on his arms and shoulders. Jonesy never asked anything of a soldier he wouldn't do himself and seemed indestructible and an all-round good guy. The rumour was, he killed an insurgent with his bare hands when caught unarmed in a battle with five armed Taliban fighters. If the story was half-right, Kieran was just happy Jonesy was on his side.

The men had only gone a few feet.

"Hold up!" Captain Dan halted in his tracks.

Kieran had to admire the captain, originally from Surrey. At 26, he'd seen and had his fair share of action as an infantry officer. After this tour, he and his girlfriend planned on settling down. They were looking forward to travelling before buying a house. Since graduating from the Royal Military Academy, Sandhurst, he'd been to Bosnia with a rifle platoon of the Grenadier Guards, he'd trained troops at Catterick and served in Iraq before joining 1st Battalion as Second in Command.

Dan always led from the front on every patrol and paid attention to every detail before advancing on any foot patrol. And incredibly fit, he would often be found running with the men around the compound during PT. As an officer, Dan had a genuine concern for his men and was a good mate. He was firm but fair. The men trusted his judgement. In the short time of being with the company, on his arrival Dan told the men that Ty, he and Jonesy were in charge, and they would be their father, uncle, brother and confessor if needed. Kieran had no reason to doubt his leadership.

At Dan's caution, Kieran felt his body stiffen, and his eyes searched the collection of dense tree-lined brush to the right of the section, scanning for hidden targets. Waiting for a flicker of movement to catch his eye.

Remembering his training: the patrolling, vehicle checkpoints, drills, and how to handle riots, which became a significant part of his survival while dealing with the sweeping for land mines, and bombs could be unpredictable and explosive at times. But he wasn't looking for those type of weapons right now; all seemed quiet.

He was about to talk into his earpiece to ask Jonesy, following up from the rear, feeling sure he knew something wasn't right when Jonesy's hushed voice came over the communication set.

"Take cover!"

Jonesy's voice startled Kieran so much, and he took a moment to react. He stared at the men as if trying to make sense of what was happening as the platoon, with stealth, made a dive for whatever cover the men could find. Kieran, following orders, heard movements a second later — it sounded like a group of people moving towards them, their voices carrying in the air. He only knew it was a heated conversation; they were still some distance away to hear everything that they were saying.

"Don't any of you make a fucking move!" Dan ordered.

Dan observed from a safe distance as he surveyed their surroundings, eyes vigilant and motionless, he rechecked the grounds; only then did he glance back to figure out the exact location of the voices. They were getting louder, and he felt the ground vibrate with the motion of heavy vehicles in use, moving at a rapid pace towards their position. His gut told him this wasn't good, and the last thing they needed right now was to be caught in open territory with no cover and outnumbered.

Instantly, the mood around the men seemed to tense up.

Captain Dan looked across at the scattered men and surveyed the open territory, taking into account his next move. "Let's assess the situation and see what's going down before we make any rash movements."

Kieran didn't need telling twice; he removed his SA80 from his shoulder and with stealth he silently settled into a small roadside irrigation ditch, relaxed, took a deep, steadying breath and pointed the barrel in the direction of open ground — weapon at the ready.

Jonesy looked at the location of the scattered men taking cover by a pile of rubble and remains of an abandoned farmhouse, and Kieran waited for orders to make their next move.

As soon as Kieran hit the dirt, his instincts kicked in — his eyes scanning the open landscape. His breath was almost silent as he waited. In the short time he'd been with the platoon his senses had developed, reacting mainly to stealth movement, instincts and sound.

The group moved steadily forward. By the sound of the voices heard, they appeared to be all men. The dust and sand blowing through the wind partially obscured them from view, and all that he could see was a silhouette at intervals. He counted around 20 men or more. Which meant it left the men outmanned and outgunned.

All of them wore black and were bearded from what he could tell. Their voices carried quickly in the wind. They weren't unusually quiet or attempting stealth; more the opposite as they trampled through the sandstorm. As they neared, Kieran thought he heard both Afghan and Pashto. Two men with granite-like features appeared to be the leaders, issuing orders and pointing an accusing finger at others while they ranted and shouted while waving their AK-47s in mid-air. Others let off several rounds of ammunition in their excitement. As the burst of gunfire echoed through the air, it was enough to set the platoon's nerves on edge. It looked like they were firing their weapons into the air for fun rather than purpose as they jabbed at the sky and repeatedly fired rounds while the others seemed to be searching for something.

From his position, Kieran watched them kicking and raking the ground with every few steps, shouting, "Where is it?" and, "Find it!" It was apparent, for whatever reason, they were searching frantically for something profoundly important to them.

The sound of the gunshots fired and the muzzle flashes sent a ripple of tension through Kieran. He gripped the SA80 more tightly and drew back further into the hard ground beneath.

The situation looked bad for them.

Dan knew this was not the best position for his men to be caught up in right now.

Another round of gunfire burst through the air shattering the silence. Then everything went silent. The flurry of fire had vibrated through the air, making Kieran's ears ring. He wasn't sure if the sound had temporarily deafened him, but suddenly there was no sound coming from the group of men at all. The voices drifted back, less aggressive this time, as they exchanged words amongst themselves.

Kieran rubbed away the dry dirt stinging his face and from his forehead while he raked his hand through his short-cropped black hair and quickly replaced his helmet. *"Was this any way for a horny single guy to spend a weekend?"* he asked himself. He'd been naive and carefree during his training days; he had his pick of lovely girls — he didn't consider himself a player, but he wasn't a boy scout either. And now, with no social life, the limited half-hour daily internet service was reduced to once a week, and the connection — mediocre at best, plus lack of electricity for his phone charger, he was only able to call his parents infrequently. He felt cut off from the rest of the world as if forgotten. He'd had an awakening as to what military combat was really like.

With the ban on batteries to run headsets and no beer, the men were left to entertain themselves by watching old DVDs of Top Gear and old movies and only bottled cold water to drink. Some were lucky enough to get sent downloaded pirate copies of the latest programmes and films showing back home, and they would all sit and watch them at night if there was nothing else happening.

The hardest thing to cope with was having to get used to the persistent 24-hour activity of men and machines. Night-time patrols and observation checkpoints were manned continuously and changed. With the tight control over the influx of troops deployed to the region and so few men in the platoon, it was inevitable patrols repeated continuously. With each person allowed two weeks' leave during their deployment, any injuries sustained and any sickness didn't make things any easier for the boots on the ground and put a constant strain on the already overstretched British troops.

Kieran realised after a few weeks in Now Zad, Afghanistan — *he had no idea what the fuck he'd gotten himself involved in here.*

Despite all this, he'd discovered the meaning of true friendship, and forged an unforgettable camaraderie with this small platoon that would never break. And although none of the men was of blood relation, they were bonded together in friendship and were brothers in arms. From the moment he'd enlisted, Kieran got to know at basic level what discipline and being part of a team was like.

When he'd first joined his platoon, he hadn't been aware of how troublesome the insurgents were and wasn't even aware who the enemy was at that time. All he could remember thinking at first glance was that every man, woman and child walked, talked and dressed the same as any other. If someone knew of a secret way to detect the insurgents and other combatants — they were keeping the secret for themselves, because he sure as hell couldn't spot one. Besides all that, he couldn't help but give an understanding as to why the people fought so fiercely to keep the land they were born to and rightfully lived there.

Before he arrived, Kieran had only heard about the war in Afghanistan by the TV news reports and read in the newspapers the same as anyone else at the time. That was before *9/11* and the intervention of the Americans in Afghanistan. He 'd heard the insurgents were opposed to foreign troops being in *Hell Man's* province as it became known by the soldiers, and the area was under complete Taliban rule.

News from around the world reported the country was unstable and one of the poorest states in the world, stricken with extreme poverty; some young children died before reaching their fifth birthday. While others lived in disease, filth, squalor and lawlessness in major cities, most under terrorism rule were influenced by profiteering in war. According to news reports, it started when the Taliban was operating under their law, outside government ruling. When news came that the Taliban had killed several civilians, accusing them of working for the government. the Afghan government requested urgent foreign aid be sent to maintain order.

Taliban, or *insurgents*, as they were also known as, was mostly made up of tribespeople and drug traffickers, afraid that their valuable crop would be destroyed and the opium trade eradicated by the ISAF troops. With climate issues of extreme heat in the summer and severe cold in winter, most of the dirt-poor and illiterate farmers of Helmand had little or no other opportunity open to them other than growing poppies. This supplied the massive demand of the addicts across the world. And most likely drove every Afghan person reliant on the poppy crops into providing money for arms and support for the Taliban in their operations. And with the *invasion of foreign aid* and *peacekeeping*, the insurgents decided to take matters into their hands.

The rest of Kieran's platoon joined C Company, and by spring were to be deployed to Iraq to operate as part of Force Reserve, *Operation TELIC*, formed in Basra City South Battlegroup. This was to involve many dangerous high-profile arrests and strike operations. Iraq was reported to become one of the largest Ops and British deployments of service personnel since World War II.

Even with the influx of the resident NATO and coalition troops, the Afghan government rule only extended to the capital of Kabul. There was no doubt that the civilian population were living under a tight rebel rule. Something needed to be done to help the people.

With continuous attacks and the death toll rising to approximately 500 deaths a month, suicide attacks were on the rise too. Some deaths were the result of kidnappings and captives killed by their captors. It became apparent more troops were desperately needed to defeat the insurgents.

By the end of March 2007 — the 1st Royal Anglians trained for ground support, and the first part of Kieran's battalion, A and B Company of the 1st Battalion were the first to be deployed.

The majority of the conflict was in Afghanistan's eastern and southern provinces, with an increased number of attacks against civilians and aid workers. To worsen the situation, another growing concern — believed to be using a form of weaponry used in Iraq — insurgents were now making their own IEDs and using roadside bombs and posting video evidence on *YouTube* for everyone to see the devastating effect.

With the situation deteriorating in the south of Afghanistan, a further 3,300 troops were promised to be deployed to Helmand province with specialised training to cope with the increased IED (Improvised Explosive Device) attacks.

Making up this brigade formation would be the 1st Battalion of Grenadier Guards, Light Dragoons, 2nd Royal Tank Regiment, Royal Artillery Regiment, (29th and 45th Foot) Worcester and Sherwood Foresters Regiment, and further regiments included Logistics, Medical, and Engineers. Many of which included bomb disposal IED experts such as Explosive Ordnance Disposal, and were now in the heart of the fighting capital of Kabul.

The actual amount posted as part of a NATO-led operation of the promised 3,300 troops were 1,700 British soldiers deployed overseas in support of a scheduled clearance patrol. The primary mission was preventing the insurgents from gaining total control of the province, by aiding the ISAF in support training situated in the central capital of Kabul. Working in collaboration with 18 other countries as part of a contingency plan with foreign peacekeepers, this was to aid the Afghans to maintain order and bring peace. Since the arrival of the British Army, the attacks on the ANP had ceased.

Still, Kieran felt it was best to remain vigilant at all times. Today, he had a bad feeling that all was about to change as he lay in the dirt. *Fuck! That fucking dust and dirt get everywhere!* Confirming what he already knew. Fear and adrenaline coursed through his veins as he lay in the ditch waiting for them to make their next move.

That morning, his section had been ordered to an area some miles out of the city centre to observe and patrol an engineering water pipeline and irrigation location. Reports relayed and confirmed the Taliban were active and seen in the area. Unfortunately, this was the enemy's home ground and strongest hold. The intelligence results revealing the insurgents had been given a premeditated advantage against the British military.

It was still early, and he gave an involuntary shake as the wind lashed sand at his face. He couldn't ignore the hot wind heading across the wild desert plains, sent from the foothills of the Hindu Kush sat in the backdrop of the province. Apart from that, it seemed unusually quiet.

Kieran surveyed his fellow soldiers; he had an uneasy feeling about this.

The group moved steadily towards the section of men lying in wait.

Due to the amount of activity, this wasn't looking to be a good sign.

They were patrolling in alien territory, unclear as to who was friend or foe. The worst thing that could happen right now was a death of one of his comrades. Was the group of men out on an intimidation mission raising new members?

Kieran glanced over the men around him, whatever their reason for being here, knowing that should they attack, all his mates were trained in the ROE (Rules of Engagement) and would know precisely the right moment to discharge their weapons. The rules were crystal clear, and no one would want to take another person's life unlawfully. It would undoubtedly mean the end of their military career and being disciplined severely, and even result in a prison sentence. But looking at another point of view, neither should a person have the right to put a soldier's life under threat and him not return fire to defend himself.

The voices drifted over their heads as they moved in closer, then the sounds, less agitated, started receding. They gradually faded until they couldn't hear anything more and the noise of the vehicles had disappeared into the distance, once more leaving silence.

He waited until Dan's voice came over the radio, "All clear!" before raising his head, clutching his SA80 in both hands, every muscle tensed in exceptional tuned accuracy, poised ready to defend himself.

After the signal told him the situation was under control, Kieran stood slowly and scanned the area around him. Not a sound. He waited. Still no sound came. An uneasiness sent a chill down his spine. Something warned him; it didn't feel right.

Kieran took a moment to orient himself, then turned north-west — in the direction of the shooting and vehicles. The trail wasn't going to last long with the wind direction against them. Faint tyre tracks left in the dust that marked the section's route in the area were quickly disappearing. One of the men took an ordnance map out of his combat jacket pocket and tried to pinpoint their exact position.

Sergeant Jones removed his helmet, rubbed his shaved head and looked over the horizon confused, before saying to the nine men under his command, "Let's go take a look around at what they were shooting at."

Dan's eyes fixed on the tracks in front of him. "Caution, men! IEDs could be anywhere!"

Kieran focused strictly on the ground around him, but the wind was increasing in strength and making it more difficult to see. If the sandstorm got any worse, they would have to return to base camp before it turned into a full-blown dry sandstorm.

Winds could reach over 100 miles an hour, and with little or no cover the men couldn't be caught out in that way.

Dan indicated he should lead the way. "Take point, Romeo. Ginger, follow behind."

A map in hand, Kieran led out on patrol. Lance Corporal Matt *Ginger* Hayes, originally from York, was a tall and gangly guy, who on occasion spoke with a broad Yorkshire accent, prepared to follow close behind with his SA80 at the ready.

Sergeant Jones and the rest of the men fell in behind in classic line patrol formation, walking silently behind him. They had been on patrol for about half an hour before they came across tyre tracks that matched with the ones from the shooters' vehicles.

Kieran noticed the freshly raked ground where the trucks had parked. He pointed. "More tracks lead east, pointing away from Now Zad." He felt everyone's eyes on him.

Taking an interest, Jonesy joined Dan and checked the soil. "We need to find out what they were doing out here."

"Maybe if we searched the ground a little further north, we might find something," Dan suggested.

Three of the men stared at him.

"Why?" Ginger asked.

"If we investigate a little closer there might be an insurgent hideout somewhere close by," Kieran offered. He turned, and took several steps north following the tracks.

"Fuck me!" Cursing himself for not seeing the obstructive stump, he straightened and looked over the obstacle. It stuck out from beneath a mound of loose dirt and sand — sizeable and dark-brown. What sort of tree would that be here in the desert? The base was big and shallow-rooted and the bark appeared dark in colour, which struck him as odd out here in this area, as such large uprooted trees were rare in the desert.

He bent forward to take a closer look, and intense disgust swept over his body. It hadn't been an old tree stump after all, and on closer examination it revealed a man's detached arm with fingers missing. Further evidence revealed a hurried attempt was made to disguise several brutally hacked body parts buried in a shallow grave. A decapitated head with eyes now lifeless was staring up at him. A clear reminder that the serene landscape was not as safe as it appeared at times.

With churning bile rising at the pit of his stomach, warning him that he was about to lose yesterday's meal, Kieran instantly realised it was the first dead body he had ever seen. Almost on cue he dropped to his knees, as the lodged bile in his throat worked loose, vomiting at the side of the dirt track.

Everyone else turned to look at the decapitated head, which on closer inspection was a stout-set man, dark-skinned, in his late forties. Examining sections of the body, it appeared to have suffered severe torture before his entire body was hacked to pieces. He was still wearing what remained of a burnt uniform that the mobile Afghan medical teams based at Kabul wore.

Jonesy combed the body to find any form of identification while half the men kept a lookout. The other half searched the ground and fanned out to look for clues and evidence. Nothing, no distinctive tattoos or marks, pockets empty with no sign of a wallet or official documents and passport. Why was that? More importantly — why had he been killed and abandoned, and left to rot and eventually eaten by the wildlife roaming the desert.

"Who do you think has done this?" Kieran looked at Dan and Jonesy for answers.

Jonesy rubbed his shaved head again and straightened his shoulders as he stood up. "I'll fucking give you two guesses."

"Fuck! What do you think we should do, Jonesy?" Lance Corporal Simon *Si* Parker asked. The rest of the group looked to the captain for the answer.

Dan looked at the men closest to him. "Let's collect whatever evidence we can find and head back to the base. Leave the body where it is."

Lance Corporal Jordan *Kenny* Kennedy nodded in agreement. "I'll see to it."

Jonesy gave it some thought. "Fine. Wrighty, give him a hand. Let's make it fucking quick."

"Something tells me we don't have long before someone comes back to make another sweep." Captain Dan told them.

"What do you want me to do?" Smithie asked.

Nodding to Jonesy, Dan organised the men. "Get the men to cover our tracks best they can. We need to buy whatever time we can. Report to the base and let's get the fuck out of here. The Afghan police will start an independent investigation."

"Do you think this man's death has anything to do with the obstruction of the main water supply problem here?" Ginger asked.

"Who knows?" Dan replied.

"Now let's make fucking tracks —"

Jonesy never got to finish his sentence. A loud pop-pop exploded from behind a large boulder 100 metres away. "Gunfire!" Jonesy yelled, and dived to the ground as a series of bullets whistled past their heads.

"Everyone down!" Dan screamed. "Take cover!" And it was as if all hell had broken loose at those words.

As soon as he heard the warning, Kieran, along with the rest of the men, instinctively hit the ground, and covered their heads with their hands as bullets zipped through the air popping at the ground around them as they fell. Crack, crack, as the shots plugged into the dirt around him, which was cracking up in front of Kieran, narrowly missing his head by less than an inch.

Fuck me! That was fucking close!

In the aftermath of the shooting, silence fell, but Kieran couldn't ignore the loud drumming in his ears. His heart was pumping frantically. His breathing was so rapid as the noise and dust settled around him, he thought his heart would jump out of his chest any moment. He tried taking a couple of deep breaths to help slow his heart rate while trying to remain alert to what was happening to the men around him.

There was no doubt about it, lying in the open like this made them sitting targets for the gunman. The last thing the men needed was to be pinned down by sniper fire.

Kieran turned his head; he spotted Dan, Drews and Wrighty within a few feet.

He raised a hand and carefully pointed to Signaller Lance Corporal Daniel *Smithie* Smith, about 20 metres away, and his radio pack lying in the open. It might as well have a target on it.

"Who the fuck is shooting at us?" Kieran whispered through his radio headset.

"A fucking sniper, you, stupid bastard!" Jonesy cursed, as he spotted a dark figure in the shadows of the trees with his binoculars. Pointing towards a clearing, he added, "I've spotted the fucking tosser. He's about 1,500 metres north, behind a boulder to the left of those rocks."

Kieran looked over in that direction — visibility was limited — he couldn't see anything moving, and he couldn't risk raising his head because if the shooter were trained with any accuracy at all, he'd be able to detect the slightest of movement.

Kieran, spotting the VHF radio lying on the ground; he shifted, making a reach for it and missed. For a minute, he thought the shooter had not detected him as the silence grew. But the movement was enough to attract another round of gunfire. The bullets popped at the dirt in front of him, sending up small clouds of mushroom-shaped dust and sand into the air, missing his head by less than an inch.

That fucker was too fucking close! The sniper's aim was improving.

While Jonesy got a location on the sniper, he called out, "Everyone OK?" Taking a quick headcount was instantly followed by more gunfire as it exploded in front of them. Relieved the headcount voices were all accounted for and unharmed, he asked, "Any of you get a clear shot off at this fucking arsehole?"

2IC (Second in Command) to Jonesy, Corporal Steve *Drews* Andrews reacted quickly; it was his job to find out where the sniper was firing from and how the men were to shoot back.

Lifting his head, Kieran looked around; they all had weapons, but there was no doubt about it, the newbies were scared out of their wits even to move. If anything, Jonesy didn't seem surprised by their action. After all, most of them had not been in contact with the Taliban before. What could he expect from fresh-faced eighteen-year-olds that were more suited to the iPod and mobile phone era than combat?

Slowly, Kieran slid his SA80 in front of him and managed to give off a couple of rounds. Smithie used the distraction to make a grab for the radio and send a message to the rest of the platoon that had trailed behind with the light machine gun and long-range rifle, but they were some distance back.

Smithie spoke into the VHF as quietly as possible. "Charlie. Under attack by sniper fire!" He relayed the coordinates. Trying to avoid bringing attention to the group. "Delta. We need long-range fire support at this location." He repeated the map coordinates over the radio. Then relayed the message over until someone responded.

"Read you, Charlie. Easty here," a voice replied, as it cracked through the static.

"Got that. Help is on the way. Sit tight!" Lance Corporal Ben *Easty* Eastman came back from the base.

"Got it!" Smithie laid the radio beside him and stared at Kieran. "They are on the way."

Corporal Drews shifted the VHF to the side of him — a move that instantly drew fire to him; the pop, pop, pop as bullets hit the dirt close to them. Kieran fired back in return the moment the muzzle flashes from his rifle gave away the sniper's position. From his vantage point, he knew the shooter was too far in the distance to do anything other than distract him with his SA80.

"Save the bullets, Romeo; he's too far away," Jonesy ordered.

Reluctantly, Kieran lowered his weapon. All he'd done was provide a distraction. "Good effort," he heard Dan say.

"Yeah," Smithie's voice muttered, "Would have been better if you'd hit the fucking wanker."

He smiled at that. "Sorry. I'll try better next time, you ungrateful twat."

A few spontaneous chuckles came from the men. The banter seemed to ease the tension slightly, but not dismissing the seriousness of the situation.

"Why do you think a sniper is taking shots at us?" a freckled-face soldier, Private Alex *Al* Myers asked. "Is it because we are checking up on the tracks of the dead man?"

"I wouldn't think so. My guess, the dead man was in the wrong place at the wrong time," Jonesy replied.

Ginger raised his head of ginger hair slightly. "That doesn't make sense to waste all that firepower on us when we are so far away. Doesn't seem likely we will find anything anyway."

"He's not trying to miss. The sniper will kill us all if he gets the chance," Captain Dan told them sternly.

A few rumbles of complaints went around the men.

"Settle down," Dan called out, in a low voice, trying to calm the men. It wasn't the first time he'd been pinned down by sniper fire and it was starting to feel all too familiar. "Keep your fucking heads down!"

"The shooter is more likely protecting a Taliban operation of some kind. Probably opium," Jonesy observed.

Fucking great! was all Kieran could think at that moment. There was no mistaking that this info put the men decidedly on edge. And why shouldn't they be? If the large numbers of Taliban were not to be exaggerated — should they decide to return and attack — the platoon would find themselves most likely outmanned and outgunned.

"Fucking calm down, you bunch of fucking pussies! The firing only means the shooter is most likely buying time for the insurgents to move location."

"Why? All the sniper needs to do is wait and pick us off one by one." Corporal Drews questioned the sergeant's explanation.

"I'll get us out of here — so keep fucking quiet. Stay low until the guys can get here. A deaf man could hear all you fucking chattering. Shut the fuck up!"

"How long do we have to wait, Jonesy?" one of the men asked.

"About 30 minutes," Smithie relayed.

An uncomfortable silence settled over the men.

Just as Kieran was getting used to the stillness, another round of shells hit the ground; the silence shattered around them. He heard Jonesy call out, "Heads down!"

"Yeah, they will come to our rescue real quick." Ginger had the last word.

A distressing silence fell over them and faces hit the dirt once more. Kieran closed his eyes. Briefly, he had a feeling it was going to be a long bloody half-hour. Try as he might, it was hard to ignore the irony in his mate's comment. Besides, it was true.

At that moment, a flurry of explosions and rapid fire could be heard. No one could see anything through the dense bush, but they could listen to it all the same. Firepower that could equal the distance of the sniper was in full force knowing help had finally arrived.

The radio crackled, and Lance Corporal Ben *Easty* Eastman's voice came back over the radio. "You guys sent for the A-Team?"

A series of massive sighs of relief went through the men. "You fucking arsehole," Jonesy replied.

"Been quiet since last activity but can't see anything," Smithie replied.

Static crackled over the radio. "Have your backs covered, when you're ready." The sound of the British armoured Snatch protected patrol vehicle came to a grinding halt in front of the men, placing it between the sniper and the men, with a WMIK Land Rover (Weapons Mount Installation Kit) beside it.

Swearing under his breath, Kieran cautiously pushed himself to his knees. No sniper shots popped and whizzed through the air, and he gave a massive sigh of relief.

"OK, men, move your fucking arses. Let's get fucking loaded up and head back to the compound quickly." Jonesy organised the men. "Let's go!" he said, as the men threw the equipment inside the vehicles and huddled inside while he searched the ground around them gathering up some spent shell casings from the sniper. Jonesy examined the cartridges closely.

Dan took a closer look at what Jonesy was holding. "What you got there, Sergeant?"

"39mm. Most likely from an AK-47." Confirming what he already suspected.

Kieran glared at Jonesy for a moment, and the evidence only confirmed what they already knew. He then turned his attention to the horizon. Taliban was out there for sure, and probably watching them. "Time to get the fucking hell out of here and pretty damn quick. Let's get a fucking move on, men! Time to peel back."

Scrambling for the vehicles, the men didn't need telling twice. It was nightfall by the time the platoon returned to the compound. Weapons cleaned and ammo counted before scoff. It was after 2100 local time by the time Dan called them all for a team debriefing.

Jonesy passed around chilled water bottles as they all tried to sit within a confined tent. Some of the men sat on plastic chairs, as others stood and lined the wall of the accommodation tent, or sat on their beds. Body odour after a day's activity mixed with dirty, dusty clothes and the heat of the confined tent left Kieran in desperate need of a shower. But at least they all came back alive.

Chapter Three

The next few weeks followed a pattern.

Since their arrival, the men had come under a constant stream of random gunfire attacks over the past two weeks. Lone shooters would pop up and take pot-shots at the men day and night. The night-time attacks of bullets fired into the perimeter wall were the hardest to deal with.

Lack of vital working equipment was another obstacle. And with the constant lack of working night-visionary surveillance equipment, the men found the attackers harder to keep track of. Single shots involving small arms fire were taken at the men as they walked across the compound or went about their duties. Luckily, none of the men was hit or injured by further attacks, but morale was low.

While the war in Afghanistan continued, the ground infantry troops became severely stretched, undermanned and constantly under fire. There were far too few troops, helicopters and air support, which put the frontline infantry boots on the ground continually at risk. Morale was at an all-time low. The men felt forgotten by the people back home as less and less was reported of their *peacekeeping* efforts.

Much-needed supplies such as night-vision equipment and tools that were vital to the mission were declined by the MOD, along with thermal imagining devices that enabled the troops to distinguish between civilians and insurgents. Working IED detectors and night-vision equipment had to be shared continuously between the men to cover around-the-clock patrols. Logistic vehicles and *Snatch* Land Rovers were outdated and continually breaking down — some of which were used to transport injured soldiers from minefield areas and dangerous frontline areas planted with IEDs.

Kieran's platoon was suffering from the same onslaught of vicious attacks from the Taliban and other militia groups. Every day, patrols would find newly planted IEDs and roadside bombs, often found buried in the shallow open ground with crude and insufficient markings, which made them lethal but effective.

Some of the men were struggling to stay awake at their posts due to the constant small arms fire happening around the clock. The biggest problem was sleep deprivation which would leave the men feeling exhausted; tempers were wearing thin.

It didn't stop the men from engaging in some traditional initiation tasks for the newbies. Everyone joined in with that one — for Kieran the task was simple — issued with white gloves, jacket and metal tray — he would act as a waiter to the rest of the men without complaint, day or night. Met with fun and banter, it gave him, as one of the newbies, a sense of acceptance and belonging, which was always received with resounding joy by the rest of the men by the end of the challenge.

To relieve tension, Ty and Dan put their heads together to think of other ways to boost morale. One of the suggestions came by way of introducing a points system. If any of the guys had a bollocking or fucked up, it was marked down. By the Friday, it was tallied up and the two men remaining had to strip down to their briefs and have a dance off. The men cheered for the winner, and the loser was left with clearing the cesspit duty for the week. Three weeks of Smithie on cleaning duty seemed to form a pattern, so the game was dropped, much to Smithie's delight. If it was a setup, no one, apart from Smithie, was complaining.

A respite to ease pressure came a few days later with the welcome arrival of food, rations, ammo and equipment, along with much-needed morale-boosting mail and care packages from home, courtesy of the Royal Mail, who introduced free posting from the UK. It was delivered by 50 heavily laden overland convoy trucks of the British Army Royal Logistics Corps *'Road Warriors'* from Camp Bastion.

Their heavy-armoured protection force escorted each convoy on a daily basis. Which wasn't surprising considering the treacherous miles they covered, along with open terrain, coping with the sweltering hot sun blazing down on them and the risk of dehydration. Sandstorms and winds would beat across the desert at 100 miles an hour, blowing swirls of sand and dirt that would cover and choke a man in seconds.

Often convoys would be delayed for hours, even days sometimes. Trucks would get stuck in soft, shifting sand and needed digging out before the convoy could continue. Sand would get lodged in engines, with them struggling to remain operational. Vehicles would break down frequently, often in enemy-occupied terrain. Despite the risks, landmines as IEDs, suicide bombers and insurgents' ambush attacks, the *Road Warriors* made those vital deliveries and equally compelling stories. As the supplies unloaded at a record pace, it came as a great surprise to most at the delivery of a massive satellite dish.

The saving grace was a TA (Territorial Army) soldier from the Logistics Corps who was a former *Sky Tv* installer and offered to get the internet up and running again if he could clear it with *Boss Man*. The previous dish, meeting with a premature end when an RPG hit the main *sanger*, was erected as a fortified lookout post and was now reduced to a pile of rubble.

The place became a hive of activity, spirits lifted and the men eagerly awaited news from back home, although it was two to three weeks old by the time it arrived. Major Tyler Morgan-Davies kept the momentum going by mail call. The earlier moods of frustrations of the past couple of weeks seemed to evaporate. The group sat on the ground outside his tent eagerly waiting in anticipation. As the CO (Commanding Officer) handed out mail and care packages with his usual style and banter, the glowing, smiling faces summed it up.

All Kieran knew was that Major Tyler *Ty* Morgan-Davies was a pretty decent guy. Always looked to be smiling and joining in the men's banter and very much a soldier's soldier. He kept his kit and himself immaculate. That seemed to matter a great deal to him. Divorced with a young son, a prime example that forces' marriages often failed due to long periods away from home. Ty came across as a solitary man, always on the move and no fixed roots to speak of.

Initially from Wales, his dad worked in the pits as a boy and always worked hard for his family, and pushed him to be all that he could be. Which he instilled in his men, His approach was always open and friendly towards the men. A well-built man with blond hair and in great physical shape for a 30-plus guy that spent most of his time sat in the Ops room. He thought nothing of joining the men on PT with full kit around the compound, and would give the men a cheeky grin when he left them trailing far behind. The only man he couldn't outrun was

Captain Dan.

Despite being a CO, he wasn't the typical officer material. No one called him Sir and everyone was told to call him *Ty* on meeting him. At the moment he had several sacks of mail to hand over, and he was acting a total arse. Kieran watched him while handing out the post and taking his time about it. Right now, Kieran had another name for him. Just like everyone else, Kieran was eagerly waiting for a postal delivery from home. It wasn't the amount of mail he received that caused him to suffer the guys' distorted jibes of humour and jokes, it was his enthusiastic joy of the items he received.

"Eh up, Romeo O'Neill is sitting on the edge of his seat, I see," said Si, as he stepped in front of Kieran and plonked down in front of him.

"Romeo, Romeo." Smithie theatrically repeated the name over.

"If you ask me nicely, I'll let you borrow Juliet this weekend." Easty chimed in with a photo shot of a blow-up doll.

The roar of boisterous male laughter from the rest of the platoon had his fate sealed. A momentary bit of larking about, and Kieran had just been given a name by his buddies, and he was never called O'Neill again.

"Shut the fuck up, you bunch of fucking wankers!" Kieran's anger was instantly met with a roar of cheering.

Smithie and Si were the two jokers of the platoon. Closely followed by Easty.

Lance Corporal Simon *Si* Parker was a 22-year-old short Scotsman, and proud of it by his opinion. He joined the army while attending university, where he was training as a vet. Si did work experience at a stable. If his stories were anything to go by, all he had experienced was getting up at 4 am to muck out stables and exercise strong-minded and wilful horses that no one else wanted to ride. He eventually got the sack when he *borrowed* a horse one evening and went riding in the park dressed as the *headless horseman* from Sleepy Hollow. It was either join the army to do something more exciting with his life, or end up in real trouble and eventually prison. He was pig-headed at times and thought nothing of standing up for his opinion — that led him to being busted down and losing his corporal stripe more than once.

Lance Corporal Daniel *Smithie* Smith was an aggravating 19-year-old heavy-set guy, and Kieran thought he looked considerably older than his years, which Kieran put down to alcohol abuse, late nights and rough women. Plus, being involved in one bar scrap or another didn't do him any favours. When he came back off leave, he always came back with at least one black eye and stories of his women escapades.

He loved nothing better than winding his buddies up until the breaking point when someone would threaten his life. Despite having a volatile temper, he could be a real charmer too and was always the first to aid anyone in or out of his platoon. Back home, whenever the men went clubbing, Smithie had to be the first to pull, and he didn't care what she looked like; the rougher the better, and he rarely remembered her name by the morning after hours of wild, even rougher sex. Married or not, he didn't care.

On more than one occasion, he was concerned and treating an itching in his genital area that was the talk of the platoon.

Above all that, he was an excellent soldier and friend. Smithie loved a good brawl, which the men had to rescue him from on more than one occasion while out on the town. But he was also a keen mechanic and always could be found with his head under the bonnet of a Land Rover or some vehicle or other for hours at a time. If he couldn't fix it — it just wasn't worth fixing. He pulled the men out of more than a few scrapes by salvaging parts from other abandoned or burnt-out vehicles en route.

Kieran put it down to a simple explanation; Smithie wanted to know what made the vehicle work and treated every part of the workings as a challenge.

While Lance Corporal Ben *Easty* Eastman was the newbie and the baby of the bunch, he'd only been at the base a week when he celebrated his 18th birthday. The eldest of six brothers and sisters he was pretty much guaranteed he always got plenty of mail from home and often shared his mum's homemade biscuits. She sent extra when someone's birthday came around. A great bloke and a keen mortar man, he formed a close bond with Lance Corporal Liam *Jacko* Jackson, and the team worked well together. Easty was an excellent marksman.

Even with all this weighed up, Easty, Si and Smithie were top British soldiers and found unique ways to entertain the men. Regardless of the times the men had been involved in scrapes, dragging them out of pub brawls and visits to the medical centre, Si, Easty and Smithie were three of the most exceptional guys Kieran could ever wish to have his back. Despite that, they were right about one thing, Kieran was a romantic.

It was almost half an hour before his name was called out and a parcel was handed to him with his name on. A large, brown shoe box-type package from home was just what was needed to lift his spirits. By the time the giant Royal Mail sacks had been emptied, Kieran was the happy recipient of several care-packages and a pile of letters from his parents and friends back home. Stuff from his mum mostly. Since being in Afghanistan, he'd asked her to send him packs of beef jerky, which he discovered could be used to pep up army rations when out on long patrols.

Kieran grew up as an army brat. He spent most of his time moving from one place to the next until his mother put her foot down and told her husband that her son needed stability and continuity in his life. His father was Irish and a proud soldier, and his mother was of German nationality; they'd met while his platoon was stationed in Germany. They had a beautiful marriage, and he'd had a happy childhood. His mother would often tell him the story of how his parents first met. His father had been a British soldier serving in Germany. He had walked into a crowded bar where his mother had been working as a waitress, and from the very first moment their eyes met, without a trace of irony, he told her she was the most beautiful woman he'd ever met, and he never wanted to live a day without her beside him. Kieran never tired of hearing their story.

It had been his dream to join the Army and live the adventure, as his father once had. When he'd told his careers advisor he was joining the army, Kieran was asked if he had a back-up plan. Positive in his thinking — Kieran knew for certain — he didn't need a back-up plan; the army was where he belonged. Kieran joined the Royal Anglian Regiment — just as his father had done. His granddad before him had been a '*Viking*', and his father before him, while his brother and two uncles were killed in the trenches of World War I. Kieran joined the regiment as his grandparents had strong ties to Lincolnshire. There was no doubt about it — the day he got his letter of acceptance to the army — he'd been *fucking dead chuffed*.

After gathering up mail, still in good spirits, Kieran sat down on his bed to go through what he'd received. The living quarter was a hive of activity, and the only downer was that the tent looked like a battleground;

packaging and paper were strewn everywhere, and everyone became very loud in the excitement. As much as he admired the guys, there were just some times when Kieran needed some alone time — this was one of them.

When the noise and excitement calmed, the men talked and shared what they had received. Firstly, came the collection of latest DVDs that the men had requested. A couple of guys had brought mini-DVD players, or laptops, with them, which was perfect for the regular section *movie night*. The last load was devoured within days by the whole platoon, including Ty.

Try as Ty might, nothing could persuade the men to watch his collection of *nature programmes* with him — no matter how persuasive he tried to be with the offer to make tea and share his mother's homemade shortbread. Within half an hour of the first, realising they were indeed watching a nature DVD and not porn, the whole platoon was left on a downer watching whales heading for spawning grounds and gorillas mating. The men decided it was best to keep their thoughts to themselves.

Not that there wasn't enough porn floating around the place as it was. Alex Myers saw to that.

Private Alex *Al* Myers was 17, and a vicar's son, who came across as a quiet man and looked the type to be horrified at the mention of porn. He shocked everyone in the platoon when he decided to share his collection of DVDs and girl-posed magazines that were popular with everyone — a supply that seemed in constant demand and circulation. His collection ranged from mild to dirty and real hardcore.

Overnight, his popularity increased throughout the compound as Al became the *go-to man*. When someone asked him how he got them, he merely smiled innocently and said, "eBay". No one knew how Al got them sent through *ethic* mail restrictions, but somehow, he managed it. Al even obtained the odd game for the guys who had brought Play Stations and X-box consoles out with them.

To be fair, lulls between patrols and keeping the guns and ammo cleaned and in constant readiness for action, while suffering long blisteringly hot days with nothing to drink but water, gave light relief to the boredom. The hardest thing to deal with when being posted in a war zone was the regular hours of downtime spent at the compound. Filling in the free time with no pubs, clubs, or alcohol; nothing to see for miles around but sand and confined to the compound, with alternative hours spent on patrol left a feeling of cabin fever at times.

The more updated supply of information and news on what was happening in the outside world was the delivery of daily newspapers, often outdated by at least two weeks by the time anyone got to read them. Top of the list was the *Sun* and *Star*, which were read from back to front in typical male tradition.

Kieran read his family mail and opened the packages that his mum had sent him. First things out of the box, pairs of new socks, were always welcome. Laughed at the news from the former mates he'd trained with, saving the newspaper for last. Like everyone else, he read the sports pages first and worked his way through to the articles until he found what he was searching for — Sophie Tyson.

"Watch it, mates! Romeo is reading his *Express*." Si pointed a finger directly at him. "*Sun* and *Star* not good enough for him."

"Yeah, best keep your fucking hands off, you fucking wankers!" screamed Kieran.

There was no doubt about it, they all knew what Kieran had meant. Newspapers, like everything else, were considered a personal item. Sure, the men shared most things, and no one was ever found short of anything. But the rule was that some possessions were valued more highly than others, and everyone respected that and treated it as a golden rule. Not taking it as such was treated in the worst way possible. A week of being ostracised and *Sent to Coventry* for the culprit if caught.

Captain Dan had his nose and ears to the ground and knew everything that was happening around his men. Dan came across a similar situation and intervened when Kieran and Si came close to throttling each other over a missing news item Romeo had pinned over his bed.

"I know you fucking have it! Only you or Smithie would fucking take it, and he doesn't have it!" yelled Kieran.

"Are you calling me a thief over a fucking old newspaper photo?" Si replied, just as heatedly.

"Too fucking right, I am. I want it back intact, or I'll fucking knock you flat on your back!" Kieran squared up to Si.

"You and whose army, you fucking immature bastard?"

"Who the fuck are you, to call me fucking immature?"

"You twat! You need to fucking back off!"

The men shared everything, but some things were personal and were respected as such. Taking something without permission — wind-up or not — would not be tolerated. There was no doubt about it, what started as a wind-up was now taking a different turn. Someone needed to defuse the situation as neither was backing down. Pride at stake, both men raised their fists, feeling it was the only way to resolve the situation.

Dan settled the dispute immediately when he entered the tent, clutching the missing newspaper in hand. It had mysteriously appeared in his quarters and was left on his bed. What surprised him more was why a young lad like Kieran was reading *Business Pages*. When a few of the men explained, Romeo was *loved up* and attracted to a female reporter who wrote a regular feature for the *Express*, that told it all.

Later that day, it came to light that Smithie had taken it after all and now faced a week of solitude. Smithie knew it wasn't just for thieving his stuff, but for not manning up and admitting it when asked. It took Si another week to forgive Smithie for his actions, and everyone noticed there was a noticeably strained silence between the two men for a while considering they were best mates. And in Afghanistan — a week of solitude felt a very long time. It was the first time Kieran and Si didn't see the funny side of Smithie's banter.

With all this, they were right about one thing, Kieran was crushing on a beautiful woman way out of his league who moved in different circles, and he had no hope ever to meet. Pity, besides, very few news reporters made it out to them. Now the engineers had got the internet set up and working, they seemed to see less and less of the press unless there was a crisis or other. There seemed a diminished interest in the war. It was as if the media back home had lost interest in the infantry soldiers that were fighting in Afghanistan.

Some of the men had started making their own video recordings, or taking shots on their mobiles while out on patrol, or faced with combat. They filmed several informative, detailed accounts the press would never see. Photos even made it back to loved ones. It seemed everyone had either a laptop or phone and gave vivid images of troops on Ops at the frontline. Kieran felt sure the MOD would confiscate everything if they found out.

Not all of the younger men were interested in using the internet for the sole purpose of keeping an image diary. They had other uses for the *net*, and some spent hours on it. Most of them joined dating sites or had social media accounts, *Facebook*, along with *Skype* held them captive, 'chatting with friends for hours on end.

Seeking adult entertainment, some found a different way to relieve their hormonal frustration, by paying for a live online adult webcam site. Si was left in no doubt their business made a small fortune from him, and from the number of troops that signed up for the site from the moment Si announced he'd signed up, and what he'd gained from it. That was until the site was discovered to be a fraud. It was a one-woman operation, fleecing men of thousands, and all the profiles and video clips were fake. After the news was made public — and a warning issued to stay clear of the highly notorious website — wisely, everyone ignored Si's former boasting. They chose a different way to spend their time, and pay less of their hard-earned money.

Of course, this didn't stop everyone else knowing Si had been shafted — fleeced by a tidy sum at that. Which left most of the section poking fun and laughing at him behind his back at the £10,000 of his retention bonus he'd spent on a girl who didn't exist. No one had dared to tell Si to his face. Through it all Si remained silent and aloof, and he spent mealtimes alone for a week. There was no doubt about it. Si had taken the whole episode pretty badly.

As a platoon, they still held up their fitness training, and once a week they would make up a five-a-side team and play a game of football. Everything was going great until someone made a crack at Smithie's *Friday night special*.

"She's not bad," Drews pointed out.

"You are fucking joking, Drews. She's a fucking slut!" Easty added, determined he wasn't missing out on the banter.

"Not as bad as that fucking fat woman you dragged out the gutter our last night out at Catterick!" Drews added.

"Piss off! She was up for it good and fucking proper," Smithie argued.

"Get fucked, you blind bastard. She was fucking ugly and old enough to be your grandmother!" Si yelled back.

"At least she was a real fucking shag. Your one was proper fucking fake!" Smithie yelled back.

With that, Si flew off the handle and kicked the ball over the perimeter fence and made a dive for Smithie grabbing his legs and wrestling him to the ground. It took six other men to pull them apart. Even if the game included a few eyeball-to-eyeball confrontations and ended in a brawl with both teams, despite a couple of black eyes and wounded egos it managed to raise spirits and finish well and no one was up on charges. And like any brothers would, the men argued then made up. More importantly, Si was back to being his annoying self.

The next morning, after scoff (food) it was back to business as usual; reports relayed by radio contact that direct combat fighting had erupted in a nearby village and was in fear of losing control of the Taliban.

A group of ANP went to investigate, and the 12 men had not been heard from since. Four hours since their last radio contact and counting. Fears were growing by the minute for the safety of the missing men and the possibility of an ambush.

Within an hour, 0600, Kieran's unit were mobile and the orders: Investigate and prepare for direct combat fire and minefield. Secure location and possible hostage capture.

Not knowing exactly what they were heading into, the men were prepared for one-on-one combat. The nine men were wearing full-body armour protection with a bulletproof ceramic plate, plus each man carrying enough rations and water for 24 hours weighing at least 50 lbs. Those with radios carried at least another 20 lbs more.

Everyone was now fully loaded up with 30 rounds of ammo and SA80s. Along with two Minimis, two underslung grenade launchers and two additional 5.56 mm rifles, the men loaded the gear into a (fully top-mounted heavy machine guns) manned Mastiff and two force protection WMIK with top-loaded manned machine guns ready to tail-end.

Joining the convoy for the first time, newly delivered from the MOD, a freshly painted, fully updated armoured PPV (Protected Patrol Vehicle) *Vector* with all the mod cons, including power-steering and two roof hatches with a mounted machine gun, and two rear doors for making an easy exit when needed, caused a buzz throughout the men.

Ty and Captain Dan got wind of the men starting a pool of how long before the Taliban put holes in the newly painted PPV. And Dan warned the men to take excellent care of it, and preferably return the Vector without any paint scrapes on the British taxpayers' investment. Leaving the FOB into the featureless, dry, sun-baked gritty distance of the desert, within minutes everyone was sat sweating in the confined heat of the Mastiff envying those inside the air-conditioned PPV.

The convoy slowly headed for the last known location of the ANP men who were reported to have lost radio contact 12 kilometres east from Now Zad and four kilometres north outside the *Green Zone* of Musa Qala, a stronghold of the Taliban. It was some 20 kilometres out from Now Zad that the lead vehicle came to a halt.

A detonated IED had left a massive crater in the middle of the road — the ideal place for the insurgents to plant fresh IEDs. After checks, for IEDs and landmines, two of the men gave the all clear to move forward. What looked like the remains of a police van had flipped on its roof and burnt out. Six Afghan policemen lay scattered around the car, charcoal body parts still smouldering, burnt beyond recognition. The second vehicle involved was a people carrier virtually untouched by the blast from the IED, which looked to be unoccupied at first glance.

While two other men, Wrighty and Ginger, guarded Kieran's back, he walked over to the vehicle, being careful to check the ground for IEDs before he stepped any closer. When Kieran opened the driver's door, nothing had prepared him for the gruesome sight before him.

Inside the van were the remains of the other six ANP men. A grisly sticky residue of coagulated blood dropped from the interior as he reached out to check further. Body parts were everywhere as thousands of flies hummed noisily in the intense heat. Just as Kieran lowered his arm to radio a response, the decapitated head of one of the Afghan policemen stared straight back at him. Kieran couldn't talk; he couldn't move. He felt sick to his stomach; this had been a real travesty and reinforced their knowledge of what the Taliban were capable of doing.

Smithie was tasked to radio FOB to request air support to lift the remains of the dead men, confirming the coordinates. The Chinook responded as it circled the area.

The rest of the men marked out the location and retrieved whatever equipment could be used by the insurgents. They tagged and named four out of the twelve dead policemen and placed identified remains in body bags and then destroyed the vehicle that remained. They didn't want the Taliban taking and claiming any of the body parts as trophies should they leave them behind. By the time everything had been dealt with and the deceased hurriedly loaded onto the waiting Chinook, the section was now running four hours behind the scheduled time.

It was evident that the Taliban *dickers* following them would be on their mobile phones or *click and press* radios picking up on their route. Unfortunately, leaving the Taliban ample time to set new IEDs or mines knowing the destination of the troops advancing towards them.

The convoy had gone no more than ten kilometres, as they drove through tracks of winding narrow roads flanked on the left by a long mud wall. The open terrain to the right was a sun-baked ploughed field with deep furrows that made it impassable. With no more than the width of an alley, they were attempting to pass through what was to be reported by the ANP as a deserted compound.

Travelling virtually at a snail's pace, no more than five kilometres per hour, the convoy had just driven clear over a bridge of a wadi (dry river bed). On entering the outskirts of the compound, the lead vehicle was the WMIK, followed closely behind by the Vector with the Mastiff truck not far behind, Smithie radioed rapid fire in the distance. When the road became too narrow for the Mastiff to continue, they set up a perimeter line to cover from the highest point on the edge of the compound to keep watch.

Following the standard procedures, with no other choice of road open to them, the remaining vehicles were forced to move onward with caution, to a clear viewpoint to assess the situation. Feeling they could be ambushed at any time, they made their way to their pinpointed destination, being a disused building no more the 500 metres ahead.

Just as the WMIK turned the bend, AK-47s began to fire into the metal sides of the PPV. With the steep, uneven terrain, the Taliban knew they were forced to stick to the track with the two remaining armoured vehicles, which were now prime targets.

Suddenly the lead WMIK was being fired upon, and Corporal Drews shouted, "Return rapid fire!" which crackled in Kieran's headset.

Jonesy knew he had to get his men to allocated position — quickly. They were coming under increased firepower and were sitting ducks inside the lead vehicle, despite the support from the top canopy 12.7 mm heavy machine gun of the PPV. Jonesy urged half of the men to move quickly, one by one, towards the nearby deserted building.

"Fucking move it!" Jonesy shouted over his radio. "Keep your fucking heads down!" Half the men had already dismounted. Al and Ginger were already set in position and returning fire.

Another band of Taliban fighters grouped, turned to the right of the convoy, armed with RPGs to cut off the men's entrance to the building. If the insurgents moved any quicker, they would have half of the men caught out in the open, making them sitting targets.

Jonesy was yelling into his radio for the Mastiff to drive through the ambush site, but they were unable to get any closer. Dan was on the radio and called for Apache helicopter support. The rest of the section was now under heavy fire and in the process of fighting back.

Kieran spotted around 20 armed Taliban heading straight for them while firing their AK-47s directly at them. He opened up the GPMG (General Purpose Machine Gun) mounted on the bonnet of the bullet-riddled WMIK.

Si spotted the silhouette of a suspected Taliban fighter; he moved slowly to the left flank of Kieran's position. It was then the shooter stepped out from the shadows.

Si pinpointed the darkly dressed, bearded insurgent wearing a dark turban, carrying an RPG launcher on his shoulder pointing directly at Kieran, and boldly refused to take cover. He shouted over the radio headset, "Contact left!" Si pumped a couple of rounds at the RPG insurgent, taking him down instantly.

It was at that moment the Taliban increased their assault and opened fire with a PKM Russian-made, belt-fed machine gun. Another RPG attacked the men across the open ground of the cultivated field, a grenade hitting the rear WMIK on impact, cutting off the exit of the convoy. Luckily, everyone made it out without being seriously injured. Using the cover of the armoured WMIK, the group made it over to the mud wall of the compound.

With the continued intense rapid fire from the popping of the AK-47s' bullets thudding at the wall and the cracking sound as they hit the ground around them, and to add the burning of the WMIK, Kieran was forced to admit they were looking outnumbered and in a dangerous situation.

Wrighty took out two more Taliban when they popped up 500 metres in front of him firing their AK-47s. Things looked worse when Dan came under fire, taking out their primary radio equipment, leaving the section cut off. The only other long-range radio equipment was in the burning WMIK. The roar of the Apache helicopter chose that moment to whoosh past, circling over the men, allowing them to take cover.

While the Taliban's attention was momentarily distracted and drawn to the Apache, Kieran chose that spontaneous chance to return to the burning WMIK to retrieve the vital radio pack.

Despite the repeated rounds from AK-47s hitting the ground around him as he went, and no doubt about the series of *fucks* he was going to get from Jonesy for being so reckless and stupid, his actions enabled Dan to send the Apache their location and vital information about the situation. So as far as Kieran thought — it was worth it.

"You stupid fucking bastard!" Si laughed.

"Have you not got a fucking brain, Romeo!" Jonesy shouted, from the cover of the Vector. With a burst of renewed fighting, taking the opportunity, Jonesy dashed for cover to join his men against the wall.

AK bullets followed his path, pop, pop. It was like everything was running in slow motion. Jonesy froze on the spot as he felt a dull thud that stopped him in his tracks, and suddenly he was on his back as he was flung backwards as two bullets hit his chest with a direct hit. With a groan, he rolled onto his side and was now lying face down in the dirt.

"Man down! Man down!" The words were shouted down the line of men in a state of confused shock.

Bullets plugged into the ground all around Jonesy, pecking at the dry, dusty ground causing swirls of dust and trying to take him out. The position of where Jonesy fell left the men in little doubt he'd been hit, but the problem was no one could see how serious his injuries were.

Taking out leaders or higher-ranking officers of the military was just what the Taliban aimed for, thinking it would cause chaos, and the men would not be able to fight back without a leader, and so would not fight back. They didn't know the British Army.

Fear did not hold these soldiers back, and no matter how bad things got — no man was left behind alone.

"*Fuck!*" Kieran tried to reach him but was forced back under fire as a frenzy of bullets popped at the ground around him. From what Kieran could see, Jonesy was lying face down wounded, out in the open for the Taliban to finish the job at any moment. "Fuck! Fuck, fucking hell!"

Kieran watched as the AK ammo fired straight at them. Round after round, with no lull as the constant stream of bullets rained down on them and one narrowly passed his head, hitting the wall beside him.

"Those fuckers hit Jonesy!" They were going to have to do something. "We have to get Jonesy out of there!" And judging by the amount of enemy engagement — pretty quickly. Obviously, the Apache could not fire on the Taliban from the aircraft's position, as fear of hitting their own men was a huge risk. The men needed cover.

Ginger and Kieran were the two closest and only about 50 feet away from him. There was no way that they were leaving Jonesy there for the insurgents to use him as target practice.

To reach Jonesy, the rest of the men opened fire on the band of insurgents and kept the two men covered by drawing their fire. With one shot to attempt a rescue and no time to have second thoughts, Kieran and Ginger made a quick grab for the sergeant, grabbed an arm each and dragged him back into cover and out the line of fire.

Somehow, they had made it back to the compound wall without either of them taking any hits. When the medic got to Jonesy, they had found his jacket had taken both bullets, hitting the chest plate, and although unconscious and a massive headache when he came round, he'd only suffered bruises and grazed knees from being dragged across the hard ground. He was lucky to be alive.

Despite that, Kieran couldn't help but feel responsible.

The helicopter pilot seemed to take forever to make the strike — but he did. There was a tremendous whoosh, the tell-tale trail of smoke as he fired, followed by a massive blast and the ground shook on impact. Everyone instinctively threw themselves down, covering their ears. The explosion was so close that Kieran's ears were ringing, and it left those closest to the detonation covered in dust, rubble and debris, which flew in every direction.

Just as quickly as it had started, the fighting ceased and everything went quiet once more. Despite the drama, and indentations — losing count after 50 spent ammo shells bounced off the new PPV — everyone made it back to the FOB alive. As Easty won the money in the Vector pool, they left it to him to fill out the damage report on the Vector with Captain Dan. Kieran didn't envy either of the men the job of telling Ty.

Chapter Four

Saturday, Intercontinental Hotel in Kabul 2100 hours.

Feeling exhausted, Sophie headed for her hotel room. All she could think of was a shower, and to slip out of the all-covering burqa. Covered from head to foot, apart from the letterbox slit for her eyes, she glanced briefly in the mirror. And, yes, despite the burqa, she still managed to get sand and dust plastered to her skin from the desert. Sophie had to admit — she'd not had the best of days as it was.

During her job as an undercover journalist, she'd discovered several high-ranking Taliban leaders ran a network of human trafficking throughout Afghanistan, by raiding poor remote villages, abducting mostly women and children and selling them into prostitution and slavery in Pakistan.

It was her job to find the evidence and expose this barbaric chain of people traffickers. The exposure was proving more challenging than she anticipated. Even after two months here in Kabul — she still felt no closer to locating the culprits than when she first arrived.

Now, a further setback, she had received word the traffickers had recently moved location, and the undercover human rights worker, posing as a medical relief worker, was out of contact range for another week.

She had an uneasy feeling about losing contact with the only person that knew her true identity, but nothing could be done about it right now; she'd have to wait out the week and see what developed. After all, it wasn't her contact's fault. Should this man be discovered, his life would be in serious jeopardy. He was risking death to aid her.

The Taliban had attacked another village and destroyed the main water pipeline, and an armed guard was needed to escort the medical staff to the locations to assess the damage and, more importantly, attend to the surviving people of the village.

Waiting for an update on the situation was so frustrating, even though the interest in the story had grown considerably. Despite that, she had to be patient and not put any pressure on the people helping with the investigation. She had been equally vigilant, hiding her identity and keeping her time in Afghanistan low key.

For the first time since getting back to the hotel, she realised she was feeling hungry. It was already past midnight when she rang room service for a sandwich and a bottle of chilled water. While she waited for the waiter to deliver her food, she glanced through her notes and interview files.

Two hours later, caught up in her research, Sophie realised room service had still not delivered her food. Oh well, she might as well get some sleep while she could.

What she needed right now was a refreshing shower, to slip on a fresh pair of shorts and a T-shirt, and free her hair from the restricting silver clip that secured and hid every strand out of sight. She turned on the shower and left it to get to the right temperature while collecting her fresh clothes from the bedroom. She was already hot — thank goodness for the rooms being air-conditioned.

At the tat-tat-tat sound of rapid gunfire Sophie gasped, trying to judge the distance between the sound of weapons fired and her bedroom. She scrambled through her handbag searching for her mobile to call the Afghan police. It wasn't there! Her hands sought the coffee table, checking through the stacks of files and newspaper clippings. Nothing.

Sophie barely made it two steps before shots rang out again freezing her to the spot — this time it was closer and longer bursts. Her gaze zipped from the unlocked door to the large, closed French windows to the balcony. It was no use, she was on the sixth floor and if she tried to jump, she'd probably break her neck. She would have to sit tight and hope someone would come to the rescue.

Screams and frightened voices echoed through the hallway of the hotel. Doors were slamming as the shouting and shots continued. The shooters were running rampage through the corridor and searching rooms. There was no mistaking the sound of fear and utter chaos. She could hear children crying and people's footsteps as they ran from their rooms eager to escape — What? Sophie tried to listen without making her whereabouts known to the gunmen.

"Where are the foreigners?"

Multiple Afghan voices could be heard above the noise as they searched each room as they swept through the building. Sophie couldn't understand it all, but by the heated tone they were making demands. Shouting in Pashto "Shoot them all!" Rapid fire followed the order.

More shots fired. Sophie covered her ears; the sounds were growing closer. She couldn't see what was happening without leaving the protective shield of the room. There was no doubt about it — foreigners were the prime target. Her only hope of escape, dressed as she was in the burqa, was that they would mistake her for an Afghan woman. But her safety was no guarantee. Living undercover as a woman in Kabul for the past week had taught her one thing — don't invite danger. That meant in this country — when you heard gunfire — smart people got the hell out before something, or someone shot you.

There was no doubt about it — she was going to have to get out of here and quick!

Scarcely enough time to stash the files and laptop before the rounds of gunfire penetrated the outer door. Fear gripped her throat, and crossing quickly and quietly into her bedroom she slowly closed the door hoping the intruders would think her suite unoccupied.

The light from her window caught her attention, illuminating the small balcony that led down to the fourth-floor main terrace and onto the fire escape below. The distance was impossible to jump, she was on the sixth floor and a fair drop — maybe she could tie some bed sheets together, which seemed her best option right now. She stepped over to the French windows to open them, trying not to make a sound.

There was a movement that caught her eye, and Sophie froze. Someone was here! She fought to keep calm and not panic. She backed away, and as she did so, a hand came from behind and covered her mouth roughly.

Sophie wanted to scream but couldn't; she knew enough of the language to understand she was in deep trouble. She was beyond fear now. A man dressed in Afghan Army uniform carrying an AK-47, wearing a suicide vest and armed with grenades and an ammunition belt stared at her.

"She has seen your face," the voice said from behind.

"No matter." His granite-like features peered at her no more than two inches from her face.

"This woman is of no use to us. Kill her now!" the first voice whispered to the other man.

"Not yet. I see defiance in her eyes." He smiled with all the charm of a viper. "I will get much pleasure from this woman before I kill her."

Sophie felt the icy chill of fear. The coldness in his eyes told her he meant what he said and would enjoy killing her. She began to struggle, twisting in his grasp as his hand held her. The two men started arguing, and Sophie couldn't understand a word.

"Hurry — We must go!" With that said she was free. "Kill her now and be done!"

The hand of the other man squeezed her face. "We have time. Killing her will be a great pleasure for me. Don't rush me."

As the second shooter left the room, he backhanded her across the face and threw her down to the floor. Although the hit wasn't that hard, with the shock of events it was too much for Sophie to take and it went dark.

Feeling a little dazed, and not knowing how long she had laid there, Sophie thought she heard an explosion the moment she hit the floor, and more voices and hurried steps before shots rang out again — this time it sounded different.

***

Sunday, 0300 hours Intercontinental Hotel.

The only thing in their favour at this moment was that the rest of the guests had exited when the insurgents had shown up and seized the hotel and occupants, and that was when the shooting started.

Kieran was pinned down behind a burnt-out car with insurgents shooting at him from across the alleyway. Unable to move closer to the entrance. *This was not the plan that was supposed to go down, was it?*

Another bullet whistled past Kieran's head, narrowly missing his right ear, and hitting the panel of the car. Right now, he wasn't sure what the plan had been, but he was pretty sure the briefing didn't include any of this. Two more bullets popped into the car, above his head, and Kieran dropped to the ground as the spent ammo left gaping holes, penetrating the car in a trail of grating metal on metal.

"Fuck me!" as he covered his head. "That almost fucking got me!"

Welcome to Kabul.

On entry to the city, judging by the amount of heavy gunfire from the militants — this was the first observation that the Taliban knew they were there and their position compromised.

Even though Kieran's section were highly trained troops in weaponry and combat situations, A Company had been ordered to support a small elite team of Special Forces, a unit primarily trained in hostage warfare situations, and they were giving the orders right now. Afghan police and British Army were called in as *support and rescue* status only if needed.

Now the terrorists had taken control of the hotel, and the guests were now hostages with reports of at least 14 civilians killed, this had been their first positive lead as to their objective since the siege began, and now smoke could be seen coming from the roof on the left side of the hotel.

Since the last suicide attempt on this luxury hotel, none of the previous searches Special Forces had followed had proved reliable to find the men responsible. Every known militant at large was suspected, of which there had been many. Each location had been thoroughly checked and then double checked, and had been false. But Special Forces were experienced soldiers and weren't about to give up and go home. The rescue operation involved over 50 men, most of them were British Army. A Company had been ordered to move quickly, followed by B Company, as the timing was vital if they intended saving lives.

At an impasse, it was unclear how many had been involved in this bloody siege, or what terrorist was responsible for such a vicious attack.

Later, intel on the attack revealed the insurgents, wearing ANA army uniforms, stormed the six-floor, 200 room luxury hotel in Kabul, and opened fire on 150 guests. The hotel security, fearing for their safety, fled the hotel without raising a weapon.

A military drone first picked up activity on the roof of the hotel, and the army was able to react quickly.

An aggressive fighter shouted threats in Pashto from a balcony of a sixth-floor room, "All foreigners will die. We shall kill them all!" as he fired his automatic weapon at the men on the ground, shouting, "No foreigner will live!"

Kieran's platoon was openly in the terrorist line of fire, which launched them directly into a head-on, full attack and fierce battle. Insurgents came at them with RPGs and AK-47s along with heavy machine guns, which ambushed them, pinning the men down and forcing them to take cover.

The direct rapid fire forced the men to abandon their *Snatch* vehicles, while the remainder scattered, taking shelter, SA80 assault rifles were checked and loaded instinctively at the ready. Some were crouching behind burnt-out, abandoned vehicles. Others were taking refuge in crumbling, decaying buildings to avoid the onslaught of gunfire and bullets, while making a tactical analysis.

At the realisation of gunfire, Kieran, while sat in the LTV (Light Tactical Vehicle), made a dive to the ground with three others, just as a bullet whizzed past him and penetrated the abandoned vehicle behind him. He checked his SA80 rifle and ammo; he was ready.

For fuck's sake! That was too fucking close for comfort.

Taking refuge in a nearby building had been his sanctuary in all this. Catching his breath, he took a moment to survey his surroundings; the entire area was mostly deserted, and checked and cleared of any wandering civilians. Many innocent civilians had evacuated before the Taliban had made a move in entering the hotel. One escaped witness told Special Forces that at least four men came to the main dining room, ordered a meal and sat down to eat. As soon as the food arrived, the men opened fire on the staff and guests, killing at least four employees.

Judging by the gunfire happening all around him, and the amount of weaponry and insurgents that had greeted them in this part of town, they were right to search this section of the hotel.

On entering this part of the war-torn city centre, Kieran noticed the few remaining people hanging around had been excited and shouted when Kieran and his platoon had first marched into the section, which was when the rapid gun battle had commenced, and forced them to engage in close-quarter fighting.

If he hadn't thought otherwise, he could have sworn that what he suspected as the *allies* was, in fact, a signal to the Taliban militants of their arrival.

Another bullet flew past his right shoulder and shattered the concrete behind him, missing him by a small fraction. *Another close call.* He needed time to contact Jonesy. Recalling the scattered men and planning their strategic defence attack had been their first call to action.

"Thought this was a fucking routine mission, pal? 'Walk in the park,' you fucking told me, Drews," Wrighty asked, where he was also taking refuge a few feet from Kieran. The barrage of bullets from the insurgency involvement kept them pinned down and from making a move against the Taliban.

"Where the fucking hell did that intel come from?" Jonesy asked the guy on his left.

Smithie was the radio operator and highly trained in warfare ordinance surveillance. "The info was good, Jonesy," he assured him.

Special Forces had been following the information on the suspected Taliban insurgent leaders carefully, and at the right time acted quickly. This had been their first positive lead on the insurgents' attacks since a suicide bombing. Kieran remembered reading about the killing in the press.

A Type 63 107 rocket was launched into a government building while defending the town of Sangin. The surprise attack had killed three women civilian workers and injured some others, while taking several hostages in the process. Two British soldiers were murdered in the blast while trying to protect the civilians, along with an Afghan interpreter that played an active role in the LEWT (Light Electronic Warfare Team). One of the fatalities was the only British-Muslim soldier killed in Iraq or Afghanistan since the fighting began. The soldier's parents told reporters that he'd been proud to be a British soldier.

"What's the matter, Smithie? Have you forgotten how to fire a fucking weapon, you wanker?" Kieran called over his radio set.

"Had it too easy lately. Gotten lazy since you had leave back in good old Blighty?" Al laughed.

"Want me to show you how a professional does it?" Wrighty teased his friend as he smacked his SA80 rifle butt and grinned broadly.

"Shut the fuck up, you tosser!" Smithie responded.

Drews laughed, as another hail of bullets sailed through the air. "Why are you complaining? Isn't this what we get paid for?" he called out as he ducked down for cover.

"And the location is hot, dry and sunny — can't beat that." Wrighty looked over at Drews.

Another rocket flew by, missing them, but penetrating the empty building close by with an explosion on impact sending dust and debris flying all around. The guys ducked down into the dirt and covered their heads.

Kieran had to agree — the location was undeniably hot. Nothing like a touch of irony. Kieran laughed, and the others joined in.

"I hate those fucking RPGs!" Drews cursed, while dusting down his jacket. "Fucking RPGs, they make so much fucking dust, and cause so much shit."

Kieran looked over at Jonesy, and he said, "Enough! For fuck's sake! Come on, guys; I've had enough of this dirt and shit — let's do something about it."

Before anyone could respond, Jonesy ordered, "Let's make a fucking move!"

Wrighty nodded. "That's more like it. We can't stay here much longer, that's for sure."

"OK. Let's make a move," Jonesy informed his men.

With their rifles loaded and hand weapons ready and raised, they made their way forward. One by one.

Kieran's thoughts were interrupted by a bullet as it whistled past his head. If he was going to stay alive, he was going to have to pay attention to what was happening around him. He touched his pocket radio button, as his sergeant's voice came through loud and clear on the line. "Stand by for action in five minutes. Keep your eyes and ears open."

"Clear," he responded into his headpiece.

Another repeating shot whizzed past him.

"Make ready to cover SFs' (Special Forces) rear," Jonesy ordered.

"Already done," Kieran responded to the order of Special Forces taking the lead in this operation.

Wrighty pinpointed to where the gunfire was situated and signalled his next move. The primary objective was to move forward to the captive building, locate the hostages and help the injured.

"What's the fucking delay, guys? Getting a little too fucking warm out here?" Al called from where he was also forced to take cover several feet away from Kieran.

"What's the matter? You want me to come and hold your hand, Al? Getting a bit too cosy for you?" Drews tapped into the line with a click. "Want me to call your mum for you?"

There was a mixture of laughter and mumbled comments.

"Keep it fucking together, ladies." Jonesy's voice came over the line.

"We are waiting for a clear visual on the enemy. Stand by," Wrighty responded.

"I was just fucking wondering. Wanted to know if there is a plan of action besides being targets for them to take pot-shots at," Al responded. "Unless the trick is we wait for them to run out of fucking ammo. Judging by the constant rapid fire, that's not likely to happen soon enough for me."

Wrighty laughed. "You never know, they might run out of ammo and start throwing rocks at our heads."

Kieran laughed and said, "Won't find anything in yours to damage then."

"Very fucking funny," Wrighty scoffed.

The men were all too aware of their orders in this operation. SFs required a diversion; this was necessary while they executed a successful rescue operation of the hostages. It had all been meticulously planned down to the last detail.

"You could try shooting back," Kieran replied. "Unless you are asleep over there."

"I thought I'd buy a car while I'm here — take my time looking around." Ginger laughed and popped his head up from behind a wreck of a torched car and waved. "Get a bargain fixer-upper."

"Strange. The owner doesn't appear to be around to ask for a test drive." Al laughed again.

"That's because everyone got the fuck out of Dodge," Ginger replied.

Everyone laughed. Despite the jovial antics, for one thing, Al had spoken the truth — with the rapid fire of shots, the gunfire wasn't easing up on them.

The enemy was holding their ground inside the fortified building across the street and had Kieran's team successfully pinned down with a barrage of flying bullets. Another bullet flew by. This entire situation was making them all anxious to end it and get the hell out of there.

The information and coordinates they received on the terrorist location had been correct. Almost three months ago, a group of hostages were taken and held prisoner. which mainly amounted to journalists and media correspondents lured into covering terrorist attacks within the city centre, and being captured immediately. Threats were made to harm the hostages within the hour unless the rebels' demands were agreed.

It all ended badly, as the hostages were all executed; one woman was beaten to death, and two UN workers were beheaded — their bodies left in a shallow ditch and found two days later. A recording was filmed of the execution and released on YouTube.

This time was different; Sergeant Jones waved a hand in the air, signalling on the earpiece. "Remember, take those fucking shooters alive if possible. Ready to go in two minutes." He started counting down.

Wrighty laughed. He looked over at Al and tapped his earpiece. "That means you will have to put buying that car on hold for now."

On the word "Go!" Kieran heard Drews groan under his breath at the banter. Drews made his way down the street making sure to take cover behind the abandoned vehicles.

Kieran and Wrighty began firing their weapons, which were aimed at the building, hoping to give Drews cover by drawing the return fire back. With the hail of bullets raining down on them, Wrighty looked over at Kieran. "I've had enough of this shit. Time to make a fucking move."

While making his way slowly forward, Wrighty, using the driver's door of the car in front rested the nose of his rifle, with its long-range sights, through the open window. He tucked himself in tight as he positioned himself, firing five rounds in the direction of the gunfire while Kieran did the same from the side of the old wreck. The return fire kept on coming directly at them.

Drews took the signal to make his move and made it across to the other side of the road and then ducked at the side entrance of the building. It worked! The terrorists were still occupied with the constant firepower provided by Kieran and Wrighty.

"Move it! Let's make a fucking move and join the party! Remember

— use caution." He heard Jonesy call out through his earpiece, as the rest of the company made their way forward to follow Drews' position with their SA80s. Their weapons ready.

Al followed up the rear with Smithie and Kenny close behind. When each of the men had made it across to the secured location, Kieran made his way over to join them.

In complete silence, Jonesy reached for the doorknob to the basement, and entered the building silently. Drews covering his back and Kieran from his left side. Rapid gunfire opened up on them; muzzle flashes from the automatic rifles spewed spent shells over the open staircase where they had been heading.

The men backed out; each of the men taking stock of what just happened. The safety of the men and civilians was above all else. Checking the wellbeing of each person, in turn, was a priority. More shots echoed from across the street, and it sounded like Al was engaged in rapid fire.

At the arrival of the remaining platoon following up the rear, Kieran and Wrighty sprinted around the corner to lend firepower to Al if he was pinned down.

Some of the men were under direct fire as they tried to make it back across the road. Kieran was relieved to see the guys unharmed — returning shots to add the cover to protect the men. Judging by the firepower, all the signs pointed it to be a small band of insurgents returning fire. And it was pretty clear to Kieran that they weren't giving up lightly.

At that moment, a flicker of movement in the hallway caught his eye. Wrighty nodded in his direction as he spotted it too. It looked like one of them had tried to make their escape before things heated up, or they got caught as a terrorist. They couldn't let him escape, or worse — set himself up as a suicide bomber.

As if reading each other's thoughts, they both raised their weapons and dashed to follow the suspicious movement. Without a word, and with precise, rapid movement, the two guys hastened after the figure that had now evaded the gunfire and made it up to the second-floor to the south side of the hotel, which looked out over the car park.

They were not sure if the man had gone rogue, or something far worse. A possible suicide bomber was trying to lure them away from the rest of the group. One thing was painfully evident as he raised his handgun and discharged it in a crazed fashion, taking pot-shots at anything that moved. Bullets were flying everywhere. Only when the man stopped shooting long enough to reload his weapon, did the guys attempt to make a move on the lone gunman.

Being careful, moving with organised precision, they headed across the hallway, one by one, but as they got closer a single shot rang out. Both men dived to the ground, giving away their position, as gritty dust covered them as bullets penetrated the plastered walls with the sound of a dull thud. Not right, being out in the open like this left them as a sitting target. It was clear to them that they were facing a lone shooter taking up a new position, allowing him access and vision to pick off the team from across the street as they made it back to the central part of the building.

Kieran looked across at Wrighty, relieved that they were both unharmed, but they couldn't stay there for long.

Drews joined them. Kieran figured he'd prefer to be helping to capture a suspected terrorist, which was far better than waiting around in readiness for the others to make their move.

"Stay down. I'll distract the shooter," Drews told the team, then made a quick exit around the side of the building and headed to the open staircase.

Once Drews was in position, Wrighty made a quick run to an open side room and the next group of gun-wrecked rooms. The building looked riddled with bullet holes and was falling apart, but perfect to take up his sniper position. Once Wrighty had Kieran covered, he then took the opportunity to make his move as he saw the suspect take cover inside a deserted room. There was no escape for the terrorist.

With trained observation, Kieran watched as the suspect waved his small handgun in the air as he shouted and cursed them. He fired his weapon at Drews and then in Wrighty's direction, missing them entirely with his random shots.

Doubting the shooter's shots and judging by his aim, neither of them appeared to be in any danger of being hit by his stray bullets. Between reloading, the three guys moved closer, still aware of their orders that suspected terrorists were needed alive.

When they were not able to safely move any closer, the men signalled to each other. Kieran called out to the man, stopping him momentarily in his tracks. He observed that the lone shooter was clean-shaven and wearing a suicide vest with grenades clipped to the belt. Looking closely, what was more disturbing judging by the distressed and agitated look on his face, he was eager to end this. And not an ounce of remorse at taking others with him.

The man called out something Kieran didn't catch. Kieran had not been doubtful that the man intended taking his life along with others, not for a second.

"Wait! Let's talk." Steve tried to reason with him. Placing his rifle down in front of him and raising his hands slowly to show he wasn't armed. "You don't need to do this. Put your gun down. Let us help you."

"What the fuck are you doing, mate?" Kieran asked, genuinely concerned for his friend's safety.

The man looked anxious, and he was sweating and fidgety. Although he was looking directly at Drews, he still didn't put his small semi-automatic pistol down. In fact, he seemed to grip it tighter. Kieran and Wrighty kept the man in their target sights, neither one of them wanted to kill this man without reason — his information would be vital to them. But should their lives be at risk, and the need arose to shoot, they would without hesitation. Should he turn his weapon on Steve, they would most certainly, especially as his gun was lying on the ground, and he was unarmed against the other man's armed response.

The man's eyes frantically searched the deserted street as if looking for another way to make his escape. He still clung tightly to his rifle that was pointing at the ground.

"Do you understand?" Drews asked slowly. He nodded to the ground. "Put down the gun and come with us. We will help you."

He was not sure if the man understood English or not, but Kieran could tell he was listening. It was necessary for Drews to get him to lower his arms.

The man nodded stiffly. Kieran began to ease his finger off the trigger, just for the tiniest motion. But it proved to be a bad mistake. Almost as if he'd reacted with Kieran's movement, it was like something out of a movie. In the blink of an eye, before Wrighty or Kieran could respond, the suspected man brought up his gun and shot at Drews and then turned it on himself and he fired.

They could only watch as Drews crumpled to the ground. The other man was dead instantly.

Oh shit! "Man down! Man down!"

Kieran could hardly comprehend what had happened. "What the fuck?" he called over his headset. "Man down!"

Wrighty cursed, "Why the fuck did he do that?" He looked bewildered.

"I don't fucking know." Kieran rushed up to Drews and crouched down to check his pulse in his neck. Despite his injury and the amount of blood soaking through his combat jacket, luckily there was a steady pulse. Kieran breathed heavily with relief. It was when Kieran turned back to the lifeless body on the ground and checked his pulse, did he say, "Jonesy isn't going to be impressed with us."

Observing the loss of the insurgent and a man down in the bargain wasn't a good result by any means. Wrighty mumbled his own words in agreement, knowing his concerns for Drews had been justified.

In a quiet voice, Steve's lips moved slowly. "I'm OK, Romeo."

Patting Drews' shoulder, he said, "That's good news, mate." He heaved a huge sigh of relief. "That's fucking great news, mate!"

"Sure fucking is!" Wrighty murmured, "I wouldn't want to explain this to Jonesy."

It was evident, by the amount of blood soaked through on the front of his uniform, Drews had been hit in his chest pretty badly, and judging by the fucking big bullet hole caused by the close-range shot of the semi-automatic pistol, Drews needed urgent medical attention. Kieran checked his jacket for morphine. Drews winced in pain as he jabbed his side with the meds, and tried to sit up.

"Stay fucking still, you idiot."

"I'll be fine, my chest feels like it's caved in right now," he gasped. He was struggling to breathe. "The medics will sort me out."

Wrighty looked down at Kieran. "We need to let the others know."

Kieran was already asking for medics on his earpiece, and then to his sergeant, "Yeah, he's dead," Kieran said, while informing Jonesy on the suspected terrorist's condition. "Medics on their way now," Kieran added, as an update on Drews. "He'll make it. He's talking, so he's going to be just fine." Kieran was silent as he waited for orders. "Sure thing. Will do."

Kieran turned to Wrighty. "Stay with Drews until medics get here and I have to join the others." Kieran nodded back in the direction of the gunfire coming from the upper level. "Jonesy wants me back with them; he thinks our dead terrorist was a decoy to lure more men away from the building for something bigger. Maybe a lone suicide bomber — could mean something worse."

He shrugged. "Not been wrong so far."

At that moment Kieran spotted the dead man's hand still tightly clenched. He checked carefully, forcing the dead man's fist to open slowly. He noticed he was holding some form of a small incendiary device, about the size of a little phone, which had been triggered to activate on pressure. Reading the small screen confirmed the device was active and counting down. An explosive device and no way to defuse it!

The findings had become painfully visible — the rest of the men were in immediate danger! He had to warn them and get them out of that building now! Acting more on impulse than brains he told Wrighty to contact Jonesy and inform him of the imminent danger.

Kieran grabbed the device and ran like hell back to the prime location. As soon as he turned the corner, he heard an explosion and noticed heavy flurries of smoke and debris were already coming out of the upstairs windows from the roof.

Smoke camouflage grenades had already been launched into the burning building, debris falling all around them — the men needed more cover in entering the upper floors of the building. Bullets were hailing down on them in rapid fire through the broken windows. They had the men cornered.

If they were going to make their move, it would have to be now, before the smoke cleared and the entire building came down around their ears. It would make it too easy for the insurgents occupying the building to take pot-shots at them, and all too quickly, pick them off.

On the sergeant's word they made their advance, the remaining men with their masks in check, ammo and guns, and once again he slowly opened a door.

Inside, everything was a blur of smoke. At first, it took a few moments for Kieran's eyes to adjust. On entering, his first instinct was to hit the floor, trying to stay low under the smoke. Despite feeling as if they had been inside the building for hours, it had in fact only been a few moments. Kieran squinted to see through the smoke. He felt Al's hand on his right shoulder, gesturing that they had located the hostages. Now it was getting to the dangerous part for sure.

The men hurriedly searched the rooms — captives were relying on the military to rescue them from the terrorists. And they would be saved, hopefully without the cost of any more lives.

At that moment Kieran saw something catch his eye. A movement. It was some kind of small figure tucked in the corner. An unconscious person. A woman or a child! And judging by the faint groans — still alive. He began to crawl closer.

She responded to the brush of his fingers on her cheek. "She's OK." A harsh whisper brushed across her ear pulling her closer. "Who the fuck would do this?"

As he held her to him, the woman started kicking and struggling in a delayed agitated response as if fighting off her attacker. He tried to quietly, but firmly, reassure her, "Fight me all you want. I'm getting you the fuck out of here." Although he spoke to her in English, his tone only seemed to stress her even more.

"She's in shock. Do something," Al's voice added, with concern.

"Take it easy. I'm not going to hurt you," trying to soothe the woman "I want to help. Trust me". He tried repeating the words in Pashto to reassure her. At his words, she became more distressed — so far he wasn't doing too good a job up to now. There was nothing left for it.

The figure whimpered as she felt a sharp prick in her shoulder as he injected her. She fought him as if to keep her senses, but she couldn't resist it, and the fight was going out of her. What he had given her was acting fast. At that moment she calmed, and her body went slack in his arms.

Jonesy was in his ear telling them all to vacate the building. Immediately!

"Everyone fucking out! It is time to get the fucking hell out of here!" he heard him say over. "Now!"

He scooped the figure up and told her she was safe now, and he was going to get her out in one piece. As the last of the rescued hostages made it out of the burning building, a loud cracking came from above. Kieran glanced up, the ceiling looked weak, and in a split second of thinking he handed the woman over to Al standing by the doorway. As he set himself to ready his escape the roof came down, trapping him beneath concrete and brick. The smoke was now too thick and blocked all hope of vision, and he could barely breathe.

Despite all the dust and rubble, he tried to free his legs and crawl to a small opening where the door was situated. At least he'd hoped he was going in the right direction of where he thought the door had been. Breathing through the mask was becoming more difficult, yet he kept his face covered and kept crawling.

Several hands grabbed him; he felt two hands grip his arms and pull him free of the dust and smoke. He felt someone tug at his mask, and thankfully he felt the sun on his face, and the fresh air filled his lungs. Wrighty and Al pulled him free, and away from the building to a safe area.

"You are one lucky bastard, Romeo!" Wrighty said.

"I'm OK, thanks for asking, you wankers" Kieran replied, coughing and spluttering and unable to get the energy to get to his feet. Deciding the way he felt, he thought he'd rest a minute.

All three men watched as the hostages were checked over by the medics. and accounted for by the remainder of the team. He heard Sergeant Jonesy over his earpiece. "You are one lucky, stupid bastard, Romeo. Do you hear me? You dumb fuck!"

For a long moment, Kieran thought about ignoring it, but he thought better of it. "I hear you loud and clear, Jonesy." He smiled weakly.

"You are pushing your luck, Romeo. I don't want you ever pulling a stunt like that again. You fucking hear me? Ever! You dumb bastard!"

"Yes, Jonesy." Sitting up, he explained about the device he'd secured. He held out his hand and dropped it in Jonesy's hand. "I think once the smoke clears, the police should take a look at that woman we found. I have a feeling her statement could be informative."

"I'll have Special Forces take a look. Our job is done here."

"OK, sir." Being wise enough to let the experts examine the

witnesses.

"Time for us to part company with Special Forces. Back to the UK for us."

"Where we going, Jonesy?" Kieran asked.

"Training. Norwich. Seems the MOD want to fucking test us to see if we are doing the fucking job right here." As he jabbed a pointed finger at the ground.

Chapter Five

One week later

Home, at last, Sophie thought, as she dropped her flight bag on the entrance floor of her house, carefully remembering to lock the front door as she did so. Once inside, Sophie found only then she could relax and take a moment to reflect.

The joy of returning home after an assignment was short-lived at the sound of a familiar voice.

"Welcome home, Wifey."

How on earth did he get inside the house without her knowing?

Sophie cringed inwardly, hating the term he used. "Hello, Simon."

Shattered from her long, tedious journey, Sophie wasn't about to let him see how much it bothered her him being in her home. "How have you been?" And above all, she wasn't it the mood to remind him that he was now her *ex-husband*.

"I'm fine. I could do with a drink. I've not touched a drop all day."

"You know I don't keep any alcohol here."

At first, it had been agreed for Sophie to stay in military housing after the divorce *"while keeping a watchful eye on Weapons Systems Officer Campbell"* as his section commanding officer had put it. She also had a job; she couldn't watch him all the time.

The problem was — Simon didn't see it that way, and the situation felt no different now than it had been before the divorce. The memory of her unhappy marriage was a constant reminder that love and happiness very rarely went together.

She had moved to Brize a little over two years ago to be with her new husband. Looking back now she had married Simon for all the wrong reasons. And it certainly felt like getting married was like the kiss of death as it quickly began a spiral downturn, looking back now. Sophie didn't know it before, but it was the beginning of the end.

Their story started like so many others. It started out filled with promise and devotion, and the fairy tale romance was turned into a humdrum routine life that affected Simon significantly. It was only a few short months ago that Sophie realised how unhealthy their marriage had become. Her life at times became a living nightmare. It certainly had elements of it.

Sophie realised now she hadn't known him well enough, and now that she did, it was too late for regret. Their broken marriage didn't mean Sophie had wanted to move out in his time of need. There seemed very little choice on leaving so she stayed, but something had gone wrong, and now things were getting increasingly more difficult to live with.

Even following an agreed amicable divorce, Simon's outlook on the sorry affair was far from judging in the beginning. After all, Sophie and Simon had grown up in the same village; he'd been 12 years her senior and lived only a few short streets away from her parents' house. She had been just a child when he had manufactured reasons to leave home at 18. He had complained incessantly about boredom within a small cramped community.

Simon joined the Royal Air Force and began training as an officer. With the lure of promises of travel he had not been able to resist the idea of adventure. From the moment she had seen him in his uniform, she'd noticed the change in him.

Over the next few years, Sophie had heard from Ruby, his mother, on how he enjoyed his life. She'd boasted of his travels around the world, and what a far cry it was from the boredom of leading a small community village life.

Some years later, it was on one of his infrequent visits home that Simon had spotted Sophie, and taken a keen interest in her. At first, things seemed pretty routine — as routine as things could be around Simon. Between overseas' postings, he kept in touch. His light, friendly letters were interesting and boasted of the many countries and destinations he saw, but never would she consider them romantic.

The next few years followed a pattern. Simon spent some time floating in and out of her life. They would write infrequently and exchange birthday gifts the odd time, but on the whole, he was an average looking kind of guy — smart and even known on occasion to show a certain amount of charm. His emerald-green eyes would twinkle as he had smiled, coaxed and flattered her with his charming smile. Her heart had melted when he told her that he would die without her. Of course, at this point, Sophie was still at university, and she had refused point blank to give up her studies or sacrifice her dreams of becoming a writer, for marriage. He had told her if her career as a writer was so important to her, he would wait for her.

By the time Sophie had turned 26, they had married and she waited for word to join him, but that was postponed for a year as Simon received a posting to Iraq for six months. Sophie remained with her job for another 18 months, and that was until he found accommodation for them at his permanent home posting at RAF Brize Norton. Unfortunately, on his return, after six months apart, it was enough for them to develop problems in their relationship.

Sophie believed some men change after they get what they want. Reading the signs today, that was Simon to a tee. Sophie had fallen in love, or she thought she had at the time, with a handsome RAF officer, slightly older, and it felt like he was set in his ways. But the minute they made their wedding vows — he had changed.

Simon became moody and possessive. He never trusted her when her job forced her to work away from home. Simon had a bad temper and always seemed to find ways to punish her, watching and waiting for things to blame her for. How had she not seen the signs before they married? It had certainly not been the married life she had envisioned or hoped.

At first, Sophie had not complained about the endless hours she'd spent alone. But unbeknown to her, what had started out as a friendly drink with the boys after work became a regular habit. Which more often than not didn't stop with the *"one drink with the lads"* either.

On her arrival, their first evening together, Simon didn't make it home after a late drinking session. She'd also believed him when he'd told her better not to risk driving home drunk, so he'd stayed at a friend's house.

He was rarely home, but when he was, Simon was difficult to be around. She would find excuses to keep the peace, and when he was away on exercise or missions she would hope Simon would come back as his old self, so she kept going. He constantly blamed his moods and bad behaviour on her.

More perturbing, he'd lost all interest in her, and stopped making love to her.

When she had approached him about their intimacy issues, he'd casually dismiss them as unimportant or fly into a rage and find something else to blame her for. He would use words to demoralise her affections. He would attack her ego, and twisted his own lack of interest in her. Simon accused her of not being interested in sex, and not caring for his needs. In his mind, she was an inferior wife by his standards. Then afterwards, he would disappear for nights on end. When it got to several more times within a month, she'd started to worry about his excessive drinking. So she tried, and instead of leaving — Sophie stayed.

The growing concern was Simon's ability to spend money like running water. With increased credit-card debts and bank loans, his lifestyle had placed them financially heavily in debt. Shortly after Sophie arrived at Brize Norton, she was able to get some work as a freelance journalist — most of it involved covering on a series of articles for the British Army as part of a recruitment drive.

The location wasn't perfect; it was based at the British Army Stanford Training Area (STANTA) close to Thetford, and south-west of the city of Norwich. The only drawback was the amount of travelling time from Brize to Norwich. But the pay offer was a much-needed boost for their depleted bank balance, despite Simon's misgivings.

The job offer came at a desperate moment in their lives when she'd discovered several bills that had been left unpaid and a severely overdrawn bank account. Their mounting debt was financially crippling them. They were living far beyond their means. And if she were honest with herself, without the military support and housing, Simon would have been kicked out of the RAF and left homeless months ago.

This didn't appease the feeling of loneliness Sophie felt at all the hours spent home alone with no friends or family to turn to other than the people Simon had introduced her to. Strangely, she didn't count Simon's friends as her own. She and Simon had argued countless times over her work and the need to curb his spending. But in the end, he had always relented, knowing how much they needed that extra income.

At one crucial point, after Sophie's pleas, Simon had begun to seek advice from various doctors, all of whom came to the same conclusion — nothing she had done had triggered off his reaction to his violent, jealous behaviour and dark moods of depression.

Sometimes things would seem OK for a few weeks. Then out of the blue, every so often, Simon's mood would swing again, and his temper would erupt and often became close to violence. When those dark moods overshadowed him, he would become withdrawn and often silent, as if fighting some demon within him. It was continually not knowing how to talk to him, as if she was continuously walking on eggshells. Out of the blue he would get angry, and if unable to cage his rage, and when he was in this frame of mind he'd find something else to blame her for.

His bad swings of violence and the sombre dark moods were what she had feared the most. The real hatred always lay beneath the surface, as if waiting to rear its ugly head. Which he only suffered after he'd been drinking heavily; it was if the alcohol enhanced the violence within him.

She would try to calm him and be patient: time and time again she would try. She had learnt early on that she had to deal with the situation, and each moment as it came along. When Simon's mood did become violent, she would try to calm him down to the best of her ability, or before he lost control altogether. Sophie had tried for so long and so hard; so much so that she had stopped caring for Simon. All she could feel for him now was pity. But Simon still needed her.

Their marriage had ceased to continue in the form of a relationship by this time. Feeling cornered, Sophie felt divorce was her only means of escape. Even after their so-called *amicable divorce*, they had formed a new friendship. But *friends* was all she could ever be to him; she felt nothing for him now. It didn't mean any more than that. And her *arrangement* she had forged with his commanding officer worked out fine. Simon needed the stability and routine that the marriage accommodation afforded.

It was important for Simon to know that Sophie supported him, and he'd convinced himself that their lives together were perfect. The only tragedy in her life was the tie Simon held over her. But she had made her bed and agreed to stay to support Simon in his recovery from alcohol abuse until he didn't need her.

But there were times when she tried to disagree and reason with him, and he would become more enraged. Simon's umbrage actions became more about control and hatred the longer she stayed with him. Not for the first time, she feared for her safety.

Some days she wondered why she bothered even getting out of bed. It certainly wouldn't have helped to have stopped working; work helped her keep her sanity and her mind active. It was the only time she could relax and allow herself to smile and be happy. At times, being with Simon, she doubted that she could ever be happy and confident to smile again. She hadn't always been like that. There had been a time that she had been a confident and happy person, and had no trouble holding her own. But that was then.

"Well, don't just stand there — make me a drink?" Simon ordered thickly, thinking only of himself as he glared at her across the entrance hall and walked ahead into the living room. The stale odour of alcohol and cigarette smoke filled the room.

"I told you..."

"I know what you told me," he interrupted angrily.

It was evident by the state of him; he was drunk again. As he swayed on his feet, his face flushed and he slurred his words through the amount of alcohol he'd consumed — his light-brown hair dishevelled and his green eyes bloodshot and ominous.

Her first reaction had been how had he gotten into her house in the first place? When she'd agreed to stay and keep tabs on Simon, she had made it clear why she had wanted separate living quarters. Which then he'd readily agreed to.

Looking more closely, from the living room she noticed the back porch door catch was ajar. The wood frame was slightly splintered, and the lock was missing from the French door and hanging still attached to the frame. Trying to take in what she'd seen, reality hit her — Simon had forced himself into her house by breaking down the door. How long had he been here waiting for her?

Panic had leapt up inside; she was tense and felt the colour begin to drain from her body slowly. She took this action as a warning — when Simon drank this much, he became unstable, and more often than not became violent, and she would often feel the brunt of that anger when he'd hit her. He didn't know or care about the limitations of his temper. However, Simon was always apologetic and begged Sophie's forgiveness the next day. The old Sophie would forgive him, no matter how much pain he had inflicted on her.

Some would probably argue and say you don't stop loving someone just because they are going through a rough time. But the Sophie of old had stopped loving him; she couldn't be sure precisely when it happened, by marking it with an actual date or time, but day by day, gradually, he had slowly driven her away. He'd dragged her into a life she didn't belong in and had no interest in living with such misery and brutality.

He had thrown verbal abuse at her and used obscenities as he directed his fixation and conversation at the suggestion she had a secret lover.

"I know you've seen him," he spat at her.

"What are you talking about?"

"I bet he can't wait for you to spend another night with him." He threw a judging scowl at her. "Spread your legs for him, did you?"

"That's a vulgar thing to say. There isn't anyone else! I don't know what you are talking about."

"You think I'm stupid! I've seen the news! I saw him carry you out that building!"

Of course! Suddenly it dawned on her. "I was rescued from a hotel siege by Special Forces. Nothing else! I was unconscious!"

"You're lying! You were staying at the hotel with some guy! I saw the evidence with my own eyes!"

There was very little chance to reason with him when he was in this frame of mind, but she needed to try anyway. "You are mistaken."

"You think I don't know about you and your lover." He swore at her again. "I see and hear things more than you know."

"This is ridiculous! I was on assignment. I told you that." She didn't want to get angry with him because it would only anger him more. "The hotel came under attack by the Taliban. You said you saw it on TV, so you know it's true. What did you expect them to do — leave me behind to die?"

"Liar! You are nothing more than a dirty slut!"

86

"You have seen the news — you know what happened."

"Liar, liar, liar! Is this what happens while I'm home alone, while I'm waiting for you to return? You come home reeking of his body on yours, smelling of him on you. Did you think you would get away with it?"

Sophie had been too weary to even argue with him. "It's not true, I wouldn't do that." She tried to appeal to his inner sense of judgement.

Simon lunged forward, falling towards her as he collapsed on top of her bed. "Don't lie to me! You betrayed me!"

"There is no one!"

"You're a bloody lying slut!" He swore viciously.

"Simon, calm down. Think about what you are saying."

"I am calm, and I know perfectly well what I'm saying. I hear what people say about you. And about how the men want to touch you. Do you think I'm stupid?" he yelled. "How many others have you seen behind my back?"

"I can't control what people say! I've seen no one!" She protested fiercely over and over, but the words seemed to fall on deaf ears. "You should calm down."

He leaned over her, swaying as he did so, His light-brown hair was slicked back savagely. He was still wearing his traditional air force blue No 2 uniform trousers. During the evening he'd discarded his blue cap, probably lost — his tie askew and dragged to one side. His blue uniform shirt was open minus his buttons and stained with spilt alcohol down the front, and he looked angry with her.

He huffed and puffed. "Don't you tell me what to do." He stumbled, and he tried to stand.

She observed him; there was no denying he looked so much older than his 42 years. Also, Sophie noticed, not for the first time, he'd put on a bit of weight. His chin had begun to look bloated and his eyes had suffered from his drinking too — once bright emerald-green and full of life, they were now dull, and heavy shadows hung low under them. There was no visible trace of the old Simon left.

Sophie didn't want to argue, not with him in this state, it was pointless. Not that he'd probably remember the tongue lashing and accusations he'd thrown at her anyway — it all felt so useless.

She turned away. Simon instantly acted on an opportunity and grabbed her forearm. "Where do you think you're going?" he demanded fiercely.

Sophie felt suddenly afraid as she tried to shrug her arm free. "To make you some coffee."

"You're not going anywhere. I haven't finished with you. And I don't want your damned coffee," Simon slurred, as his grip tightened and his fingers painfully held fast.

"Simon — stop it. You're hurting me!" Sophie called out.

He suddenly threw her away from him, falling back awkwardly onto the sofa. As Simon laid on his back looking up at her, he jabbed his forefinger into the air with such force, sending a chill down her spine, and by the look on his face, for the first time, she believed him when he said, "I hate you! I fucking hate you!"

"Simon, please!" She detested the way he would swear and curse her.

He ignored her. "What sort of woman are you?" Simon continued his onslaught — his voice so loud her ears began to ache. "You're not a real woman, not if you can't give me children. I hate the very sight of you! I despise you! Do you hear me? I fucking despise you!" he said over and over. His eyes were full of rage.

Sophie was cringing inside. He blamed her for so much. Even hated her at times. Not revealing how much his words stung and hurt her, she tried to calm him.

"Simon, let's talk. Have you forgotten our arrangement? We're not married to each other any more," she cried out to him, trying to get through to him. "Don't you remember?"

"You're my wife, and don't you forget it!" he shouted at her angrily, "We belong together, and you are going to give me what any other warm-blooded woman would give her husband."

"Simon, you don't know what you are saying." There was no mistaking the fear in her voice as it rose. "No, Simon. No!"

Pointing an accusing finger directly at her, he vented his venom on her. "You think you are too good for me, don't you? You are a prized bitch! You with your almighty ways and your posh university education," he was saying as he stumbled, trying to remove his clothes as he swayed on his feet.

"Please, Simon, listen to me," trying to appeal to his better nature.

Her pleas fell on his deaf ears as he threw himself on top of her. The weight of his body held her captive. Rigid with fright, she waited for what she knew was about to follow. Unable to tear her gaze away she looked him in the eye; there was no mistaking the cold, steely-eyed glint that was undoubtedly there for her to see.

"You are my wife! Mine! Do you hear me! You will always be my wife! Don't you even try to forget it!" Simon spat at her through clenched teeth; his breath stank of stale alcohol. At the same moment, he raised his right hand, clenched his fingers into a tight fist, and struck her hard across the left cheek.

Too stunned to cry, desperate for her safety, she began to fight him off. She had to escape, and quickly. He loosened his hold on her a fraction, and her release became possible. His face flushed as he became enraged and fought her more savagely.

His ego could not take her not wanting him, that was the one final blow to his ego that he couldn't stand. Simon suddenly stopped trying; his bodily desire had weakened as he became unconscious in her arms. There was one thing for sure — there was no way she could get him safely back to his accommodation without calling attention to herself. Or to Simon's state of being. There was nothing for it — he would have to remain on the sofa until morning. She was too exhausted to do anything right now.

For a few moments she lay there rigid while her mind slowly absorbed the situation and seriousness of what had just happened. Her mouth felt dry, and she tried to swallow a couple of time; she licked her lips and started to cry silently to herself. Sophie knew she would have to move; she couldn't just lie there waiting for him to regain consciousness.

Working her arms free she pushed and twisted beneath him. Pushing him away became an act of desperation. Freeing herself became a cumbersome task as Sophie gently rolled him off her. Sophie carefully laid a cover lightly over him where he laid on the sofa. Switching off the light she went to make some tea for herself in the kitchen and prayed he slept the night.

The events of the evening left Sophie realising she couldn't take any more of this. First thing in the morning, she would have to make preparations to see Rev. Barnes. He was Simon's local priest on the base. OK, so she wasn't his religion, but Simon needed help and the kind she could no longer give him. She needed to get as far away from him as possible.

His anger tonight had been out of control, and she didn't know how many more nights like this she could stand. One day he could seriously hurt her — and next time she might not get away from him so quickly.

Rev. Barnes would know what to do; he seemed genuinely concerned about Simon's problems. Sophie knew she couldn't go on like this, and more importantly neither could Simon; he needed professional help. She was unable to cope any longer by herself. Her face began to throb where Simon had hit her. Her lip trembled, and tears gently rolled as she put a shaking hand up to her wet cheek. Sophie could already feel the swollen, heated flesh under her fingertips. God knows what she was going to look like in the morning.

Sophie grabbed a spare blanket out of the linen cupboard and settled him down on the sofa. She went to bed, locking the bedroom door, and she slept the best way she could without lying on her left side of her face. Tomorrow would be here soon enough; she may as well try and get some sleep.

By the feel of the burning sensation on her face, she knew one thing for sure — Rev. Barnes was not going to be too happy with Simon at all, and it wasn't going to be comfortable telling him either. It had been through Rev. Barnes that Simon had first received counselling, no one had supported Simon's plight more. Apart from herself.

Even though she had divorced Simon six months previously, she had come to his rescue when he needed her. He'd begged her to stay, and in a moment of weakness she had agreed.

All three of them had made a deal. Simon had promised he'd try to curtail his drinking, and Sophie would live unconditionally at their ex-marital home, at least until Rev. Barnes saw Simon fit and able to cope alone. And in return, he would be on call anytime she or Simon needed him. And she certainly needed him now. Tomorrow Rev. Barnes would have to make alternative arrangements for Simon. His mistreatment of her made it clear — she could no longer help him; her sanity and wellbeing were at too much of a risk by waiting.

When she awoke the next morning, the bright sunshine was flooding through the window. Brushing her tousled hair away from her forehead as she sat upright and looking around the room, Sophie felt slightly disoriented for a moment. Just for a brief instant, she couldn't remember anything about the night before. Sophie looked at the small anniversary clock on the wall unit — what day was it? Was she late for work?

It was eight o'clock and she remembered it was Wednesday. She heard noises coming from the bathroom. She slowly remembered the events that had taken place the previous night. She felt the colour drain from her face in recognition. She was going to leave here today, she had decided. Rev. Barnes would have to like it or lump it. Her safety mattered more to her than staying in his good graces. Rev. Barnes hadn't been there when Simon had lost his temper last evening. And Simon wasn't going to take her news that easily either. It didn't matter to her what either of them thought of her. She was leaving — today! Each day she stayed, it got harder to break free of Simon, and Sophie felt sure he found pleasure in his life by making her miserable.

Just at that precise moment Simon came into her bedroom, entirely dressed wearing his blue uniform ready for work, and he was carrying two mugs. Sitting up slowly, she pushed back her dishevelled, dark hair. Simon halted in his tracks; he was staring at her strangely.

In total embarrassment, his face stiffened and coloured. The bright redness looked strangely funny, and in any other circumstances Sophie would have probably laughed. But the situation was too severe; his eyes, ringed with puffed-up shadows, were nearly the same distinct colouring as his face.

"Haley! What in God's name has happened to your face?"

Sophie ignored his pet name for her, refusing to let him rile her this morning. She eyed him questionably, uncertain of his mood and not entirely trusting how his mood would swing.

He placed the two steaming mugs down carefully on the small coffee table beside her. Showing genuine concern, he chose to sit on the vacant chair opposite her, instantly realising his actions were to blame. Ashamed of his behaviour, suddenly overwhelmed, he dropped his head in his hands. "Did I do that to you?" he asked, not raising his head.

She couldn't believe him! He hadn't remembered. Or had he just chosen to block it out? Of course, it wasn't the first time he had blotted out the events of the earlier night's traumas.

Simon lifted his head slowly and looked her in the eye, his eyes puffy and bloodshot and yet filled with remorse — as usual. Raking his hands through his hair, he dropped his gaze, shaking his head in disbelief.

"I'm so sorry; please forgive me, I don't know what comes over me to act in such an appalling manner. I promise you I'll never lay another hand on you again, my sweet, sweet Haley."

Trying to ignore his pet name for her by not cringing and hiding her discomfort, Sophie watched his facial expression. Sophie had heard all this before. And there was no doubt about it, Simon sounded so sincere — as always. His green eyes filled with regret; his sadness looked genuine. But then again, he always did.

"You know I didn't mean it, don't you?" Giving her half a smile. "I would never knowingly harm you."

Sophie relented and nodded. He leaned over and lightly kissed her bruised face.

"I know — I don't deserve you." Despair was in his eyes. "I can understand if you want to leave me and return to your parents. I know I have no right asking you to stay. But you won't leave, will you? Not yet? Not until I'm ready, you promised."

It was true. Sophie had promised.

She freely admitted that she no longer loved Simon, but could she walk out on him when he needed her most? She would like to think she loved him once. The divorce had been her decision alone. She desperately wanted her freedom and escaped from the shackles of an unhappy marriage and neglect. Sophie had her divorce all right, but she wasn't free. Simon needed her more now than ever. He was entirely dependent on her. She knew he no longer loved her — if he ever did.

"I won't leave you," she promised. But knowing deep down inside her, at some point, it was a promise she would have to break.

"And I promise you, I'll stop drinking. I know we can make it work as long as I have you."

Even after he said those words, Sophie had wished with all her heart that she could have believed him. And, of course, uttering those same pledges — just like all the other times — he'd meant it.

"Simon," she began carefully, "I want you to listen to me. I need you to understand something important." At least he was sober enough to listen now. While he was in an amicable mood, she thought she'd try to explain the situation more clearly. "You understand I have to work. If you want this treatment to work — we need the money. We still have a lot of unpaid bills, credit cards, huge bank overdraft. Our outgoings are unmanageable on your wages, and I can't keep up the payments on your money alone. And remember Rev. Barnes has control over your wages — at least for the time being." She calmly tried to explain using an even tone.

She had left out the part where one of his conditions was, he relented his wages to pay all outstanding debts of credit. Now he relied entirely on her for money. Sometimes, with his need, he wasn't above taking it from her by force. "For me to continue supporting you I need to work." She avoided any mention of his overspending.

His eyes widened in disbelief. "I know that. Don't stop working on my account," he said. Reaching out slowly he touched Sophie's cheek and added, "It's my fault we're in this mess in the first place." He sighed heavily. "I get so jealous at times. A sort of anger comes over me. It doesn't help me when I hear the whispers of how many men like you — and I can't tell them you're married to me." He ran a finger along the line of her bruised cheek, and she fought against drawing away from his touch.

Sophie didn't feel right contradicting him about their divorce status. "I have given you no reason for jealousy."

He smiled weakly. "I know, I know — I hear about the men that fall over themselves to meet you and talk to you — praise you, and flirt with Haley Campbell — my wife. And I know you don't want me."

There was no use reasoning with him. He'd refused to accept they were no longer married. When he got something fixed in his head, there was no way anyone could change his mind. So, it had finally come to this. "It's fine, don't worry," she reassured him. "We'll sort everything out."

It was later that morning, Simon had left for his weekly meeting with his section commanding officer, when she finally saw herself in the bathroom mirror as it reflected the cause of his embarrassment.

Her face badly bruised, her cheekbone and her left eye was a multitude of colours that made her look dreadful. She and Simon both agreed last night had been a minor setback for him. He was right — she realised that now. And he was sorry.

At the time she hadn't taken into account how poorly her eye looked and judging by the mess her face was in, no wonder he had been so shaken when he'd walked into the living room and seen it for himself.

Sophie closed her eyes briefly; now she had to convince Rev. Barnes that Simon needed more time to fight this disease. He needed her support. She had no choice; she would have to see it through to the bitter end. She could not abandon him when he needed her, but she could not stay either at the risk of her safety.

Chapter Six

"So sorry I'm late," a breathless, excited voice came from behind Sophie. Greeted with an affectionate hug. "Have you been waiting long?"

Sophie shrugged. "Few minutes." Then gave her friend a welcoming smile. "I'm so pleased to see you, Jane. I've missed you."

Jane linked arms with Sophie, and with an understanding smile she said, "Ditto. Welcome home."

"Despite everything, it's good to be back. I'm so glad you can do this with me."

As best friends, her only friend, the two of them were very close, even though Jane had a look of frailty about her, there was no mistaking Jane was Sophie's rock. Sophie had so few friends of her own she could count on.

Jane had met Sophie while involved in arranging a serving military dependants charity event. Jane had asked for some publicity cover to advertise the charity, and they had been best friends since. Jane Lister was a friendly slender-built, short-haired blonde woman with an amazingly kind heart, and an avid fan of the stay-at-home-wife and mother of three boisterous, young, energetic boys. Sergeant Lister was a heavy-set, kind-hearted, jolly man, who instantly on meeting her, had insisted that she needed a good meal and that she should stay with them whenever she needed a place to call home.

Although Jane was level-headed, sensible and kind, she wasn't afraid to stand up and criticise, or raise a crusade for any issue she considered worthy. Jane had an infectious, outgoing personality she put down to being raised on a Yorkshire farm. Sophie doubted that RAF Chief Tech Lister, Andrew — had ever had a crossed word with his wife. Andrew was also a few years older than his wife. Jane loved her husband dearly, and it was clear that Andrew carried a torch for his wife. While Jane, knowing Sophie's career, never criticised or judged her actions, and never tried to pry — they were as close as any two sisters could be.

The moment Sophie had landed, she couldn't wait to phone Jane, more importantly, couldn't wait to see her. It had been several weeks since they had last spoken. They had plenty to catch up on. The call lasted a few minutes, but it was good to hear a friend's voice after weeks of solitude. Jane didn't lose a moment in telling her she had seen the siege of the hotel on television.

"I've been watching the news. I've been so worried about you. I want to hear all about Afghanistan. Meet me outside the church hall tomorrow." Jane was using her stern voice as if she wasn't going to take no for an answer. "Let's say 10 am."

The next morning Sophie had driven her car over to the Royal Air Force military base, arriving at Brize Norton, Oxfordshire, on a chilly but cloudy day in late April. Despite her many visits, because of the high level of security of the base being on *Red Alert*, Sophie was required by military police to leave her car at the visitors' car park, situated some way from the main camp grounds. Which unfortunately for Sophie meant a long walk across the camp grounds.

As she left the car park, Sophie felt quite conspicuous, if not a little ridiculous. Dressed in fashionable casual attire, she made her way to the base. Her jeans fitted her snugly on her hips and tight on her slim legs. She wore stylish high-heel ankle boots and a slim-fitting T-shirt and black leather jacket. Sophie had chosen to leave her hair hanging freely — dark, thick, curling in a wild, long, unruly mane around her oval face.

Her over-sized dark glasses designed for a bright summer's day were now intended as a prop to stop prying eyes and made her feel ridiculous.

Thankfully, she didn't have to wait too long before Jane turned up to meet her. Sophie's only regret was she was attracting far too many admiring glances, along with a few whistles from the passing military-clad soldiers as she waited. Soldiers from all ranks and ages stared at her; some were cheeky enough to give a wolf whistle.

Sophie turned as she felt a light touch on the shoulder. "I'm so sorry to be late. Have you been waiting long?" Jane said, a little breathlessly.

"No, but I've had my fair share of interested looks, and some a little on the lecherous side," Sophie replied, shrugging her shoulders.

Almost on cue two male airmen passed them and smiled; one even commented, "She's a looker."

"Well." Jane looked her over. "That is your fault. And being a 30-year-old *looker* helps I suppose." Jane laughed at Sophie's outraged face, and her eyes followed in the direction of a brick building situated behind them. "If it helps — most of these have just landed after being deployed overseas. Haven't seen a woman in months. Anything female with a pulse is probably fair game to them. Don't worry, they are only here for two weeks of training, then they go back overseas."

"Thanks a lot." Sophie laughed. "Such a lovely compliment?"

"I'm right though," Jane teased.

Sophie grunted playfully. "You are enjoying this." Thankfully, if Jane harboured any ill thoughts on Simon's recent behaviour and mistreatment of Sophie, Jane said nothing.

"Come on; we can pop in here," Jane suggested lightly, "we have enough time for a cuppa in the NAAFI before we meet with Rev. Barnes. In the meantime, you can fill me in on what's happened with Simon." Jane threaded her arm through Sophie's and patted her arm reassuringly. "Come on! Cup of tea, I think. A strong one."

As if not believing her ears, "Jane," Sophie gasped. "Never mind the tea. What about these?" She pointed to the large sunglasses situated on the bridge of her nose. "Didn't it enter your head that I might look rather stupid in these over-sized bumblebee sunglasses. Especially on such a cloudy day. I feel foolish."

Following close ahead of her friend, Sophie started to walk towards the red brick building. Looking over her shoulder, she was so absorbed in deep conversation with her friend; she'd failed to notice a group of soldiers all dressed in a desert combat-style uniform that had gathered in front of her, obstructing her way.

"Excuse me," she murmured, trying to skirt her way past two of the taller soldiers, who were in high spirits and busily arguing in raised voices over the football game that had been broadcast on television the night before. "Excuse me," she said, again. Nothing.

Just as Sophie stepped past the first soldier who was still absorbed in his conversation and not looking at her, he turned to the side to let her pass and opened the door for her to enter. She turned to thank him, but as he was still immersed in deep conversation, she doubted he would have heard her.

"Look out!" Of course, Jane's warning had come a little too late. *When — wham!*

Winded and stumbling, she suddenly felt like she had walked into a solid brick wall, which she discovered confirmed her worst fears — a man's broad chest knocking her back on her heels against the entrance glass door.

The shoulder strap of her shoulder bag-type-briefcase caught on the door handle, jerking her shoulder back and yanking her bag from her grasp. Folders, newspapers, pens, her mobile phone, business cards, papers and her diary tumbled to the ground.

"Now look what's happened, Jane. I told you these sunglasses would be a stupid idea." Sophie dropped down beside the now scattered contents. A crowd had now gathered in front of the doorway.

Jane gave a little shrug and a short laugh. "Apart from the small detail that you can't see where you're going — I think they look pretty good on you." She smiled wryly.

Sophie gave a small laugh. Trust Jane to see the funny side of it. Sophie chuckled again while she and Jane took pens, papers, mobile phone and files out of several pairs of hands. Sophie leant forward and reached for her diary behind Jane's right foot, only for her to be knocked off balance by someone from behind. She tried to steady herself by grabbing an army combat green uniform-covered thigh crouched down beside her to keep from falling on her face.

"Thank you," she said, managing to gain her balance and turning to the side.

"You're welcome, ma'am," said a man's velvety, warm voice.

Sophie found herself drawn to a voice she'd felt sure she had heard before. Gazing up into the mesmerising, ebony eyes of a young man, wearing the most disarming, dazzling smile she'd ever seen.

From the first moment she'd seen him, she'd noticed he had the most amazing dark eyes, and they were staring straight back into hers. And there was something so familiar about his eye contact. And judging by the look he was giving her in return — he'd sensed it too. Suddenly feeling conscious of her staring, she dropped her gaze. Clumsily, she tried to stand, and in a razor-like reaction, the soldier's arms swept around her to steady her.

There was no mistaking that his arms felt like bands of steel as he held her tightly. The heat from his body and his strength seeped through every pore of her being. With the force of the body blow, not to mention his disarming smile, it took her a moment to regain her breath. As soon as she did, Sophie tried to apologise.

"I'm sorry; it's my fault entirely. Please, accept my apologies," Sophie said, a little breathlessly. "I didn't see you," Sophie murmured, shaking.

He nodded, still smiling, his tall frame still blocking her entrance. He leant closer and quietly whispered, "I know it's none of my business — but I think you would see a lot better if you removed those fucking ridiculous sunglasses."

His voice was deep and had a velvety texture about it; she found herself lost in its smoothness, even if he did sound annoyed with her. But before Sophie could think of a suitable reply and without a moment's hesitation, treating her like some opposing military objective, he grabbed the sunglasses from her face.

Instantly, his jaw dropped. "What the fuck!" The rest was left unsaid. He stopped short, both of them realising with a sense of shock at the consequences of his reflex actions. There was no doubt about it — he recognised her instantly. To his horror, there stood before him was a beautiful, petite woman with a swollen, bruised left cheek with an enormous black eye, and her face turned up towards him in a sort of doe-like expression. The sight tore at him.

The view of a dead man hadn't moved him and sniper fire had got his adrenaline pumping, but it didn't get to him the way Sophie's bruised face and sad, beautiful, brown eyes did.

There was no doubt in his mind — he recognised her immediately. He'd read about her the same as everyone else and knew all there was to know about her as a journalist, but nothing had prepared him for seeing her face to face, feeling all the power she emanated from her small frame. She was gorgeous. Even with a bruised, swollen, red cheek and colourful, bruised eye. Which thanks to him was now clearly visible to all.

It hadn't taken him to be a genius to have figured out how angry Sophie was. Hurt, huge-as-saucers, chocolate-brown eyes appeared as if they were shooting poison darts at him, or something just as bad.

Shocked and embarrassed at what he was facing, his face froze. He had seen that same hurt look before!

Sophie could only stand and watch the young soldier's reaction. It was though he had never seen a black eye on a woman before. Perhaps the soldier hadn't, who knows. And she didn't care.

With rapidly growing red tint to his cheeks, he awkwardly placed the glasses in her small hands carefully, unable to take his eyes off her face. If this was his way of apologising, he was finding it difficult.

"Fuck! I'm sorry," the soldier began, his eyes never leaving her swollen face — his embarrassment was evident in his voice. "I just didn't think there would be a valid reason for wearing those fucking horrible things." He tried to apologise clumsily as a rise of colour was staining his cheeks.

Sophie was feeling a little uncomfortable. Luckily, people were now disbursing as they'd lost interest in the public display and were moving on. Currently, there was just the three of them standing there.

Sophie gave a wry but brief smile as she matched his gaze. "What did you think? I was wearing them for a fashion statement or something?"

Kieran flushed, he felt a prized arse and considered himself reprimanded by her blunt response. And who could blame her?

He was suddenly aware how close they were standing — kneeling on the ground he hadn't been that close to her. Was that the reason he hadn't seemed so tall then as he did now. In the doorway, surrounded by other soldiers coming and going, they hadn't seemed to have stood that close. Not like now, standing so close, he filled every inch of her vision.

Preoccupied, and distracted by other events taking place was the reason why she didn't remember his chest being as broad beneath his army green combat cotton shirt. And try as she might, she couldn't come up with a rational explanation as to why this man should look so familiar to her and so damn sexy — and so young! And to Sophie — that was precisely the way he seemed to her too.

Even though he looked young and not much older than a boy, she needed to crane her neck to look up at him. He was a good few inches taller than her tiny five feet two inches. He was by no means thin and gangly. This soldier was an adult and all man in every sense of the word. His black hair was partly hidden by the regular issue green army cap that adorned his head. In fact, his full attire consisted of the traditional combat green army issue No 2 uniform. To say he was pleasing to her eyes would indeed be an understatement.

Even when he stepped closer, he was so close that she had to tilt her head right back — she couldn't bring herself to look away from his eyes. She couldn't for the life of her ever remember any man having such sparkling dark eyes filled with so much experience.

The secondary movement of his arms around her as he aided her balance was more a feeling than an image — the flex of a shoulder and the crinkle of crisp green cotton of his uniform shirt.

Sophie realised one thing, he was far too good-looking for his own good. And he probably knew it also. She had seen that same look of interest on so many of the men before. And the way he was staring at her gave the game away and sent alarm bells sounding in her head. Guys like him liked the challenge — crazy for the chase, and a novelty to him. Even if she had the time, she wasn't about to play his game. She was better to stay clear. But there was no denying, for a brief moment, there was something so familiar about him that made her question her opinion.

Trembling, as Sophie breathed profoundly, and as she inhaled, she caught his essence of him: he smelled so delicious. The smell of apple soap and freshly laundered clothes mingled and teased her senses, and waited for his touch.

Almost as instinctive, his knuckles lightly grazed her bruised cheekbone. His large palm sizzled against her skin; his fingers spread across her face to behind her ear. Angling his head towards her, he said in no more than a whisper, "I'm sorry." There was that look again.

His breath stirred the wisps of unmanageable hair curling on her fringe; the contact was no more than a gentle brush of air on skin. "It looks painful."

"Not so much," she lied. Sophie shivered and stepped back. Sliding a hand from her face down to her shoulder, he wrapped his fingers around her upper arm, steadying her. He released her and backed a step away.

"Still..."

With the return of her space she came to her sanity. She wasn't about to discuss her life with a perfect stranger. "It's all right. Just a little accident." Sophie laughed when she noticed how embarrassed he felt.

"No damage."

He gave a courteous nod, taking the hint she didn't want to talk about it further. "Good." He tapped his cap as if to salute each of them in turn. "Ma'am — Ladies." He smiled respectfully, nodding once more.

The warmth of his smile tickled her skin, and she smiled in return. His smile, his kindness and caring nature were far too disturbing for her to cope with for the present. Sophie, replacing the dark glasses on the bridge of her small nose, turned to her friend. "Come on, Jane; I do need that cuppa now." She smiled back at the young soldier.

When he still didn't move, Jane took charge of the situation, apparently amused by the event. "Don't look so worried, soldier," as she glanced directly at Sophie, "you didn't do it." Then proceeded to take Sophie by the arm to lead her past the young man, and this time safely into the building and the NAAFI coffee shop. Pausing for a moment at the door, she slipped the sunglasses onto the edge of her nose and peered over them for one last look at the soldier as he marched across the concrete to join some friends.

Entering the coffee shop, they saw part of the restaurant area was reserved and closed off in preparation for the lunchtime rush of military servicemen and women. When they got served and stepped inside the enclosed area, one of the men sounded a low whistle aimed in their direction. Jane's eyes followed the sound of the noise and noticed a group of soldiers dressed in military combats who were occupying a table on the opposite side of the room and suggested they went elsewhere.

Sophie shrugged her shoulders. "We don't have time to go somewhere else. Besides, it's only a cuppa," Sophie said, in a quiet voice.

As they occupied a small booth, Jane and Sophie sipped their teas. Sophie smiled as the group spoke in a subdued conversation.

The room was relatively quiet, so they became audible where Jane and Sophie sat in silence. Sophie had guessed their hushed whispers had something to do with her wearing dark sunglasses indoors.

After what felt to Sophie like several hours had passed, she sat and sipped her tea in silence thinking over the events that led to her being here. Her thoughts were interrupted when the young soldier with the fantastic, warm, ebony eyes, broad shoulders and muscles that she had met briefly now joined the group. "*Muscles*," Sophie opted to call him and watched as they all huddled around the table with their heads fitted tightly together.

Jane smiled reassuringly at Sophie as pieces of their conversation drifted to her ears. "Seems you have caused a bit of a stir," she said, over the rim of her cup as she sipped her tea.

Sophie chuckled wryly. "It seems that way."

"Looks like you are the talk of the town," Jane replied.

Although they spoke among themselves in hushed whispers, due to the quietness of the room their voices carried over to where Jane and Sophie sat. "I noticed." Sophie smiled weakly in return. "Pity they don't have something better to talk about." So much for trying to feel inconspicuous.

"No, I'm fucking telling you," *Muscles* was saying, "there's something wrong. The woman has an enormous black eye. I'm telling you — that was no accident."

The group of men were silent for a long moment, until the ginger-haired guy burst out, "What a bastard."

"What twat would fucking do something like that to a woman?" Another added to the conversation.

"Seriously?" Someone questioned.

Within moments the conversation became a mixture of voices.

Another joined in, "I don't believe you."

"OK then... if you don't believe me..." He leant back in his chair to give the matter some thought for a second. "Fine. You go over there and see for yourself."

"Not a fucking chance. Too obvious." Apparently not rising to the challenge.

"You do it." Someone suggested back at him.

"I've seen it, you fucking idiot!" Muscles gave a burst of laughter, followed by the others joining in.

"OK," said another. "I'll go."

"Take notice — it's on her left cheek."

"What would I say?"

"Ask her to pass the salt or something," he suggested lightly, and he shrugged his broad shoulders.

Another chimed in with his say on the matter. "Oh yeah, what a fucking dumb idea. As if that's going to fucking work." He laughed.

Muscles shrugged his shoulders. "Well, I don't fucking know. Think of something, you useless wanker!"

All the men in the group joined in on the conversation, sat huddled around the table, heads bent and talking in low-key whispers. Then, when satisfied with the plan, they sat up straight.

"Right!" Another soldier, with light-ginger hair, rising from his chair, was agreeing to accept the challenge. "I'll do it." The scraping of chair legs moving across the terracotta tiles echoed around the room. The group immersed in conversation as they chatted around the table.

One thing she noted — for young men — they liked to use the *F-word* a lot.

Sophie took another sip of her tea. "Excuse me, miss." Sophie glanced up over the rim of her cup. A soldier with huge green eyes and a crop of red hair stared back at her. He looked anything but relaxed as he muddled through his words. "Sorry to trouble you, but could we borrow your sugar, please? We seem to have run out on our table." He smiled, as he asked so politely.

Sophie glanced over the dozen or so rows of tables he'd passed before getting to hers, spotting the recently freshly filled sugar canisters on the unoccupied counters. Slowly, she lowered her cup and rested it on the table. "What about these?"

"Checked, all empty," he responded.

She removed her glasses and stared directly back at him. For some reason, their comments stung her. It was like she was part of their little game — something to be ogled and pointed at, or even laughed at if it suited them. "Sure," she said, as she smiled brightly, entirely bowling him over.

He had been unable to take his eyes off her more noticeable features. Caught staring at her more prominent black eye and swollen cheek, he turned several shades of red then turned away with a hurried, "Thanks."

"Hey, soldier." She stopped him in his tracks. He turned around perplexed. "You forgot your sugar." She smiled again, wryly, making her whole face seem softer and younger. Unaware of one young soldier paying particularly close attention to her.

Later, after what turned out to be an eventful day, Jane had decided they needed some serious lubrication.

"Let's have a pick me up," Jane insisted, "I'll pay." And by all accounts, she told Sophie — they deserved it.

There was no mistaking, the first person they came into contact with inside the bar area was the young soldier, and he'd spotted her as soon as she stepped into the bar. The soldier, she thought aptly named, *muscles*, dressed now in a similar state of attire as herself. Dark-blue jeans hugged his male body; dark-green T-shirt stretched and fitted perfectly across his broad chest. Suntanned and tattooed, his body was magnificent, his teeth shining between his tanned cheeks. His firm, generous mouth smiled in welcome, showing a flash of perfect white teeth. His friendly face and open smile topped him off perfectly.

He nodded in greeting to Jane before turning his attention back to Sophie. He touched her arm gently; maybe she had been mistaken, and she thought for what seemed a mere pause in time, he'd given her the most frightfully admiring grin as she shrugged off his hold.

But instead, he said, "If we're going to keep meeting like this, I think we should at least know each other's names — I'm Kieran O'Neill," he offered, as his dark brows rose persuasively. "And you are Sophie Tyson, journalist," he confirmed, without hesitation.

Sophie stared at him — her mouth half-open — she had been in this situation many times before; single men, sometimes even married men, on occasion, would hit on her. Over time, she had hardened to any advances men would make towards her. Being nice didn't always get the message across; Sophie learned early on that she had to be firm at times. Although for some reason this young man seemed different, but she had been wrong to trust before.

Sophie's eyes narrowed as she cocked her head to one side, as if trying to figure out if he could be trusted. Then she did something entirely out of character for her. She smiled warmly up at him in return. "Yes, I'm Sophie Tyson. You know me?" Sophie extended out her right hand for him to take.

Taking her small hand in his, he grasped it firmly. "Pleased to meet you, Sophie Tyson," he said, repeating her name wryly. "Not really, you probably don't remember me. Our paths crossed a few weeks ago in Kabul."

"You met me in Kabul?" Sophie asked, confused. "I don't remember."

"There is no reason you should," Kieran said. His pride was a little wounded, but why would she have reason to remember him. "I was involved in the search and rescue op — I pulled you out of the hotel. You were out of it for a while. Then you were transported to Bastion hospital, and I didn't see you again."

She smiled, nodding in return. "You saved my life?"

"Not really, just in the right place at the right time I guess." He nonchalantly shrugged his shoulders.

"Well, thank you for saving my life and helping me. I'm pleased to meet you, Kieran O'Neill."

He frowned as if something was on the tip of his tongue, but for the life of him he couldn't figure out what it was he wanted to say. Instead, he asked, "Is there a Mr Tyson?" Kieran was still grasping her hand in his.

Putting her on edge by his question, she struggled out of his hold. "No, not really." She pointed to her bruised face, indicating with her forefinger. "A simple disagreement with someone."

He leant towards her for a closer inspection of her left eye and grimaced in distaste at what he was seeing. "Doesn't seem that simple. I suppose he'll get away with doing that won't he?" he asked, and waited for her response.

"He?" Sophie never mentioned who.

He gave her a deep penetrating stare. "Men punch, and women slap. It doesn't look like a slap to me."

There was no mistaking the meaning behind his words.

"Yes, I suppose you're right," she replied softly. She looked at Kieran suspiciously as she waited while Jane ordered them something tall, multicoloured and mysterious. Jane handed her one of the two glasses she was now holding. She pretended to take a sip of the orange concoction, then she looked over the top of her glass swirling the contents as the ice clinked noisily.

His eyes became thoughtful for a moment, as he stood towering over her. There was no mistake that he was angry; he was having a hard time accepting that a man would treat a woman this way.

He looked down at her, smiling. The concerned look was gone, and with his dark-brown eyes sparkling, encouragingly he said, "You need cheering up." He gave her a breathtakingly warm smile. "Why don't you and your friend join us for a drink? Help celebrate our return to UK soil with us?"

Sophie hurriedly shook her head. "Oh, no, we couldn't intrude. We need to leave soon — actually," she said, as she turned round to look for Jane anxiously. It wasn't the first time a soldier had hit on her. "We only popped in for one drink." As handsome as this man was, she wasn't there to flirt with muscle-bound young men in tight T-shirts and even more comfortable jeans. No matter how good his intentions. Sooner or later they all reveal their real plans.

"Please, stay. No one will say anything to you while we're here. I promise," Kieran told Sophie, his hand resting on her arm gently. There was no mistaking his open friendliness, or his flirting. "Just one drink?"

Sophie felt like a jolt of electricity had surged through her entire body as she felt the warmth of his hand on her forearm. Never in her life had she had such an odd reaction from a man, especially one so young. Which prompted her to ask, "I don't mean this to sound insulting, and please don't take this the wrong way but — how old are you?" Sophie said, while taking a sip of her drink from her glass.

"I'm 18," he chirped, as if he explained it all. By which of course it didn't. As he gave Sophie the most charming grin, he asked, "Why?"

"No reason." Sophie shrugged. "You don't look 18. I was expecting a little older." She swirled the contents of her glass.

"Really?" His brows rose as if pleased by her response.

"Yes," she replied quietly.

"How old do you think I look?" With a quizzical frown, he asked, "What about you?" Kieran kept his eyes fixed on her face.

"I don't know. Around 22. Early twenties, I would guess."

Kieran's directness knocked her sideways, ignoring the second part of his question. He had a lot to learn about the art of conversation with a woman, including asking her age, she mused.

"Fuck! Really? I will be," he laughed. "In a few years." Kieran continued to stare at her with the most alarming and brilliant smile.

His answer revealed a little of his immaturity, and Sophie smiled to herself. What could she expect? He was still very much a teenager to her — even if his body shouted out otherwise. She would do well to remember that.

It must have been the look on her face that revealed her sobering thoughts which triggered something inside him as he remembered what it was, he'd wanted to say. "I could say —" he continued gingerly, "I was expecting you to say younger too. The picture of you in the *Express* doesn't do you justice at all. You are much prettier in person."

Sophie felt a sudden rush of colour at his directness. "Really?" Feeling uncomfortable with his boldness, she added, smiling, "That's the press profile photos for you."

Sophie felt strangely flattered by his genuine compliments as he continued to discuss her work. It was odd; she had never felt overwhelmed by flattery from other people who so enthusiastically admired her work — she had always been wary of men hoping to date the elusive Sophie Tyson.

Most people said and did all the right things, but she was a shrewd judge of character and never let any of that sort of stuff faze her.

Much of her work relied on interviews: details of what it was like working in the background with the British and allied forces and their family life. Her work was highly popular and fruitful. But what appeal did it have for a boy of 18 she didn't understand.

"My father is a huge fan of your articles. He thinks you have an honest and direct flair that is both creative and truthful."

Which now explained why he knew so much about her work. "Thank your dad for me."

"You should meet him; I know my dad would love a chance to chat with you about some of your work."

Clearly, he held his father in high regard. "That is a lovely thought, but I don't get a lot of free time that allows me that sort of thing..." She glanced at her wristwatch. "In fact, talking of which, it's getting late, and I do need to be heading home."

He smiled broadly. "Oh, where's home?" he asked boldly.

Sophie sighed. Smiling, she gave in to his inquisitive nature. Friendly or not, she wasn't about to disclose her address to anyone. "I'm renting while I'm working on a series of articles locally."

To her relief, Jane chose that moment to appear at her side. "I think we have to leave now, Sophie. Remember, we have to retrieve your car."

Sophie placed her unfinished drink on the bar. "Of course, and yes, I'm ready," Sophie replied instantly. She thanked him for the chat and gave a brief farewell.

"You're leaving?" His hand rested gently on hers on the glass. "Look," he said, as he halted her movements. "I'm going home this weekend," Kieran explained quietly. "My folks don't live far from here. I know this sounds like something from a movie, and I can't think of one reason why you should even consider what I'm about to ask you seriously for one moment…"

He removed his hand from hers when she tensed briefly and pushed his hands into his jeans' pockets. He floundered over his words. And for the first time, Sophie sensed he doubted his confidence. But she said nothing.

"I just thought — if you needed to get away for a few days — well, you know — it might be something of interest — possibly consider — if you want — coming with me for the weekend?" *Fuck! That was hard work.*

Sophie, touched by his kindness, reached out and touched his arm in a reassuring, friendly gesture. She didn't want to hurt his feelings, but for apparent reasons aside, she couldn't accept.

"That's very kind of you," she began, choosing her words carefully, while trying not to dismiss his kindness carelessly. She continued, "but I'm not sure that would be appropriate. I'm deeply flattered, but I just can't."

His face coloured the moment she said the words. "Fuck no! I don't mean…" Flustered, he ran his hand through his short, black hair. "I apologise. I just supposed if you wanted somewhere different to escape to, somewhere private, my parents' home would be a safe place for you. And, of course, you would be chaperoned the entire time we were together." He quickly scribbled down his mobile number on a beer napkin and handed it to her. "Think about it."

The smile she gave him was shy. It was hard not to respond to his warm generosity and his innocence. Taking the paper napkin from him, Sophie reached out and rested her hand on his forearm in response to his friendly gesture. She felt a heel giving him a flat out — no. "I'll think about it — thank you," was all she could think of to say.

She turned to walk away, and Kieran reached for her hand, stopping her with a touch of his hand on hers. The feather-light touch felt as if he never wanted her to go. "Please do."

Then Sophie left without a backwards glance.

All the same, she felt his eyes on her as she left.

Mercifully, Jane let the matter drop, without a word.

Chapter Seven

The days had come and gone several times over before Kieran had to accept that *Sophie Tyson, journalist*, was not going to contact him.

Kieran crossed behind his mate Drews, stepped over a fallen mess-hall chair, pulled another out from the long table and grabbed his phone from Matt's hand. "What the fuck are you doing, Ginger?" he asked, taking the seat beside him.

His friend gave him a wry grin in return. "Don't call me that. I keep telling you I'm not fucking ginger! I'm strawberry blond," he protested earnestly.

"Yeah right." Kieran dismissed his objection with a light shrug. But he wasn't going to be swayed. "What the fucking hell were you doing with my phone?"

"You know what I was doing, you useless twat!" Ginger returned in a wry, matter-of-fact manner. "I'm making the call you're too afraid to make."

Hearing nothing but a dial tone, he cuffed his friend on the shoulder. "I don't fucking think so."

"Why not for fucks' sake? Someone has to," Drews argued. "You fucking don't seem to be doing anything about it, you spineless bastard."

"If he's too spineless to make a move — I might ask her out. She might fancy a fine figure of a man like me." Smithie laughed. Trying to get a rise out of Kieran.

"I bet Romeo has her number on speed dial." Ginger laughed. "Don't you?"

Kieran forced himself to remain silent, trying not to confirm or deny his friend's suspicion by the growing heat in his flushed face.

Wrighty glared back at Kieran. "Soft bastard, grow a pair of balls. We all know you want to call her, don't you?" He pointed an accusing finger. "If not. Mind if I do?" The guys congregated around the mess hall table joined in with the ribbing.

"Maybe I'll have a crack at her," someone else chimed in, "give you a run for your money, Romeo."

Another chuckled beside him. "Maybe I'll beat all you fuckers to it and go after Sophie Tyson myself," Al contributed to the banter.

Everyone laughed. "Bollocks! What you going to do with a woman like that, Al? She'd eat you alive." Some of them threw screwed up paper-napkins in Al's direction.

"I could ask her who supplies her with her porn DVDs," he joked.

"Going to be fucking hard work that one. Besides, Romeo, the daft bastard, has his heart set on going after her," Smithie announced, "And once he makes up his mind no one will stand a chance."

"I don't know — she spoke to me and smiled," Ginger boasted, "I think I'm in with a chance."

"Yeah, yeah, yeah," Kieran scoffed.

"I don't know — I wouldn't be surprised if Ginger isn't in with a chance," Al suggested.

"Stay the fuck away from her, Ginger!" Kieran roared, as he slammed his fist down on the table.

The men met his anger with a cheeky round of applause and cheering.

"You can all fuck off!" Kieran retorted. "You bunch of wankers!"

His response was met with boisterous laughter.

"Not interested, eh?" Wrighty teased, swinging his leg over a chair to sit the other side of him. He raised his hands. "Can't blame you. Too much of a woman for you to handle. She looks top fucking class. A perfect ten, and you wouldn't know what to do with a woman like that."

Kieran came back with, "Who said anything about going after her? I haven't called her yet."

"Probably lost your number by now," Kenny added to the conversation. "Most likely forgotten your fucking name."

The banter was starting to get annoying. There was no doubt about it, Kieran's mates were getting their money's worth.

"Ungrateful cow! Save a woman's life, and that's the thanks you get." Ending with a mocking "Tut-tut-tut."

"You do right not calling her," someone chimed in.

"More like he knows her number by memory," another teased.

Kieran neither confirmed nor denied the banter.

"You like her, don't you?" Wrighty asked, in earnest.

"I'm not sure." He shrugged in response. Already wishing they hadn't seen through the lie as they all gave a boisterous laugh.

"Fuck off! Now we all know you're lying!" Drews teased.

"Well then, I'm just helping you on your way. For fucks' sake! Call the woman — ask her out or something. Talk to her. You know you want to. Put all of *us* out of *your* misery," Wrighty ordered, pointing an accusing forefinger.

Kieran tried to ignore his friend's banter. He sat up straight, ramrod stiff. "Don't know what the fuck you're talking about."

"Oh, come off it," he argued. "Since meeting the woman, you haven't stopped going on about Sophie Tyson. You've hyped her up that much even I have fantasies about her."

"Shut the fuck up! You're fucking exaggerating." Kieran shrugged.

"I think not — we all know when she dropped her bag Al saw you pick up one of those business cards of hers and keep it," Wrighty retorted.

"That's fucking true. Ever since then you have been stomping around and moping about the place in a foul mood acting like a right fucking prick!" Al confirmed.

The blond guy with a cheeky, round face smiled and nodded. "That's true," Smithie confirmed. "You never stop talking about her."

"Who else in their right fucking mind reads out-of-date business pages of the *Express* newspaper while deployed, Romeo?" Drews asked.

"Look — you can all mind your own fucking business!" Kieran snapped.

Kieran knew they were telling the truth, but there was nothing he could do about it. She hadn't called, and he wasn't the type to invade someone's privacy.

"Don't be a twat. You should call her. Women like it when you take the initiative." Wrighty smiled in return.

"Oh yeah. And what made you such an authority on women? You're still a fucking virgin and don't even have a girlfriend," Kenny added to the conversation, laughing.

Wrighty was unfazed by the jibe. "Don't put it off. Don't let her get away if you like her. And we all know you have the hots for her. You fucking talk about her all the time."

"Shut the fuck up, Wrighty!" he fumed. Fighting down his growing anger.

Drews grabbed a tray of burgers and fries from the food serving area of the mess hall and slammed the overflowing food tray down on to the table. Several hands grabbed the food all at once.

"Don't be a twat by having a go at Wrighty. You're the one sulking because this Sophie Tyson hasn't contacted you."

He tried hard not to let their playful banter get to him. But it did. "I'm sure the lady is just busy."

"Bollocks! That was fucking days ago. What's wrong with you? Snap the fuck out of it. Face it — she's not interested, mate. Move on or do something about it. Life is too fucking short."

It was no good. "I wish the lot of you would shut the fuck up!" he shouted at him.

Meeting Drews' gaze, there was no mistaking his friend knew him well. "No need for that!" Pretending to be hurt by his words.

Feeling ashamed, Kieran turned back to Wrighty. "Sorry, mate." His apology was genuine.

Wrighty flashed his cocky 18-year-old grin. "Yeah, well — we figured when she didn't call you as you'd hoped there would be shit hitting the fan at some point. We were all expecting you to go off on one." He shrugged. "With one of us at least. Should have kept my head down."

"Have to admit, she is pretty gorgeous." Al confirmed what Kieran already knew.

Great! Tell him something he didn't know.

Kieran watched in a distracted way as Tim's hands made a move for some French fries lying on the tray. The sad thing was Wrighty was right about one thing — he had sulked for long enough. Kieran leaned back and closed his eyes. She was perfect beyond compare, and just looking at her made his blood sing.

Drews snatched a burger off the tray. "Come on, mate. Get real; this isn't like you. Forget her — go and get yourself an entertaining girl for the evening," he said, taking a huge bite out of his burger.

"I think you should call her — don't be a fucking idiot!" Wrighty called out. "Take a risk. You want to call her, don't you?" he pushed.

Kieran shrugged his shoulders. "I suppose," trying to sound more confident than he felt.

"Well then?" Wrighty pushed. "Don't be a fucking useless prick!"

Trying not to show how he felt, Kieran said. "I think I should give it a go and call her—"

Drews' crew-cut red-head was shaking from side to side in a disagreeing stare. "Big fucking mistake. I think you should forget her."

"What the fuck do you know?" Wrighty grunted. "No, he's right to call." Clearly against Drews' advice.

"That's crap," Ginger argued. "Mate. You are making a mistake." He pointed directly at Kieran. "Come to the NAAFI bar with us. Get yourself a shag from one of those newbie recruit girls that's just arrived." He winked.

"Yeah, one of those would be better than fucking mooning about some woman reporter that you only spoke to once." Drews laughed wryly.

Kieran shook his head and dismissed the idea.

He didn't want to say it out loud, but he felt it all the same — he didn't want just any girl. And Sophie Tyson was far from being labelled a *girl* — she was a woman. And as far as his feelings went towards her, he knew the moment he laid eyes on her, brushed her face, the way she had smiled at him and lit her face up which made her eyes come to life. There was no way Kieran was going to walk away when he'd seen her smile at him that way. No, she was the only woman for him.

Sure, her beauty struck him hard. Just as much as the first time he had seen her. There was no denying the sight of her got his testosterone going overtime. So much so he had dreamt about her every night since. Not seeing her or hearing from her only made things worse.

Her beauty had captivated him, but there was something more to Sophie — she was intriguing, intelligent, mysterious and gorgeous. What man wouldn't want her for his own, but when he'd touched her there was that moment that something told him she had been both repulsed and petrified by a man's touch. And no wonder, judging by her bruised face. He hadn't wanted to pry back then; now he needed to know more.

Kieran placed both his hands on the plastic table and rose from his seat. "No thanks, mates." He rejected them lightly. "Fuck off and enjoy yourselves. You never know — Al might even get a sympathy shag. I'm settling for an early night." Trying to sound nonchalant.

With a scraping of mess hall chairs, mixed with laughter, the guys started moving. Wrighty got to his feet, playfully punched Kieran in the arm, and walked with rest of the guys heading for the door. "He's going back to the block to toss it off and call his girlfriend, aren't you?" Wrighty gave a provoking broad grin.

Drews added mischievously to the banter, "Yeah, she's going to need someone to baby sit her ten fucking kids while she goes on the town with her tosser husband."

"Very fucking funny," Kieran mumbled sarcastically, aware that his mates were ribbing him, but Drews was already halfway down the road with the rest of them, and out of the way of Kieran's retaliation. "Piss off!"

There was no doubt about it, the guys were right about one thing, since meeting Sophie Tyson she had his mind and his heart tied up in knots. He couldn't eat, and his sleep was suffering too. It was as if he had a one-track mind focused on Sophie Tyson. And if he was going to save his sanity, he was going to have to do something about contacting Sophie sooner or later — even if it was purely to satisfy his curiosity and restore some order with his pals.

Leaving the mess hall — Kieran gave a passing mock salute to the eight guys heading in the opposite direction. Crossing the parade grounds and going directly to the accommodation block, D block was where he'd called home for the past week before being posted back to Afghanistan.

Thinking about it now, he'd acted on impulse. Taking the woman's business card that morning hadn't been a crime, but not returning it wasn't typically his style. It was as if he'd been acting entirely out of character since the moment he'd laid eyes on her.

That serendipitous moment catching him off guard as she did. Leaving the NAAFI, on his way to meet the guys waiting outside he may never have met her. Glancing up at what some of the guys were signalling to him through the window, distracted by the antics of his pals fooling around. Before he could do anything to avoid his actions he had collided, delivering a full-body blow, with a small petite figure coming in the opposite direction, and staring into a pair of dark, large, bumblebee-shaped sunglasses.

When he had removed those huge, infuriating sunglasses, he was instantly spellbound when he had found himself staring at the most amazing, captivating, large, brown eyes he had ever seen. Topped off by the wavy, waist-length hair that was the colour of burnt sugar made Sophie perfect and so angelic.

When she had finally spoken, it was with a voice that reminded him of soft summer rain. And the smooth tenderness of her skin beneath the trail of his fingertips had felt electrifying to the touch and made his entire body shake from head to foot.

As if consumed by her mere presence that had knocked the breath out of his entire body, he couldn't breathe. Of course, he wasn't under any illusions that she'd liked him after meeting him in such a way. He must have acted like a real immature bastard coming on to her that strong. Meeting her, she'd been everything he had envisaged, even dreamt about, although he never actually thought the opportunity would arise to meet her face to face.

Reading her column and seeing images of her appearing at some interview or other had been his only link to her. He'd admired her skills as a writer with her directness to rewrite the unknown facts against the terrorists and the revealing real stories of a soldier's life, but nothing had prepared him for seeing her in the flesh.

Her slim, petite frame; her shapely legs as she bent down to retrieve her belongings; the beautiful face flashed upwards towards her friend, with a radiating smile; the power she had over him that radiated from her small frame. He was wrong. She wasn't just gorgeous. No, she was much more than that. She was perfection.

He stared at her as she moved, watching the gentle sway of her body, the long, wavy hair that hung down the length of her back, and he had to fight the sudden urge to run his hands through. He had been captivated as he watched her hands gather and stuff papers and other items into her shoulder bag, brushing stray wisps of long, dark hair from her face with her fingers. He'd watched the rise and fall of her breathing, and the way she tugged at her T-shirt when she twisted to pick up her scattered items.

He'd seen her smile to herself, then glance up to see if her friend had caught the act. He'd seen her frown when the sunglasses displeased her, and her amusement when her friend stood in front of her and announced that she'd thought the dreaded sunglasses suited her. And because Kieran couldn't see her response, he'd looked closer. At the shoulder bag tucked at her feet, the paperwork spread all over the pavement, noticing her casual clothes that no doubt cost a small fortune.

Still, he looked. He couldn't move. And for a split second, he'd thought Sophie had looked up and seen him too. But she'd been smiling up at her friend, while they both gathered her scattered belongings. People had begun to gather pens, pencils, newspapers and other pieces. And then he spotted something lying on the ground in front of her feet. And for once in his life, Kieran had made a snap decision without spending hours planning it.

Kieran shook his head, still unable to figure out why he'd done what he did. An idiot! That's what he was. *An idiot.* He should have dropped the business card straight in the nearest waste bin he'd seen after he'd picked it up. That's what he should have done. Kieran headed to his room and closed the door.

An hour later, he'd taken a long cold shower and towelled his hair dry. Exhausted, he flicked off the bedside light, and he slid naked between the sheets. But he couldn't sleep. He flopped over, his hearing alert, and his heart beating so hard his throat ached. He mentally argued and wrestled with himself over the reasons why he shouldn't or should call Sophie.

Don't be a fucking idiot, Kieran. You can't call her — you just can't! What reason would he give for phoning, for starters? What if she didn't want anything to do with him? Facing the fear of rejection was far worse than facing the unknown, or was it?

He closed his eyes and breathed deep, ticking off the minutes until his alarm sounded. Thirty minutes later, he turned on to his back, grumbling under his breath, tossed off the cover and tried again. Another hour of restlessness passed before he became determined he had to do something about this, or he would be heading for a bout of insomnia. Swinging his legs to the floor, he figured he had to take action now before things got so twisted that his work suffered. With a flick of the switch, he turned his bedside light on, holding his phone firmly in his grasp.

Fighting to deny his inner negative thoughts, he glanced at his watch for the umpteenth time within the last few minutes. It was late. Some of the guys would be rolling in from after final orders at the bar, rowdy and full of good spirits endued by alcohol no doubt, Kieran thought.

The military block where he lived was still reasonably quiet at the moment. There was the odd plodding of feet milling past his room on the way back from the showers, and with everything so still were all signs of people settling down for the night which had a sort of calming effect on him. Now would be the perfect time to make a call.

In the privacy of his own dimly lit room, he pulled her business card from his wallet, rubbing gently to remove the creases with his thumb and forefinger. Ever since meeting her, he had just wanted to know more about her.

No doubt about it, he was taking a considerable risk. Sophie could report him to his commanding officer if she wanted. Or was it something else — a thrill? Or was he merely acting out of stupidity? Whichever it was, he was going to find out; he just needed to hear her voice one last time.

Sitting upright in his bed, with an intake of breath, he propped his mobile on his lap and laid back on his pillow and tried to relax. OK, this is it. Now or never. Instead of bitching about it, he'd get on with it. The worst she could do was refuse to talk to him. There was no doubt about it, he'd been on active duty in Afghanistan but nothing scared him more as his actions right now.

His hand trembled on the keypad as he slowly tapped out the numbers. He tapped the wrong digit twice due to nervousness and had to redial.

The connection clicked at the fifth ring, stopping Kieran's heartbeat.

Chapter Eight

"Hello?" Snatching the phone from her nightstand, cursing this untimely interruption, regretting that she didn't switch it to silent mode.

Sophie answered with an annoyed sigh, glancing at the small brass carriage clock revealing it was after midnight. Most ordinary people who worked regular hours would probably be tucked up in bed by now. Luckily, she would consider herself as not in the class of ordinary people.

It had been the first night she'd had a chance of uninterrupted peace in months. Who on earth would be calling at this time of night? All she could think — this better be worth my time. Reluctant to answer her mobile phone at all.

"Hello?"

She answered a little breathless in her voice, slightly sleepy, and the sound raised the hairs on his arms. Kieran hesitated a minute, almost losing his nerve at the tone of her voice — too late now.

Exhaling he gave a simple, "Hello," in response.

He cringed at the sound of his male, gruff, almost inaudible voice and damned the nervousness in him. Sounded like he was calling for phone sex. Great. The guys would get a big kick out of him making a hash of this.

"Is someone there?" came a soft reply, filled with nervous apprehension.

"Yes, I'm here — sorry," he mumbled, cursing himself for stumbling over his nervousness.

"Who is this?"

Despite the sound of noticeable caution in her voice, Kieran couldn't help but feel triumphant. He'd finally had the courage to phone her. The problem was he didn't know whether she sounded thrilled or annoyed at the prospect of talking to him.

He glanced at his watch again. Oh, fuck! Kieran cringed. It wasn't eleven-thirty as he first thought — it was twelve-thirty!

"Who is this?" She asked again.

She was starting to sound more than a little anxious. Kieran knew he would have to say something, or he was going to blow it at his first words. He hadn't been prepared for this.

"Yes, I'm sorry. I don't know if you remember me — my name is Private Kieran O'Neill. We met recently." He stumbled over his explanation. Feeling confident she would remember him.

When she didn't speak, he feared the worst; he had to think fast. Not letting it deter his confidence when she hadn't recognised his name. Then he remembered something else. "You may remember us meeting a couple of weeks ago outside the NAAFI — I criticised your sunglasses — while you were still wearing them."

He heard a deep intake of breath of recognition which gave a small laugh in response. "Oh, yes, the dreaded sunglasses episode," Sophie gasped, realising instantly who the caller was and she gave a light giggle. "I'd forgotten all about that." She had been lying of course but no need for him to know that.

He felt himself cringe again. Sophie might have dismissed their encounter, but he certainly hadn't. He relived image by image and frame by frame to remember every crucial detail to the last.

"Really," he sounded so impatient and breathless as he hurriedly tried to explain. "Please don't be angry. It's just that I haven't seen you around camp. I called to ask if you were feeling all right and if everything is OK? If you remember, you had just returned from Afghanistan — we met in Kabul."

Stunned into silence. Unbelievable! Was this guy for real? Sophie couldn't believe he was calling her this late to inquire about her wellbeing when he should've been more concerned with his own.

"That was days ago — but yes, thank you, I'm fine. I've been busy with work since I got back." She took another deep breath before asking, "What of you?" She didn't want to pry but felt compelled to ask. "Busy training, I believe?"

Kieran was surprised to find she'd been interested enough to ask. "I'm OK now. I'm back home." *And talking with you*, he'd wanted to add but then thought better of it. After all, he didn't want to scare her off. "Rested up on a few days' leave while the army puts us through our paces."

She raised her eyebrows. He made light of his training but Sophie had seen the vigorous training at STANTA. It wasn't that easy. "I forgot I was talking to a tough British soldier."

Kieran laughed. "So, how have you been?" Polite chit-chat was all he could think of; he might as well start somewhere.

"Do you know what time it is?" Slightly bewildered by his call.

She sounded more irritated by the time of his call and not annoyed that he had called at all.

"Yes." The male voice was gruff, slightly tired and the impact of his one-word response was enough for the small hairs on the back of Sophie's neck to rise.

"Well — as nice as it is for you to concern yourself with my wellbeing — it is very late."

"Is it?"

She kept her tone as firm and polite as possible. "I'm sure you must have work tomorrow. I know I do, so if you will please excuse me when I say goodnight." Trying to end the call quickly. She wasn't in the mood to be some guy's late-night booty call after the bar closed.

He shrugged more for his benefit than anything else. Hurriedly, he said, "I'm so sorry; I normally don't phone girls and especially beautiful women."

"I see." Ignoring, what she considered a half-hearted compliment. "So — you usually expect girls to call you instead?"

"I just wanted to hear your voice for myself and know you were OK." Sophie found that hard to believe.

He quickly went on to say, "I don't know any other women but you. And the girls I do know I can never get them to call me back after the first date. I may be doing something wrong, I guess."

Trying to suppress a laugh. "Maybe you should brush up on what time you think it's acceptable to call a girl; you might have better luck."

"Fuck! I think you are so funny; I like that in a girl."

"And I think you like to swear a lot."

When Sophie chuckled — the sound made him feel warm inside.

"Sorry. I work with soldiers that think it's the one word that fits every occasion. I get so used to saying it that I forget myself sometimes."

He chuckled. "And I'm sorry if I sounded like I was calling for phone sex."

"And are you?" she answered, in a smooth tone. "Some light stimulation, maybe?"

After everything she'd been through lately, she wasn't about to trust a soldier who'd probably just wanted what every other guy wanted from her, and that was not going to happen. She decided being blunt was her best option.

"No! There was something about meeting you the way I did that day in Kabul, then again outside the NAAFI. I was just wondering — was it fate?" His voice seeped through her, wickedly low and deep.

"That was a coincidence," she said. "My being in the middle of a hotel siege during a war was just me in the wrong place. You were deployed, and in Kabul. It just happened."

Sophie didn't believe in fate — too bad he didn't think that. Kieran didn't say anything for a moment. "The truth is I found your business card on the ground outside the NAAFI; I thought I would call and ask how you were doing? Tonight, is the first opportunity I've had to call you."

She couldn't help but admire his honesty. "I see," was all she could think to say.

Remembering staring into the dark depths of his fathomless ebony eyes, she found herself swallowing the lump that had formed and lodged in her throat, which seemed harder to do than she'd thought. Sophie tried closing her eyes for a moment desperately trying to block out the image. She opened her eyes again. Time to think of something else. "Do you phone all the women you rescue from hotels this late?" she asked.

It was apparent in her tone that she felt he was another bored serviceman looking for a cheap thrill. More like thought him crazy, and he was more interested in the challenge, and a novelty for a short time until he got bored again.

He would show her differently. "No, I don't usually call women, beautiful or otherwise, at all. I've been in my room for a few hours, trying to work up the courage to call you for the last couple of hours or more," he said, calmly. "I chickened out a few times."

What did that tell her? "You were taking a risk calling me this late.

A possibility I may not be alone. Do you often take chances like this?"

"Not very often. I think you're the rule."

"Lucky me." Noting her dry tone, she sounded anything but impressed.

He chuckled, almost a low rumble, nothing immature about the sound and all man. Pure unadulterated temptation, which unnerved her. "I find it easy to talk with you."

"Maybe you feel you have some misguided honour because you saved my life?"

"I'm just trained to protect and serve without prejudice, view or political gain. It was my instinct to protect civilians. I like to think my military training will help put a stop to some of the violence."

"Thank you for saving my life all the same." Sophie hesitated, then added, "I must admit — you are a strange one." She laughed.

"Maybe I act a little impulsive sometimes. When I know something is right." He laughed outright as he heard her intake of breath.

She was shaken by his directness and it was obvious. "As I said, thank you for saving my life," she said. "But you have no claim on my life."

He'd said the wrong thing. "I didn't mean it that way. I just meant—"

"What exactly did you mean?"

"I meant — I was there. I thought you could relate to some of the problems the people are facing in Afghanistan during troubled times. Just talk."

Slowly he exhaled and said, "Being in Afghanistan changes you. Lives saved and lost. Face new challenges every day. Difficult choices have to be made. Orders followed. Events set in motion where you are left with no alternative but only to hope you are making a difference in some small way."

There was no mistaking the anxiety in his words. "Does it bother you talking about the things you experienced?"

"At times," he paused, "it's hard to explain how it is over there. One day in Afghanistan can at times feel like a month back home. Especially if the day happens to end badly."

Sophie noticed a change in his voice. "I'm sorry if talking about it bothers you."

"Talking about my time over there only bothers me when a mate is injured or worse. But I know my mates always have my back. And we know what is important to us and where to draw the line. Especially if they have their sights on a beautiful woman that is out of bounds to them." He laughed, and his mood suddenly lightened.

"Like me?"

"Like you," he responded earnestly, and then laughed at her shocked intake of breath.

The teasing quality of his words and his laughter made her smile. Sophie curled her toes into the mattress, settled deeply between the two pillows and pulled her sheet to her chin. Surprisingly, she liked the sound of his laughter; it was something she didn't expect to feel. It sounded as if filled with warmth and generosity. She knew she would have to watch her step.

"You like poking fun at me?"

"No, laughter is a great sense of stress release. I would never poke fun at you. I would just like to talk with you."

"I guess I find it so unexpected from someone who's gone through what you have been through recently to be so laid back about the whole experience."

"There are some secrets I will guard with my life and probably take to my grave. Some things I should probably talk about and don't. And then other things I never will. Secrets I can't discuss for reasons I'm sure you understand. It's rare to find someone who has insight into what it's really like over there."

"I must be just lucky you want to talk to me."

"Yes, lucky you." He laughed again. "I trust you."

There was a small trace of concern in her voice as she spoke. "This is all very nice of you." She paused, giving her answer some thought. As much as he appeared a nice guy, she still had her privacy to think of. "I have to say I don't appreciate strangers calling me late at night. Knowing where I live and texting me."

"We're not strangers. And I don't know where you live — I have your name and phone number. I didn't plan on calling."

She responded with, "Then why call me at all? You could have simply thrown the card away. You didn't really need to call to inquire about my health, did you?"

She waited, anticipating his answer, wondering if it was what he'd seen that prompted his impulsive move. After all, you didn't see a woman with a huge black eye and bruised cheek every day. He merely felt guilty at the way he'd removed the dreaded sunglasses. At least that was what he was telling himself.

"Honestly, I'm not sure why I called, but I'd like you to help me understand." He breathed into her ear. "If you'll just give me a chance."

Over the phone, Sophie could have sworn she heard the creaking of bedsprings. Was he in bed too?

Sophie closed her eyes; she wondered whether he was a pyjamas-bottoms type of guy. Or the kind to sleep in the buff? As she pictured him, a delicious shiver seeped through her body as she recalled the vivid image as she had stared into his piercing dark eyes, and felt his charming, warm smile with his handsome, youthful expression.

Blocking out the vision she opened her eyes slowly again; there was nothing to be gained from such images. She had enough unhappiness in her life at present without creating more unnecessary problems.

There was no denying, she didn't need any distractions or added complications in her life, and right at this moment she already had one too many. She could ill afford distractions at such a critical time. She'd tried marriage and settling down with a man who'd claimed he loved her, and it had been disastrous. But there was something about this soldier that made her think.

Trembling, Kieran listened to her breathing as he waited for her reply and the creaking of what — bed frame? Maybe she wasn't alone. "I'm sorry, it's a little late for this kind of conversation. Did I wake you?"

"I was working on a deadline," she replied, a little wooden.

"I shouldn't have called so late. I'm sorry." Again, he was apologising; this was becoming a regular habit.

She remembered his previous words, and she suspected he needed to talk with someone. He'd been through a lot recently while in Afghanistan. There was something about him that reached out to her.

"Hmm, I don't think it was a particularly good idea or a well-thought-out plan considering the time of night. What about you — don't you have to get up for training, exercise or something equally energetic?"

"I'm fine." He sounded almost desperate. "In fact, I've thought about you a lot since we met."

Sophie didn't say anything — couldn't say anything — and as much as she wanted to deny it, she couldn't form the words. He was flirting with her.

When she didn't say anything for a minute he asked, "Does that surprise you?"

Sophie found herself frowning, and using caution she explained. "I have a lot of guys tell me they think about me. Try to date me. Ask me to go away with them for the weekend—" She reminded him of his invitation to a no-strings-attached weekend away. It wasn't meant to sound conceited. She valued her privacy above all else.

"What you're saying is — you think I'm no different from them."

When she didn't respond with anything but a heartfelt sigh, he sucked in a deep breath. There was no way of describing his feelings at being slightly wounded by her words. "I don't know you."

But since meeting her he wasn't surprised, she'd had every right to form her own opinions and be suspicious of men. His friends warned him that they'd heard the rumours about scores of men asking to date her, and how they were politely, but firmly rejected for their futile efforts.

"Is that what happened to you? Did your ex find out the guys that were hitting on you, so he hit back?" he asked, instantly regretting his question, then hurriedly added, "Forget I said that. I'm sorry. It's none of my business."

True.

"You're right; it isn't." She confirmed.

"I'm sorry. I have poked my nose in where it isn't wanted." He didn't want to pry. He just wanted to understand why a man would hit the woman he's supposed to love and respect.

"My ex-husband is my business. He only has a problem with guys wanting a relationship with me. Or asking me out on a date." Sophie laughed. "And you aren't are you?"

Suddenly his hands were shaking and his palms were sweating. Kieran tried to imagine that laugh. He took a long time to consider what she'd said. Kieran wanted so much to assure her that he wasn't like the rest. And above all be with her, and he didn't want her feeling threatened by his eagerness, so he took his time in replying. "I'm not sure I know you well enough for a relationship — as for the other — not yet."

It was the delayed *not yet* that made the hairs on the back of her neck stand up and prickle in apprehension. "Is that what you think this is — the start of something?" Sophie questioned.

"No." He laughed. There was no denying this lady was quick to make a snap judgement. He would have to watch his step if he wanted her to take him seriously, so he explained a little more cautiously. "More of a prelude to a first date."

She laughed again — a gentle tinkling sound. "I see. A prelude, eh?" He sounded so confident for one so young. "Do people prelude a date over a phone call?" *Yes, he was definitely flirting with her.*

"No idea. What do you think?"

"I wouldn't know; I haven't dated in some time, and I'm out of touch. Maybe you should tell me what people do on a prelude first date phone call."

He couldn't breathe. Oh shit, he couldn't breathe! With a shaking hand, he shifted the mobile over to his other ear relieving the ache from the one that seemed on fire. He took a deep, steadying breath. Trying to keep his voice natural, but it was a hard task. "I don't know. It's a new one on me. Let's start with something easy. You could ask me a question and vice versa."

"Interrogate me more like?"

"No — just someone with interest in your wellbeing."

She thought for a moment. Sure, right, as if she believed that. Seemed to know a lot about it for someone having limited knowledge on the subject. Ask him a question. She thought for a brief time as she mulled over some ideas in her head. What sort of things did you ask a guy that calls you out of the blue, and past midnight? Keep it simple and not too personal. "Do you live in the camp?"

"Yes. Do you live alone?"

"Yes," she assured him. Not wanting him to know anything about her problems with Simon.

"Great," he added gleefully, "that's great."

Sophie felt a deep yearning like she'd never felt before. Which by her standards seemed an odd reaction for someone she hardly knew.

Especially with a guy so young.

"So, Miss Sophie, Sophie Tyson, the journalist, where do we go from here?"

The yearning deepened as she listened to his warm, velvety voice. "That depends on what you want from me?"

"Whatever you want to give me," he replied eagerly.

She sighed heavily. "Are you seriously asking me for a date?"

"I most certainly am," he said excitedly.

"I see." Trying not to be harsh in her response. "Well, thank you. But, no thank you," she replied evenly.

"*No thank you!*" Kieran repeated. "Oh, come on!" Then asked impatiently, "Why not?"

"Before considering anything else, there are quite a few reasons why we can't see each other."

"Like what?" he returned anxiously.

The situation was getting ridiculous. OK. This soldier asked for this — being nice was not getting her anywhere. She needed to focus on getting her life back on track. She had a lot riding on it. "For starters — if I'm honest — there isn't just the chronology to consider and the generation gap between us. Besides that, you are much too good-looking and self-confident for me to be associated with. And while you seem a very nice guy, I really can't afford any distractions right now." She had obligations too.

"Seriously? Are you for real?"

She ignored his glib comment and continued. "Secondly, I work all over the country with military officials and staff every day, and I wouldn't appreciate the gossip. Thirdly, the reasons why you wouldn't want to get mixed up with me would probably fill a book, and if all that wasn't enough to deter you," she paused, "you would see that I don't have the time for a relationship with anyone or a prelude phone date for that matter. As I said, thank you—"

"You think I'm good-looking?" Kieran interrupted.

She gazed up at the ceiling and gave an exasperating sigh. "You're not listening."

"Yes, I am." Hurt by her dismissive tone.

"Then what did I say?"

"You gave me a lot of sensible reasons why not."

"That's correct." She agreed firmly.

What didn't help was that he was choosing to ignore anything he considered irrelevant to his mission. "Where are your reasons why we could?"

"There are no positive reasons. I like my privacy."

"Then — there's no one special in your life?" He ignored all her negativity.

For reasons she couldn't comprehend he wasn't hearing her protests. "You aren't listening to me. The last guy I dated — we got divorced some time ago. I haven't had much free time for a social life since then."

"What happened?" He asked what he swore he wouldn't and instantly regretted it when the conversation came to an abrupt halt.

Seconds passed and turned into minutes, and Kieran's heart counted every one. Sophie replied slowly, "I married too impulsively, and I shouldn't have. I thought he loved me — I made a mistake."

"You're afraid you will do the same thing again? Trust the wrong man, I mean."

More time ticked by, and then softly she whispered, "Yes."

"Tell me about it?" he calmly invited.

"Never mind. It's a long story." She dismissed his question as unimportant.

"Then let's forget it," he said, with renewed enthusiasm. "I'd rather know what you would like to talk about."

"There's nothing else to know."

The sound that rolled from his throat was a growl of deep-seated hunger and protest at her simple dismissal of *nothing else*.

"You are wrong. There's you, Sophie, Sophie Tyson the journalist — I want to know you, both inside and out," he paused briefly, and then went on to say so slowly, "but I don't want you to think I'm like the rest. I'm not that shallow. I can wait. Let's forget I asked you out and start over. I will settle for being friends — for as long as it takes for you to trust me. We could spend our whole lives being terrific friends. If you think that's all there will ever be between us. Do you agree?"

There he goes with that directness thing again.

And it was if suddenly she couldn't breathe. The air became trapped

130

in her lungs. She couldn't breathe. Kieran was leaving the decision up to her.

"Sophie?"

With a shaking hand, she shifted the mobile to her other ear — the one that didn't feel like it was on fire by his words. "As I said, I don't date military—" she started, then sucked in a gulp of air as she caught her breath. "And I don't know you."

"Then you shall get to know me — as a friend. I'll make sure of it. That way when we decide to start having a relationship, I want you to know what you're getting into when the time is right. You might be surprised."

Silence met his answer.

Not a good sign. Maybe he'd pushed too far. Or, Sophie was having more of a difficult time with her ex than she'd admitted to him. He didn't want to frighten her away. Not after coming this far. Maybe he'd overstepped the mark. She was right, after all, she didn't know him for the guy he was. That would be up to him to show her. He knew what he wanted — and he wanted her.

"What is it you want?" he asked, as he let his voice trail off, hearing what he thought was a strangled whistle of breath.

Sophie made a small sound. "What I would like is to have at least six hours sleep, if I can get it."

"You still haven't answered my question."

"What question?"

"You know what I asked — don't go trying to change the subject on me."

Sophie gripped the phone tighter and drew her knees up to her chest. "I've heard it all before. I took a chance on someone who I shouldn't have. I believed in him — that was my mistake, and now—"

"And now — you're afraid to try again thinking you might make the same mistake of trusting someone?"

She nodded, then softly whispered, "Yes. I also don't have the time or room in my life for anything other than friendship." Sophie ran her palm caressingly over her duvet. "And now if you don't mind — I'm exhausted. I'm going to turn over and go to sleep."

"Are you in bed now?"

Oh dear, she knew where this might be heading. She heard the gentle rhythm of his breathing down the phone. She couldn't speak.

"Sophie?"

His velvety, warm voice encouraged her to speak. "Yes," she answered slowly, touching her tongue with her upper lip.

"Talk to me. Tell me what it's like, tell me about your sheets and what your bed feels like." Kieran breathed slowly against her ear. "I want to know."

She gave a small tinkle of laughter. "I don't think so."

He knew he was in dangerous territory for their first conversation, but he was teasing her, and the game was innocent enough — risky, a little crazy even. "Come on, Sophie Tyson, tell me. Lighten up. Enjoy the game. I dare you!"

She swallowed hard. "I'm too old for games. You can't teach an old dog new tricks and all that."

"What dog and who's old?" He laughed, knowing he considered her far from old, and as for the other — no way — a perfect lady.

OK, she allowed herself a small smile. He wanted fun at her expense, did he? He might have wanted a bit of fun with her — but she would teach him a fun lesson he wouldn't forget so quickly. Maybe it seemed harmless enough. Nevertheless — it felt like fun teasing him and very, very naughty.

Fun was something she hadn't experienced a whole lot of in her life up to now, and this was a little naughty for a conversation this time of night, and especially in a dimly lit bedroom. Her heart was racing at the thought — not sure what she had talked herself into. She blew out a slow breath and smiled to herself once more as she lifted the sheet and duvet and glared at her nightgown — she'd chosen the perfect one to wear for this game; Sophie allowed herself another smug, wry smile. Dare she!

"It's a short nightgown, in a two-tone pattern of deep crimson red and black. Soft and feminine. The body has a fitted bodice of black lace over a layer of crimson silk, which moulds to fit my body perfectly. It's cut low with thin, black, lace straps. It fastens down the front of the bodice with a row of small pearl buttons and ties with laces at the base of the low-cut back."

"Do the laces go all the way down the back?" Even as he said the words, thinking of her wearing the garment was enough to send his heart thumping wildly against his ribcage.

"No, the laces tie at the hips, and wearing such a luxury garment feels so sleek, cool and so light — like a caress against my skin. It fits perfectly; it allows me to move in my sleep."

"What else?" With added confidence he breathed into his phone. "What else are you wearing?"

"Nothing."

"Do you sleep on your back or your side?" he asked — his voice like gravel now.

Enough was enough. What started as a game and fun was quickly turning into something else. "Why do you want to know?"

This time his breathing was raw and ragged with need. "I want to lie beside you. I want to feel your silk and lace next to me; to unlace your nightgown and pull you hard next to me, and never let you leave my side."

The arrogance! Sophie pulled the sheet up tighter and trembled. Sophie closed her eyes tight for a moment and then opened them slowly. Exhaling, she said, "You frighten me, Kieran O'Neill."

"Do I? Are you sure it's me and not yourself you're afraid of?" He asked in no more than a whisper.

"I don't know," she breathed, reluctant to confirm or deny anything. "I can't deal with this game playing right now, especially at this moment. I'm not ready for a relationship or dating. Not with anyone, especially with someone so young."

"Trust me. You can." When Sophie didn't answer, Kieran continued, "Then you can sleep on it; I'll call again, or whenever you want. But I will call, I promise." He was playing it cool; he'd left the final decision to her. "Only if you want to talk with me again. Tell me. It's up to you."

"I won't allow you to do that."

"Do what?"

"Bully me."

"I won't need to." Sophie could almost feel his warm, sensual smile as he teased her. "You will come to me willingly."

"This is just what I'm talking about," Sophie sighed, for the first time showing she had a stubborn streak. "I won't allow you to talk to me this way."

"You won't allow! But — what if I want to call and talk to you?" he responded lightly. Not waiting for her to reply he added, "So, it's a date then?"

"Is that what this is — a phone date?" She sounded shocked at his directness.

He sounded amused. "Could be."

She laughed. "Before I make those sort of decisions as to whether I would like further phone contact I think I should sleep on it."

The line went dead in his ear. Setting his phone on his bedside locker, he reached up and flipped off the lamp and smiled to himself. He'd done it; he'd finally found the courage to call Sophie Tyson.

The realisation set in all too swiftly. Fuck me, why had he called? Why on earth had he called her at all? His life had been so organised, so on track, and so mapped out, so — ordinary.

After Sophie hung up, he found he couldn't sleep; Kieran decided he'd got some thinking to do. She appealed to him in so many ways, and at levels he was yet to discover. He was still restless. He punched his pillow and, lying in his bed, he imagined the classic lines of her body, moulded to her lovely shape in a nightgown that was held together by lace strings.

His mind focused, wanting to remember every last detail of their conversation and what he'd gained at the risk of sleep deprivation. There was no denying it, Sophie was relationship shy, which he felt sure probably had something to do with her ex.

So, how far could he go without making her doubt his sincerity and scaring Sophie off? He couldn't believe some of the things that had come out of his mouth while talking to her. But he'd been propped up in bed naked — the quilt cover across his lap doing nothing to hide the effect she had on his libido. And he'd wanted her to know what he intended from the outset. He certainly didn't want her thinking him immature. He'd wanted her to take him seriously; his feelings weren't those of a boy — in fact, they'd only intensified. He would prove to her their age difference meant nothing to him.

Kieran grinned to himself; she was nothing like what he'd thought she'd be. She had surprised him, and the way she'd spoken to him in response. Her sharp wit and no-nonsense attitude. What is not to like about a woman with a great sense of humour, but also able to challenge you mentally?

The truth known, he loved it: probably a little too much. She'd excited him so quickly; his heart beat faster — more than he'd thought possible, and Kieran was undoubtedly looking forward to their next conversation. He wondered what other surprises she had in store for him because he knew he was going to enjoy finding out.

Chapter Nine

Kieran surveyed the waiting men who were being pinned down with heavy fighting from the insurgents across the street with their AK-47s and RPGs.

"Gun! Rooftop." Kieran spotted from his position.

Wrighty's eyes spotted him. "Seen him."

There was no mistaking; the Taliban were not making things easy for them. Kieran kept a close eye on the nose of an AK-47 peering over the rooftop of an occupied Taliban secured four-storey building.

Kieran slid closer to the dry, dusty ground as a bullet whizzed past his head and penetrated the dry mud wall behind him. "Fuck me!" For a moment he thought that bullet had his name on it; thank fuck the shooter wasn't an accurate shot, random at best. But any weapon can kill when someone is trained to pull the trigger. He wasn't in the ideal position to do anything else than keep a watchful eye on the bastard.

Surrounded by AK-47s and RPG fire raining down on them was not the way he had first hoped to spend his weekend.

His immediate thoughts went to his previous conversation with Sophie and promising to call her again felt like he'd made a colossal mistake. He hated giving his word and breaking it. But in his defence, he didn't expect to be shipped out, back to Afghanistan, at a moment's notice either.

Going to sleep each night dreaming of her had eaten him alive. If he were honest, since that night, he'd continuously thought of nothing else. Even now, over three weeks later, he could still hear her voice. How soft and warm it had been when she'd relaxed. There had been no mistake when he'd recognised how anxious she'd been when talking with him at first, which he had put that down to the lateness of his call. But as time passed, the more they spoke, she'd lost some of her anxiety and tightness in her voice and became more jovial.

They had ended their call on a light note with a promise to call her, and Kieran had felt high when she'd agreed to speak again. But would she feel the same today — after all, that had been over three weeks ago?

Now, he was here and unable to call her as he'd promised. For that, he felt a heel. Kieran's thoughts were interrupted as a bullet whizzed past his head. If he was going to stay alive, he was going to have to pay attention to what was happening around him.

It didn't help that the section was still one man down with Drews on sick leave. The last report said he was doing well and safely on the mend.

Kieran touched his earpiece as his sergeant's voice came through loud and clear on the line. "Stand by for action in five."

"Clear," he responded into his headpiece.

Another repeating shot whistled past him popping at the ground, narrowly missing Kieran's right leg, leaving him to curse and call out another round of fucks.

"Can someone take that fucking shooter out? That bastard is so fucking annoying!"

"Got my eye on him, Jonesy," Wrighty called out catching sight of a bearded man who looked to be dressed in a black dishdash with a large ammo belt hung from his shoulder. He didn't appear to be seeking any cover as he took random shots.

"Located," Ginger added while fixing his Minimi focused on the rooftop.

Wrighty pinpointed to where the gunfire was situated to back up with the second Minimi. Within the time it had taken the two guys to set the guns ready, an RPG was launched directly at them.

"Grenade!" Jonesy spotted the small, metal, oval-shaped object hurling towards them roughly the size of a medium potato, and everyone made a dive for cover away from the Mastiff and two stationary WMIK. The last thing any man wanted was to be caught standing next to a vehicle when the grenade went off.

"Take cover!"

"Fucking hell!" Kieran didn't wait to be told twice.

In a desperate scramble to take cover, everyone threw themselves down into the nearest irrigation ditch and covered their heads. Another moment passed and just when Kieran started to suspect the grenade was a dud — Boom!

A flash of light, a shaking of the ground caused by a shock wave and the ear-shrieking explosion happened all at once. Dirt, rubble and dust came hurling through the air spreading the debris across the compound, covering everyone with layers of dust and dirt. Fortunately, no one was seriously hurt or shouting man down and, more surprisingly, the vehicles were untouched.

In the silence that followed the explosion, the ringing in Kieran's ears was so loud he was sure he had gone deaf.

Time to get the hell out of this place, Kieran thought, and pull back pretty fucking quick. Kieran turned his head to look at the mud and brick building across the filthy street that served as the insurgent's' headquarters.

"Anyone see where that fucking grenade came from?" Jonesy shouted.

Everyone seemed to confirm at the same time. "Nope."

"What's our next move, Jonesy?"

Having their arses kicked was not part of the operational plans. The troops were only supposed to follow the AFP and keep a watchful eye on the 'Op'. If the Afghan police came under attack, the men were there for their safeguarding only. The British Army was sent in to prevent the Taliban from making any premature attacks. That didn't seem to be working.

Captain Dan came up with a plan; he wanted the men to concentrate on the kilometres between the two points known as the *Green Zone* — prime poppy cultivation land. 'A' Company patrolled the roadless desert between Now Zad and Sangin to help the AFP locate the farmed fields and irrigation ditches, suspected as a newly planted crop of opium poppies. The area was found concealed and surrounded by eye level dead grass and dense shrubs by a sniffer dog.

The primary objective was to move forward to the fortified building and locate the suspected terrorists and take the fight to them. The men were all too aware of their orders in this operation. AFP required a diversion; it was necessary while they executed a successful operation to capture the insurgents. It had all been meticulously planned down to the minor details.

"Make ready to cover AFP's rear," Jonesy ordered.

"Already done," Kieran responded to the order of Special Forces taking the lead in this operation. "Ready to make a move to the position."

More gunfire exploded seconds later to the left of their position. From Smithie's vantage point from a nearby irrigation ditch he was able to see where the gunfire was coming from. He shifted and grabbed the radio. "The second shooter to the right," he confirmed, "Top window."

The long barrel of a second shooter RPG poked through the open window on the third floor as the others pinpointed the shooter at the same time.

Another round of bullets of increased rapid fire kept them pinned down. They almost had their balls served to them on a plate.

"What's the hold-up, guys? Things are getting warm out here," Al asked, from where he was also forced to take cover about 50 metres away from Kieran.

"Let's take that annoying fucker out!" Kenny tapped into the line with a click. There was a mixture of laughter and mumbled comments.

"We are waiting for a clear visual on the target. Stand by," Wrighty responded. "Waiting for someone to take the shot for Ginger. He'll probably miss as he's a blind bastard."

Ginger rested the nose of his L7A2 (GPMG) fitted with the C2 optical sight with its long-range ability, fixed on the tripod bracket and tucked himself in tight on the dusty ground as he positioned himself, firing one shot in the direction of the gunfire. "Very fucking funny, you cheeky bastard," Ginger scoffed. With one shot he had taken the Taliban shooter out.

Jonesy looked over at the building; the gunfire had brought about 20 insurgents flocking to the windows with fully loaded weapons. All of the AK-47s were pointing in their direction. The grenade had been the signal to begin firing.

The enemy was holding their ground inside the building across the street and had Kieran's team successfully pinned down with a barrage of flying bullets. Another bullet flew by narrowly missing its target. This entire situation was making them all anxious to end this and get the hell out of there.

The info and coordinates they received on the terrorists' location had been correct.

Almost three months ago, a group of civilian office workers had been taken as hostages and were now in forced labour to tend the poppy fields. Others were less fortunate at the discovery of dead mutilated bodies found in an unmarked shallow grave located two kilometres from where they were first taken.

Now was the time to end it. But right now, their position had given the terrorists an advantage. Something the enemy wasn't giving up on so quickly. Thankfully they weren't brilliant shots, but a bullet could kill on contact if it hit you. At least everyone was wearing full-body armour protection. The AFPs, poor bastards, were not as protected.

Sergeant Jones waved a hand in the air, signalling on the earpiece. "Remember, rescue the civilians alive if possible. Ready to go in two." He started counting down.

The men checked their SA80s were fully loaded using 5.56 mm rounds while two men stayed behind to back up with an 81 mm mortar support weapon and LMGs (Light Machine Guns). But it didn't matter what gun a bloke carried — it was important every firearm was well maintained and cleaned every day in readiness.

While making his way slowly forward, Ginger slid behind the back door of the vehicle wreckage 200 metres from the rear entrance to the building, while Kieran did the same from the side of a burnt wreck 500 metres to his left. The return fire kept on coming directly at them — the LMG firing 750 rounds a minute.

Jonesy took the signal to make his move and made it across to the other side of the road, and then ducked at the rear of the building while the rest of the men covered with back-up to the firepower with single shots directed at the shooters.

It worked! The terrorists engaged fully and were occupied with the constant return shots for shots provided by Kieran and Ginger.

"Move it! Let's make a move and get these fucking insurgents to reveal their hand." He heard the sergeant call out through his earpiece as the rest of the section divided, and others made their way forward to follow Jonesy's position with their SA80s. Their weapons ready.

When each of the men had made it across to the secured location, last man behind, Kieran made his way over to join them.

Jonesy signalled for Kieran to take the lead to Lance Corporal *'Si'*

Parker.

In complete silence, Kieran reached for the doorknob. Smithie covering his back and Wrighty from his left side. As he opened the door, a spray of spent ammo popped at the wall, and met him with rapid gunfire on the open staircase where they had been heading.

Each of the men headed for cover taking stock of what just happened. They knew to secure the safety of the men, and the rescue of hostages was above all else. Checking the wellbeing of each man, in turn, was a priority.

At the arrival of the remaining platoon following up the rear, Kieran and Wrighty sprinted forward the moment the door opened a second time to secure a firing position on the first floor.

Some of the men were under heavy fire as they tried to make it back to the landing. Kieran was relieved to see the guys unharmed, and returning firepower to add back-up to protect the men.

Judging by the massive firepower, all the signs pointed there to be around ten suspected terrorists returning fire from an open balcony window. And it was evident to Kieran that they weren't giving up lightly. At that moment, a flicker of movement caught his eye as a lone figure hid in the shadows of a darkened room one flight up.

Wrighty nodded in his direction as he spotted it too. It looked like one of them had tried to make their escape before things heated up or being caught as a terrorist. They couldn't let him escape, or worse, set himself up as a suicide bomber in another unsecured room. The worse speculation would be for the suspect to execute the workforce to stop them from admitting anything to the police.

Kieran glanced at his mate; he was taking cover from inside an open doorway across the landing. As if reading each other's thoughts, they both raised their weapons and raced to follow the suspicious movement.

Without a word, and with precise, rapid movement, the two guys hastened after the figure that had now taken to hiding in the disused loft of the building. With no sign of the mysterious figure, they were searching the attic for him. Because even though the room had no windows or electricity, 'Kieran had been able to visualise an image of the darkened room on entry.

Just thinking of a shooter lying in wait to ambush the two of them like some coward was fucking annoying him. Along with the intensified heat. Kieran wiped the sweat from his forehead, surprised how many sweat droplets had dropped from his gloved hand. It was as if someone had turned the sun up another 40 degrees in the room and was trying to micro-cook them.

Kieran was not sure if the gunman had gone rogue, or something far worse, and got rid of the people who tended the fields, which meant no witnesses to tell of the drug pipeline. For the time being. The fear of reliving the confrontation of a suicide bomber that resulted in Drews getting shot still stuck firmly in Kieran's mind. One thing was painfully evident as the gunman positioned his AK-47 and rested it on the floor and discharged it in a crazed fashion. He was taking pot-shots at anything that moved in the darkness of the room. Bullets and flashes of light from the muzzle were flying everywhere.

Only when the man stopped shooting long enough to reload his weapon did the guys attempt to make a move on the lone gunman.

"Let's go," Kieran whispered. Being careful and moving with organised precision they headed across the vast, darkened, dusty room. He worked his way across the poorly lit room using the dirt walls to guide him, trying to get his bearings.

A faint clicking noise sounded to his right. Listening to every sound the two men edged closer and kept to the wall. Half-dried mud crunched like sand beneath their dirty boots, giving them away as to their position. Kieran shifted to his left; he flattened himself against the wall. He eased one foot in front of the other, and he moved cautiously with Wrighty close behind to back him up.

For a brief moment, Kieran thought he heard a clicking sound again. At that moment Wrighty lost his balance, and as he went to lower his body to lie on the floor, a gun nozzle flashed and a single shot rang out. Both men dived for the ground, narrowly being missed by whizzing bullets hitting the wall behind them.

Something wasn't right — being out in the open like this left them a sitting target. It was clear to the two men that they were facing a lone shooter taking up a new position, but for what purpose still evaded them. At this point, one thing was a priority to make their place secure — a light was essential without giving away where the two men were situated and compromising their safety. At that precise moment, there was a deafening crashing noise, followed by a blinding flash, and it felt as if the whole building was caving in around them. It was as if all hell had broken loose.

For an instant, Kieran saw the clean-skinned young boy, who looked no more than 12 years old, wearing black dishdash, black turban and supporting an AK-47 that seemed as long as the boy was tall. The small boy looked terrified, anxious and confused and was pointing the AK-47 directly at them.

Fuck me! He's just a kid for fucks' sakes!

Taking advantage of his confused state, Kieran jumped up and tried to dash for the boy's gun. But the boy was too quick, and he was able to get a shot off before Kieran could get out of harm's way. Instantly, Kieran felt a burning pain in his arm as the bullet hit.

Wrighty had his weapon raised and the kid in his sights. "Put your gun down!" He wasn't even sure the kid understood. Wrighty repeated the warning, but the boy remained steadfast.

Kieran slowly raised his Glock17 sidearm and kept the shooter in his sights. At this critical stage, he could not be underestimated for any reason.

The boy froze. He turned and looked at Wrighty with such a look of male hatred that put Kieran's nerves on edge. He'd seen the same look on the suicide bomber just before he shot Drews. And a look that would never go away. But if the boy surrendered his weapon now, Kieran was prepared to live with that to save lives.

Wrighty lowered his weapon carefully, keeping his eyes fixed on the boy who still seemed in the state of nervous confusion; his attention was divided for just a moment as he looked over Kieran's arm.

The boy took advantage of it and grabbed Kieran's gun. He shoved Wrighty, barely managing to push him aside; his actions were enough to disarm Kieran and swing the gun up towards Kieran.

Scrambling for his gun, Kieran made a desperate attempt to regain possession of his sidearm. After all, he was twice the size of this nimble kid. But with his arm weakened from his wound, it became a huge task to avoid anyone getting either of them further wounded or even killed.

Now engaged in the desperate struggle for control, the boy was able to get a shot off before Kieran could gain control, and before anyone realised what had happened, the boy fell dead against Kieran's chest.

Further to the examination of the body, it looked like the bullet had projected upward, hitting the boy in the face. On exit, the shell left a massive hole in the back of his head. Kieran felt it was a sad loss of a young life. Another fatality of recruiting a boy to fight in a man's war. Despite that, Kieran would never have let him kill Wrighty or himself should it come to the death shot.

Just as the two men thought they were clear to leave, Wrighty heard a faint click that sounded behind him, like two ticks of a clock, Kieran had an uneasy feeling about it.

"Fuck!" Time to leave, and pretty fucking quick if his senses had anything to go by. Kieran said, "Let's get the fuck out of here!"

The two men ran to the door.

The explosion rocked the very foundations of the building. Wrighty had just placed his hand on the door to make their escape when they found themselves thrown back against the dusty, dirty wall, which was crumbling to the ground around them.

They were covered in dust but alive. For a moment Kieran couldn't breathe, hear or see anything, Wrighty tried to get their bearings while feeling along the floor, as they both leaned back against the wall. Kieran closed his eyes for a brief moment — thank fuck he was still alive. Disintegrating building particles covered every crevice; everything seemed to be happening in slow motion and in all directions.

Kieran tried to follow Wrighty as he began moving towards the attic door. Trying to fight off the feeling of sickness and the constant ringing in his ears.

On the exit of the building, Jonesy was striding straight for them. There was no doubt in their minds, the two men were in for a round of — fucks!

"Can either of you dickheads, explain what the fuck the two of you think you were fucking doing?" Kieran knew this was coming and Jonesy wasn't holding back. "Have you lost your fucking minds?"

Wrighty said nothing as he sat in the chair across from Kieran at the med centre, holding the open wound pad against his arm where the bullet had grazed him and was still bleeding.

"Don't know what you mean, Jonesy," Wrighty answered flippantly.

Private Tim *Wrighty* Wright was a great soldier and good mate, but he was crap at lying, Kieran observed. He talked the good talk when it came to women, but Kieran found out through getting to know him that he actually knew nothing, and was quite shy around girls. Kieran suspected he'd never had a girlfriend. As a 20-year old he was happy most around people he knew best. He kept his equipment and himself top-notch. Even when the men hit the town on one of the group's legendary nights out, many of them returned to the base shit-faced, but never once had Kieran known Wrighty to get legless. He was always the responsible drinker. And as an only child, the army suited him, he was well liked by everyone, and there was nothing he wouldn't do to back up a mate.

"Are you fucking kidding me?" There was no misunderstanding — Jonesy was mad as hell. "You think I'm fucking stupid?" He leaned over Wrighty. "Don't let me ever catch you both playing fucking solo heroics again. Or I'll have you both transferred out of this section in less than an hour — you fucking pair of dumb bastards! Do I make myself fucking clear?"

Without a word, they both nodded. Too intimidated to do any other. Jonesy left without another word.

The doctor patched his arm and at first glance at the wound, deemed him unfit for work for two weeks.

"Looks like you are going home for two weeks, soldier," Wrighty said, "you can finally ask that reporter lady out on a date," he teased. "Shame you had to get shot to get the chance."

"Yeah, right," Kieran shrugged. "If she ever talks to me again."

"If she doesn't show any interest in you, I might try for her myself." Wrighty smiled. "Pretty, little thing with those big, brown eyes and a perfect smile that lights up when she walks in a room. A real-life cute angel."

Kieran grunted. "Stay the fuck away from her," he warned.

A burst of laughter met his response.

Leaving him to realise he was being ribbed. "Shut the fuck up!" Kieran barked. "I still have one good arm, you fucking wanker."

Silence met his rebuff, taking the advice to remain silent and not say anything else about Sophie Tyson.

Wrighty ignored his anger. "I'm sure she's heard by now of our situation." He rubbed the dust away from his face and hair. "If she is half the woman you think she is, I'm sure she'll at least give you a chance to explain."

Kieran wished he had Wrighty's optimism. Right now, he could only hope. After the last few weeks without contact from Sophie he'd got a feeling that he was going to have a difficult time of convincing her to take his phone call.

All he could think of right now was returning to base and handing over their intel to other forces. One thing at a time.

***

The next day passed in a working blur of activity. Firstly, the infantry section finished returning the equipment to the stores. And then he filled in the report for the ammunition used. Completed the stack of paperwork and data checked and doubled checked it. Rifles, handguns and all weaponry needed counting and logged in. Locked up the stores and handed in the keys. With all that done he'd only thought of calling Sophie Tyson a dozen times more since his return.

Being wounded he thought of going home to visit his parents, but his mum would have given him those sorrowful looks, and she would have had a hard time concealing her worry as she fussed and fretted over him. He couldn't stand to see that on his mother's face. He couldn't bring himself to tell her it was the hazards of the job. So he chose to spend the time in camp until his wound had healed enough to remove the dressing. Kieran figured a week on the base should fix things, then he'd think about facing his parents.

Once he'd joined the others at the mess hall, he found he wasn't in the mood to eat. What he wanted to do was take a shower and clear his head from the events of the day. He picked up a sandwich and bottled water and headed back to his room. On returning to his room, Kieran had eaten his chicken sandwich and quickly headed for his shower hoping to eject the remaining dust and sand from Kabul out of his hair. Jumping out, he towelled off and pulled on his boxers and a pair of jeans once he'd half-dried.

Kieran knew he wouldn't be able to rest tonight until he'd called Sophie. He wanted some answers to some of his questions. He'd tormented himself for long enough. Tonight, he promised himself, when he called her, he would make sure things would be different from the last time. He would make sure of that.

No way was he going to get caught out calling her that late again and give her the opportunity to refuse not to talk with him. And after last time, there was no way in hell he was going to speak to her naked, not this time. No way was Kieran going to let the conversation get out of hand either. He was going to be in full control. That sinful conversation he'd stirred — their previous conversation that had ended up leaving him so turned on and so frustrated, which he had dreamt about for all those nights since.

What in the hell made him do it last time?

Kieran had no idea what had made him do it, but the sound of her voice and the image her words painted on the blank canvas in his mind had been more than he could stand. He'd never been so turned on by a woman's voice before, not while in his room alone.

Kieran had no problem giving her all the time and space she needed to figure out what she wanted from this, and how far she wanted to take things with him. But all he knew of her was a name on a card, *Sophie Tyson, Journalist* — a card he kept like a treasured possession and was with him always.

He'd told her the truth when he told her he didn't know anything about her apart from the obvious. He didn't know where she lived. She'd cautiously kept that withheld. And her not trusting him bothered him. A lot. But the last conversation had started out in one direction and quickly taken another.

And it had been his first involvement with a woman he'd ever had that involved him being so infatuated based on such a short acquaintance. Not to mention ever spoken with such an intelligent, beautiful woman on the phone. Phones made him nervous for some reason. He certainly didn't want to blow it now.

Kieran sat on his bunk and watched as each second ticked by. He took a steadying, deep breath and picked up his phone and dialled.

147

"Hello?" he heard her say softly.

He couldn't speak, feeling strangely intimidated, and he froze at the sound of her voice. When Kieran didn't speak, she sighed, which sounded like a breath of a kiss.

Met with silence, something told Sophie who it was. "Kieran?" she whispered.

He couldn't believe it! Kieran had got to hear her voice, and he'd become totally immobilised before uttering a sound. For a guy who had served in war zones, he was surprisingly uncomfortable talking to her.

Sophie took another breath and calmly asked again. "Kieran?"

At the sound of his name, he sucked in his breath. "Yes," he exhaled slowly.

"How are you?" Sophie asked, with genuine concern.

"I'm OK," was all he could say. All these weeks and that was all he could manage to say. "I didn't call you because—"

Sophie interrupted quickly, "I'm talking to a British soldier. I understand. I've seen the news."

Wrighty was right about her — she did understand. "Then you understand why I —"

In no more than a whisper, she said "Yes — I understand. The news reported your unit searching for known Taliban leaders taking refuge in a village. The women and children were calling out to you, begging for food for their sick, dying children."

"Yes, we couldn't understand what they were saying to us, but the begging and pleading glances told us that we were their last chance of survival. We gave them some food and some blankets. It was all we could do for them until help arrived. Our troops were there to take control over the insurgents."

"They were alone, scared and in desperate need of help. I'm sure you did what you could to help the people."

Kieran couldn't believe why he was telling Sophie this, as he took a deep breath. He had never spoken about his tours with anyone before, except with the guys, but for some strange reason he wanted her to know. "Their husbands had been taken by the Taliban and crops destroyed. The women were repeatedly raped by the insurgents and left to fend for themselves. Children were sick and the other half had died of malnutrition. We had to help. We couldn't leave them that way."

"You did what you could."

"Was it enough?"

Sophie had never heard Kieran talk this way. There was no mistaking the sound of regret. "The Taliban need people to plant, water and weed the crops. Human trafficking for any purpose is a huge business." It was a subject Sophie knew something about, but she had to use caution. Sophie's attempt to make him feel better about his efforts had only added to his thoughts.

"So the Taliban seized men from their homes just so the women would tend these fields?"

Sophie didn't know why, but when she had heard the sadness and hurt in his voice, tears formed in her eyes. He'd shown her such kindness and respect, but whatever he'd been experiencing as a soldier was far worse than anything she was going through as a single woman. "It happens."

"I guess so."

"What now?" She felt reluctant to ask. "You have plans?"

"Now?" he whispered. "Now, I ask the questions," he said, jumping in quickly before Sophie had a chance to utter another word.

Sophie released her breath in a long, slow, awkward sigh. "I don't think that's a good idea. We have tried that."

"Then we try again. You can start by telling me all about yourself. What have I missed on TV? The weather. Whatever you want."

She gave a small laugh. "Not such a good idea. I don't like talking about myself. I'm a very private person."

"All right. Whatever you say."

After several seconds ticked by, she chuckled softly. "Are you always this agreeable?"

"Ask my mates, and you'll get several mixed comments about that. But I've been looking forward to calling you from the moment I got back in the UK this morning; I've waited all day. As long as you're talking to me, I don't care." He relaxed enough to sit back against the headboard and rest his head against the wall. "I'm agreeable to whatever you suggest."

She laughed. There was no mistaking the eagerness or the

enthusiasm in Kieran's voice. "I see."

"What's so funny?"

"Nothing. I don't want to discuss anything too personal."

Too personal. Kieran paused, then took a deep breath. He was prepared to tread carefully, as above all else he wanted her to know she could trust him. "The way we ended the conversation last time, I didn't think we had anything too personal that we couldn't discuss."

"Old wounds." She gave a self-conscious, little laugh.

Old wounds? He considered her few words. *What the fuck did that mean?*

"I feel sometimes people don't see the real me," she said slowly, taking a deep breath. "I'm a solitary person."

He thought of how many times he'd thought of her throughout the day, picturing her in that nightgown — removing it from her small frame. Kieran got to his feet. He turned off the bedside lamp, plunging the room into near darkness. The shadows made his confession somehow easier.

"From that first day, the moment I saw you, I don't know what happened to me. I looked into your eyes and saw something that resembled hurt to me — maybe — I don't know what I felt, Sophie. You looked up at me, and there you were. Beautiful. Elegant. Nothing made sense to me. I don't know what else you expect me to say."

Sophie hesitated, her voice growing frantic. Her answer revealing she was clearly disappointed in his response. "You saw what everyone sees. That isn't the real me."

He sat back on the edge of the bed. "What you told me the last night we spoke showed me more. I liked it."

She gave a small laugh. "I'm not talking about that." Realising that it was beginning to lead towards sex talk. "I'm talking about personal stuff. Believe me when I tell you I'm much too busy for a personal life. Now, future — and in the past."

"What about now? What are you going to do about my feelings?" He stopped at the foot of the bed and closed his eyes. Leaning his head back, closing his eyes briefly, trying to swallow the lump forming in his throat — longing and need had risen deep from within him. "Give me a chance to show you I'm different." He was rushing her, he knew that, but he couldn't help it. "Just one. That's all I'm asking. If you don't want anything to do with me after that, I'll accept your decision."

She didn't speak.

He needed her to know how he felt, but he also suspected she was reluctant to trust anyone. "Tell me where you are, and I'll be there, I promise! How about Saturday? I'll pick you up anywhere you say. Name it. I promise you — no strings attached. We won't talk about anything that you don't want to. All I'm asking for is a chance to show you."

"Just like that? I can't go on a whim. I have commitments — deadlines. What about your friends?"

"Screw them. The mood I've been in lately. My mates can handle me not being around them for one weekend." Leaving out the explanation of him being unfit for duties was something he preferred not to share with her right now.

"Wait! I don't know anything about you."

"You know what I look like. Isn't that enough?"

She seemed to hesitate. "Kieran?"

He melted at the sound of her voice; he loved it when she said his name in that breathy way. "Yes?"

"What are you thinking?"

He laughed — it was payback time. "What do you think?"

"I don't know unless you tell me." She wasn't biting.

This sharing of information was not going the way Kieran had planned. "I've been thinking about you, dreaming about you every night, Sophie Tyson, journalist."

"Kieran," Sophie sighed heavily. "This isn't working. I should go."

"No, wait!" The same longing and frustration that filled his voice filled his jeans. He couldn't go on not knowing more about her.

"What?"

"You haven't said yes or no — I need to know."

For a moment, he heard nothing but breathing, then she whispered, "Yes."

Kieran expelled a huge, deep breath of relief. Perfect. She'd said *yes*!

"OK, Sophie Tyson. It's eight o'clock, and I'm in desperate need of a shower." He didn't bother telling her he'd already had one, or that Kieran pictured her beside him standing under the spray, or that he' wanted her with him now. "Don't suppose you'd like to join me, would you?"

She sucked in a sharp intake of breath.

When she didn't speak, half-joking he said, "I could use your help washing my back."

In a voice so low it became almost a whisper, she replied, "I always have trouble washing my back, getting to those hard-to-reach places. You know — between the shoulder blades and back of my calves down to my ankles."

Kieran dropped his head back and stroked his urgently building need. "Sophie—"

She gave a small, confident laugh as she continued, "I like standing under the warm spray and letting the water run slowly down my body in a warm caressing motion as I soap my body all over with a sweet-scented apple soap."

"Enough!" He flipped his bedside light on, flooding the room with light, which appeared to make their conversation a little less intimate.

"Wet skin is so refreshed and smells so sweet," Sophie went on, her voice as sweet as honey, "especially when the water is warm and soothing."

"We have to stop this now!" Reaching down, he pressed against the ache growing heavier with Sophie's every word.

"Yes," she giggled. "I agree."

A strange calm relief left Kieran. He glanced down at his erection. Yes, aroused but calm. He was right to put a halt to their conversation. "Shall I call you again tomorrow about the same time?"

"I have plans tomorrow."

"Thursday then."

"Busy."

"Friday? We can discuss where I'm to meet you on Saturday." He hated the thought of her seeing anyone but him, but he didn't want to frighten her away, so he ignored it.

"As long as it's not a date. It's not what I want."

"OK. Trust me. We can go to my parents' home. I promise you it will be the best non-date weekend you have ever experienced. I give you my word that I won't touch you. I won't even come near you if you don't want me to, I promise. And if anytime you feel uncomfortable and want to return home I won't argue. I'll turn around and bring you home with no questions asked, and I won't bother you again. I'll respect your privacy. Will you trust me — just this once?"

Her voice dropped to a low murmur, "I trust you, Kieran," she replied, then severed the connection.

Kieran snapped on the leading light and shrugged out of his jeans, returning to the washroom for a long, cold shower.

Chapter Ten

From the beginning of the weekend, there was no doubt — the weather had been glorious.

True to his word, the whole weekend Kieran had pampered and cared for her. Sophie had never felt so utterly at ease, and for the first time in months, relaxed. And as the weekend progressed, she learned how to be at peace with herself.

A sort of calmness — peaceful tranquillity — had slowly drifted over her. She somehow felt different with Kieran, more relaxed, lighter and happier than she'd felt in a long time. Sophie couldn't remember the last time she had felt so good about herself.

She had a felt a strange sense of freedom in everything they did together as a family. And for the first time in months, she wasn't living on tenterhooks every time she made a move. She certainly didn't need to guard herself against Kieran's moods or suspect his every motion.

Kieran, not once, ever showed he had an ulterior motive for being in her company. Equally, at that same time, she didn't have to look over her shoulder, suspicious of a man's motives at every movement.

It helped that his parents were kind too — she had warmed to them instantly. They had a strong family closeness that was unique. Kieran clearly held his parents in such a high regard. No one else could live up to that.

His father, Sean — she could never bring herself to call him by his first name, had been open and friendly from the beginning. If he didn't approve of their friendship, he never commented on it. Even if he'd thought it strange that their son was bringing a girl home with him for the weekend, they were polite enough not to mention it.

Sean was two years younger than his wife, and although Ingrid's background had been different with her German upbringing compared to her husband's Irish, dirt-poor-farming background, as he'd put it, this had only added a particular attraction for them both. Anyone with half a brain cell could immediately tell they were both still madly in love.

It was clear by their actions over the weekend that Kieran was their only and much-adored child. It had been on that Sunday morning, while the two men had gone off fishing in the early hours that she and Ingrid sat drinking coffee around the kitchen table, and Ingrid confided in her, by explaining she'd been unable to have more children, and that they were thankful every day for their son.

Her sadness for not being able to have more children had touched Sophie's heart. They were a warm, friendly, close family and, as Sophie expressed to Ingrid, she was all too well aware of the disappointment at not being able to have children. She had also wanted children, but after what Simon had told her — and after weeks of tests that she had subjected herself to — the results had been conclusive. The military doctors had confirmed that Sophie and Simon would not be able to conceive a child of their own. Something else for Simon to punish her for and he delighted in doing so.

As their only child, Sophie could fully understand why Kieran's parents wanted the best for him. Ingrid's honesty and Sean's frankness were a refreshing change for her, and she could see where Kieran had got his honesty trait.

Her life as a journalist had become unfulfilling and empty, just like the sham of her marriage to Simon had become phoney. Making her realise one thing that was painfully obvious — for the first time in her life, Sophie felt lonely.

Meeting Kieran with his zest for life and adventure had given her a new lease of life. She came away from the weekend feeling refreshed and invigorated. Sophie realised one thing — she wanted so much more out of life than the mundane existence she had gotten accustomed to over the years.

But becoming attracted to an 18-year-old boy was out of the question. Kieran was her friend; their association was a friendship worth far more to her than to risk everything on a brief, casual affair. Especially with such an impressionable, young guy, and it seemed unfair to him to assume he was like many other guys of similar age — functioning more on hormones than brains.

When she had first met Kieran, she had labelled him as a player.

Sophie realised now that had been a snap premature judgement on her part. And true, the longer she knew Kieran, the more she liked him. He was also charming, humorous, respectful and courteous at all times. She had also come to realise that Kieran was also much more relaxed and content in his natural home and family surroundings.

From the very moment she met Kieran she had noticed a strange and rare quality about him that only enhanced his attraction. There was no doubt in Sophie's mind, Kieran also seemed a lot more mature than some of the other soldiers his age. And although he'd spent most of the weekend observing her from afar, there was no mistaking his attraction for her.

Even though Kieran never said anything about it to her during the weekend, there was no mistaking those adoring glances he cast her when he thought she wasn't looking. Sometimes she would be doing something and she would feel a strange urge that someone was watching her. She would glance up and find Kieran's eyes on her, silently staring at her with those adoring, deep, dark eyes. Sophie had to stop herself from staring back at him.

But — facts were facts, she could ill afford others seeing her running around the countryside, or anywhere else for that matter, with an 18-year-old boy. She would do well to remember that.

Most of the weekend passed in a blur of various activities, such as basketball, fishing and tennis. After dinner, they all took a walk to visit Sean's traditional local bar. They all sat on the patio while listening to the band playing time-honoured music; his parents preferred to sit holding hands and listen to the music, while Kieran and Sophie danced.

As he went to take her in his arms, she wound her arms around his neck. She sensed a growing change between them. Something froze inside her.

There was no mistaking he'd sensed it too. His steps stumbled momentarily revealing his nervousness, his body rigid — no mistaking he found it difficult to relax.

Consciously, she had erected a barrier between them, and Kieran had sensed that. Her mind was steadfast. Their friendship would have to battle all the elements that he wasn't equipped to deal with.

One day Kieran would understand why she felt the way she did.

Kieran had his whole life ahead of him; sooner or later, he was going to thank her for this. Then, hopefully, one day he would find a young woman more suited to his age. So why wasn't Sophie congratulating herself? After all, she had achieved what she'd set out to do. Sadly, knowing this brought her no comfort.

By the Sunday morning, she had known what she must do. Sever all ties with him. Would she be able to convince him enough? Other than friendship was not possible with this association. But for the moment the knowledge of that gave her nothing but pain and torture.

Sunday evening — Kieran had dropped her off at the train station to retrieve her parked car with a casual, friendly farewell.

Of course, it had helped that Simon was away for the entire weekend. And as part of Simon's recovery process, he was ordered to take a regular assessment course, arranged by Rev. Barnes. Suspecting he'd arranged this more out of concern for Sophie, giving her a thankful and much-needed break from her constant worrying over Simon's state of health, and a respite from his unscheduled and uninvited visits to her home in Norwich. Sophie wished things could have remained that way forever.

Simon had left early on Friday morning filled with high spirits and hopes. And the main thing about it — he wasn't due back until late Monday afternoon.

With a massive breath of relief, and for the first time in months, she had slept soundly in bed that night without the worry of what state of mind Simon would be turning up in on one of his impromptu *'flying visits'* as he called them, with an excuse or other of that he needed her.

Over the next few days, things seemed a little less tense. Simon had returned enthusiastic about his trip; she thought she'd seen flashes of the old Simon as he *'called in'* to tell her all about his weekend. As he chatted and laughed, he looked younger and healthier; he'd become more like his old self again.

Yes — the break had undoubtedly done him a world of good.

His black moods seemed to have evaporated. Sophie hoped that things would stay that way. His constant visits and unwanted phone calls had dwindled down to no more than a trickle.

His progress improved so much over the next few months, which enabled Weapons Systems Officer Simon Campbell to return to work as ground crew under supervision. He still wasn't allowed to fly, but he was prepared to work his way through as long as he could be involved with his old flight crew — familiarity was crucial to his progress. His CO had been confident in his judgement — to let Simon resume his post with limited ground duties would be considered the best for him.

Sophie observed as each day followed. The seriousness of the situation was evident to him — if he failed this time Simon would no longer be the Royal Air Force's responsibility. But Simon surprised everyone; he hadn't failed — he was getting stronger, and going from strength to strength with each day.

It was evident to her that Simon no longer needed her, and judging by the continued string of phone calls he'd received from female friends — Sophie knew she'd made the right decision to be free from the bonds of marriage.

Now would be the best time to make her move.

Secretly she arranged a meeting with Rev. Barnes; she didn't want Simon to get wind of the appointment for two reasons. One, she didn't want him slipping back, not after all the excellent work he'd done with getting himself back on track. The second, Sophie hadn't wanted Simon trying to talk her out of moving closer to her job. It didn't mean she didn't want to support Simon with his recovery — it was just — she needed more independence. So when she had been offered accommodation on the military base in Norwich, she accepted.

Rev. Barnes was a small, stout man with receding, white hair and had been her lifeline while at Brize. He had a jolly nature, and Sophie had liked him from the first. They had often worked together in the past, through either her commitments with various charity events or his continued support and counselling with Simon. There had been no end to the man's generosity.

Her job became more focused in Norwich and surrounding areas. Unfortunately, Kieran's platoon was stationed at the same Norwich base until further orders were released.

Although she had tried to stay clear of Kieran since that weekend, he made it visible he found her attractive. Everything about him made it evident as if silently drawn to her like a fish to a hook. Despite this, she dared not raise his hopes; it was too risky for either of them. With her history and his youth they could never be allowed to form a romantic relationship. His infatuation with her had to stop.

Her first move was to distance herself from him, although there had only been a couple of phone calls from him, she'd put a halt to the late-evening telephone calls the moment he arrived in Norwich.

Not only did she need to disconnect specific forms of communication, but their growing attraction was becoming impossible to control while he had insisted on calling her.

As for the rest — she would ward off his attempts one by one with the best of her ability.

Kieran's countless reasons and tactics to spend any spare moment alone together proved confusing at times. His innocent adoration and affection would only surface as a weapon for Simon to use against her should he so choose.

If Simon should ever find out about the friendship — as innocent as it was — it would be disastrous for both concerned. Simon's jealousy was her main reason she could never risk a relationship, or encourage Kieran's attraction.

No, she was right to be cautious of forming friendships — with anyone.

Over the next few days Kieran — it would seem — had other ideas. He seemed to dog her every step, and every which way she turned Kieran would be there, watching, waiting to snatch a chance to steal a moment alone with her.

Sophie suspected, judging by his ability to turn up at the least likely events, Kieran had allies in many places, as they were continuously meeting at the unlikeliest events.

Some days later, after many attempts to unsuccessfully evade him, suddenly Kieran was confined to base. Worrying news came through to her — Kieran's unit was going back overseas. His outfit ordered to return to Afghanistan at a moment's notice. The redeployment was for a minimum of a six-month tour of duty.

Part of a significant combined-force platoon, the troops found themselves redeployed, and in the central city of Kabul, Helmand Province, at the heart of Taliban badlands. The situation was critical. Not for the first time, they were to be involved in a major operation. The battalion often patrolled some of the most dangerous and feared parts of the capital.

Their main aim was to keep order and support ISAF on foot patrol and train the locals — making them independent of British forces' influence during the ground patrols for the operation to have full effect. The hardest part was distinguishing civilians from the Taliban. It was a distressing time.

Kabul was continuously under attack by the Taliban and other militant forces.

Reports relayed, that came via Sophie's media connections, didn't reveal much, but told his remaining platoon were lucky they made it out alive. Sophie spent days and days worrying about Kieran, waiting for news of his safe return. Even though he'd sent her a constant stream of letters to his family, his mother had kept her updated continuously with whatever she knew, which wasn't much. Deployment didn't just happen to the troops — it affected the whole family.

Sophie hadn't revealed to a soul that Kieran had also sent her letters through her media contacts. She had not opened or replied to any of them; she dare not. It pained her to treat him this way, aware how much her cold-shoulder treatment must have hurt him, and desperate to know he was safe and well. In spite of this, she had convinced herself it was better that way — it was no use encouraging him. There was no future in it. She prayed he would understand and eventually forgive her.

Unable to sever her connection with him completely, Sophie did, however, call his parents on occasion to inquire about his wellbeing and offer her assistance, should they need her support. More so, she promised his parents if she heard important news of any related specific events taking place involving Kieran's platoon, and could relay minor incidents, she would tell them immediately.

Ingrid thanked her repeatedly for her updates, even though news feeds revealed very little about 'A' Company or their mission. All Sophie knew was he wasn't having too much of a good time of things. Sophie, like everyone else who had a serving family member or loved one, prayed Kieran would come back home safely.

From Sophie's confidential source, she'd been able to read that Kieran's unit had suffered casualties. One particular report she'd been privileged was harrowing to read. Her heart had saddened at the news.

***

It had been a long blistering hot day, and everyone was exhausted by the intense heat beating down on them.

Kieran wiped the beads of sweat from his forehead with the back of his hand. He was that wet with sweat that droplets fell onto the ground as he walked on it.

He was hot, thirsty and hungry. On top of that, Kieran felt a foot blister was now painfully aggravating underneath his right foot, and with about two miles to go he couldn't wait to get back to base. Everyone was exhausted by the endless walking, and now to add to that there was a sandstorm blowing south and heading directly for them.

Being out in the dry, flat desert with virtually no cover was enough to raise the hairs on the back of his neck. Something about the situation didn't feel right. The men could ill afford to be caught out in the open like this.

In spite of that, after hours on patrol covering miles of open desert, he was like the rest of the men, ready for food and fresh water. Despite the possibility it was leftovers from the previous evening meal, or Pot Noodle, and warm bottled water. He didn't care, warm or cold — it would serve his need right now.

A crack of gunfire echoed through the outskirts of the dry, sun-baked ground with a tiny strip of a ditch, some six kilometres from the OP in Kabul. The first pop-pop sounds of gunshots sent a rush of adrenaline to his heart.

"Ambush!" Kenny called out from lead position over the radio.

"Everyone fucking down!" Jonesy shouted. "Fucking move it!"

Heart racing a thousand beats a minute, he could hear the sporadic sound of shooting in the distance. Kieran struggled to control his breathing and to push the fear aside. Rather than panic or worry, he did what the rest of the infantrymen did — instantly reacted at the sound of gunfire, and headed for cover. The only form of protection was a small, dry ditch.

"Everyone ready!"

Kieran gripped his SA80 more tightly and buried himself closer to the dry, dusty ground pinned down by direct fire. Unable to see who was shooting, before the men could return fire and fight back, the shooter needed to be located and identified as Taliban.

Unfortunately, by this time, the two point men Kenny (2IC) and Drews were some 30 metres in front and now cut off from the rest of the unit and caught in open terrain with no cover; there was nothing the men could do. The two men had walked into a small band of around five insurgents with guns and ammunition straps around them. And the two men were now under heavy fire.

Jonesy, as the sergeant was *'tail-end Charlie'* was one of the last men in the patrol. He ordered to engage fire as two of the men were pinned down by enemy fire. There was limited visibility as the wind blowing against them swirled the dirt and dust; the men instinctively reacted as they threw themselves onto the ground, while the rest of the men opened with rapid fire.

Using the muzzle flashes from the insurgents as target indication Drews and Kenny started engaging in return fire. Tat-tat-tat as they returned bullet for bullet in repeat, rapid fire. Judging by the multiple shots, the Taliban had the upper hand. Sending up swirls of dust into the wind as each spent bullet thudded the dirt.

The patrol was now under full attack by the Taliban. Engaging in full-on assault, employing small arms, heavy machine guns, rocket-propelled grenades, mortars and rockets.

"What's the position, Drews?" Above the noise, Jonesy tried to assess the situation over the radio.

"Can you fucking hear me? What the fuck is going on, Kenny?" Jonesy asked.

As the wind had increased, it now made it difficult to hear or see anything.

No reply came back.

"Repeat! What the fuck are you two playing at?"

Nothing.

"Drews? Kenny?"

Nothing.

Fearing the worst, Kieran had taken two steps towards the men before muzzle flashes stood out again. Followed by more shots, closer this time, multiple and in bursts across the two acres of desert land. Kieran heard the tat-tat-tat, as his eyes eagerly gazed out across the open terrain of what looked like deserted land.

"Get a visual on those two fuckers!" There was no mistaking the desperation in Jonesy's strained voice. "I want to know what the fuck is going on!"

Al searched the area through his binoculars and estimated around 20 Taliban had surrounded the two men.

The insurgents had now divided into three groups leaving the section exposed from all sides, preventing Drews and Kenny making any successful attempt to return fire.

Next followed what the section feared and dreaded — the news came over the radio headset. "One man hit! Man down! Man down!"

Jonesy was shouting, "Who the fuck is it?"

"It's Kenny!" Drews answered.

Something had to be done and urgently.

With stealth, Kieran slid up across the ditch into kneeling position, grabbed the Minimi, and set the LMG in place and opened fire, spraying around 700 to 1,000 bullets a minute against the oncoming fire. Although he couldn't see much of anything, he heard movements a second later. It gave the troops the advantage to move forward.

A second rapid burst of multiple shots rang through the air, ringing in his ears.

One thing was clear, the insurgents knew they were there. Terrorists had known of their presence and had taken advantage of the situation, pinning them down while out in the open, low on supplies and returning to base tired and hungry. Ground cover was limited. The Taliban had the upper hand as gunfire erupted along with a section of IEDs and landmines exploding beneath. A Taliban sniper gunman had split from the group and now had Drews and Kenny cornered.

With two of the men cut off from the rest of the section, one injured, possibly severely, they had to act quickly. The plan was for the remaining seven men to move forward and add the firepower and cover to retrieve Drews and Kenny who were isolated from the rest of the group. Five of the men advanced forward to rescue Drews and Kenny.

Smithie and Wrighty would be the ones to hold the ground from the rear with the 81 mm mortar engaging in enemy rapid fire, and two of the men with SA80s with the UGL — a Heckler & Koch AG-36 40 mm grenade launcher, which consists of an optical holographic sight. It enabled the men to operate the UGL as a dual-purpose weapon, allowing the grenade launcher to deliver accurate fire at up to 400 metres firing as a single-shot SA80.

However, the disadvantage was the chamber restricted bayonets fixed for close-contact firefighting, so the remaining men attached the blades to their SA80s in readiness to engage in close-contact combat.

It had been the first time Kieran had ever fixed his blade to his SA80.

The men made their way forward to secure a safer position, along with Smithie and Wrighty, and Kieran was preventing the sniper from taking out any member of their unit.

When the men advanced enough to gain an advantage firing point, they located Kenny, and he was in a bad way; he'd been kneeling down when he was shot twice in the chest and the shoulder, and was now bleeding out. By the time Jonesy and Si were able to administer medical treatment Lance Corporal Jordan *'Kenny'* Kennedy died due to extensive blood loss and wounds. He didn't regain consciousness.

There was no way the men were going to leave his body behind for a trophy to be used by the Taliban; they prepared his body and carried Kenny back with them to a safer location.

Faced with intense fighting from the enemy, Smithie showed tremendous courage while supporting his platoon sergeant, Jonesy, keeping the insurgents at bay while the last of the platoon moved to safer terrain. Wrighty and Smithie prepared to join their pals as they peeled back to the last man.

Pinned down by enemy fire, Smithie provided cover with the Minimi. But before Smithie could make his final move, something went wrong — the LMG failed on him and stopped firing. As he stood up to make a run for it, a single shot to the chest from the sniper hit his heart, killing Lance Corporal Daniel *'Smithie'* Smith almost instantly — he was cut down as he withdrew from his position.

After sustaining fierce fighting from the Taliban, the company, all but two, made it back alive. Two of Kieran's mates had been killed in one day. The entire platoon mourned their loss of two professional soldiers and close friends.

***

When Sophie had spoken to Kieran's mother on that occasion, she'd confirmed what Sophie had already known and established as accurate. He was distressed over losing two of his friends, and two of the men he'd trained with. There was no doubt about the danger he faced every day. The whole section grieved their loss.

The last communication she had received was in May, a week after suffering the loss of two comrades.

***

Gereshk region of Helmand Province, May 2007.

Kieran's platoon was divided into two. The first company were ordered to take part in a secret operation to transport a small number of detained, proven terrorists — high-ranking Taliban figures — to a secure location within the Sangin Valley.

The remaining members of Kieran's battalion were sent on a routine clearance patrol close to Sangin.

With the Taliban on the offensive in several parts of Sangin, it was putting extra responsibilities on the military as the troops often became engaged in heavy fire. It wasn't unheard of for the patrols to be ambushed while in open terrain and cut off from their prime position.

"Gunman left flank," called Jonesy.

Jonesy was the first to spot the shooter from his position in the open hatch of the six-wheel drive, heavily armoured Vector.

"On it." The gunner from the follow-up WMIK vehicle swung 360 degrees to fix his GPMG (General Purpose Machine Gun) on target.

"Got that," replied Wrighty, from the rear station of the support WMIK vehicle. Pointing out the 40 mm GMG (Grenade Machine Gun) directly ahead of Jonesy, keeping the gunman in his sights, he manoeuvred to support their comrades and outflank the enemy.

As Kieran heard this over the radio, his eyes fixed on the bearded, crater-faced gunman on top of the building. Wearing black dishdash and turban was an immediate concern, as there was no mistaking the markings of a Taliban foot soldier.

There was no mistaking the two-storey brick and mud building with well-fortified iron bars at all the windows and tall, metal gates on the entrance.

As soon as the WMIK and Mastiff approached the tall, full-metal gate, the nose of an AK-47 poked through a firing-hole in the metal gate. As the barrel gleamed in the sunlight less than a metre from the man in the line of his vision, with the restricted movement to give the man any choice of target, it pointed directly at Jonesy in front of him.

Jonesy immediately suspected the section had been part of a plan to ambush British Army soldiers.

Radio contact with Dan ordered the reverse of the WMIK. The PPV Vector concerned could be left immobilised in the soft sand — it was parked at least a hundred metres back due to uneven, narrow lanes. Other AKs came to the main wall of the compound making Jonesy a prime target.

Before any one of them had a chance to move or say a word, the insurgents all started ranting and waving large blades, pointing the knives at them as the shouting and ranting grew.

Fuck! Things didn't look right.

Things were getting heated, and adrenaline was fuelling them to boiling point.

Just as Kieran thought things couldn't get any worse, things escalated rapidly when several of the men brandishing knives mimicked the actions of slitting their throats. They thought it was time to move away from the compound and reverse back to join the Vector.

Fuck! Jonesy lowered himself slowly, and away from the gunman's sights. It had taken him no more than a few seconds to act when the WMIK came under attack.

It had taken Wrighty less than a minute to return fire from the GPMG on the top cover of the WMIK.

Si was reversing the vehicle with the aim to get them out of the line of fire. Wrighty was on the radio to get the Vector to give them cover. Two newbie's, Matt and Connor, reacted quickly and returned fire with a Minimi, spraying the compound walls with bullet holes. Within less than a minute the WMIK crew were involved in fierce engagement with the insurgents. On top of that, the Taliban looked well prepared for the attack as if they were expecting them; they were wearing large ammo belts, small arms, heavy machine guns, rocket-propelled grenades, mortars and rockets when they attacked the platoon.

What was worse, the lead vehicle WMIK of the patrol had been cut off from the rest of the platoon and was pinned down by insurgents' heavy fire.

The Vector attempted to move closer and got within 20 metres of the men, hoping to provide cover while delivering GPMG rounds, followed by 12.7 mm heavy machine gun fire.

Kieran's remaining section manoeuvred the WMIK to rejoin their comrades and try to outflank the Taliban insurgents. As they neared their comrades, a group of fully-armed Taliban fighters launched a full-on attack on the right flank of the armoured vehicle.

A fierce fight erupted, killing only a small handful of rebels in the attempt to retreat. It was at that moment an RPG launched a grenade with a direct hit on the side of the Land Rover as it rolled underneath the vehicle which was far from bombproof.

"Get the Fuck out!" Jonesy shouted, forcing the men to abandon the WMIK. The men jumped behind the vehicle making a run for the Vector knowing their lives depended on it as they scrambled for cover behind the Mastiff.

Within a second there was a massive boom blowing up everything in its range. And all at once, there was a blinding flash of the detonated grenade, followed by a pulsating shock wave and a deafening bang taking the men off their feet and into the air tossing them onto the ground like rag dolls.

Shrapnel flew in all directions at the same time covering the men in hundreds of small metal pieces, mixed in with dust and oil as it flew across the compound. Pieces of metal pinged at the metal gates and compound walls, smashing windows and what was left of the now burning remains of the WMIK.

When Jonesy took account of what happened, and the men stood up and were counted while taking in what had just happened, the men had responded well. With a massive release of nervous adrenaline rushing through his system, cheers went up; it looked like they had got away with no more losses of men.

Jonesy was still head-checking that every man was standing clear of the wreckage. Then a bleak look on Jonesy's face, told something different.

It had taken Kieran a few moments to realise not all the men had managed to get clear of the attack.

Alex Myers was caught up in the explosion less than 15 metres from the rest of his platoon and died instantly. Parts of his body had been blown off in the blast.

Despite the seriousness of the situation, and putting themselves in extreme harm's way, the men refused to leave without Al's body. Only when every part of him was accounted for — the men drew back. There were 12 body parts in all.

The loss of Private Alex 'Al' Myers was hard for the platoon to take. Not only did they lose an outstanding infantry soldier and a true friend, but a young man losing a life in such a tragic way was hard to take.

Captain Dan had paid him a touching tribute. Christian beliefs were always close to his heart. Al, always the *go to guy*, provided a morale boost to the men on many occasions and was a great friend and dedicated soldier.

***

Reading between the lines of his letters home to his family — there was no doubt in Sophie's mind that Kieran was in severe danger and battled constant attacks against the Taliban militants. But something deep inside her told her he would come back safely.

After that incident Sophie lost contact; the military had tightened its security, and she could not do a thing but wait. That was the hardest part for anyone.

Simon, however, at this time was suffering another setback. Unbeknown to her, Simon had started drinking again, and one day things took a turn for the worse. Simon was missing and was now AWOL (Absent Without Leave) which was a severe offence. Simon was now a deserter — this was serious!

Sophie had been approached by the MP's (Military Police) concerned over his whereabouts and state of health. Sophie decided to trace him herself and tried to convince the military it was best for Simon if she could talk him into returning to his Squadron CO before the military police found him and arrested him.

With the support of the military, she'd found out that he'd gone back home to Corby Glen. To help Simon, she would have to return home immediately; there was no alternative route. Her family at least deserved to know the truth about her relationship with Weapons System Officer Simon Campbell.

Chapter Eleven

Despite the fact she hadn't been home in a while — the village of Corby Glen, tucked into the heart of Lincolnshire, was having its share of bright September weather. As the sun shone brightly, a warm breeze brought the taste of late summer. Gone now were the early morning hard frosts, and the storms and icy rains of winter, as she remembered her last visit home.

As Sophie drove through the lanes slowly, she recognised, as a small child, how she had played in those same fields, where she heard the echo of children's laughter as they played.

Corby Glen wasn't a large village by any means and the people that lived there had been there all their lives. Sophie doubted more than a couple of hundred people lived in the tranquil village. Sure, it had the usual small church, a manicured green designed for bowls and the main street where the village shops were strewed.

The post office occupied one half of the main road and sat to the left of the shop, which was situated next to the White Horse pub where the World War II crew from the RAF 633 Squadron used to spend time, and period photographs decorated the walls as proof. To some, it was more important to host the monthly heritage meeting there as it was the only pub in the village.

The other half of the village was occupied by small, pleasant cottages that faced each other, which mainly belonged to retired couples wanting to escape the busy city life. Only two roads led up to the main street, while colourful, flowered gardens decorated most of the village's' larger and older houses.

Above all this, Corby Glen was a quiet place tucked away in the deepest part of some of the world's most beautiful countryside. Situated some nine miles from the historic market town of Grantham, its rural surroundings came dotted with farmland, which stretched as far as the eye could see. Since the village was not far from the main A1 route, it was easy to find her whereabouts even if she hadn't been home for about three years.

Sophie stepped out of her VW Golf hire car and took a deep breath, taking in the rural beauty of her surroundings, and at the fondness of her parent's' house — it was just as she remembered it. A white trellis fence led up the stone path to the front door. The large, wooden, carved door opened.

Her mother's hair was now silver, but her slim, petite figure had remained the same. Right at that moment, seeing everything unchanged, it was as if she'd never been away, and all the worries and unhappiness of the last few years ceased to exist.

"Hello, dear." Her mother hugged her tightly. "Had a good trip? Your old room is all made up and ready for you." Christine Tyson helped her daughter with her luggage. "Simon is over at his mother's. I take it that's why you're here?"

"Mum," Sophie had sighed, "can this at least wait until we get inside before we start having this conversation?" She had insisted. "I don't want to talk about Simon in the middle of the street."

Half an hour later, mother and daughter were both sat in the dining room drinking tea along with eating her mother's homemade scones.

"What do you think? What are you going to do about him?" Christine was asking.

"I'm not sure, Mum. Simon is a very sick man; he's suffered terribly. He needs medical help urgently." She felt terrible for speaking about Simon this way, but she had carried the burden of his secret long enough. "I'm only here long enough to try to talk some sense into him. It's better for him to return with me while he can. If he doesn't — the military police know where he is."

Her explanation met with a gasp. "You're telling me Simon's AWOL!"

"The MPs are giving him a chance to turn himself in voluntarily. It will go better for him if he turns himself in sooner rather than later, but they are going to arrest him at some point."

"I don't understand any of this," she said, shaking her silver head. "Simon's always been such a good man to you in the past, was he not?"

"Yes, you're right." She agreed with her mother, not wanting her to think too badly of Simon. She certainly didn't want her parents' relationship to change with Simon's mother because of the way he'd treated her.

Her mother was an astute woman when tuning into her daughter's wellbeing. "What aren't you telling me?"

"In the early days, he used to care for me a great deal." Sophie paused while clutching her mother's hand for support, still reluctant to turn against Simon when he needed her support. "Some things have happened between Simon and I that you and dad are better off not knowing."

Her mother patted her daughter's hand as if coaxing her. "Has he become physical with you?"

Sophie lifted the teacup to her lips and gave a weak, sad smile before taking a sip of her tea. There was nothing that got past her mother so she might as well be honest.

"Let's just say there were times Simon could be less kind and loving than he would like people to believe."

"Is that why you paid so few visits to us after you were married?"

Sophie merely nodded. She explained in the briefest of detail about the life of abuse and brutality she had endured at his mercy. It wasn't easy telling her mother of the frustration and desperation Sophie felt. Most of all, the isolation and loneliness she suffered in the beginning to make him feel secure in their relationship.

After she had finished telling her mother about the events leading up to her visit to Corby Glen, her mother asked wisely, "With everything that's happened do you think it's a wise move going to see Simon alone?"

"I have to, and I need to make him see sense," she replied, determinedly. "I don't have long." That was true.

The civilian police wanted Sophie to explain to him that it would be better for him to turn himself in. Sophie only had 24 hours to convince him, and if not the military police would come and arrest him. His arrest would finish him and his career would be over — that would kill him.

She sat thoughtfully for a moment. "Besides, Simon wouldn't hurt me, not with his mother to witness his actions. Ruby wouldn't stand by and let him hurt me."

Her mother was not convinced. "Just the same — it would be safer to make sure you're not alone with him in that house," she had warned. "I want you to make sure Ruby doesn't leave you alone with him."

"I'm sure I'll be safe enough."

"Promise me you won't be alone with him." There was no mistaking the obvious concern in her mother's voice. "You can't trust him."

Sophie gave a reassuring smile. "I promise."

Monday morning, Sophie managed to catch Simon at home, but as she cautiously stepped over the threshold of his mother's house, in the quietness, Sophie became painfully aware that he was at home alone.

Her voice trembled as she spoke. "Simon," she began, and for a second she almost lost her nerve. "I think you know why I'm here."

"Do I?"

"I've come to ask you to return to Brize with me."

"Well — I might not be ready to return to Brize."

There was no mistaking the flippancy in his responses. At least he was calm.

"I think you should know you're in a lot of trouble — I've come to warn you."

"And why would that be, my sweet, adoring wife?"

She ignored that. "The military police are searching for you," Sophie tried her best to reason with him, "you're in serious trouble, Simon. The police are going to arrest you."

Simon stood to observe her quietly. He stepped closer, more focused on her now than he had been a few seconds ago.

Silently, he stepped aside and invited her in with a sweep of his hand, but she was not permitted beyond the hallway entrance.

At first he'd said nothing and he'd merely closed the front door firmly behind her. Since then he'd not gestured to move in further. He stared at her with a sort of glazed look, as if he hadn't heard her words at all.

"Simon, please, let me help you before it's too late," she pleaded.

Something inside him seemed to snap and boil. Simon spoke for the first time in a low, menacing voice, "Don't you come here trying to sweet-talk me, you cheating bitch!"

Ignoring his anger, she said calmly, "I'm trying to help you."

Leaning closer, he snarled, "Help me?"

"Of course I want to help."

"You want to help yourself more like it."

"That's not true."

Almost as if he couldn't stop himself from touching her, he reached out and grasped her chin in his right hand and squeezed. "What's true is that I've discovered a few things too, Haley. I knew all along you were hiding something from me. Now I know everything! All those lame excuses for not seeing me. You had to work late. Charity events. Pathetic excuses."

Despite his hold, Sophie pulled her head away, and Simon's eyes narrowed. "That's not true!"

There was no mistaking the pure hatred that he directed at her at the point of questioning his reasoning. "Not to mention all your cosy weekends shacked up with your little lover boy. I should have known something was going on behind my back. No one is as sweet and kind as you pretend to be!"

"Simon!" She tried to interrupt. "I had one weekend away in three years."

"Don't bother trying to lie to me — I know! And all the time you were so convincing about having no lover, you—"

"Simon!" She tried again, as her hands balled into fists so tightly her knuckles showed white. She wasn't going to allow him to sway her so easily this time by his insults. "You don't know what you're talking about."

His voice raged on. Sophie's denial only seemed to anger him more. "The truth always hurts, doesn't it?"

"It's not true."

But Simon wasn't listening. "I suppose you think you are clever, don't you? To think how easy I made it for you getting rid of me so easily. Rejecting me, and divorcing me! All because you wanted your freedom to get your bodily pleasures elsewhere with some young squaddie."

"That's not true," she whispered, tears falling down her face.

"Yes, it is!"

"You don't understand. If you're talking about the same solider that I think you are, we're friends. He's never laid a hand on me — he wouldn't do that." Feeling justified in defending Kieran and being careful not to mention him by name, Sophie couldn't reveal anything that might give Simon the upper hand.

"I don't believe you. You're lying to me! Stop lying to me!" he shrieked.

Suddenly, the rage in him exploded. He grabbed Sophie's arm and dragged her along to an empty living room. She tried to call out as he instantly placed a hand over her mouth to stifle her cries. Sophie desperately tried to think of something to calm down the situation: wriggling wouldn't help the case. She tried to calm herself and think about her next move.

It seems her mother was right to have suspicions of Simon.

If only he hadn't been home alone when she had called. If she could break free of him, she could try to escape. Her elbow connected somewhere in the upper region of his ribs. His muffled groan gave her time to escape as his hand over her mouth loosened.

She tried the knob on the door, pulling frantically; he gave a cruel yank on her hair. In a vice-like grip he brought her arm up behind her back in a brutal, agonising twist. She was caught unprepared for what came next, as a quick blow came to the side of her head. It made Sophie cry out.

A sudden backhand on the left sent a shooting pain ringing in her ears, and she seemed to lose her balance quickly. Somehow Sophie ended up on the floor, unable to move as he kicked her with one trainer-clad foot in the back. Sophie cried out in pain and tried to half-roll and half-crawl away from him. He grabbed the front of her T-shirt to stop any further movement. Simon was straddled heavily over her. She felt a cruel yank on her hair.

Before she had a chance to realise what was happening, his fist was aiming for her midsection. Doubled with pain, she sobbed. Tears were rolling down her face. Simon ran a finger down her cheek, and she flinched — she couldn't stop herself. He rewarded her with a slap. "I could kill you now!"

He bunched a fistful of her hair tightly and banged her head repeatedly on to the floor until she appeared to lose consciousness.

When she came to, he was slapping her face from side to side. Groggy and unable to move, dazed and feeling like the room was reeling, she tried to reason with him. She felt sick, and tired, really tired and her body ached all over. It wasn't just the beating that tired her; he'd done far worse in the past.

Her voice was calm but she was rigid with fright. "Simon, you don't know what you're doing." Sophie tried to look him in the eye and stay focused. The same cold, steely-eyed glint she had seen so many times before was indeed visible.

He gave her another backhander across the face. Although it didn't feel as hard as the previous, it felt like her face was exploding on impact.

Fear bound her as tightly as his hand was now gripping her right cheek. "Does this look like I'm not in charge of my faculties to you?" he said, as he landed an agonising punch on her right upper arm, catching her shoulder. She cried out in agonising pain. He landed another full-body punch to her midsection again. "Or this?"

"Simon — don't!" Sophie shouted, as he continued to land another blow in the same region, even harder than before. Her head was in agony.

"Simon — you're hurting me!"

Her words seemed to fuel his fire as another blow landed heavily on her arm. He sneered at her cries of pain and laughed as he mimicked her voice. "Simon, don't! Simon, you're hurting me!"

"What of you? You hurt me. A wife doesn't turn against her husband." As he hit her again, he added coldly, "You hurt me when my friends told me about your soldier lover boy you have been carrying on with for months. How they laughed at me. Taunted me with their jokes about not being able to control my wife."

He gripped her jaw and hit her again. "But let me tell you something — if you so much as speak to that boy again — I shall ruin him and kill you! Do you hear me?" he snarled, giving her another backhander.

There was no doubting he intended to make good with his threats.

"You see — I know things too. Your soldier has big plans for the future, doesn't he? Professional soldier through and through. Doesn't his family have big dreams of him becoming an officer? So proud of their son." He sneered down at her tear-stained-face with bitterness and rage burning in his eyes. "Such a clean military record he holds at the moment."

Untouched by her sadness and pain he continued with his vindictive onslaught.

"Oh yes, I know all about him. You would be surprised what I do know," as Simon hit her again.

The pain was becoming unbearable, and she was growing weaker by the moment. She tried to reason with him. "He's a friend, Simon, why won't you believe me? Why hurt him?" That was the truth.

A thin, angry line appeared on his jawline as he clenched his teeth before saying, "Because you care for him. And for that reason alone I could kill you!"

Sophie tried desperately to keep her mind focused on Simon's anger.

There was no way she could admit her true feelings. If Simon suspected anything, there would be no reasoning with him, because while filled with so much hatred, Simon was quickly becoming a danger to even himself. "You have it wrong."

"Oh, I know what you've been up to — you two-faced, lying, cheating bitch!" His anger had taken a twist. "There are words for a woman like you — you ruin good men and their careers."

"I haven't done anything," she denied, but it was no use.

"Do you think he'll want you once he finds out you're responsible for ruining his military career? And once word gets around you are a married woman stringing him along?" he chuckled. "Do you think he'll want you then?"

"People won't believe you. We're divorced, Simon. No one will listen to you." She froze waiting for him to strike her again, but he didn't.

He merely said, "They don't have to believe me." Simon chuckled again bitterly. "The doubt will be cast. That alone would be enough. The damage would have already been done. He'd be finished."

"Why would you want to do that?" Sophie was aghast.

"Because you care for him!"

"That boy has never been intimate with me, in any shape or form." She took a deep breath. "Have you gone mad?"

At those words, his eyes darkened, and he leaned in so close she felt his heated breath on her face and she looked him in the eye. Sophie sucked in a breath; it was then she knew she had pushed him too far, and instantly realised how much danger she was really in now.

He placed his hand on her throat. The look of pure rage destroyed his handsome looks. Slowly his grip tightened. "You will find out. If I can't have you — I will make sure no one else will want you."

Sophie panicked as she began to find it hard to swallow. She kicked out frantically, trying to dislodge his hands as she clawed at his arms in a desperate attempt to free herself.

The room started to spin. Sophie 'began to feel a growing sensation on her tongue and a swelling in her mouth and his voice could be heard in the distance. There was no mistaking his hatred for her, or severity of events now happening.

She tried to lick her lips but was unable to. She attempted to swallow a couple of times, but it had become too painful. She started to shake. His low, menacing voice was telling her he was going to kill her.

For the first time, she believed him. Tears ran down her cheek; she was going to die. Her body began to grow limp. Terrified, she waited for her death to follow. Slowly, she felt her consciousness slipping away.

In her last effort to fight the darkness, she had heard her mother's voice coming from somewhere far away in what seemed a fathomless, dark place. Desperately, she clung to the sound, "No, Simon, stop! For God's sake stop this now!" She thought she heard her mother crying.

In a semi-conscious state, a comforting hand felt soft and reassuring. The cold, sobering realisation of what had happened drifted through her mind. Someone was shouting — calling her name. She neither had the energy nor the desire to speak; she couldn't face what had happened to her. She felt tired; she wanted to sleep — if only she could sleep.

"Sophie! Sophie! Sophie, please answer me." Her mother's voice was calling to her: sounding full of anguish. She felt the soft, cool, soothing hand brush her heated face.

"Mum?" she thought she heard herself say in a hushed whisper.

A soft hand continued to brush her face. She felt her mother's hand, gently soothing and 'reassuring against her tear-stained cheek. Her eyes opened slowly, reluctantly. Christine was kneeling beside her on the floor, helping to support her arm. Panic and fear tore through her and cramped her stomach.

She tried to speak, but her throat was dry and sore. She attempted to sit up, which caused a bout of coughing, and her raw, swollen throat throbbed sorely, as she continued to cough. Sophie's mother fetched her a glass of water. She drank slowly, as it trickled down her throat and slowly eased the pain.

Her mother helped her as she tried to sit up. But she couldn't make her body respond. Sophie knew her legs would never support her if she tried to stand. They were far too weak.

"Mum!" She gripped her arm in sudden panic. Forcing herself to say, "You have to leave, please go! Just go!"

"It's fine. There is no need to worry. Take it easy — everything will be all right. Sophie, you're safe now," her mother soothed.

She breathed deeply and gulped some air. Trying desperately to ignore the pain in her throat. "No. Simon has gone crazy. You're not safe here."

Her mother patted her arm reassuringly. "Don't worry — Simon's gone." She hesitated. "I found you both here. I was out at the shops when I spotted Ruby out in her car. I guessed he was here alone. I came here as soon as I could."

Sophie put her hand to her throat. "He could have killed me, Mum. If you hadn't come, Simon would have—" She paused, unable to continue as fresh tears began to blur her vision.

"I'm just so glad I found you. After everything you told me about Simon, I couldn't trust him not to hurt you." She patted her hand. Christine's worries had been justified and she had called the authorities on finding her daughter beaten and in a terrible, stressful state. Tears had begun to run down her mother's cheeks. "Besides, you're my child. Any mother will protect its young no matter how old the child."

Sophie tried to smile and gripped her hand tightly. "So, where did Simon go?"

"I don't know, and I don't care. After I walked in and found Simon leaning over you, he took flight. He ran out through the back of the house." Christine patted her hand. "I've rung the doctor; he's on his way. I've also rung the police." She tried to take control of the situation and reassure Sophie of one crucial point. "You will never have to see Simon again."

"You think so, Mum?" she asked feebly.

"Yes."

"I sincerely hope you're right, Mum — but I have my doubts."

On her return to Norwich, she was to spend the next several hours answering questions by the RAF Military Police, SIB(N) (Special Investigations Branch) officially based at RAF Cranwell, Lincolnshire.

By the end of the day, she was weary on her feet; she just wanted to fall into her bed, back in her own house. The SIB police had ideas of their own.

"I'm sorry this is taking so long, Mrs Campbell." He introduced himself. "My name is Detective Dent, and I would appreciate any information you can give us to help locate your husband. I understand it must be a terrible experience and a terrible ordeal for you. But you do understand the urgency of finding your husband. When you're feeling up to it, we would like to get you to write everything down in a statement. Then we will see about getting you home."

Bleakly, she nodded. "I understand."

"That's good." He was smiling at her. "Now, Mrs Campbell, why don't we start with you explaining what happened while in your mother-in-law's home in Corby Glen."

"I will — but I think I should tell you something first," She licked her dry lips. "Simon and I are no longer husband and wife. We divorced over three years ago. And my name is Sophie Tyson. I reverted to my maiden name."

The detective stared at her blankly. "I don't understand. How does this explain about him living in married quarters at Brize Norton if you're divorced?"

She bit her lower lip nervously. "Rev. Barnes organised everything. I think you should have a word with him about our arrangement. He was aware of Simon's problems and tried to help him. He suggested that if Simon remained in our former marital home, it could be of more help to him if he maintained balance and continuity. At first, I stayed in the house with him. I was there for support mainly. Someone for him to talk to, come home to, and to keep a watchful eye on him. Make things as normal as possible. But when things became increasingly difficult, I decided to leave."

"Did he abuse you often, Ms Tyson?" Dent asked.

She felt such a traitor. "Sometimes. That's why I had to move out. I was offered living quarters near my place of work in Norwich. But he would visit my house regularly. I could handle the abusive telephone calls and text messages that went with his mood swings. After he returned from his last treatment session things seemed to alter. He seemed much happier in himself, and I thought things were finally improving for him."

"But they weren't?"

She shook her head. "No."

"Why didn't you come to us at the time when the abuse started?" He was looking at the dark bruising on her neck, which made her feel conspicuous. Subconsciously, she placed a hand on her neck and tried to pull the collar of her blouse up in an attempt to conceal her injuries.

She thought it her duty to try to defend her decision. "You have to understand, in the beginning, I was there to help Simon. Rev. Barnes had arranged for treatment for Simon, and he seemed to respond well for a while. That to me was a good deal," she retorted.

Detective Dent replied slowly, but with some trace of doubt. "You are a courageous woman. Either that or a foolish one." He sighed heavily, "by this I mean Simon isn't capable of knowing his limitations. Which can have dire consequences if left untreated."

The shock of his words echoed in her ears. "Why didn't someone tell me?" Her voice felt strained as she spoke, and no other sound came out.

"Because what Rev. Barnes did or didn't do was entirely off his own back. He wasn't capable of knowing how ill Campbell was. That's why we need to find him and soon."

Fear gripped her. "He'll blame me for what's happened to him. And you think he'll come looking for me?" She tried to sound calm, but feeling anything but she asked, "Do you think I'm at risk?"

He eyed her steadily. "Yes," he nodded. "I'm afraid I do. He's fixated on you. That's why we must find him, and the sooner the better. He's beyond anything you can do for him now. Without the proper treatment, his condition will only worsen."

She licked her lips. Her mouth was so dry and feeling so parched again. She sat with her shoulders hunched and looked down at her trembling hands placed loosely in her lap. Her lower lip trembled. It had all been too strenuous for her; she immediately burst into tears.

Hours later, she sat on the sofa going over everything that had happened. Sophie could remember briefly someone taking her home. The hordes of military-style-clad feet trampled through her house as they checked it for any signs of Simon's presence. Her luggage bags were now deposited inside her front door. As she sat on the large, leather sofa, she tried to think clearly in the quietness of the room. It had been the first time she'd been alone in a place in days and had time to think.

Right now, she had one single thought going around in her head. She strongly suspected if Simon was indeed that sick, then there was no doubt in her mind that he would keep that threat to destroy Kieran's career. She had to do something to prevent that, but what? A loud knocking sounded on her door and interrupted her thoughts. Slowly and without any enthusiasm, she went to answer it. Her legs were barely supporting her as she made her way to the front door.

On opening the door she felt a sudden burst of colour run through her body, feeling a rush of panic: Kieran was standing before her. As if out of a dream Kieran appeared, his eyes filled with more questions than she could answer. One thing was for sure — he wasn't going to make it easy for her. And by the look of grim determination on his flushed, tanned face, he'd undoubtedly come looking for answers. By the look he was giving her now, he had no intention of going anywhere without getting what he came for, and making things more difficult than she had imagined.

His ebony eyes shined a dangerous brilliance, as her skin began to prickle all over her body. She had been so afraid her face would betray her. There was no doubt by the look in his eyes that left her without question — Kieran meant business.

For his protection, and if it took every ounce of her breath and willpower, she was going to have to send him away. Ever since the night they had first danced together and he'd held her, every day she was getting in deeper and deeper; she had to admit, she had already fallen deeply in love with him.

Those dreams! Those dreams had been responsible for her feeling this way — dreams she had of him while he was on deployment. They had been a signal, from the start. How many times during those long, lonely nights that he was away she had dreamt of Kieran holding her, kissing her, making love to her. She didn't have any control over her

182

dreams. She did feel guilty having fantasies about a man that was considerably younger than herself. Hopefully, seeing Kieran in the flesh would help her to regain her composure.

She was still an independent woman, and she had to remember that at all costs, she was going to show him she was stronger than he. The most significant mistake she had made was inviting him in. Looking at Kieran now, she realised it had been the fear of what Simon was capable of doing to them both that frightened her the most.

And she was about to discover Kieran had a will of his own.

Chapter Twelve

It hadn't taken Kieran less than a second to detect he wasn't wanted here, or a genius for him to figure out Sophie was giving him a wide berth.

Since the weekend at his parents' home, she was certainly playing it cool as far as keeping him safely at arm's length. He just knew her actions had something to do with their weekend away. And Kieran wanted to know what had changed between them to make her treat him so differently, and so coldly. And he had feelings for her that were not reciprocated and tearing him apart.

Before his deployment, he had sensed a growing change in their friendship and she was freezing him out. Something was bothering Sophie and placing her constantly on edge. Not wanting to upset her he decided to play it safe and give her time alone to deal with whatever problem concerned her so.

But even on his return from Afghanistan Sophie was still trying to avoid talking to him. For the life of him, he couldn't think what he'd possibly done to make her act this way. He figured out even before his departure things had notably changed between them.

It had been by that early spring, just before the start of that long, hot summer, and a whole month since Sophie's visit to Kieran's family home, that things had taken a turn. When he had tried to approach her, Sophie had told him she was busy working on a particular feature which consumed most, if not all, of her time.

Her friend Jane had invited her to stay most weekends at their home; this being so that Sophie could be close to the garrison for her press interviews on Afghanistan conflict and upcoming military manoeuvres.

If she thought it strange that Kieran also preferred to stay on the base at weekends too, she never commented on it. She had always been so courteous and indifferent whenever their paths had accidentally crossed, although Sophie may not have been as friendly as he may have hoped.

Now — thinking back — her actions seemed odd as occasionally he sensed she seemed withdrawn and living in the shadows, almost like she was afraid of something — or someone. She continually appeared on edge, always looking over her shoulder.

It was right, they had spent a lot of time together, but never alone; Sophie made sure of that. And there was no denying he'd wanted more than friendship, and the longer Kieran knew her, the more he desired her. He had no idea what he'd done for her feelings to change so dramatically.

When she'd asked him, he'd agreed to cease making the nightly phone calls. Disappointed of course — it hadn't been his choice and he understood that. However, he'd decided to give her time to think things over. But he was now getting impatient for her response; his body ached to be close to her. When she wasn't there, he'd look for her. His mind refused to function properly without at least seeing her. He felt his life was in turmoil — and he couldn't do a damn thing about it.

To make things worse, his friends and most of his battalion guessed how he felt about her. If not by his mood swings when he wasn't able to see her, it was his constant obsessive behaviour to be around anywhere close to her. It was as if his senses would react like radars whenever she was within a 20-mile radius of him. The smell of her perfume as she passed by, and the sound of her laughter as she shared a joke with others.

It didn't matter how hard he tried to act nonchalant around her — he would fail. How could he do any other when there was always something there to continually remind him of her. Just the very essence of her presence aroused his interest and made him deliriously happy and deeply sad all at the same time. He tried going on leave for a week and staying off camp at his parents' home. Not seeing her for a week became unbearable and he couldn't wait to return to base.

He and *Soph*, as he liked to call her, in the act of desperation, thanks to his trusted allies, were paired continuously off together at social events. He was painfully aware of her keeping her distance, and since their weekend at his parent's' home, she'd changed.

On their return, she'd told him there could be no more nightly telephone calls. No cosy little chats alone. She'd used some stupid-half-cocked excuse that she heard people had talked and made accusations, and she'd prefer it if they'd not give others room to gossip. He'd promised to honour her privacy.

In fairness, she'd never encouraged the attraction he felt for her. But it had hurt when she hadn't sensed his growing friendship was turning into something more than just an infatuation.

More so of late she seemed to merely tolerate him; she became increasingly out of reach. It was as if her actions were to dampen any growing attraction; all his attempts were becoming futile. He saw less and less of her; he was growing desperate.

His mother and father, thank goodness, had not found it strange that he should wish to stay in camp with his friends at weekends. As their only son, he'd been unspoilt as a child; they had given him all the freedom he needed to pursue his life and career in the army. Never revealing how they worried about his safety on more than one occasion. When he did finally go home one particular week, he remained solemn and withdrawn. Preferring to spend his free time in his bedroom, playing loud, sultry rock music.

His parents never questioned why he preferred to stay on the base. If they suspected something was going on between him and Sophie, after meeting her, thankfully they never let on. It might have been because he left them to draw their own conclusions about extending his career in the army.

With his ability to speak several languages fluently, he had often been called upon to attend conferences as an interpreter for the army. He even gained a couple of promotions to go with it. His station commander would often invite Sophie to those same morale-building events, as he hoped it would supply the base with good press coverage. Also, it allowed Kieran to meet Sophie formally without her knowing of the growing affection he had for her.

With all her apparent displays of detachment, he sensed that Sophie wasn't as detached and indifferent to him as she tried to portray. Occasionally, he would feel his senses twitch as if someone was watching him, only to catch her staring at him with a downhearted expression in her large, sad, doe-like brown eyes. But as soon as he caught her eye and held her gaze for a moment, she would react, blink and quickly look elsewhere.

Of course, on the odd occasion she was left no other choice and was obligated to dance with him at a ceremonial function or other. At one particular formal dress Grand Ball he'd given her no escape route by asking her to dance in front of the commanding officer. She could not avoid such an open invitation in front of the CO. Though treating her with absolute politeness was getting him nowhere. She had danced with him as though she was under torture. Her natural grace and beauty had been visible with his CO. As he watched her danced around the floor, he felt a strange alien feeling of jealousy as his CO made her smile so happily.

Not once had she relaxed and smiled at him, and her stiff and unyielding body had been only a shell of a woman. Her distant politeness almost crushed him, especially when he was so besotted with her.

Just after his 19th birthday, he had returned from a mission in Afghanistan. He hadn't seen or heard a word from Sophie in all those weeks. Now he was back after completing a challenging deployment.

Although he'd missed celebrating his birthday at home, his parents had arranged for the special occasion not to pass unnoticed. His mother had informed him although they had invited Sophie to his party, unfortunately, she was unavailable; she'd been called away on some urgent family business. He didn't want to believe this, something in his gut convinced him that she was trying to avoid him.

It had been a simple explanation to him. What was self-explanatory was the turning of his age had frightened Sophie, and she had taken flight.

In those last few days in Afghanistan, he'd seen the horror of war and was involved in events that had changed him. He'd lost mates over there, good mates. Kieran cleared his throat, pushing away the memories that always hit him when he was least expecting them. It had been a terrible time for his whole battalion. He had matured quickly.

Military manoeuvres had been a constant challenge.

On one particular routine patrol, Kieran's section had been hit by rapid fire; smoke had billowed around them, obscuring his vision to almost nothing. He walked, not even able to see the men in front of them as they all dashed for cover. He tried to take cover, he stumbled and fell to the ground. He looked down at something covered in dirt and sand, and realised he'd tripped over another human being — lying face down in the sand was his mate, George.

He'd joined up with Private George Lawson, and he'd miss his banter and good humour. He'd been 17 when he joined up and never lost the ability to annoy the fuck out of Kieran, especially when he'd teased him, and, yes, infuriated him over his feelings for Sophie. But Kieran had returned safe and well, and there was one thing he'd learnt overseas — live your life to the fullest.

He had many fond memories of all the good times they all shared. There was nothing like facing the reminder that he could no longer share the everyday events that bonded them more like brothers. He would miss the camaraderie and the bond they shared with the fallen. Until that deployment he hadn't realised the sacrifice the forces make.

Returning to Sophie had been his only lifeline. He hadn't seen or heard from Sophie in those weeks, and he was desperate to see her. He wanted to tell her, and show her. His time had come, at last; he had found out from a friend that Sophie was coming back to her work. He wasn't going anywhere, and she had no place left to hide from him.

His self-assurance and his arrogance appalled him now.

It had never entered his head he could have been wrong about her. After all, she had never once given him any reason to think she had any attraction towards him. He'd been so sure of himself. Then, his innocence had made him arrogant and cocky from the very start.

For one thing, he hadn't seen her since the night of the ceremonial Grand Ball, and before he could create a practical plan to see Sophie again, his battalion was on 24-hour standby and restricted to base. There had been no time for goodbyes. Before Kieran knew what was happening, he'd received orders and was shipped out to Afghanistan on *'Special Ops'*.

While there, keeping his mind active seemed crucial to his perseverance survival. He did everything he could to stay positive. He contributed to all the available activities organised by the allied forces; it had been a difficult and incredibly trying time for him emotionally.

He had not known a moment of peace. When he hadn't been on patrol, he hadn't been able to think about anything other than seeing Sophie again.

The way things were going for 'A' Company, he felt he may never get the opportunity to tell her of his feelings — sometimes it became almost unbearable. When he laid in his bunk at night, he was plagued by unholy thoughts of the risk that she may meet someone else while he was away.

The week of his return, and at the first available opportunity, Kieran had approached Rev. Barnes. He'd concocted an excuse to contact Sophie about a social event and how he'd misplaced her address. OK, it had been a white lie. Thinking about it now though, it had not been the most sensible thing he'd ever done. Should Rev. Barnes have checked on Kieran's story, he would land himself in so much trouble with his CO. But the relief he felt when Rev. Barnes handed over the address to him meant it had been worth it.

Until that day he had never known where her house was. And he hadn't had to drive too far out of the city limits of Norwich to find her home. But the one thing that had never entered his mind was that she would refuse to see him. But she didn't. She could have reported him at the base, and worse still to his CO, but she didn't do that either.

He wondered what she had thought when he'd turned up so unexpectedly and uninvited on her doorstep. She must have known his battalion had returned to the garrison, and that same day as their arrival from Afghanistan. He had been so desperate to see her that he'd not stopped to question his actions.

When she opened the door of her house, she revealed no evidence of having any real feelings for him whatsoever.

"Kieran," she said. "What a surprise." And Sophie looked as she'd told him, surprised. Making him think he had made a severe mistake coming to her house in the first place.

Sophie had been wearing navy-blue trousers and an equally dark, matching, long-sleeved, high-necked silk blouse. He remembered her long, dark, glorious hair hung loose; the unruly locks of dark brown curls were cascading down her back to her waist. Her make-up had been perfection itself. She never looked more beautiful to him, and he instantly knew he could never be free of her hold on him.

He noted her jacket and her handbag in her hands; he thought her dressed and ready to go out. "Come in. I'm sorry about the mess," as she waved him inside. "I've been away — as you can see." Indicating to a pile of unopened mail she had discarded on the coffee table, she added, "I've just got back myself."

He congratulated himself; his timing had been perfect. And the fact Sophie had even agreed to let him in only fuelled his passion.

"How have you been?" she asked politely.

He fixed his stare on her. "Good." Which was a lie of course?

Sophie had unconsciously shown him into the living room. In keeping with the military housing, the living room was spacious and orderly with large windows on two opposite walls. The carpet was a deep-pile rustic red. The view from the windows gave a glimpse of life in the city. The far wall, while illuminating the room with soft lighting, was tastefully decorated with rare pieces of cut glass from all over the world. It was apparent that Sophie had made this place her home.

"I have been watching the news. I was sorry to hear about the loss of your friends."

He said nothing; he didn't know why he needed a moment to think. Losing his friends meant he'd known and felt pain and grief like nothing she'd ever felt. What he'd experienced and seen as a soldier had given him memories that he'd never be able to be rid of, not that he wanted to forget.

"It was full of challenges I hadn't expected to face," was all he could say.

He glanced over at the room as if needing a moment to gather his thoughts; he'd noticed how she had a large choice of plants strategically placed around the room. An eight-seat, charcoal-grey, leather, corner sofa, was situated in the centre of the room around the coffee table. A large screen and audio system were discreetly placed in the wall unit that was designed as a cupboard. All the coloured glass and Italian porcelain figures revealed her love of different cultures and her visits to far-off places.

His eyes caught the attention of a closed door. "That's my study," as she followed his direction, "and it's very untidy like the rest of the house."

"Fuck no, it's great!" he said enthusiastically. Then slightly coloured as he realised how immature he sounded. "What I meant to say — it's great."

Pushing a hand through his hair, he felt his palms were sweating, so he decided to rub his hands down his jean-clad, long legs, then he felt like a child caught playing truant.

She smiled sweetly. Gracefully draping her jacket and handbag over the arm of the sofa, she sat and clasped both hands together in front of her and asked, "You like my home?"

Then it suddenly dawned on him, Sophie was nervous. But of what? Would it have been so inconceivable to believe she was worried about being alone with him? He couldn't believe his luck. What if he was mistaken, and maybe it was too good to imagine?

"So, what brings you to my home, Kieran?" As she walked over to the impressive built-in wall unit, she asked politely, "Can I fix you a drink?" Taking two glasses out of the cabinet.

"Yes, please," he replied eagerly, then hesitated for a moment before making his selection. "I'll have a tequila sunrise, please." He knew it was her favourite drink. He'd observed her drinking a tequila sunrise at several functions; he'd never seen her drink anything else.

"Oh, on the cocktails now?" A small, sweet smile moved the corners of her mouth.

"I just happen to like the drink, and it makes a change from beer." He felt he had to prove himself.

"You do? So, tell me what is it you like about it?" Sophie handed him his drink, rising to join his playful banter.

Swirling the glass, he observed the contents. "It reminds me of you. Sunny, sweet with hidden depths and deeply pleasurable from the first taste." He smiled a small, impish grin over the rim of the tall glass. His dark eyes dancing mischievously.

"How would you know that?" Sophie's smile widened in return, throwing him completely off guard by saying, "Is that what you've heard — or have you come to find out for yourself?" She challenged him as she sat down on the large sofa, leaving him to follow suit.

This situation was all wrong; his comment had meant to sound fun and harmless, but had the opposite effect judging by the look of disapproval on her face. He had to be more sincere. "Truth is, I heard a guy tell a woman in a bar the same thing."

"And you thought that you might use it to soften me up?"

Kieran swallowed, not sure where his confidence was coming from but he needed to know what Sophie thought of him, and by the look on her face, and the way she was reacting to him it was no more than platonic.

Filled with a sinking feeling, he sighed. "I've heard nothing from you in months. I had to see you; I've missed you," he rushed, instantly regretting his outburst. Whatever else he'd have wanted to say to Sophie, it had probably not been that. He had to tread carefully — Sophie might ask him to leave, and after coming this far he certainly didn't want that.

"So I see."

"I couldn't call. I kept my word to you."

Her face flushed and she took a small sip of her drink noticing the ice clink in the tall glass as she did so. Sophie forced herself to raise her chin and meet his stare. "Well, that's very kind of you — but you don't need to worry about me — I appreciate your concern, but it's not necessary—"

Kieran interrupted, "Wait!" He tried to bring his urgency under control. He had so desperately wanted to see her, and had missed her beyond words, and she was talking to him as if she was reading from a restaurant menu.

He tried to keep his cool, but she wasn't making things easy for him. "Shit! I don't want you being grateful!" he exclaimed. "I'm telling you I missed you. I needed to see you, and when you didn't come to my birthday party, I thought something had happened to you. I know my parents invited you, Sophie, so why didn't you come?"

He was finding it hard not to behave like a petulant child. Why had he' been so abrupt with her? Never in his life had Kieran spoken to others in such a rude way, nor behaved so childishly. But he had nothing to lose.

Sophie turned pale, disturbed by his behaviour no doubt, and for that he was sorry. He watched as she swallowed and placed a small, delicate hand on her throat. It was such a simple gesture, but at that moment all he could see was her beauty and how, right at that very same moment, it had been beyond compare. He watched spellbound as her hand brushed slowly across her throat.

"I don't think this is a very grown-up way to behave is it?"

"We are doing nothing wrong. I want to talk."

Minutes passed, and she remained silent.

He laid his glass on the table, and before he could look up, she said, "I understand that. But I thought you knew — I sent your parents a reply explaining I was away on family business," she told him. Her reply seemed delayed for so long that he found himself doubting her sincerity. What was he to learn from that?

Standing up slowly, he asked, "Are you telling me — if you had been here — you would have come to my party?" Kieran pushed his hands deep into his pockets. He had to show her he could be assertive; Kieran had come wanting answers to questions that he'd not dared to ask so many times before. And who knows what he might discover if he succeeded in pushing a little.

In an almost hypnotic gaze, Kieran could only watch as Sophie sat silently for a moment as her tongue appeared to moisten her lips. The impact of that simple movement caused him to feel as if something dealt a full body blow instantly. The sight of Sophie's pink tongue — sensual and disruptive — as the tip brushed along the line of her lips. All sorts of images crept into his mind, and the heat was surging through his entire body — all of which showed at this moment and were of no help to the situation at all.

Sophie lifted her shoulders in a slight shrug. "Maybe. I can't say now — can I?" she said finally. "I'm sorry, but this is becoming embarrassing."

Kieran's blood had boiled in his veins. He began to worry about any reaction his body made to her sexually. He didn't want her thinking his attraction for her had become anything more than purely a sexual thing.

"I'm sure no one realised I wasn't there," she told him, leisurely taking another sip of her drink, placing the glass carefully on the table.

Raising his voice in anger wasn't going to help but he couldn't seem to stop. "I fucking well knew!"

Sophie flinched at his raised voice. "People probably thought—"

Kieran snapped angrily back at her, and impatiently he added, "Fuck them! I don't care about what other people thought — I wanted you there with me celebrating what should have been a great birthday party." His eyes searched her face.

Sophie was now standing too. "Kieran, look—" she began, and she slowly ran a hand through her hair as if thinking about what to say before she spoke. "That's very sweet and considerate of you—" she paused again as if searching for something polite to say without hurting his feelings, but her voice remained firm. "Kieran, I want you to listen to me very carefully. I am very fond of you. And I'm extremely flattered that you thought of me on your birthday. But as you and I are friends — I don't want you thinking as such you have the right to come here and try to interfere in my life. My private life is my business." Taking a deep breath, she continued more sternly, "I'm sorry if you mistook my friendship to mean something more, or you harboured any thoughts that you and I could extend our friendship into meaning something more, but we are friends — simply that. Nothing more. It could never be more than that."

"Have I?" Kieran stared at her; her shoulders seemed stiff, and a tense, nervous look appeared to lie on her face. He should have known better — coming here had been a mistake. Glancing at her face, he saw he'd made a huge mistake. "Have I got it wrong, Sophie?"

Taking a deep breath, he realised there was nothing left for him to stay for after all. "OK, before I go — will you just tell me one thing?"

"I will if I can." Sophie smiled reassuringly.

He rubbed his stubble chin, deep in thought of whether he should ask a specific burning question, but Kieran knew he had to ask anyway. "While you were on this family business, did it involve your ex at all?"

"Yes," she replied quietly.

How that one word crippled him inside. So, that was how things stood; he had been so stupid. It was this ex-Mr Right she still cared for, not him. He should have seen the signs. The deep-seated need for her to keep him successfully at arm's length — how could he have been so wrong about her?

"I'm sorry, Kieran." Sophie was talking to him with a sort of sadness in her voice. "If you think I've deceived you in some way," she was saying, "I've enjoyed your friendship, and our fun times together — I sincerely have. But if I've hurt you because of that friendship, I'm truly sorry."

With his head bent, he simply said, "I see."

Steadying her breath before saying softly, "It was never my intention to take advantage of you or our friendship, so I hope you don't think that of me; or because of your age, you're wrong. I admit — you being 12 years younger could have given me some concern if we had become involved, but under the circumstances—" Sophie gave another heartfelt sigh before concluding with, "it remains impossible to consider any further involvement other than a distant friendship. And I sincerely hope we can stay friends? Please forgive me if I've misled you to believe otherwise."

Slowly, he pulled his hands out of his pockets and smoothed his palms down his thighs. "Thanks," he struggled to reply. *That's it! He felt his whole world coming to a bitter end, and all he could think about saying was thanks!* "I'm pleased we had a chance to talk things over," he said cynically. "I feel so much better for knowing that." Which of course was a huge lie.

Sophie bit down on her lower lip and stared at him through pain filled, doe-like, brown eyes. It was as if something like regret passed through her gaze. She exhaled slowly and breathed his name. "Kieran?"

"I know," he sounded almost congenial. Even though he'd felt like his entire universe had come abruptly to an end, he remained conscious of her every movement and breath she took. "I know. I must have sounded like such a loathsome jerk." He looked into her eyes and added with injected bitterness, "Do you still love your ex? I need to know."

Sophie stiffened again, as she looked straight up into his eyes, causing her head to tilt back. "I don't mean to hurt you or be cruel. That has nothing to do with this. Or indeed you."

"It has everything to do with me."

Her eyes flashed with sudden fire as she exclaimed swiftly, "You know nothing about my life or my relationship with my ex-husband. How dare you!"

Kieran couldn't believe what he was seeing as he observed her taut expression and tone. "I need to understand what hold he has over you. In all the time I've known you, not once have I ever heard you talk about him. Not once have I heard you mention his name. Why — Sophie? Why is it such a secret?"

Sophie's eyes took on the same wounded look as before; her beautiful eyes took on such a pain-filled expression it was hard to feel so detached. The hurt and pain were visible in her voice as she spoke. "I — I can't — please don't ask."

The expression on Sophie's face and the sadness in her wide, brown eyes seemed to give him renewed hope. Hope that there was something deep inside him that told him her feelings for him were not as platonic as she'd professed.

"Let me get this straight — are you telling me if it wasn't for your ex — things could have been different between us?" Kieran took a steadying breath; he had to finish what he had started. After all, he was here to get answers. "Tell me, Sophie — could we be more than friends?" His voice was barely audible but firm.

"We are already friends, Kieran," she replied, with an anxious voice.

Now he was angry; she was avoiding answering him, trying to make light of his torment; for torment was what it was. "Don't treat me as stupid, Sophie. You know what I'm asking. You're an intelligent woman, now — answer the question, damn it." He tried his best to sound forceful.

"No," she said decisively. Kieran noticed that she struggled to compose herself; she walked up closer to him refusing to let him take advantage or intimidate her by his arrogance.

As she came closer, he could almost feel the warmth of her body as she stood close to him. With a deep sigh, Sophie ran a hand through her long hair. "Kieran, you have no idea what you are asking of me. Please, try to understand it's not that simple for me."

"Why — why isn't it that simple? Is it me? Don't you find me attractive?" The words were out before Kieran could halt them. He studied her carefully; he wanted so badly to hold her in his arms.

"You shouldn't ask questions that are irrelevant." She dismissed the question as unimportant, and that hurt his feelings.

"So — that's it? You think after all these months of having me wrapped around your little finger that my feelings no longer matter to you? You have me so fucking confused I feel I don't control my life any more. Shall I tell you what I think—"

Sophie cut in; she didn't like where this conversation was heading. "Spare me the sob story, Kieran."

Kieran wasn't listening; he'd lost her anyway, so what difference did it make. "I think you're afraid of your feelings. I certainly think you're afraid to face how you feel about me. Equally, what might happen between us if you let go of the hurt and relaxed a little. What is it Sophie, afraid you may discover you care for me? Admit you may even like me more than you protest?"

Something like anger flashed across her face. "Don't be absurd. You don't know what you're talking about; you have it all wrong."

"Have I?" He waited for her reply. There was no mistaking the deep, angry, glint of challenge in his eyes. "What about the fact that I love you?" he blurted out.

There was a long silence. Wide-eyed, Sophie could only stare at him open-mouthed. When she finally regained her composure, she merely sighed.

"I think we've just about exhausted this conversation, don't you? I think it's time you left. I want you to go — now." Sophie gave another heartfelt sigh and took a step back; it was as if the fight was going out of her.

He shrugged indifferently; his black leather jacket grew tight across his chest as he moved. He was trying to appear as if it didn't matter to him one way or another. But it did matter. "Sure, if you think that's for the best."

"Yes, I do," she assured him. "I'm sorry, Kieran. I think it's for the best."

"I don't understand it. What have I done wrong?" He was feeling totally bewildered.

"Nothing, absolutely nothing. You have been very kind. I don't know how you think you can be in love with someone you hardly know."

"It wasn't as simple as that?"

"OK, I'll talk you through it." She boldly matched his stare. "We meet purely by accident on the camp. We meet again briefly in the NAAFI bar, and I politely take your number. Then you decided to call me out of the blue and make a childish nuisance of yourself."

"Oh, I see. Asking you to come home with me on a weekend break wasn't what I would consider as making a childish nuisance of myself." He repeated her words angrily.

She gave an indifferent glance. "No, Kieran. That was a very kind and thoughtful gesture. But I take it you weren't in love with me then?"

He appeared thoughtful for a moment as he looked down at the floor briefly before looking directly into her eyes. He always prided himself on telling the truth; there was no reason to feel any different now. "No

197

— it happened later."

"It couldn't have happened later. We haven't spent that much time together. So, what happened? Did you spend too much time alone in Afghanistan? Someone drop something on your head?"

"No, nothing like that. It was before that. On the return from my parents. When I'd got back to the barracks after I'd dropped you off at the train station. We ended the weekend with a casual goodbye, and I felt something was wrong. It was as if I suddenly realised it was because you weren't with me. It was just this feeling — something deep-rooted inside me. It was telling me that my place was beside you, and I wasn't. It was as if I knew we belonged together. Even while I was overseas, I just knew something was wrong, and I should have been with you. I needed to talk to you. Nothing important to say; I just wanted to see you and be with you."

Sophie stared at him in a bewildered daze. "I don't know what to say. I can't believe you're saying this. I don't think I can believe you. Seriously, what's so attractive about older women for goodness sake?"

His voice rose. "This isn't exactly easy for me. And I don't go for older women. I'm in love with you, and I have never in my life felt like this for any other girl." He took a deep, steadying breath as he spoke; his intense, dark-brown gaze fixed firmly on her face. His gaze dropped and he ran his hands through his hair. "When I first saw you on the doorstep, I was completely bowled over. I nearly died on the spot. I couldn't speak. It felt like I couldn't breathe. My hands started sweating, my heart racing—"

Sophie dropped her eyes to the floor. "This isn't right. It's all well and good as a fantasy, but there are too many obstacles in the way when it's real life. I'm sorry. I don't mean to hurt you or be intentionally cruel. And I'm deeply flattered...." She raised one hand to her chest and put her hand over her heart as she was talking.

"This is fucking crap!" he burst in. Taking a steadying breath, he continued, "I don't want you being flattered. I think you're the most wonderful, fantastic and intelligent woman I've ever met and I want to have you close and be with you. Why can't you see I love you?"

Her eyes fixed boldly on meeting his gaze. "And it just so happens that I'm happy with my life the way it is. So, for me, please, don't call me or contact me again. You have to leave; I want you to go. You've said enough!"

She turned her head away, and she tried to avoid touching his body in any form as she tried to manoeuvre past him. Naturally, she aimed to show him out. Acting purely on impulse, his body instantly reacted as he swayed towards her. As he obstructed her path, he reminded himself that she was all alone here, there were going to be no interruptions.

His one real aim was to get Sophie to understand his feelings for her, and he had this deep-rooted need inside him to get to the truth and know if she cared anything for him other than friendship. His gut instincts told him she did. If Sophie genuinely didn't care for him, he was willing to put her feelings to the test. He wasn't on duty now, and she had no one distracting her attention from him. Whatever happened here now was strictly between the two of them.

Shaking slightly, she said, "Kieran, what are you doing?"

He didn't move; he didn't speak — he couldn't.

Sophie sidestepped back a few paces. As she looked up at him, her chin raised in defiance, her brown eyes narrowed as if appraising the situation for what it was. Kieran's intense, dark eyes bore into her. Remembering the closeness of her body on the occasions when he had danced with her. The way he'd held her in his arms had become unforgettable.

"Kieran, I want you to leave. I think this is getting rather childish."

Her words were accusing and as anxious as she sounded, Kieran never thought for one moment that she might have anticipated she was in any danger from him. Well, he couldn't go back now, not with her this close.

"I want you to stop this right now!"

In reply, he lifted his hand and gently trailed his fingertips down the length of her cheek. Kieran's touch on her skin felt incredible; her skin felt so soft and delicate. The deliciously silky texture made his hand tremble slightly. It had been the first time he had voluntarily considered making such a bold move. All his caged emotions fought against him, desperate for release.

Her response became choked. "Don't!" She chased his hand away. "You have to go; I don't want you here." She stared at him angrily.

"You're making a terrible mistake, Kieran."

Was he? He wanted to believe her, he did. And he tried to listen to her, but all those months he had spent longing for her, all those respectable admiring glances he had bestowed on her... Only a few months ago he would have obeyed her every command, that was before Afghanistan. He'd grown up since then.

Now, knowing she'd been back to see another man, realising she still loved but one man had been more than he could tolerate. Something inside him had changed at that moment. How could he have been so stupid? All the time he had held back, ever since that weekend at his parent's' home — it had all changed since then. She had kept him at a safe distance ever since he'd taken her home with him. It had all gone wrong after that.

"Am I?" he scornfully replied. "Are you sure about that?"

She tried to dismiss his comment and sidestep him, but he had anticipated her move, and he had been too quick for her. His hands reached out to her and grabbed her forearms to stop her falling back. He held her firmly in his grasp. Sophie tried to wriggle out of his grip unsuccessfully as he held her fast.

"Kieran, please, let me go — you're hurting me," she cried out in an anguished voice.

Chapter Thirteen

He felt her body stiffen and grow rigid beneath his hands as she called out in such agonising pain.

There was no mistaking her pain, as he watched the blood drain from her face twisted in agony. He let go instantly, dropping his hands to his sides.

"What the fuck!" He couldn't believe his strength. "I've hurt you. What the fuck have I done?" He watched as her face twisted with torturous pain. "Sophie, I'm so sorry," as he watched her gently massage the tender flesh and her face filled with renewed pain as she gently massaged the area. "Let me see, please."

Kieran felt so guilty; he hadn't meant to handle her so roughly or be so brutal; he didn't realise he'd held her that tightly.

Unsteadily, she replied. "It's nothing. I'm fine really." As he watched her face colour slightly under his stare, he knew she was trying to hide the pain from him.

"You're lying to me," he argued. In a deep, velvety voice and with as much force as he could muster, he said, "Now, show me — or I'll remove that nice silk blouse myself."

As he eyed the delicate fabric of the blouse, Sophie knew he meant every word of his threat. "I don't think so."

Kieran stepped closer, saying, "I think so. And I promise, it won't look as good as it does at this moment by the time I've finished," he warned.

"Kieran! You wouldn't?" Sophie gasped, and there was no mistaking the look of shock visible on her face. Something in his tone told her he was serious.

He was acting purely out of concern for her wellbeing; he faced her head on. "Shut up, Sophie, and do it!" He had hurt her and knowing that was more than he could stand.

Sophie raised her hands to the front of her blouse, and he watched as she gradually unbuttoned the silky garment with shaking hands, button by button. Realising that she was wearing the same dark-blue coloured bra as the filmy fabric as it left her shoulders, his eyes following in the same motion as the blouse as it slid down past her right arm. He sucked in a deep, agonising breath.

"Fucking hell!" Shocked at what he was seeing, Sophie laid a hand defensively on her upper arm. "What the fuck happened to you?"

He couldn't believe what he was seeing. The anger inside him was overwhelming. Whoever had put their hands on Sophie, and hurt her to this degree, he wanted to severely beat them in return and see how they liked it.

Part of her shoulder, her neck and half her arm down to her elbow was severely swollen and bruised. It looked dreadful, as his gaze followed the trail of multiple colours of purple and various swellings on her body. On her torso it was hard to say which bruise ended and where the other began. Looking at her now, no wonder she had been so apprehensive at allowing him near her. She must have been in such terrible pain.

Stammering, she smiled weakly, and finally managed to say under his intense stare. "It's not as bad as it looks." Judging by her attempt at humour she was trying to play down the situation and what had happened.

His wide ebony eyes strained to take in her appearance. "Really? Fuck! Is that supposed to make me feel better — because it doesn't — it looks fucking bad from where I'm standing. I've seen guys survive combat duty and not look as bad."

Slowly and cautiously, he reached out and pushed her hand down as he gently placed his fingertips along the lines of the bruised area. He felt so sorry for her that he'd wanted to draw the pain out of her body.

"Have you seen a doctor?" he demanded.

"Yes, I'm fine. No cracked bones or anything like that. Just a few bruises. Honestly, I'll be fine."

"Sophie," he implored, "this looks more than just a few bruises. What happened! What's going on — and please don't insult me by telling me it's nothing. We both know that's not true."

"Kieran, you're asking something of me that I cannot discuss with you." She had looked at him so appealingly and almost waif-like that it had been so hard to remain untouched.

Confused, a frown formed. "Why the hell not?"

"Please. If you care anything for me at all, you will not ask me anything else." Tears formed on her lashes as she waited for his answer.

The sight of her tears had pushed him over the edge. "Damn it, Soph." He gathered her gently into his arms and kissed her mouth so gently. At the first taste of her lips, his head had grown dizzy. It was like shock waves pulsed through his entire body.

"Kieran, I'm too old for you," she managed, breaking the kiss and taking a step back and looking him directly in the eye.

"Not to me you're not."

"This isn't a good idea," she whispered against his mouth.

"I know," Kieran said, "but I've been fighting it for some time."

"Maybe we should both fight it a bit longer."

"I don't think that will help."

"Maybe things will change, and it will pass," Sophie said, trying not to let him see her true feelings. Denying it may convince him enough to send him away.

Kieran stepped closer with his eyes fixed on her. "After all this time — do you think that will work?" he asked.

Sophie took a deep breath and inhaled his scent: the smell of denim, leather and Kieran teased her nostrils. She swore to herself. "We should try harder to make it work."

He reached towards her and skimmed his hand over her shoulder, and down her arm to her side, linking his fingers with hers. "Is that what you want? I'll leave now if that's what you're sure you want."

Sophie felt everything inside her shift to tilt; she hadn't expected him to be prepared to fight back. Sophie closed her eyes tightly and fought for sanity.

"Why do you want me?" she asked, fretting. "I'm not willing for you to add me as another notch on your military bedpost."

"You're not," he said, with no hesitation. "I won't let that happen."

"God's gift to women," she quoted. "Isn't that what they call squaddies?"

"That's not me!"

"You say that now because you want something from me."

"It's not like that."

She felt his conviction echo inside her. She hoped it was true. So many had treated her as a challenge in the past. Said and done the same thing over and over.

"I don't know, Kieran. It could all end badly. There are so many reasons why we shouldn't."

"We could promise always to be friends."

"How could we do that?" she asked. "If we make love — it will change everything."

"That will only happen if we want it to. I'm just happy to know I am near you. Before I left for overseas, I stayed away from you to show you my feelings for you were not just a sexual thing."

"I see."

"No you don't — you have no idea, Soph, how many times I wanted to see you and tell you how it was for me. I wanted you to understand how I felt about you. Because I know I couldn't feel the way I do about you if you didn't feel the same way too."

"I'm not sure how I feel. It's all very sudden." She felt so confused.

"Yes you do," he said quietly, "it might scare the hell out of you Sophie, but you know."

Shyly she smiled up at him. So, it had come to this. Sophie stared at him for the longest time. "I don't know if I'm ready for this."

Of course, she knew. If she should succumb to Kieran's charm, Sophie knew how she would feel if he lost interest in her after tonight, and walked away in the morning knowing that was the end of it. And the next time she saw him — he cuts her dead after this night. Even worse — makes her the butt of all his jokes with his friends. What would she feel? Heartbroken — because he'd hurt her so. There was no denying she'd miss him. And where would that leave her?

He lifted his hands to cup her face and drew her closer. "Yes, you are. Trust me. You know I make sense," he said, lowering his head so his lips stopped inches from her own.

Tears pricked the back of her eyes. She felt the moisture drop from her soft lashes onto her cheeks; there was no denying, Sophie wanted to believe him so much. "I've missed you so much while you were deployed in Afghanistan, Kieran," she said, admitting defeat. "I felt so incredibly alone without you," she sobbed.

He ran his fingers lightly through her hair as he spoke. "You have no idea how much I've missed you too. I wrote to you, but you never replied — not once."

"Believe me when I say if it had been possible, I would have."

"What stopped you?"

"It's complicated."

"All I could think was how much I wanted to hold you and kiss you."

"I've waited so long for you to kiss me. Just once."

She felt his warm breath on her tear-stained cheeks as he spoke. "I'm not sure if I can stop with just one kiss," he warned. He smiled sweetly and brushed Sophie's cheek with a brush of his thumb and his hand cupped her chin lightly.

"Let's not overthink things any more." she demanded. and smiled sweetly. She barely got out the words before he captured her mouth with his own.

Kieran pulled her up against him.

It took every ounce of strength Sophie had to ignore the pain of her aching body, but he felt so solid and male next to her skin — the pain was worth every caress. Sophie couldn't keep from rubbing herself against him. Only in her most inner secret thoughts had she imagined touching him this way. Kieran felt so firm to her touch. So intoxicating, and so male.

He groaned softly, breathing against her lips, as he whispered against her mouth, "You feel so good to hold."

Wanting to feel every inch of Kieran, she strained against him again and opened her mouth to him.

"Oh," Kieran broke off for a brief moment, and placed one of his legs between hers as he continued, "you're so perfect." He kissed her again. Sucking all her doubts into oblivion.

Lying in his bed at night, Kieran had thought of kissing Sophie for so long. Only deep within his realms of fantasy he dreamed about her on so many lonely nights while in Afghanistan. Kieran half-expected to wake up any moment. But, this wasn't a dream, he could never have imagined such tenderness as her mouth moved gently against his, filled with such tender passion. She tilted her head back to make it easier for him to kiss her.

His fingers caressed her head as he slid his hands into the silky softness of her hair. When his hands moved slowly down to her waist, he'd hardly taken into account what she was doing to him. His brain had gone numb as his mouth searched hers. Her mouth opened as his tongue probed and tasted her. She sucked gently on the tip as she held it between her teeth, teasing him with delicate strokes with each motion.

As he felt her breasts pressed tightly against his chest, she had to cling to him for support. His whole body began to beat to a hot persistent rhythm, and his heart beat wildly against his ribs. He could feel her fingers digging into his waist.

The knowledge of her standing before him minus her blouse and the sensual feel of her lacy, blue bra rubbing against his chest brought a sudden wave of heat in his loins. A sudden explosion of emotions raced through his body. He hoped he would be able to control himself long enough to please her.

Sophie's fingers travelled upwards; she felt his back warm to her touch, and she swayed closer.

His jeans were becoming increasingly and unbearably too tight. Maybe she knew of his inexperience of pleasing a woman, Kieran thought. He'd hoped not, as he tried to dismiss the idea out of his head in denial.

"Kieran," she whispered. With that beautiful sound of defeat, she wound herself tighter in his arms. He knew she was having a devil of a time trying to keep her emotions under control.

With trembling hands, he touched her breasts. Delighting himself with the smooth, sensitive flesh that instantly came to life under his fingertips. He buried his head; she shivered under his touch.

He wanted her to touch him, but most of all he didn't want her to stop. She raked her hands through his short-cropped hair, slowly massaging and caressing the back of his head. She was driving him to the limit. Sensuous longing filled his body, tormenting him beyond his endurance. His legs felt strangely weak, as he was aware of them sinking onto the large, low, padded, leather seat of the oak table behind him.

Kieran felt the soft brush of Sophie's legs against his thighs as she moved closer to him. A strange alien feeling was intoxicating him, filling him to the very brim of his body. Her tongue appeared and fused him again. There was no turning back now. He shrugged quickly out of his leather jacket, letting it fall, not caring where it landed.

Her hand moved up to the front of his chest and very slowly she ran her fingertips lightly over the row of his pale blue shirt buttons. Unhurriedly, with a feather-light touch, releasing each button in turn until his shirt was free.

As the shirt left his broad, tanned shoulders, Sophie dragged her fingernails down his spine — the action in itself proved provocative, as he watched her with each sweeping motion of her small fingers. He removed her front fastening bra, and as he did, he groaned as her breasts tangled and rubbed against his chest hair.

He lifted his head to face her, fixing his gaze on her, staring into her warm, brown eyes. His palms slid over her breasts with nervous anticipation in slow caressing motion, and he felt the urge to suck. Kieran bent his head, using the tip of his tongue to brush the fullness, gradually taking the full tip in his mouth.

Her hands pulled tightly at his hair, and she groaned at the pleasure of his mouth on hers, forcing him to look at her face; their eyes met briefly before their mouths met and fused with moistly heated passion — the sort of emotion that Kieran had not believed possible.

"No more running away from me?" he asked breathlessly. "I want you so much," he paused. "I don't want to lose you, not now. Not after this. I want you in my life always. You are the most precious thing in it."

Deeply touched by his sweetness, she replied, "No. No more running away. I promise."

He needed to explain how he felt but he couldn't. "I don't want to hurt you — I would never..."

Sophie smiled warmly. "I believe you," she whispered against his mouth, "you don't have to worry about being protected — if that's what you're asking? I'm safe on that score."

He frowned for a moment before he realised what she had meant. Damn it! He hadn't thought of protection. It had never occurred to him. For starters, he never thought he would have gotten this far with making love to Sophie. How he desperately wanted to make love to her. Holding her in his arms, kissing her like this was no longer an unprocurable dream.

He removed her trousers, and the delicate lace underwear followed.

Feeling her soft, heated skin as he ran his fingers down the smooth, creamy flesh of her inner thighs, he felt a sensual feeling that was far beyond anything he had ever experienced. Nothing was beyond his reach now; today she would be his, and tonight would hopefully be the first of many to come.

He felt her fingers move to the fastening of his jeans. Kieran realised, there was no going back now for either of them as she leisurely ran her fingertips over the buttons of his jeans. Proving to her the force of his arousal was apparent enough, as the lightness of her touch sent a tremor surging through his body; he drew a trembling breath and exhaled slowly. How difficult it had suddenly become to breathe.

During his tour in Afghanistan, Kieran could remember he had been through some terrible, terrifying ordeals. During his deploy, he'd been involved in may dangerous explosive situations, and been scared and often feared for his life. The army had taught him to expect the unexpected and trained him for many eventualities; some had scared him at times, while some shocked, horrified and surprised him and sometimes thrilled him. But, what followed next was like nothing he'd been taught, short on being hit by a tank! Nothing he had experienced in the army could compare, or excited him more than being here with Sophie.

She skimmed her breasts against him and opened her legs for him. She wanted him in every way. Kieran lowered his mouth to her throat, and let his tongue slide over her skin. "You taste so good," he whispered, as he continued his crazy onslaught trail down to her breasts.

The sight and sensation of her against him took his breath away. He lowered one of his hands between her legs and instantly felt her swollen, wet, feminine, heated flesh in desperate need of his touch.

"I need you!" she whispered, against his neck.

The composed, friendly discipline she had enforced so rigidly got sucked into oblivion. Now, they had both turned into two people obsessed with seeking pleasure from each other. He was impetuous and demanding; his own need to plunder had become what he had desired most. He had devoured her from the beginning; his blind hunger was pushing him, building towards a premature climax. As he drove open her thighs then lowered himself into her, he felt her melt lovingly around him.

The impact of that first thrust of his manhood and the way she welcomed him so willingly made him feel it would stay with him forever. Her small, delicate frame had moulded so perfectly to his own, and nothing but the gentle rhythm of her breathing and the beating of her heart could be heard.

She reached up and plunged a hand into his sweat-drenched hair. The wave of tenderness shook him as her fingers gently stroked his hair — every motion her body made increased his desire tenfold. "Are you still sure this was a good idea?"

He lifted his head and looked at her with substantial, sexy, dark eyes. His pupils dilated, there was no mistaking the raw hunger deep within. "I think it's an excellent idea. Besides, we've only just begun. I haven't finished with you."

His curiosity about her body had proved insatiable, and he knew he could no longer postpone the hunger to satisfy, feeling the need to crush her body against his — feeling his dominant rhythm building as it drove them to the very brink of satisfaction. Finally, feeling the overwhelming exuberant satisfaction as his own body quivered, shaking with one last thrust of his sex. With his final climax spent, he collapsed in her arms. His sweat-drenched body rested against hers as he lay with his head buried in the curve of her neck.

Kieran couldn't speak; he couldn't move, overwhelmed with the feeling of being complete and he couldn't bring himself to do anything but lay there secure in her arms, while she gently ran her fingers through his short, sweat-drenched, black hair. Remembering at least she was now his — gloating with satisfaction. Nothing could come between them now — he was sure of it — not when he loved her so.

Sophie lay awake well into the night, her head on Kieran's shoulder, her small hand pale in comparison as it rested on his chest. She could feel his heart beating, feeling the gentle rhythm of the rise and fall of his chest as she thought about what they had done. There were no regrets; she had none. Kieran had shown her how it was to be loved by a man. And for that alone, she could never have regrets.

But with it came new worries, she still needed an escape plan from Simon — and when that happened, she would most likely never see Kieran again. And as much as she didn't want that, it was for the best.

She didn't want any awkward goodbyes between them, at least that's what she'd hoped as she lay beside him thinking.

"Stop! Don't do it!"

Sophie jumped almost out of her skin, pushing away from Kieran as he tightened his hold on her in a vice-like grip. He convulsed, and she pushed his body forcing herself away from him. She grabbed the sheets and pulled them up to cover her naked body. Eyes fixed on the man she'd been cuddled up to so peacefully moments before.

Sophie blinked twice before her eyes fully adjusted. She could make out Kieran's body glistening with sweat, his fists tightly in balls and raised across his chest; he was waving them about as if trying to punch his way out of a fight.

This was not good. What was going on here?

"Get the fuck out! Take cover!"

His voice was louder this time, and the meaning was clear. Sophie felt the pangs of fear running down her spine; there was no mistaking the panic in his words as he barked orders.

"Watch out!"

The cold realisation of his words meant she knew that it had to be a dream and a nightmare that had something to do with a traumatic event he'd been through in Afghanistan. But she'd lived with a violent man and his unexpected behaviour had scared her rigid. So much so, cautiously and as quietly as possible, she rose off the bed, grabbed her bathrobe from the nearby chair and escaped to the bathroom and was violently sick.

Sophie knew without a shred of doubt Kieran wasn't like Simon, but what if he hurt her and hadn't realised? She was undoubtedly scared of what was happening. But she didn't want to be on the receiving end of another man's fist, scared of being hurt by someone who had inflicted pain without reason. No, she couldn't stay close to Kieran, and she sure as hell wasn't going to risk waking him to explain. She would explain tomorrow.

Besides, she'd heard and seen enough about troops returning from war who have PTSD to spot the early warning signs.

The last thing Sophie wanted was for him to wake up and think her the enemy. Trained in combat, he could probably kill her with a single blow and not know he'd done it. She watched frozen to the spot as he tossed and turned. He kicked out at such force that the sheets tangled around his legs. She wanted to help him but wasn't quite sure how, or if she should. She kept a watchful eye until the dream had subsided.

Dressing quickly in the dark, she went through to the kitchen and sat sipping tea until the light came through the windows.

Chapter Fourteen

Kieran had woken that following morning with a sense of unfamiliar surroundings. He cast an eye over the other half of the empty bed, stretched and yawned.

He smiled sheepishly; somehow in the middle of the night they had managed to make it to her bedroom, and the vast four-poster bed that welcomed them. Showing their cravings and insatiable appetites they had for each other. Again and again, their bodies fuelled each other's desires; she had made him feel incredible and sexy too.

In the heat of their passion, his life had got infinitely so much better; she had made him feel whole. Life without Sophie had been far beyond anything he could ever fathom. Now, with her back in his life — it was complete — nothing else mattered. He could achieve anything with Sophie beside him.

Last night, while submerged in a shared passion, he'd hoped he'd shown her, and revealed, how much she'd meant to him. And yes, how much he loved her, and would always love her. Everything he felt for her was his world — nothing outside it and nothing beyond it mattered to him, nothing but his Sophie. And it had been the first good night's sleep Kieran had had in months.

In the light of day, looking around her room, he noticed the plain, cream curtains and the sun appearing through large French doors that looked over a balcony and with the curtains pulled back, he smiled again — they had made love with the shutters open. He smoothed the matching creamy duvet; he couldn't help noticing how it matched Sophie's life, flawlessly. Even down to the simple choice of furniture — uncluttered and large, oak pieces of furniture could hardly be classed as feminine, and yet it seemed to slot so perfectly into her personal life.

He pushed back the bedclothes and shrugged into a bathrobe, which was far too small for him. He went in search of her. It wasn't hard — he just followed the delicious smell of fresh coffee and warm bread.

When eventually he'd found her, she was perched drinking from a large mug at the kitchen table. Her hair was damp; she had already showered, he guessed. Pity, he smiled — he couldn't help it, as his eyes trailed over the length of her body. Slightly disappointed as he noticed her nice, elegant business suit, and dressed for work by the look of her. But it was Sunday. Didn't everyone at least deserve one day off?

He didn't care; he was happy for whatever time they shared, and he wanted her to see it. He smiled, remembering the way they had made sweet love just a few hours before.

"You look disgustingly smug this morning. What is it?" Sophie said, boldly.

"It's the thought of sleeping next to you every night," he replied, delighted with himself as if it was the perfectly normal, regular thing to happen. "Slept like a log afterwards, so you most certainly wore me out."

Sophie looked at him oddly, and he had no idea why.

"Every night — would suggest plural. I'm only aware of one night. Something you're not telling me?" She smiled nervously.

"I said nights — I meant nights." He leaned over the table and cupped her chin, holding it firmly, "Give me time, we have the rest of our lives to catch up on the other nights we've missed."

"I see," she shifted in her seat. "going to spend a lot of times having a sleepover, are you?"

He laughed and straightened, letting his forefinger trail slowly across her soft, flushed cheek. "Believe me, after what has happened over the past 24 hours and introducing me to the pleasures of your delectable body, I'm not letting you get away from me so easily again."

Sophie's flush deepened as her eyes searched his face. Came another, "I see."

"Good, I wouldn't want to think I've disappointed you in some way. Can't have that, can we?" He smiled and winked mischievously.

"What is it?" She laughed, teasing him, delighting at his touch, and her eyes sparkled. "Not sure?"

"If I've disappointed you, I will simply have to do better tonight."

"What makes you think I'm free to see you this evening?" she snapped suddenly. "Or do you plan on staking out my home again?"

In return for her comment, he smiled sheepishly, ignoring her tone.

He didn't feel like sparring this morning; he'd felt like that most mornings since his return, but was too exhausted to question why. "I simply meant I have no way of knowing if I've satisfied you unless you tell me — if you know what I mean?" He winked again.

Sophie stared at him, an odd expression of disappointment crept across her face. "What are you saying?" Her voice was now void of humour.

Something told him he was pushing his luck with her. He turned and picked a cup up from the drainer and poured himself some coffee. He had to think quickly; he didn't want her asking him to leave. Turning back to face her, he smiled cheerfully. "It's not important. Let's talk about something else, shall we?"

He could feel her eyes boring into his back as she said, "I'd like to know your answer to my question first."

He turned slowly and leaned against the drainer. Judging by Sophie's stare he felt nothing was going to sway her. There was nothing left for it. "Going on the last couple of years, I'm just saying my relationships with women are what you would call experienced. In the past, with what few girls I've known, if I met a girl I liked, we went out, then we'd have sex. It would trickle to nothing after they realised what my job involved. They would move on to a guy that was around more. That was fine by me, until now. I haven't kissed a girl since the moment I met you. I knew at that moment something had happened to me, to us. I didn't plan on what happened last night, but I'm so glad it did." Kieran watched her beautiful face colour under his stare. He wanted her more with each passing second.

Her eyes narrowed as she stared at him. "Makes it sound like I'm a means to an end." The words she feared most by the look of judgement on her face.

It wasn't like that with Sophie. Her words tugged at him — the softness of her voice, the hurt in her big, brown eyes... Kieran was seconds from breaking point.

Coffee pot in his hand, he watched as he poured the coffee into the cup. Anything to take his mind off her face and wanting her. "I'm just saying — judging by our actions last night — I'm out of practice and I want no other but you. I have feelings for you, Sophie, you know that."

She tried to smile and make it look genuine, relieved by his answer. "Well, that's all right, then." Relief flooded her face, and for an awful moment she thought he was going to tell her something else. By the look of the colour of her already flushed face, she needed to ask a straightforward thing, "I thought you were going to tell me you were a virgin."

Spoken like someone who dealt with lies and deception regularly. Kieran liked that about her. The adventurous journalist that lived each day without regret or denial in seeking the truth.

She sat watching as he stood gasping and choking with the shock of disbelief that she'd asked such a question. "No, course not."

When she stood up, she shook her head. "I thought for a minute—" Their conversation was interrupted by the distant ringing of the telephone, which caught her attention, and she left to answer her call.

She had left, with no time for him to explain further.

Some time had passed, and Kieran sat in the kitchen and waited for her to return. After about an hour, she had not returned, so he went in search of her. Time was getting on; he glanced at his watch for what seemed like the umpteenth time. He hadn't wanted to leave without saying goodbye. That felt too much like a one-night stand. No, he'd wait.

He glanced at his wristwatch again, and the door leading to her study opened suddenly. She strode out and stopped dead at the sight of him. She had been unable to avert her tear-stained face as he saw her. Frowning, he crossed the room to her side; he asked, "What is it? What's wrong?"

"Nothing. I'm fine," Sophie said, in a bid to avoid Kieran's eyes and his questions, "I think I might be getting a cold or something," she added, as she purposely walked past him to take a tissue from the box on the coffee table.

He scrutinised her every movement. She'd been perfectly fine right up until that phone call; he was beginning to hate the word. "Was it serious?"

She looked at him strangely; it was if it was on the tip of her tongue to tell Kieran to mind his own damn business. Of course, he always had in the past, but last night had changed all that. "It's work. I've had some sad news about a missing co-worker. I have to leave for a meeting soon

— this needs my urgent attention."

"I see." His reply questioned her honesty. Without question, the look on her face told him something was worrying her. Ex-husband troubles or not, she wasn't about to confide in him or trust him.

Her mouth twisted. "Hell! Don't start thinking you own me because we've slept together, and just because of last night I owe you some explanation," she took a deep, steadying breath. "Because if you do, I can tell you now — mind your own damn business," she spat at him sharply.

He eyed her closely. This side of her was so unlike her. She had never spoken to him in such a way. "Soph — what's wrong? Whatever it is — let me help you," he said, as he suddenly tuned in on her abrupt change of mood. "Please, tell me. You can trust me." Something told him she was acting out of protection and not to punish him.

She shook her head. "It's not easy for me. I can't tell you anything." She touched his arm lightly; a simple act of his care for her wellbeing was enough to make her realise Kieran was not her enemy. She squeezed gently, and as she did so it was enough to send shock waves through his body. "I'm sorry."

"Why?" His voice sounded shaky.

"Please don't ask me to break a confidence." She smiled up at his face. Her face was pale and looked determined. Her tear-stained face had an overwhelming effect on him. He didn't like it, but he had to abide by her decision. His heart melted instantly, as his arms reached out and gathered her to him, and her arms slipped around his waist.

Her body pressed against his, arousing his passion anew. His mouth planted small kisses along her cheek and down her neck. "OK." He looked deeply into those chocolate-brown eyes. "Soph, I have to leave soon too."

Her head tilted back. "Yes, you're right. You had better leave; I have work to do. I can't do that while you're here distracting me."

"OK, why don't we meet later for a drink?" He cupped her chin as he reminded her of their shared passion. "I want you to understand — I have no regrets about last night, Sophie. It's my choice. I like being involved with you, so don't try pushing me away. I will tell you now; I won't allow that to happen. I'm here to stay."

He kissed her lips gently and blew warm breath over her skin, and as quickly as the kiss had begun, it was over. And it took every ounce of strength and self-control he possessed to step back.

"Do you know the pub, Marshall's? It's down the road from here. I'll see you in there at two." He wasn't asking her.

"I'm not sure..." A frown appeared.

"That's settled then," he said lightly. He placed another light kiss on Sophie's lips. "I have to get a shower and get dressed."

"A shower?"

"How about you join me?"

She blinked. "Join you?" she echoed.

"In the shower," he said. "We just about have time, don't you agree? Besides, I could use your help to wash my back. Remember our phone call?"

He lowered his mouth to hers, and she immediately opened her lips. Even thinking about being with her made his legs weak. His tongue slipped into her mouth, and he slid his hands down the sides of her body.

"I'll take that as a resounding yes," he said, and he began to undress her.

***

Kieran had sat in the crowded restaurant; he was waiting not so patiently for Sophie, totally oblivious of the chatter and bustling going on around him as he caught a glimpse of the woman coming through the stained-glass doors.

She'd stopped to speak to the Maitre 'd as she quickly scanned the restaurant. She looked stunning! He smiled at her elegant, black suit as he sat casually in a black, leather jacket, well-worn jeans and a dark-green T-shirt.

He gave another small smile. He could sense Sophie's struggle to hold her thoughts under control. It was as if he could almost read her thoughts then. He watched as she slowly crossed the floor to reach his table; the smile fixed firmly on her face never wavered.

Kieran remembered her cool, reserved manner which had revealed a highly sensual and sexy woman the previous night. He had demonstrated to her he had no firm moral objection towards her divorce: quite the reverse where Sophie was concerned. He'd freely admitted he had female friends in Catterick, so his claim of his casual acquaintances had not been well received by her and she treated his confession as nonsense.

From the first moment he had touched her, he'd never known he had possessed such sensuality in his nature. The heat generated between them had burned inside them both since that very first morning. That single moment when she'd accidentally collided with him at Brize Norton.

He hadn't dared to confess that he'd seen her around the camp many times before that, and how desperately he'd wanted to meet her. The trouble was now, his bombshell had her believing he had a warped and unpredictable sense of humour. It was almost as if she had expected him to burst out laughing. The trouble was — he wasn't smiling. And what was worse — neither was she.

Maybe she wasn't taking him seriously? He felt a sudden rush of colour creep into his face as the hot image of Sophie and him in the shower slammed into his mind — warm and wet, and kissing and touching her. He smiled, recalling as they lathered each other with soap. Kieran was too busy sliding his hands all over her, lingering on her breasts and lower between her legs. He made her so hot and needy she could barely stand it.

She licked the drops of water from his chest, and he groaned, unable to breathe, as he kissed and caressed her nipples and then kissed his way down the rest of her body. When he took her with his mouth, Kieran couldn't remember feeling so erotic and robust and powerless to her moans of pleasure.

When she cried out, he lifted her, pressed her back against the tile of the shower and thrust inside of her. The invasion sent ripples of shock surging through his body, yet sinfully delicious. He felt her wrap her legs around his waist tightly as he pumped and then locked her gaze on his face as she watched him and saw his face as he went over the edge. Raw, unadulterated, sexual pleasure. There was no denying he wanted more of her. He would always come back for more.

Now she was here, meeting him in the restaurant, he observed her as she stopped to exchange a few pleasantries with a male diner, before reaching their table.

Fuck! She looked so beautiful, and even more so sexy. And judging by the adoring looks from most of the men in the room as their eyes followed her, they thought so too. There was no denying he felt such a rush of jealousy as she had smiled so sweetly at the male sitting grasping her hand — he had to look away.

Sophie looked up long enough to see a glare of jealousy in Kieran's eyes.

He was looking directly at her; now his absorbing ebony eyes intensely focused on brown. She searched his face gravely. If any of the other diners had spoken to her at that moment, he doubted she would have responded. Her long, dark, wavy hair glistened like spun silk; her elegant poise showed how much in control she was. He could only surmise she was on a mission.

"Hello, beautiful." He flashed her his most brilliant smile, and the look was gone. When she didn't respond he slowly picked up a menu; she lowered her eyes as she came to a stop in front of Kieran. He sat for a moment in silence — was she going to stay? Suddenly he felt her poise crack under strain. She smiled a warm, radiant smile that changed her whole face. There was no mistake, she looked beautiful in her lightweight, black suit she wore for work, finished off with a high neckline, black, silk blouse.

He had seen the dark bruising on her neck. Hell, he'd examined the severe bruising covering virtually 70 per cent of her body, but she had refused to explain or comment on it. He didn't want to force her to confide in him; no, he hadn't wanted that — he wanted her to come to him of her own free will.

Angling his head towards her, Kieran reached across the table, and trailed his thumb along her lower lip, tugging on the centre until she wet the spot with a flick of her tongue. "Cat got your tongue, Sophie Tyson?"

He didn't think for one moment she had worn that outfit for him, no matter how damn sexy she looked. He wanted her to find him more appealing than just a lover.

He wanted so much more from her. He wanted it to mean more than a casual affair and having great sex. He didn't want her ever to walk away from him. To suffer the grief to one day lose her, or to be treated no more than a casual affair, would be more than he could take. He could never have walked away from her without his heart left unbroken.

"Don't I deserve at least a welcome?"

Her brown eyes bore into him. She seemed wryly amused, rather than scolding. Had she been just as unsure of her ground as he had been?

"Hello, Kieran." She sounded reasonably calm. "I'm sorry I'm late. I got held up." Sophie sat down beside him. She seemed oddly distracted. She looked briefly at the menu. "Do you know what you're having yet?" She sounded more nervous than he first thought.

It was obvious to Kieran, clearly, after a few hours apart, Sophie was starting to get cold feet about the whole affair. He flashed her the most disarming smile he could manage. "No, not unless you want me?" Kieran couldn't help teasing her; smiling mischievously, his voice dropped to a husky tone. "I could be the main course, and then if you're starving, we could try for dessert." His eyes searched for a glimmer of humour. She avoided his stare. "What is it? Are you afraid to look at me?"

Sophie kept her eyes fixed on the menu. "No, I'm not!" She cast the menu aside.

"I can't stay long. I have to get back for a press meeting." Not divulging the details, she leaned forward and crossed her arms over the table.

"Yes, I figured you might be busy."

"What's that supposed to mean?" Unfolding her arms, she placed both hands palm down on the table as she absent-mindedly smoothed the tablecloth.

He leaned back in his chair, not taking his eyes off her face. He laid a hand casually over hers. "Are you going to tell me anything about this ex of yours? Or what happened to you? I worry about you. I want to know you're safe."

"I would if I thought it would be of any use to you."

Her words cut him deeply.

She bit down on her bottom lip. "I'm sorry. I didn't mean to say it the way it came out. It upsets me discussing him, so I would rather not." She tried to reassure him.

"I can understand why when he's hurt you so. But don't push me out, Sophie."

"I'm not. Truly, I'm not." Sophie looked up at the bright lights above, wishing she could tell him what she had meant.

"Yes, you are," he insisted. "You may not realise it, Sophie, but I have to disagree with you."

She sighed heavily. "I'm sorry if you feel that way. But for now, I feel bad enough about what's happened between us. And right at this moment, I would feel awkward talking to you about my ex."

"I can understand that. But I don't know what you expect of me, Sophie?" He leaned forward and said quietly, "Do you have any regrets about last night?"

She frowned. "No, of course not."

"Then what are you afraid of?" he started, reminding himself of the real reason he'd wanted to see her. Kieran sighed and changed tactics.

"Nothing." Something inside him told Kieran she was lying.

He picked up her small hand as it had laid under his. Although she flinched as he'd held it firmly in his, he asked, "What do you want out of this relationship, Sophie?" His instincts took over, as he suddenly wanted to do more than hold her hand. "If you told me what your expectations are, I would stand a better chance of knowing what I'm up against. If you're worried about the age thing — it doesn't matter to me at all. I didn't plan last night but I'm glad it happened."

"I admire your honesty, very much."

He'd hoped that he had met some of her expectations the night before. "Of course, I want more from you than just the sexual pleasures that we had both enjoyed last night." He smiled at her shocked face. "Unless you have any complaints on that score?"

She sat bewildered. "No, none."

"Good. Because since the day I first met you, understand I've wanted no other but you. And how desperately I've waited for you. I wanted you to take my affection seriously; I'd hoped you wanted me too. Now, I'm sure you care for me in some way. I'll take whatever you want to give me. You may think I'm too young for you, but I work hard at the things that are important to me. I love you. I want you more than anything. I'm just asking for a chance. But, don't try sending me away or dismissing me as a mere boy, Soph. Because if you do, you'll be making a big mistake."

"I won't," she swiftly replied. Not doubting his word for a moment. "Kieran, thank you for being so frank with me."

Maybe he should have been cautious as she'd replied so sweetly, but she had utterly bowled him over. Sophie had become an addiction to him from the very first taste of her. After one taste of her sweetness, he had known he had to have more to feed his burning, insatiable hunger.

"I'm not ashamed of how I feel about you, Soph, and I don't care people knowing about us either." His fingers had locked in hers. "But I won't lie for you. And I won't tell anyone about us if that's what you want. You only have to say how you feel." He had wanted her to feel loved and cherished. Most of all free for her to choose.

"What about the rest of the men you work with?"

"We are a close-knit unit, but some things are still private."

She smiled — the tension seemed to ease out of her. "That's good to know." Kieran seemed concerned about her feelings, and she couldn't ask for more. She barely knew what Kieran was saying any more.

He had been looking at her amused face as if waiting for the unspoken punch line of a crude joke. "My life is private and I am a solitary person at times. I don't like people knowing about me or making fun of me at my expense. Trust and loyalty are a huge deal with me."

"I would never have told you something like that to lie to you. I chose to tell you because not only are you the most beautiful woman I've ever met, but you're caring, intelligent and I'm already in love with you. I had hoped last night had at least meant something other to you than pure lust. No, Sophie, I don't want to make fun of you, or intend turning us into a circus act."

"But — I don't understand. Why me? Surely you have had plenty of opportunities with girlfriends closer to your age?" Catching sight of a passing waiter, they ordered and Sophie lapsed into silence.

"How many younger men friends do you have, Sophie?" The question tore at his insides, but he had to make her see reason.

"What's that going to do with anything? Surely, you're not trying to tell me you haven't slept with any of those girlfriends you speak of?"

"OK. I won't. Have you slept with any of those so-called boyfriends of yours?" he replied, only half-joking.

"What's that supposed to mean?" she asked, apparently put out by his light, pithy tone. She didn't sound amused at all.

"You're the reporter. You believe what you want to believe."

"For goodness sake. You're in the British Army! We've all heard the stories of what soldiers are like, especially the playing away from home."

Something told him Sophie was talking about a particular episode she had confronted during her time here. "That's no excuse. I only live about ten miles down the road."

"Then, why me?" Sophie asked finally, as she sank back in her chair and lapsed into silence again.

"Why do you have such a hard time believing me? I find you interesting and beautiful. I like being with you. Since the very moment you exploded into my life, I haven't been able to get you out of my mind." He had murmured as he vividly remembered all those erotic dreams that had filled every sleeping moment he'd had since meeting her. "I wish you would believe me when I say I only want you." He grinned broadly.

She had no idea how it made him feel being with her like this. He had held her hand as she became aware of the environment around her. She gently pulled her hand away from his. It was almost like she was ashamed to be seen with him.

Kieran decided not to mention her simple action hurt his feelings.

"I— I can't afford uninvited complications in my life," she told him. "Although, I have this strange feeling you're laughing at my expense," she had pointed out sharply.

Sophie had a point though; he liked to make her squirm a little. "Does that mean because you're the most experienced out of the two of us — that I have to place my young body in your capable hands?"

"Oh, God!" She gave him a small, nervous laugh. "Can't you at least be serious for one moment?" It was obvious the conversation was making her uncomfortable.

"Well, I guess I could, sometimes, when it matters," he said, as he slipped her a quick wink. "Besides, everything I've learnt I owe you. Just think, you're the woman who took an innocent, young boy and turned him into a man. The only woman who taught me about giving real pleasure. The only woman whom I considered worthy of giving her my treasured youth." *So, all right — he was taking advantage of her embarrassment, and he may have laid it on a bit thick, and now sounded utterly wicked at making light of her discomfort.*

He just wanted her to feel as he had felt. He wanted her to know she was the one woman he loved deeply above all others and loved with all his heart. She had been unforgettable, not only had she been his first love — she was his only love.

He sounded suddenly impatient. "Why don't we get out of here?" he had said, as he had watched her prod and push her salad around on her plate. "I could make us something to eat at your house."

Sophie didn't say anything straight away. "I'm afraid it will be a late dinner. I have to leave," she said, as she glanced at her wrist. "I really do have that meeting to attend."

"Don't you want me coming home with you?"

"It's not that, Kieran," she was saying. She knew what was going through his mind, wondering if it was the same doubts that he harboured earlier.

"Would you rather we didn't see each other until tonight? I know you must have other friends you would like to see."

"Yes, I do." He had known he could stay calm at those words, but he refused to take the bait. Then mildly she said, "But not tonight." A tingle of delight shot through him.

"You, my lady," he laughed and winked wickedly, "have what's known as good sense." He smiled warmly. "Let's go." He had held out his hand. Slowly, she placed her small hand in his. He knew they had just taken a giant leap forward.

It had been right — she had class, and she was a lady. Sophie was in a class all of her own. Her formal, black suit and black high-heels somehow added inches to her height. Her dark, wavy hair looked beautiful, even tied back in the type of an elegant braid that hung down her back. She had looked good, too good. And the glint in his eyes must have revealed something of how he felt.

He remembered her bruised arm and shoulder; how he'd been so angry at the sight of her injured multicoloured flesh. She had been a victim; she had worn the marks of a man's hatred, but why?

Kieran had wanted to protect her, but never permitted beyond the boundary of a lover. But, how could he have protected her when she would never confide in him enough to reveal the details of her attack or the attacker's name.

Each time he approached the subject she would clam up. She would grow considerably paler, almost ghost-like, and her dark, soft, brown eyes would fill with fear. He would be shaken by her response and by the look of dread on her face. Watching her beautiful face become taut and filled with fear was more than he could stand.

Her pose and her beauty combined with her intelligence meant she was indeed a force to be reckoned with, and yet something inside him told him that deep within her hid a frightened little mouse. For such a fiercely strong, independent woman, she intrigued him, and above all, raised his curiosity as to what this beautiful, business-savvy woman needed to hide away from the rest of the world. And if nothing else he was going to make it his mission to find out.

Between training and deployments with his unit, Sophie had consumed him. They were in constant touch. They'd spent almost every available waking moment together. But it didn't matter how much Kieran loved her, there always seemed to be a distance between them. It was·if she was keeping a very dark secret from him that she could reveal to no one.

***

It wasn't long before Kieran was deployed back to Afghanistan, and as much as he regretted being apart from Sophie, it was a mission that was vital to the war on terror. And it was his job. A job he loved. Orders were orders.

In the week he was away from Sophie he'd been unable to sleep or eat without thinking of her. At night he'd missed her wrapped in his arms.

"Snap out of it, Romeo," Private Adam *Scotty* Scott '' brought him back to the present.

"I'm good." Kieran surveyed his surroundings and bent down and patted the dog's head as the liver-white Springer spaniel sat at his handler's feet, wagging his tail.

Crackling static came over the radio. "Stand by."

The city centre of Kabul was filled with a waiting crowd, many waving and cheering, eager to celebrate the arrival of the American and English troops with lots of media coverage. Kieran wasn't so sure all this attention and crowded streets was a good thing. After the last few days spent in the desert on patrol, lugging his backpack, he sure wasn't going to complain about such a cushy number as this, not even if they asked him to stand about for another six hours.

"Troops are ready, Jonesy."

Kieran touched his headpiece as the other soldier's voice came through on the line.

"One final check in five."

Kieran moved down the street checking that all the people were securely behind the low, temporary barriers erected. A few feet from where the parade would pass, some local law enforcement officers were on guard; everyone was vigilant over the number of people in the crowded street.

The security was tight. And snipers were in position, sitting up above on rooftops within 1,000 metres of the location, keeping an eagle eye on the people. All the reserve soldiers had been pulled in for this one. It was a significant event. Every spare member of the armed forces was vital to the mission.

Kieran moved slowly, watching the crowd as he did so, and made his way down to where his Snatch Land Rover was parked. Kieran had already stated he'd meet the four-man crew at the checkpoint at the appointed time. They needed to do one last check for explosives, and then the primary objective was to escort the 'Chief of Staff' safely from his car to the main building.

"I have a visual on the lead Snatch." Before heading to the rendezvous point.

The lead Land Rover pulled up with four soldiers on board. Adam stepped forward with his dog to meet the jet-black car with tinted windows behind. Kieran went to take a step closer, and that was as far as he got.

The crowd were now waving and cheering excitedly, pushing their way through the fence. A lone figure forced his way forward. Kieran noticed that he was acting differently from the rest of the crowd. The man stood a distance from the cheering people in the street, standing silent and alone. His attention was on watching two children playing closely to the Snatch as Kieran kept a close eye on his movements. His gut instincts told Kieran something was not right; he touched his headpiece to advise Adam to observe him.

Before Adam had a chance to *Confirm,* the man had rushed up to the Land Rover and thrown a small object at the base of the wheel, and before anyone could react...

Kieran's face turned grim. He'd been too far away, and the noise from the crowd was overpowering; his radio headset had lost contact. He felt helpless. As if in slow motion, he could only stand and watch, powerless.

The device exploded immediately on contact as the Snatch blew up in seconds, sending debris, swirls of smoke and bodies hurtling through the street. The impact of the explosion shook the whole building, and the sound was deafening.

For a moment he couldn't see or hear anything. He struggled to get his bearings. Dust seemed to be settling everywhere around him.

The Land Rover, or what remained of it, was a ball of fire. Kieran could see the smoke billowing from the wreckage. Pieces of rubber tyres and chunks of metal thudded and pinged as fragments of the Land Rover hit the road, while oil and fuel sprayed across the street in all directions.

The suicide bomber who had done this had undoubtedly done the job by placing it close to the petrol tank. The flammable liquid had ignited. The whole thing had exploded within a fraction of a second.

Screams and wailing from civilians could be heard above the sirens as they ran through the street searching for cover as the panic grew. People were pushing and shoving, and crying out in terror as the fear spread through the road sending chaos through the crowds.

With action-like reflexes, Kieran had cornered the street as a state of emergency so that the emergency vehicles could get through. When Kieran finally got close enough, he realised the suicide bomber had killed himself, along with the two children that had been playing close by, and seriously injuring four of the servicemen in the vehicle.

Adam was lying in the street, caught in the full blast, and it was apparent he had been killed instantly; his body burnt and hardly recognisable apart from the plain gold ring on his wedding finger. His dog was lying beside him. Although the dog was unharmed by the blast, the shock had been too much for his loyal sniffer dog, Sasha, to handle, and she died within seconds from heart seizure.

Kieran knew he was of no use to Adam now. Seeing through the smoke and heat, he watched the firemen cover the dead bodies of the children and his friend.

If the explosion had happened five minutes later, he would have been in the vehicle too. The only thing he could be thankful for right now was that he wasn't in the Land Rover also, or he would be dead, or severely injured for sure.

"You OK, Romeo?" Came Jonesy's voice. "The situation is fucking bleak. Get the fuck out of there, Romeo, and let the bomb disposal team handle it."

Kieran shrugged. "I was going to check if there was something I could do." His throat tightened as he said the words. Kieran straightened himself, forcing himself to cut off his emotions. Since his time overseas, he'd become an expert at disguising his feelings over the years. The truth was — there was nothing he could do.

"Get the fuck out!" Jonesy ordered. "Fucking let the guys do their job."

Jonesy was right; he needed to back off. It was too dangerous to be out in the open like this after such a tragic event. They needed answers as to how this happened, and he couldn't do his job if he were dead.

This terrorist suicide attack on Kabul city centre had been well planned, no doubt about it. The Afghan police were not ruling out a possible inside job. Leaving 29 people dead and 81 civilians wounded in the attack on the people, and seriously injuring four servicemen and one dead. Sadly, for the team, they had lost another valued member of their platoon.

This proved the Taliban were capable of launching attacks on civilians and troops in urban city centres with not an ounce of regret at the loss of lives.

As Kieran stood watching the fire-fighters and soldiers put the last of the flames out, and sort the wreckage out for further investigation, he knew exactly how lucky he'd been. Although upset over his friend, he was glad it hadn't been him, too.

With everything going on around him — all the noise and chaos, all the danger — all he could think of right now was returning to Sophie. He couldn't wait to hold her in his arms. He knew then everything would be alright.

***

On his return, spending time with Sophie had been the one good thing in his life to come out of such tragedy of losing his friends. As the week passed, he was happier than he'd ever been.

And as the days turned into weeks, he'd grown even more deeply in love with her, and with every day he became even more infatuated with her. So much so, she had also agreed with his constant, gentle persuading to attend the upcoming Grand Ball with him. Although he'd loved her madly, she drew the line of him moving into her home.

Even though he'd spent most nights with her, she had clung to the belief that she needed her independence. And he loved her so deeply he would have agreed to give her anything. No matter how much he begged and pleaded with her. He only decided to drop the issue when she threatened to stop seeing him. The expression on her face told him she meant it.

Keeping their relationship behind closed doors became almost unbearable for him. He wanted to shout from the highest rooftops of his love for her. For her to finally agree to go to the Grand Ball with him was a breakthrough.

Her decision to keep it from everyone she knew other than her two closest friends became increasingly difficult. He met Jane and Andrew on the odd occasion, which wasn't easy for him, but they had welcomed him all the same.

Sophie had been continuously invited to their home on weekends. On meeting the couple for the first time Kieran could well understand how close their friendship was and how protective Jane was of her friend. The couple were kind, generous, and thought highly of Sophie, and undoubtedly would have done anything for her. Kieran, however, realised the couple had known specific privileged and guarded information that he did not, which came to light one evening when he'd overheard them talking in hushed whispers whenever he came within earshot. There was no doubt about it, her lack of trust in him hurt him, but he hadn't pushed her for answers. He figured she would tell him in her own time.

Chapter Fifteen

This is a huge mistake!

As she looked judgementally in front of the mirror, she applied her make-up carefully, before running the brush through her hair. She couldn't help but think this was a huge mistake.

The moment a knock sounded on the door, her heart skipped a beat. She gently smoothed her hands down the sides of her dress, and she smiled at her reflection; there was no denying she felt and looked great.

On opening the door, the look of open adoration on Kieran's face told her she had made the right decision in taking the extra effort in dressing.

The night of the Grand Ball had arrived. After weeks of Sophie living in a panic over their undercover love affair, he had finally talked her round, and she relented and agreed to attend the formal reception with him.

Kieran remembered that had been the first time he'd seen her wearing red. The long, flowing, red, silk, strapless, evening dress had been sensational. The tight glitter bodice moulded to her body as the skirts floated around her shapely legs. She looked beautiful beyond words. The colour complemented her creamy, porcelain skin and waist-length, wavy, burnt-coffee-coloured hair to perfection. Overwhelming.

The occasion warranted him to wear a full, dress uniform. Every brass button and every stud shined to supremacy. As her arm had rested on his, escorting her to the ball filled him with a sense of pride; feeling her close was a dream come true.

The atmosphere had convinced him he had chosen the right evening to lay his foundations for their relationship to advance for the two of them.

He and Sophie mingled, danced, and laughed with just about every other guest in the grand reception room.

That night, as he escorted her home, he stood on the doorstep and looked longingly into her eyes. His arms had slid about her with great pleasure. He instantly felt the heat of her body through the bodice of her dress. He could feel her heart beating against his chest. Just holding her made him burn with wanting. His aroused body pressed against her stomach. His erection strained against his trousers. His mouth burned as he placed tender kisses on her neck.

"God! Soph, I've ached for you all evening," he told her huskily, as his teeth gently brushed her heated flesh. Tasting her as he continued with his kisses he asked, "Can I stay tonight?"

Her brows arched. "Why?" Her voice seemed shaken with emotion.

"Why?" he repeated, a little bewildered by her response. "I thought it was obvious. Why? Because I love you — that's why." He smiled at her in a lazy, suggestive style that he knew she loved.

Kieran leaned forward and began to pull her slowly and sensuously towards him as he whispered close to her ear, "Sophie, you feel so good." He looked down — their bodies touching. He smiled at her triumphantly. He sensed her apprehension. "You're shaking — are you afraid of me?"

"No — it's not that." She laughed, not entirely convincingly enough.

"Then it's because you're a naturally nervous person."

"It's not that either."

"Then it's because you're worried what people might say if they see me leaving your house in the early hours of the morning?" He nuzzled against her throat and placed a single kiss at the base.

"Something like that." She smiled weakly.

"Perhaps you wouldn't feel such an old-fashioned prude, Sophie, if you and I got married," he suggested spontaneously.

"I've told you, it's not for me," Sophie replied flippantly.

He brought his head up and glanced at her face. "You haven't been married to me," he replied calmly.

She pulled out of his arms slowly. "Kieran, don't joke about things like that," she told him solemnly.

He'd been planning to ask Sophie to marry him for weeks now, and he'd thought to ask her tonight had been a perfect time. But he hadn't counted on being so impatient that he'd blurted it out on her doorstep of all places. He'd been so eager to ask her that he hadn't thought of her response.

"Is that a yes?" was all he could think of saying.

"Kieran. You don't know what you're asking of me." She looked at him through pain-filled eyes.

"Yes, I do," he bit back.

"Have you given any thought, Kieran, to what people might say? There are your parents to consider for starters. What do you think they will say to their only son of 20 years of age wanting to marry a 30-something-year-old woman and a divorced one at that?"

"That's OK; you can adopt me." His quick-fired wit was supposed to inject some humour into the conversation — it had the opposite effect.

She sucked in a shocked breath. "I'm not kidding, Kieran. No."

"Why would we give a fuck what people think or say?!"

She stormed off inside the house, leaving him on the doorstep. He found her in the sitting room looking despondent. "I won't marry you, Kieran. I can't marry you." Her face flushed with anger.

"Was that can't or won't?" he asked lightly.

Sophie straightened her shoulders. "Both." Sophie looked him squarely in the eye. "It's impossible."

"I see." He smiled as he loosened her red, silk shawl off her shoulders. "Then..." he said huskily, before continuing, "I have the rest of the night to try to change your mind and make it probable."

He looked down at her triumphantly as he towered over her. Slowly, and with great finesse, he pulled her into his arms, and she leaned towards him. He began to loosen her dress slowly. His shaking hands started to slide inside the front of the delicate fabric as it fell to a pool of shimmering silk at her feet. Bare skin on skin was sending him wild with wanting. Making him shake with longing and need. "I have a feeling that I just might enjoy seeing you change your mind."

His urgent need to feel her against him grew. His hunger to feast on her flesh became almost unbearable. The heat of his erection was crying out to eagerly be inside her, as he wanted to satisfy them both.

Since the first time they had made love, he had wanted to give himself so thoroughly. Without any restraint, with a lifelong commitment at stake, he gave it his all.

In their time together his experience had grown enthusiastically by leaps and bounds. His hands and mouth had done extraordinary things to Sophie's body as she melted against him.

Later, thoroughly spent, and leaving him exhausted, sleepy and happy, she collapsed into his waiting arms.

Sophie lay awake long into the night, her head on Kieran's shoulder, and her hand resting on his chest as she listened to the rhythm of his breathing, feeling the gentle rise and fall of his chest as she tried to clear her mind of what just happened, and thought about what she had done. She had given him hope of a future together, and that was wrong of her.

Kieran stirred lightly, but to her relief he didn't wake. He just uttered "Let's go!" in his sleep.

He turned restlessly onto his side. "Get the fucking hell out!" he shouted. He kicked out of the sheets — arms and fists flying as if he was fighting for his life. "Don't go near that device, Scotty!" he called out. "Don't fucking go there, Scotty! Get out now, you fucking wanker! Move it!"

Sophie jumped off the bed naked and pushed herself against the wall, her eyes fixed on him as she stood watching him for what seemed a long time. She grabbed the top cover and wrapped it around her body as she watched him from a distance.

It became all too clear.

His dreams were of the time spent on missions in the army. There was no mistaking — the visions felt real to him as if reliving the terror of what he'd been through; he sounded to be warning the men of oncoming danger.

"Don't fucking do it! You fucking moron, get the fuck out now!" he called out. The order was clear, and his voice much louder this time. "Sasha! Get them the fucking hell out of there!" His body convulsed, twisting and turning. His body was soaked with sweat within seconds. He punched his fists in the air as if he was fighting for his life. "Get the fuck away, you stupid bastard!"

Not for one moment did she think Kieran would knowingly hurt her. But she had seen the strength of a violent man before and felt what a troubled man was capable of inflicting on someone first-hand. Hurt by the one you trust most. And she had lived to regret that terror.

She waited, wanting to help somehow, but felt if she went close to him he might mistake her for the enemy and without realising it and lash out at her. Worse still, take hold of her in a deadlock and choke the life out of her. And Kieran certainly looked like he needed help. She'd heard things and read reports of service personnel having symptoms such as this happening when dealing with PTSD. There was nothing she could do at present but wait.

Kieran was calling out again, tossing and turning; the agony in his voice and the desperation was almost deafening to hear. His body glistened with sweat as he fought furiously against the tangled sheets. He rolled so near to the end of the bed that Sophie dashed to his side.

"Kieran!" Sophie called out, trying to shove his body back onto the bed.

One moment she was wrestling with him and the next he was sat upright, looking disoriented with his hands shaking his head.

"What's wrong, Soph?" His voice was almost normal. Still dry from his shouting. "Did I wake you?"

She didn't say anything for a moment. Instead, she reached for some water for Kieran to take a drink. Leaning forward, she said, "here, drink this. It will help."

Kieran was starting to feel anxious. He reached over to flick on the bedside lamp, illuminating the room so that he could see her more clearly. "What is it? What did I do?" he asked.

Sophie wasn't sure what he remembered, so she took a deep, steadying breath before perching on the end of the bed next to him. "I think you were having a nightmare. I didn't want to wake you, but you were on the verge of falling out of bed."

Kieran's expression changed, his face became withdrawn and masked over. "I'm sorry to have frightened you. I don't know what I was dreaming about."

She placed her small hand over his as it rested on the bed beside them, clasping his fingers. "I think you do." Trying desperately not to hurt his feelings. "This has happened before. The first time we slept together, when I left you alone to sleep that morning, it was because of this. I didn't know how to deal with what you were going through."

He pushed the tangled sheets off his legs and swung them off the bed; his head lowered into his hands as he sat next to her. His body was glistening with sweat and shaking as if cold.

Sophie wanted so desperately to comfort him but wasn't sure how her action would be received. It was a problem he wasn't that comfortable talking about with her.

"Have I hurt you before?" he asked, as he raised his head. "When I woke alone that morning after we spent such an amazing night together, I had the strangest feeling I'd done something wrong, and I frightened you."

"You didn't hurt me. It frightened me because I didn't know how to handle it."

As if embarrassed by his actions, Kieran stood and paced the room. The mere size of his frame seemed to dwarf the room.

"I'm sorry. It wasn't intentional. I don't even know I'm doing it. I sometimes go to sleep, and it happens, if you understand..." Kieran's voice drifted off as if haunted by a painful memory.

"I'm not blaming you. None of it is your fault. Remember what you first told me?" She reminded him when he looked at her with puzzled eyes. "Things from the past cannot hurt us."

He walked up to her and knelt before her resting his head on her lap. She stroked his face. "I never meant for you to be afraid of me, Sophie. I'm sorry I put you through that."

"Tell me about it. Let me try and understand."

Kieran made a sound that came from his throat. At first, she thought he was going not to reply. He was uncomfortable with discussing the dreams, but then his body seemed to relax.

"Adam, 'Scotty' we called him, was one of my best and oldest serving friends. We met when I joined the company in Afghanistan, and we both have seen some bad stuff. We both lost friends that we were close to on missions. He was one of the decent guys; he lived with his wife and two kids when home, near Cambridge. He liked his drink and enjoyed nothing better than a good football match in front of the TV and spent all his leave time doing family stuff. Scotty was an excellent soldier, and you knew where you stood with him, and you knew he always had your back covered."

"Something bad happened to him?"

"Yes, killed on our last mission along with a couple of kids."

She watched Kieran's hold as it tightened. It was clear this was something he wasn't comfortable with; it was as if he'd not discussed it before.

"And he's one of the men in your dreams, isn't he? The one you are calling out to?" Sophie hoped she wasn't prying too much. "Who's Sasha?"

Kieran gripped the covers tightly — his fists white showing how hard his hold was.

"There were a few of us that joined up together and formed good friendships. We were out on a special mission when we came under enemy fire. Five soldiers were injured that day. One soldier, great guy, was part of the BAVC (British Army Veterinary Corps) with his explosives' sniffer dog, Sasha. Scotty and his dog both died that day."

She couldn't speak, she didn't know what to say. No amount of words of sympathy would be able to console the loss of Kieran's friends.

Kieran looked at her with misted eyes. He shrugged, and she knew he wasn't comfortable and wasn't finding it easy going back over some of the things that tormented and haunted him during the night.

Tears pricked at her eyes. She tried to hold the unshed tears at bay. The last thing she wanted was for him to misinterpret her love for him as sympathy. "Kieran, I'm so sorry for everything you've lost and been through."

"When I came back on leave, things were difficult for me for a while. Then Jonesy, my platoon sergeant, got me back on track and sorted me out. Since then we've met up with some of the guys from my platoon. We meet up when we can and chat about the 'laugh about the good old days', but we never discuss what happened or mates we've lost. I guess you could call it a guy thing. We never truly talk about the hard things we had to face and the hell we went through on missions."

"Understandably. You have been through a lot. Some people find it easier to ignore I guess." She knew what he meant exactly.

"I think I should leave," he said. As he raised his head, she could see his tear-stained face. His cheeks wet, and his eyes red and swollen. She had never seen a grown man cry before, and she couldn't take her eyes off him.

"No, don't go like this." Her heart was aching for his sorrow.

"No, I'll go," he whispered. "You need some rest."

"Wait a while. Lie back and rest a little longer. If you still want to leave afterwards, I won't stop you." There was no denying she felt guilty Kieran leaving like this. But he was fighting some severe inner demons, and that was something with which she couldn't help.

Later that morning, as he felt her sleeping, her long, soft, silky, dark hair strewn across her pillow reminded him of their wild night of passionate love they had shared, stirring his loins anew at the mere sight of her.

She had silently watched him through half-closed eyes.

He slowly and quietly walked across the bedroom floor entirely naked. Sophie's eyes fixed on his broad shoulders, long, smooth back, and his muscled legs with their coarse, dark hair along the calves.

He moved around the room with an unselfconscious, masculine grace. Kieran glanced over to where she lay; no man had ever made her feel so sexy and so cherished. The intimacy of the situation was enough to make her heart beat frantically.

Sophie had to turn away; she could hear him as he moved about the room picking up his clothes. Hastily he dressed. She couldn't bear to turn and watch him dress back into his uniform and leave. There was something about the way Kieran wore his uniform that made him look so damn sexy.

He was upset with her. They had talked about marriage, him wanting to marry her, wanting her, needing her. She pictured him using words of love. Sophie knew it was hopeless to deny to herself she was in love with him. He didn't need to take her to bed for her to know that.

Kieran sneaked out of the house hoping not to wake her, and he raced back to his barracks to change. Whether she agreed to marry him or not — he wouldn't give her up. He couldn't. There would be time to discuss it with her later.

An hour after Kieran had left that morning, Sophie took a leisurely shower. Afterwards, she slipped into her towelling robe. It was far too big for her; the sleeves were too long, the shoulders too wide, but she liked the length that covered her well-shaped calves.

She padded across the hallway on her way to the lounge. She stopped dead in her tracks. She hadn't been prepared for the sight that greeted her. Her heart stopped as she saw someone standing in the centre of the room, and his face looked cold and stern as if carved from stone.

"Simon!"

When Kieran had arrived at her home a week later, he found something he shouldn't have. After he returned to base the men had been called on a week-long exercise and he had been unable to contact Sophie. That evening, filled with hope for their future and a ring in his pocket, nothing had prepared him for the shock as he had found it completely deserted.

Every piece of furniture, crockery, clothes, books — gone. Not even a light bulb remained. Kieran never forgot the sound his footsteps had made on the bare floorboards as he walked across the living room floor. The memory of total abandonment filled his heart.

The memory of that night haunted him repeatedly.

Despair became part of his world. Loneliness was his only companion. As each day passed slowly by, and with no trace of her, he found it more and more difficult to believe Sophie would leave without a goodbye. Facing each day filled him with despair and dread that something awful had happened to Sophie. He clung to the belief that Sophie was somewhere safe and well.

His job began to suffer as he sank deeper and deeper into a depression. His only saviour, as it turned out, was some weeks later when the truth finally hit him. Sophie was not coming back; nor was she ever coming back to him. He moved back to his parents as soon as possible. He found living in the camp had made his life difficult, along with friends giving knowing, sympathetic looks which made it unbearable. Too many reminders.

His parents must have thought he'd lost his mind.

Weeks of solitude and moodiness from what he could only describe as suffering from a broken heart. Everywhere he went, everything he did — all painful reminders. He had to get away from everything that reminded him of his time with Sophie. Throwing himself into his job, he knew just what he needed.

Then, three months later, on a cloudless, hot, dry and windy summer's morning, he realised she'd controlled him long enough. It was time he made a stand and pulled himself together. It came to him as clear as day: no matter how he searched for her — she was not coming back to him.

All in all, thinking about it, it seemed such an easy decision to make when it had come right down to it. It just took a crap day to realise. A really fucking shit day as it happens. It didn't start out that way, but it sure did end pretty bad.

On Saturday morning, Taliban radio was intercepted and translated, warning anyone opposing their leadership would face their wrath. Intel had confirmed a growing number of the insurgents had banded together from neighbouring villages to join the fighting, and the Taliban were confident they would have driven out the troops of Sangin. They relayed a menacing threat. The Taliban would kill any captured coalition forces by sundown. Worse, anyone caught would be beheaded and videoed live and the recording released on YouTube.

Although the troops were informed it was no more than propaganda, it was taken seriously all the same.

The 'Op' was the most extensive British-led military plan, originated by the ANA and the ISAF. It set to drive out the Taliban in one of the most occupied and dangerous strongholds in Helmand Province, southern Afghanistan.

Major 'Ty' Morgan had the idea if he marched small bands of men for over ten miles to the location, loaded with as much kit as they could carry overnight through hostile territory, some carrying 80 lbs of equipment, supplies and rations — to their appointed destination, it would gain an advantage over the Taliban in a remote part of Afghanistan.

Shortly before dawn, the platoon had successfully moved into position, surrounding the insurgents from all sides, blocking their escape routes as the ANA, with a heritage spanning as far back as the 18th century, and known for their fearlessness in the face of danger, drew them out.

Dwellings were situated in the middle of the town. The district centre was a cluster of low buildings made up of cement and mud surrounded by a compound perimeter wall that was less than six feet and that provided less than adequate protection.

The intention was to win over the local people by supplying an overwhelming amount of military personnel of over 2,500 men. This action appeared to have the opposite effect, causing many of them to flee the area. And despite the influx of NATO troops and the assurance that the British Army were there for their protection — the Taliban continued to maintain their hold over vast swathes of territory and often revealed they were capable of launching regular attacks on the troops at any time.

British forces' intelligence observed the Taliban had begun to circle along the outskirts of the town. Each evening the insurgents would return to make several attacks with small arms fire and RPGs.

For a precautionary measure, British forces started extending the patrols in the area in preparation for the battle. No longer content to be sitting targets for the insurgents to take pot-shots at, so the soldiers made their own plans and made their presence felt.

Kieran stood by his post to watch while the two front men, Private Ryan Greenwood and Lance Corporal Ashley '*Benny*' Benson walked down the street inspecting everything.

Their job was to set up a cordon around the town with Vallon metal detectors, sweeping everything as they left nothing to chance. Bomb devices could often be detected in the smallest and isolated areas. Every piece of rubbish, building and vehicles needed to be treated with caution and suspicion on every patrol.

The Taliban had planted landmines and IEDs as they reinforced their position to defend their stronghold on the town. For every one found and destroyed — the insurgents would often return as soon as the men had left the area and plant others. Locating IEDs was an ongoing battle.

Once the area was given the clear, he'd heard the voice on the line of his headpiece, "All clear this location."

Kieran touched his radio headset and responded, "Clear" and crouched down behind a derelict brick wall of a two-storey ramshackle former luxury hotel and waited for the remaining troops to arrive in their vehicles and get themselves into position in the south of Sangin.

This '*Op*' was part of a carefully selected company of infantry troops, conducting a joint forces' operation with ANA soldiers, to fight for control against the Taliban in the dominated areas that posed as a serious and dangerous threat to British forces and the local people of Afghanistan.

Kieran heard a dog bark in the distance; he located the lone soldier walking with a black Labrador dog that was sticking close to his side.

There was no doubt about it, Kieran had to admire their courage; even the sniffer dogs were brought in for added security. He sure didn't envy his job. Sniffer dogs often became targeted by the Taliban and shot while on patrol as the dogs could detect insurgent strongholds and opium growers, which led to the destruction of poppy fields.

Part of the Royal Army Veterinary Corps, the soldier spoke to the dog by name, and without hesitation the dog instantly responded to his commands. The dog and handler worked closely together as any team would. At first glance, anyone could see the dog had a special bond with its handler, and there was no mistaking the professionalism. Both were highly trained in locating all sorts of bombs, explosives and ammunition devices hidden in any vehicles, including bikes and buildings, along with other IED searches and routes.

For the past year, the men stationed across the southern and eastern parts of Afghanistan had been witness to an increase in the amount of IEDs and roadside bombs planted — often devised as crude but effective and often with deadly consequences.

Kieran looked up at the sound of several scraping noises along with a couple of thuds above.

Instinctively, he flattened himself against the wall, keeping deathly still as he tried to peer up at the rooftop on the second floor of the house. Heart beating so loudly, he was sure someone would hear him breathing. He pushed himself flat against the wall.

A voice came over his headpiece. "In position, Jonesy."

Jonesy's voice came back loud and clear. "You have support company, Romeo."

Relieved, Kieran's tension in his shoulders relaxed. "Heard the patter of tiny footsteps, Jonesy. I did wonder."

"Just setting up family plan in motion." Realising the empty building across the street gave two of his guys the tactical advantage from the flat rooftop.

The sudden quietness on the rooftop told Kieran the men had finally settled in for the duration.

Since the advanced warning leaflet drop, judging what looked like half the town, and an amount of people he'd never seen before, had chosen today to make an appearance to evacuate the town. And it didn't take rocket science to guess why. They were anxious over the number of coalition forces who were patrolling the streets. To top it off — if the townspeople knew the troops were in effect you could be sure the Taliban knew too.

Team briefing prepared the troops for a different strategy. This *'Op'* had to be handled differently from the other times. Military engagements often resulted in the loss of too many non-combatant civilians. The Afghan government had concerns at the loss of casualties and fatalities since the trouble began in 2001. There were too many civilians to take chances in such a populated area — the evacuation was going slowly. They would have to hold their position and wait.

Kieran was starting to realise the two men lying on the rooftop above him were busily setting up their GPMG. Kieran didn't need to be told what this meant. Judging by the amount of equipment being hauled about, the men were not going to be caught with their pants down when the fighting started. They were going to be prepared and outfitted for anything that could happen on a larger scale. Kieran was sure the only weaponry to cope with a massive operation was the L7A2, operated by a two-man crew firing 750 rounds per minute, and with a range up to 1,800 metres, sustained fire (SF) role, and mounted on a tripod, fitted with the C2 optical sight to provide ground troops with support cover when needed.

It felt oddly reassuring that if they were going to be involved in heavy-gunfire fighting, Kieran was glad to know the two men were up there and watching over them.

The British military ground troops were carrying SA80 rifles, some with UGLs, Minimis, and other heavy machinery transported into place.

There was a cautious atmosphere; everyone was filled with nervous excitement at the thought of something BIG happening today. And the civilians knew it too. It was as if they were afraid, and didn't want to be caught up in it.

It seemed to take forever as Kieran waited for the remaining forces to get in place. Standing by for orders, his eyes observing, and vigilant of his surroundings, his ears picking up every sound amplified by every movement, intensified by the nervous adrenaline pumping through his entire body. Kieran was sure he wasn't the only man feeling this way.

Kieran watched the town's people going about with their busy, everyday lives. Something about the crowds made him uneasy. His gut instincts were warning him to be cautious, and his gut had not let him down before. Something felt amiss. It paid to keep his eyes and ears open.

Someone whistled from across the street. QRF (Quick Reaction Force) and ANA troops were finally set.

Jonesy waved, signalling with his hand, and his voice came down the line of his radio headpiece. "This is it."

Kieran checked the ammo of his SA80 rifle. He tapped the butt of his gun and answered. "Ready!" he confirmed along with the rest of the unit.

Members of the QRF had assembled to talk to a bunch of local people. The conversation seemed light and unthreatening, and the group of children continued playing in the street. One of the children had found an old ball, which they used as a football and kicked it while others cheered. It was good to see the children at play, but this wasn't the right time. What was more surprising was the QRF didn't appear to be in a hurry to move the children on.

Just before 0600 hours Kieran observed a lone, young boy busily working in the street. He'd been moving a wheelbarrow from one new build to another for a couple of hours. The boy of about 13 years of age pushed the wheelbarrow along the road and rested close to where the QRF was standing. The boy paused for a break and looked up for no more than a blink of the eye. Without warning, a bomb he was carrying was detonated, causing a massive explosion in the wheelbarrow, and instantly killing a group of civilians, including some of the children that had been so happy playing.

It was then all hell had broken loose. As if the boy had been the trigger for the Taliban to attack while the troops had been distracted by the explosion — catching them off guard.

The insurgent's' tactics showed they were equally prepared for war. Large groups of Taliban fighters began to attack from all sides: intense, full-on frontal attacks as they threw grenades directly at the men and to cut off the town entirely.

The British forces were there to support the newly trained ISAF against the insurgents, but they too had now become engaged in open warfare to protect themselves in combat.

The Taliban made direct attacks at the British-held compound with not more than a ten feet wall to separate them from the insurgents — attacking the troops with RPGs and small mortar rounds, and often engaged in bouts of small arms fire at close quarter combat.

In the midst of confusion, the militants armed with a rocket grenade fired it onto the rooftop at the two soldiers covering sniper fire, killing them both instantly and taking out their vantage point.

The observation posts and changeovers suffered severely; each man put himself in the direct line of fire as they found themselves being a constant target for the fighters to aim for.

Without rooftop cover they were now relying on mortar firepower set up behind a low compound wall. It proved to be sufficient to a degree. The only drawback was it needed two men operating indirect fire weapons. The positive side was it was able to provide accurate explosive mortar — the long-range L16A2 81 cannon, covering maximum 5,650 metres, permitting disengagement efficiently, to move swiftly to set up a new active-firing position.

The cannon proved useful to say the least.

Taliban casualties were a considerable number. At this point, the insurgents increased their attacks with mortars, RPGs, and sniper fire putting up a front. The Taliban were here to fight to the death, at whatever the cost. And the loss was devastating for everyone involved, with an increased chance of getting injured or killed.

It became all too clear from the off — A Company did not have the troops or the air support to hold off the constant heavy barrage of firepower from the Taliban attacks.

"Man down! Man down!" came the desperate cry from the radio headset.

A mortar shell hit a Vector, causing a massive explosion in the north-eastern outskirts of Sangin. Three of the unit were returning from a patrol during which they came under vicious enemy fire when a mortar struck their Vector vehicle.

Lance Corporal Ashley 'Benny' Benson, Private Callum Wallis and Private Tony 'Rose' Simpson were all blown from the Vector as it instantly burst into flames on impact.

Lance Corporal Ashley *'Benny'* Benson had been hit directly on the head from a fragment of the hull of the burning Vector as it hurled large chunks of metal and rubber through the air, seriously injuring the two other men as the wreckage came crashing down. The Taliban fighters fired directly at the soldiers, pinning the three men down close to a derelict building leaving them no room for escape from the inferno.

Benny, 20 years of age, had only been with A Company for two weeks after returning from training, earning his sniper badge. He loved being a sniper as much as he loved being in the army. Benny was an excellent shot, and was so proud to be a British soldier. The three men were airlifted to Camp Bastion to the ISAF hospital by emergency response helicopter, but sadly Benny did not survive. Despite Private Wallis's injuries he survived, but was medically discharged.

With so much intense fighting the men had no chance to mourn the loss of their friend as the battle continued.

The fighting continued throughout July and into August, as the routine patrols faced the increased danger of newly planted IEDs and road bombs that were continually set during the night by insurgents and which claimed casualties almost every day. By the end of three days of intense battle, the town had virtually collapsed through the destruction of fierce fighting. Along with the high cost of casualties came a ceasefire.

Sangin mourned the death toll of the civilian people and children as they were laid out. The covering of so many innocent bodies lying dead in the street and so many injured was more than Kieran could take. The accurate count was not known as to how many Taliban died as a result of the fierce fighting. The insurgents blamed the loss of civilian lives on the British troops and claimed to kill 17 men of the ANA and ISAF.

A few days into the ceasefire, morale suffered a blow at the news of other British soldiers in the north facing a standoff against large numbers of Taliban. Cut off from reinforcements and much-needed supplies the troops were undoubtedly down on their luck.

For A Company, this sudden inactivity meant they spent the first couple of days cleaning up, making brews and cooking unmentionable concoctions on campfires from whatever food rations were considered edible, and clearing away debris.

To lighten the mood Captain Dan decided to rally round the men in the search for ideas to relieve the boredom by suggesting a sing-a-long after evening scoff. The men wanted to test their physical strength in a sports contest; one other suggestion was an emptying the cesspit of human excrement by hand without vomiting competition.

The other idea was to retrieve the burnt-out wreckage of the Vector and make a sculpture out of any salvageable bits they could recover — a job they'd put off until now. Pieces of metal, rubber and engine fragments of the Vector were strewn all over the compound in the explosion during the heavy firefighting, and the lads had been keen enough to do the clear up. But the promise of a reward by way of the CO buying the first round of beers for the winner when they hit UK soil was too tempting to refuse.

It was the first time the men had seen the wreckage since the ceasefire. What visibly remained of the Vector through the debris and metallic body wasn't much. The bullets had left a shower of indentations in the armoured sides and the RPG had blown the undercarriage and engine entirely to smithereens, taking all the latest techno equipment inside with it, costing the taxpayers thousands. By the end of the day, it left the men in no doubt that there was nothing left to salvage.

There was no question about it, Kieran didn't envy the report 'Ty' was going to have to write about the demise of the newly assigned PPV Vector and the loss of the taxpayers' money. And what once was a state-of-the-art PPV now stood as a large, upright sculpture resembling a giant finger posed in an obscene gesture. It stood on the roof of the main building, pointing in the direction of the town — 'Up yours Taliban' was painted on it.

Disturbing intel also positively confirmed heavy firefighting in the north had increased, and the Taliban had regained control of Musa Qala and surrounding areas. With the growing concern of shortage of boots on the ground, medical support and equipment, it wasn't difficult to realise that a full-scale operation was the only way to relieve the garrison. The men were weary and had suffered losses, but most of all, they felt they were sitting targets for the Taliban to attack.

It was Major *'Ty'* Morgan that informed Captain Dan Hale that the troops were no longer going to wait for the Taliban to come and pick them off — the British Army was going to take the fight to them.

With the ceasefire, it was decided instead of the entire platoon travelling en masse to the remote British FO (outpost) Inkerman, north-east of Sangin in the *Green Zone*, and without making a move too conspicuous, or leaving the compound unprotected, each section would again send a small band of men on designated foot patrols. Their active role was to send out small infantry patrols to cover the district and surrounding area.

On arrival of the first men, one thing was clear to them as they viewed the remote compound, exhausted and hungry — "the place is a top prize, fucking shit hole" was the radio message relayed.

Unfortunately, there were no mud or brick huts, and the area was covered in filth and offered no other security protection but the perimeter walls.

Despite the ten-mile trek the men had just done, they set to, storing away any supplies and equipment they'd carried with them, before making preparations to make the compound secure before the rest of A Company arrived.

Finally, it was Kieran's turn. When he arrived, Inkerman Garrison was a hive of activity. Within a day, the soldiers took over the centre building in the compound, set up an Ops room, and erected three sangers as vantage points, spotting at least five Taliban fire-points pointing directly at the British garrison.

Orders were simple — the men were to cover a 24/7 operation to patrol irrigation sites to protect the workers. Allowing the aid workers to lay a pipeline to connect water to the remote areas to improve the quality of life. The soldiers gave a presence to reassure the people.

Most of the time the rest of the men spent their days involved in continuous enemy contact surrounded by insurgent fire. The troops were continually under attack. The Taliban hit the garrison and guarded outposts with small arms, RPGs, mortars and 105 mm recoilless rifles along with the AK-47 rifles. Engaged in repeated heavy fighting with the Taliban, despite fierce opposition and struggle, the troops continued their advance, clearing the Juysalay area of Helmand Province, and pushed them north and forced them out of the Sangin Valley. The insurgents, who chose to stand their ground and fight, were decisively defeated at the cost of lives.

Shortage of troops and air support became held up when severe firefighting broke out across Op Afghanistan, stretching the infantry and resources to the max.

Taliban raids increased around Inkerman, Sangin Valley in the north. And due to the remote location, nothing could be done to assist the men; the platoon would have to hold on until supplies could reach Inkerman garrison. They were on their own.

They were armed with only what they had brought with them, which included .50 HMG (Heavy Machine Gun) mounted on tripods, and placed in three prime positions to protect the compound. Also included were GPMGs and sniper L115A3 long-range rifles, which had deadly accuracy when engaged in long-range shots in support of the British Army issue SA80 guns.

Kieran was out on patrol with Platoon Sergeant Jonesy and eight others heading for an irrigation plant when they came under direct attack. As AK-47s fired repeated rounds at them, followed by mortar fire, the sound of rapid fire sent men diving for cover where they stood. The men tried to take cover in the nearby irrigation ditch — but all hell broke loose at the explosion of an IED. The blinding flash, dust and smoke of the roadside bomb explosion had been less than a few metres in front of Kieran. He was acting point man to the captain, and armed with his SA80, was blown flat on his back, and although winded — thankfully — was unharmed.

He was in more danger lying out in the open, covered in the dust and rubble from the dirt road track with Jonesy, both men firing their SA80s. Taking a quick look around him, judging by the firepower, mortar shells and RPGs — they were under attack. He knew he wasn't in the safest position. "Fuck me!" *He might as well have a Taliban target on his back.*

At the first opportunity, Kieran made a move to take cover, half-expecting Jonesy to follow him to the nearby ditch — but Jonesy wasn't behind him. "Fuck!"

This wasn't looking good.

Then came the words he dreaded most. "Man down! Man down!"

Kieran heard another "Man down!"

Radio chatter confirmed Sergeant Andy Jones, "Jonesy is down!". He was injured when he stepped too close to another IED, which severely

249

wounded him in the leg and instantly killed another soldier in the blast. Jonesy was pretty messed up and had part of the flesh blown off from his knee downwards, including leaving a gaping hole in his thigh with fragments of explosive embedded.

Private Tommy Thompson suffered from head wounds and even though the men did everything they could, Tommy had died at the scene.

The men fought back from their position with everything they had brought with them. Engaged with enemy fire for more than two hours, the Taliban hit them continuously with every weapon they had — bullet after bullet and mortar shells rained down on them again and again, with no lull in their attack. The radio was alive with activity requesting air support for the five men wounded. Unluckily for the men, there were no free aircraft available to carry out air support. Nothing could be done to help them at this time.

As quickly as the barrage had started, it ceased.

All Kieran could hope for was that the bastards had run out of ammo and decided to make a quick exit.

Kieran, adrenalin reeling from the attack, looked over at the scattered and injured men, taking in that it was quiet enough for them to help Jonesy and check on the other wounded men.

Four British soldiers were injured pretty seriously, and one had lost his life during that day of the siege — his unit lost comrades they had known only a few weeks.

For the first time, Kieran felt sick to his stomach.

Eventually, Jonesy was airlifted to HQ Camp Bastion along with the rest of the men in need of medical treatment. Jonesy was operated on for 13 hours, and he managed to survive. Kieran had been hugely relieved to hear that while Sergeant Andy *Jonesy* Jones had sustained devastating leg injuries he was now making a rapid recovery.

Despite the respite, that wasn't the end. The next day things took a turn for the worse causing the garrison to be on lockdown.

Kieran observed, at first, the ground attacks were random — a single-round shooter would pop up like a meerkat, try their hand and then fuck off into the nearest hole, or small groups would come at them with about five or six men, and try their luck at firing RPG mortar at the sangers. The attacks were poorly organised and not in any order at this point and inaccurate, counting the number of pot-shots hitting the perimeter walls.

That all changed when the Taliban hit the garrison with a surprise attack — hitting them with intense fire and heavily armed, engaged fighting with every weapon the Taliban had.

Major 'Ty' took to the Ops room leaving 'Captain Dan' in charge of the front line. For a clear view of the action, Dan took up position in one of the sangers to support the defence stronghold and ordered everyone to take cover behind the perimeter wall.

With A Company down in numbers, the platoon was now severely undermanned and spent most days involved in enemy contact, sometimes for hours, surrounded by enemy fire from all sides. The Taliban hit the troops hard and fast. The men continually held off insurgent attacks as they frequently attacked the compound and manned outposts with small arms including semi-automatic pistols, RPGs, machine guns, with 105 mm recoilless rifles along with the AK-47 rifles, often emptying a full magnum into the compound wall.

Kieran knew, just like the rest of the platoon, their biggest problem was the constant firing of fucking inaccurate mortar fire from RPGs.

There was no denying the insurgents had upped their game and were hitting A Company with a continued barrage of mortar launched at them throughout the day. They lurked in every mouse hole and ditch, enabling them to get close to the compound virtually unseen to engage in close-range fire. Their aim was simple — take out anyone going about their duties inside the garrison.

Despite the increased heavy fighting, and being under intense firing from large groups of Taliban surrounding the base from all sides, and taking into account that the men were largely outnumbered at least 4 to 1, the garrison returned fire. The men fought hard, but after hours of enemy firefighting, the biggest concern was — would the ammo last until supplies could reach them?

Armed with only what they had brought with them, which included .50 HMG mounted on tripods, placed in three prime positions to protect the compound on top of mounted sandbags to reinforce the sangers. Also included was GPMG Mortar 81 mm mortar, an indirect fire weapon capable of firing high explosives with deadly accuracy when engaged in long-range shots, in support with the standard British Army issue SA80 rifles, but Kieran knew that supplies were desperately low.

Initially 30 strong, sickness and injuries now reduced the platoon to around 20 men, who were now heavily pinned down by constant enemy fire, desperately lacking equipment and living on basic rations — which wasn't much — with the fear of troops becoming severely dehydrated by running out of fresh water to drink. They were now reduced to living on emergency daily rations of Pot Noodles. Urgent, distressing reports were relayed back to Camp Bastion during the constant assault that the soldiers at Inkerman garrison were suffering from exhaustion and facing challenging, ongoing situations.

Rescue attempts were sent to relieve the soldiers, but each met with failure.

While the men waited for reinforcements and supplies, the garrison was reduced to basic emergency rations to stay alive. To make matters worse, ammunition and equipment were now severely depleted, with virtually no night vision due to lack of batteries, and emergency ammo was also critically low.

On the north side of the compound came a round of RPG mortar fire hitting the main sanger full on. The shell ripped through the reinforced box as if it was paper, causing a massive explosion as the men were blown from the sanger. Due to the severity at what had happened, the men closest to the area ran to help. They had to wait for the smoke to clear and the fire to be extinguished before they could assess the damage and recover the wounded.

The mortar shell had hit Dan and he was in bad shape. Covered in blood, his wounds gave off the smell of smoke, gunpowder and burning flesh, and he looked to be in horrific pain, but luckily, he was alive. And while the mortar fire injured six others, Dan refused morphine so he could keep a clear head until all the men under his command had received first aid treatment.

Air support of a Chinook helicopter was requested to evacuate the injured along with urgently needed medical assistance, but it was unable to assist immediately due to heavy fighting in the north. There was no mistaking the urgency as the men were in dire need of reinforcements.

Refusing to leave his men facing the enemy alone without a leader, despite his injuries, Dan returned to the fighting, his men being his primary concern. For a man in such a crap state, he held it together for some time. It became evident to a few of the men that Dan was gradually weakening under the pressure of his wounds and was fading in and out of consciousness.

The men worked tirelessly to save his life, and attended to him best they could, but with no medical officer, their knowledge was limited. Moments later Captain Dan was dead. Only the day before he'd delivered a touching tribute at the loss of their friend and comrade, Private Tommy Thompson. The entire unit mourned their leader and the death of a great friend.

The situation was now critical. By the time a rescue mission could be mounted — it was clear to the reinforcements — A Company had fought courageously under adverse conditions.

Their platoon suffered nine fatalities during their deployment. The cost of fallen comrades and brothers in arms was a high price to pay. Quietly and respectfully, A Company mourned the loss of their closest of friends.

When it was over — things were never the same.

Chapter Sixteen

Afghanistan 2018

So this is it. Back to where it all started, Kieran thought.

Quietly, shoulder to shoulder, he observed the rest of the troops around him. The Hercules C-130 was packed to the hilt with every portable piece of equipment the soldiers could carry, along with 98 fully-armed personnel.

Looking out of the Hercules window at the vast sandy, arid land, he sat taking in the view between Helmand and Kandahar provinces in the south-western region of Afghanistan, and below him were the mountains stretching far into the north.

The monotony of dry sand went on for miles, broken only by occasional patches of green land — an oasis *'green zone'* and irrigation ditches and muddy wadi. If the return deployment was anything like last time, it made him wonder how people could live in such decimated land, with sparse vegetation, let alone the terror of insurgent attacks.

In a few hours, thankfully, they were going to land at Kandahar under cover of darkness, as the aircraft were prime targets in daylight, and risks of being shot down in mid-flight were still high. A few more minutes and they would be flying in under total darkness, all internal blinds would be closed ten minutes prior to the final descent.

Kieran didn't give much thought to the RAF until he got to look first- hand at some of the stressful, life-challenging situations they faced each flight. He'd considered them a means to an end, and never thought of them other than self-absorbed, glorified chauffeurs, carting kit and supplies backwards and forwards, taxiing from one airbase to another. But it wasn't like that at all. Any aircraft landing and taking off were constant sitting targets for the Taliban. And the bigger the aircraft, the better the goal for the Taliban to hit. The Chinook helicopters were often at the frontline and continuously came under attack.

During an assault on Musa Qala, one particular harrowing story he heard was of a Royal Marine helicopter pilot, who came under attack when attempting to evacuate wounded from enemy territory. While flying in *'fast and low'*, the aircraft came under direct fire by the Taliban and was hit by ground fire. The rescue mission had to be stopped. On return to Camp Bastion they found four rounds had hit the aircraft, and one of the rotor blades was severely damaged. But the pilot, despite this, managed to land the helicopter safely. Undeterred, the pilot refused to leave the wounded behind, and he returned with another aircraft. Despite being under renewed heavy Taliban fire he airlifted the injured.

Yep, Kieran had to admit he had respect for those flyboys.

"I don't get you, Romeo."

He folded the letter he was holding and looked at the man sitting to the right of him. "What the fuck are you talking about, Jacko?" Liam *'Jacko'* Jackson was a 36-year-old northern lad from South Shields. He joined the army after being made redundant from his factory job where he was making car panels. He found the job mundane and wanted to travel. Single, and he liked to keep it that way. The army gave him the freedom and excitement he loved.

Jacko manoeuvred in his seat and picked up one of the pieces of paper from the open folder lying on Kieran's knee that had held his friend's full attention since leaving Brize. He didn't care what the platoon sergeant thought of him, but he was going to have a chat with him. Romeo O'Neill couldn't go on like this.

"You know," Jacko started, "ever since you got word that woman was located in Kabul, you've been in another world. You need to snap out of it and move on. She's fucked you over, mate."

Kieran snorted. "You don't know what the fuck you are talking about. This is none of your fucking business, and can I suggest that you leave me the fuck alone."

"Hold it! I'm thinking of you. Whatever it is she did to you has fucked you up good and proper. It's been ten years, mate! You know what the rest of think — time to move on!"

"Enough! I'm OK." He punched the holdall in front of him, and with a few verbal comments in response.

Jacko laughed. "OK. Sorry, Sergeant." The anger in Kieran's voice went a long way from reassuring Corporal '*Jacko*' Jackson. Maybe Kieran needed to find her, and then perhaps he might be able to heal himself. And O'Neill had lost some good mates back in 2007, and he desperately needed some closure and understanding of losing his girl too. Guess it was hard to come back from all that happened. "I guess you know what you're doing with this girl, you dumb fuck."

"And her name is Sophie, and she's not just any girl."

"They are all just girls, mate. Lose one, the next one is pretty much the same as the last."

Kieran shook his head in disagreement, said nothing and went back to reading the newspaper in front of him. He glanced over at the discarded papers on his reading pile, which were failing to capture his attention. There was no denying, Kieran felt an emptiness in his life. His thoughts were of the lives lost in 2007, and he wondered how many more lives would be lost, or remained untouched by the tragedy of this war on terror that seemed impossible to win. The surviving men he'd bonded with on that deployment dealt with the hell they'd lived through in their own way.

The major — '*Ty*' Morgan-Davies finished his tour and resigned his commission on medical grounds. No matter how many times the men invited Ty — he never did turn up to join them for a celebratory get-together pint. Jonesy did suggest he'd taken Captain Dan's death hard. To lose so many fine soldiers was something he found hard to face.

As for the rest — they remained in touch as often as they could and their jobs allowed.

Jonesy stayed in the army and was posted to Canada as a senior instructor, where he met his Canadian wife, Amy. He spent his time between raising a family, training and flittering back to the UK for army recruitment drives. Along with the occasional drink with the lads to talk about the *good old days* where most of them just sat around the table and didn't really speak that much about it at all. They toasted their lost brothers and shared their funny stories as if to keep their fallen brothers' memories alive, as if it was an unwritten code of honour between the men. No one ever spoke of the real trauma, or the ordeal they had lived through as they had fought so valiantly and survived against remarkable odds.

Corporal Steve *'Drews'* Andrews and Lance Corporal Simon *'Si'* Parker saw out their time and turned their skills to work in private security in Qatar as bodyguards to the wealthy. They were doing really well too. Travelling the world and protecting the rich and famous and getting well paid for it also if the stories Si and Drews told were anything to go by.

Ginger, Lance Corporal Matt Hayes, like Kieran, stayed with the platoon. He was now a corporal. *Ginger* eventually got a date with a school teacher from York and married her two months after their first date. They now had three kids.

While *Easty*, Lance Corporal Ben Eastman, the once baby of the section, was now a marksman and still with the unit. He jumped at the chance to return to Afghanistan, as long as they didn't give him Pot Noodles to eat was his only stipulation.

Despite everything that happened to the mates lost and injured — Kieran considered himself as a British soldier and proud of it. He was doing the job he had trained for and loved. He couldn't see himself doing anything else.

The Hercules started to lose altitude at that moment. It was now time for him along with the rest of his unit to join the several build-ups of troops in preparation for the *'peacekeeping'* deployment. And judging by the history of previous battles in the area, he was going to have to keep his wits about him to keep the peace.

The first impression was that Camp Bastion had changed a great deal since his last deployment. The camp had grown tremendously, not just in troop movement, but there were now fast food restaurants and pizza houses and the place was a bustling metropolis. No doubt about it — things were certainly different — and for the better — but time would tell.

A week later, Camp Bastion was buzzing with activity and whispers of a *'spring offence'* carried out by the Taliban. Launching a string of attacks on Kabul killing 71 people and injuring hundreds in the process, the Taliban and Haqqani network carried out the assaults.

To make matters worse, Kabul was not only the capital of Afghanistan but by far the largest developing city in the eastern province, situated in one of the densely populated trading and thriving neighbourhoods known. More importantly, it occupied some of the most significant military and government buildings located directly in the centre of town.

During the entire month of April, the allied forces' top brass observed, attended briefings and inspected the incoming intel and updates on Taliban and militant activity. Whenever possible, the troops watched live video footage, sometimes distressing, as they observed disturbing activity. Images flashed across the whiteboard as what to learn from previous attacks in the area resulting in the cost of casualties, both military and civilian.

Even though the militants increased attacks on Kabul, the Afghan military and joint coalition forces carried out an estimated 19 counterterrorism attacks on the insurgents.

While the Afghan police force and the Afghan Army continued with the burning and destruction of opium poppy fields, there were growing concerns as other harmful illegal crimes exploiting the less fortunate people in Afghanistan grew.

As Kieran read through the intel provided by the ANA and AFP, he realised that the trafficking of people for sexual purposes was an illicit business and was thriving.

Often distressing reports filtered through of children between five and fifteen years of age that were frequently sold and trafficked through Pakistan for destinations in the Gulf and Iran. Elsewhere, children were sold as wives to men sometimes three or four times their age, or as prostitutes. Along with females, young boys were also trafficked through channels and regularly shipped to Saudi Arabia for sexual exploitation and other illegal purposes. Inhumane acts of neglect, abuse and violence against children often resulted in premature death, and very few reached adulthood.

Initial reports revealed that three of the primary ways people became drawn into trafficking usually stemmed from family poverty (family debt or drug addiction), young boys sold as sexual entertainment to wealthy men, and women offered the prospect of employment only to find them sold into prostitution. Victims of rape and forced prostitution tagged them under the Afghanistan law known as 'Zina' which condemns sexually exploited victims.

Young boy soldiers were sometimes promised enrolment in Islamic schools in Pakistan and Iran, but instead sexually exploited and trafficked to camps for paramilitary training.

Traffickers were often found actively running under the protection of corrupt police officers in many areas. No province was virtually left untouched by this. Troubling media news came through the government that border police officers would regularly take bribes from traffickers to allow them to cross borders with groups of people in tow.

Undercover media reports of inhumane acts came through that children deemed unfit to be sold (those aged 12 to 16) were used as suicide bombers by the Taliban. Some were tricked or forced to carry explosives and bombs detonated remotely. It was more commonly known that children were used as currency and bought and sold to satisfy the prolific degenerate desires of those in need. Regardless of world awareness, the Afghan government had seen minimal improvement in reduction of activity since the arrival of foreign aid workers, supported by NATO and coalition forces to central provinces in Afghanistan.

As the situation worsened, the coalition planned an 'Op' to arrest the traffickers and other militant groups, and to cut off their organised route by setting up Afghan military and civilian HQs for issuing IDs and erecting secure detention centres. Since the battle of Musa Qala, the increasing presence of coalition personnel and long-distance patrols raised new problems for the traffickers.

On the eve of the crackdown, the influx of 600 troops was redeployed to Kabul, with orders for the coalition and NATO troops to continue to southern Afghanistan, transported in helicopters, including the Chinook on loan from the Americans, Blackhawk troop carriers and escorted by Apache fighter helicopters. This manoeuvre was a significant part of the operation in support of the US troops and enabled them to move forward and advance with Afghan soldiers to prevent Taliban strikes on heavily protected sites.

Without the cost of more civilian lives, the military objective was to drive the Taliban and other militants, including Islamic State extremists, out of southern Afghanistan without forced combat, leaving a secure, fixed military presence in the area.

A NATO airstrike was launched on the Taliban in Musa Qala, killing Mullah Ghafour in February, and ten days later another airstrike killed a Taliban leader, Mullah Manan.

The Taliban was growing in numbers and reinforcements arrived for the insurgents, increasing the enemy's strength to 500 strong. Wanting revenge on the killings, the Taliban launched a string of attacks throughout southern Afghanistan; these insurgents had now changed tactics with some deadly results. The insurgents warned the media they planned to attack several spots in the city, including high-ranking military facilities, army convoys and crowded civilian areas. The cost of lives would be high.

Afghan Intelligence thwarted several attempts at suicide bombings to attack some government buildings and bases used by security forces in Kabul.

The first brutal attack was led by Taliban followers dressed in military uniform as they stormed a police compound south of Kabul, killing at least 41 people including a local police chief, and wounding many others in a fierce gun battle that lasted hours leaving chaos in their wake.

In Gardez, Paktia province, another severe attack followed when a suicide bomber detonated two car bombs outside the compound injuring around 100 people. The Taliban occupied two towers to inflict harm on civilians and police in the area. Around the same time, in Ghazni province, the Taliban claimed to have killed a further 25 government security officers and five civilians when a suicide bomber drove a vehicle into a government compound.

The Afghan intelligence agency revealed several other attacks, including smaller attempts at suicide bombings in Kabul, leaving a further 74 people dead.

The most determined assault by the insurgents was when a suicide bomber drove a laden ambulance filled with explosives. The Taliban drove past a police checkpoint in a secure zone, harming 600 people with another 158 people suffering injuries.

The US troops carried out a drone hit and were able to break through the Taliban defences, and this paved the way for the Afghan police to reinforce their defence positions. Regularly coming into conflict with the insurgents, a coalition airstrike killed a known Taliban leader, along with 20 of his followers.

Wanting to exact revenge, the Taliban leader, heavily armed, led a group of 200 to 300 militants and wreaked havoc on the town, executed elders and destroyed the government buildings in the process.

Although a further air strike killed at least 20 extremists, the Taliban remained in full force and inflicted anarchy on the people without empathy or fear. With continued control and mistreatment of the locals, while operating drug trafficking and tribal rivalries, it did not surprise anyone that the situation became volatile.

Later in February, in Kabul centre, a suicide bomber killed at least 95 people and injured 158 others in the capital. The Taliban carried out the deadliest attacks since killing hotel guests and staff when the insurgents drove an ambulance loaded with bomb explosives. A lone insurgent drove through a security checkpoint leading to a crowded shopping area filled with people on a Saturday lunchtime close to a hospital. The bomber, telling police he was taking a patient to the nearby hospital, exploded the bomb outside the second checkpoint between some government buildings and foreign embassies.

The aftermath of the explosion, on examining the number of dead bodies, was catastrophic. A mass of human scattered remains, many burnt, were caught in the blast, and due to the intensity of the blast, bodies could be found for almost a kilometre away. No one could understand how the Taliban had got through strict security checkpoints.

Afghanistan accused Pakistan of providing support to the attackers, and it was rumoured the US cut its security aid to Pakistan believing they failed to take action against the Taliban on Pakistan soil.

The scale of the attacks continued when 300 people were injured, and as many as 30 others were killed when a suicide attacker bombed a military HQ in Kabul in early spring. Security became breached when lorries loaded with a significant number of explosives rammed into the compound where Afghan military officials and government VIPs were situated.

In Tehran, over 100 Afghan police and soldiers were killed when ambushed by the Taliban insurgents close to the city of southern Helmand province when they tried to retreat from the fierce attack. When investigated, it raised the question — was this an insider attack? It wasn't the first time the insurgents had dressed as Afghan police to kill government workers.

The coalition and NATO forces joined in agreement with the Afghan government, and due to the intensified attacks, the Taliban carried out horrific offensives around the country and several attacks on the capital. Despite causing so many civilian deaths, the Taliban were increasingly using complex and suicide attacks in highly populated areas. The attacks continued, each one more sinister and deadly than the next.

The British forces had been trying to stabilise the situation since and before social media attention escalated the problem. It was a matter of time before the press picked up on the destruction and continuous and senseless killing of the people in Kabul.

In ten years, along with redeployments to Afghanistan, Kieran's platoon had conducted operations in Kuwait, Iraq, Sierra Leone, Bosnia, Cyprus, and now British forces were back, mainly on checkpoint duties, while others were in a joint Afghan mission to hunt down insurgent groups involved in known bomb-making and illegal people trafficking.

About 30 men in all returned to Kabul, and Rawlins' orders were simple: with a small platoon of British soldiers — *Support the ANA. Take down the Taliban stronghold. Crack down on the leaders, and finally decimate the traffickers by closing the chain, cutting off contacts.*

The platoon of men settled into a disused compound outside the town's limit, in direct line of the trafficker's primary link between the hills and surrounding villages. The idea behind the op was to remain as inconspicuous as possible. Rawlins was taking no chances of any info leaking of their mission and playing things very hush-hush.

In spite of the soldiers being dropped from Chinooks under cover of darkness, and staying clear of being drawn into provoked attacks, the locals seemed to know they were there as the men endured persistent attacks of small arms fire and rocket-propelled grenades.

By the end of the second week, things had eased off, and it was as if the town's people had lost interest in the British soldiers. It was as if the insurgents had realised the soldiers were staying put and going nowhere and attacks had ceased.

On Thursday, the men were called to the central part of Kabul to assist the ANP in a shooting. A lone Taliban shooter was reported to be perched on the rooftop of a four-storey nearby hotel firing random shots into the fleeing crowds.

The men arranged themselves inside the two heavily armoured Mastiffs and two armoured Foxhound Land Rovers. Now fully loaded with body armour jackets, rifles, rocket launchers, radios and all necessary kit to see the men over 24 hours, the troops were ready.

A kilometre from where the reported shooting had taken place, the men sat inside a metal sweatbox on wheels waiting for intel on the situation in Kabul city centre before they could make a move.

It was 1243 hours, and a media bus carrying journalists from a press conference had just exploded. At least seven people were confirmed dead, and many others injured.

Instantly, the men's orders changed. It became clear at that point that the lone shooter was a distraction, leaving the people unprepared and left reeling from a further attack.

"At the ready, men." Captain Henry Rawlins' voice came over their headsets. The view from the hull was far from a pretty sight, and the pungent smell of dead flesh stuck to his nostrils and turned his stomach. "Go!"

The doors of the Mastiff flew open, and the soldiers on board reacted instinctively. As soon as Kieran's boots hit the ground, he was nearly half-blinded by the number of lights flashing on emergency vehicles parked in the area, and overwhelmed by the chaos of the immense crowds of injured people wandering the streets and the uncovered dead bodies lying openly in the immediate area, as the ANP tried to identify and cover the remains.

Instinctively, Kieran's training kicked in. Without delay, he cornered off a perimeter and stopped a uniformed Afghan policeman getting any closer to the wreckage until IDs were confirmed.

Observing him thoughtfully, if anything, the man looked nervous as he searched his pockets for some ID and when he flashed his badge at Kieran with a smug smile, in the end, he let him through. Which saved Kieran the problem of pulling his gun on the policeman, because without the correct ID — there was no fucking way some unidentified person was getting any closer to the perimeter.

Chaos reigned as Kieran stood back far enough away not to let the policeman see him from his vantage point. Kieran watched closely as he jogged over to a small group of men who seemed to be more interested in the havoc it was causing than directing people safely away from the explosion. Which seemed odd behaviour for a man of his ranking.

Behind them, Kieran could see the bus laid on its side burning — the concentration of flames were most extensive in the centre undercarriage. Smoke billowed from inside where the seats used to be. Kieran realised no one could have survived that awful wreckage.

He drew his attention back to the crowd of uniformed men; sure, they had the valid ID, but something about their jovial manner didn't feel right, and it made them suspicious.

Kieran turned about, not to let them have a visual on him as he radioed Captain Rawlins. He was in no way near half the man 'Ty' was, but decent enough all the same, and until Jonesy' decided to return to the platoon as the new CO — Captain Rawlins was all the platoon were getting.

Some part of Kieran knew something was wrong. "I think we need to make an assessment," Kieran told the 'Captain' as he preferred.

Captain Rawlins looked over to where Kieran was stood, and then over his shoulder to where the group of men were standing, almost joyful in their stance. "Hang on." Captain Rawlins spoke into his radio again and waited for a response. "Afghan Security Forces are going to have a closer look."

It was hard for Kieran to imagine the insurgents were brazen enough to remain so close to admire such a devastating disaster. "OK," Kieran murmured. He turned his head back to the group. But where was he?

***

"Mohammad Yasin!" She couldn't believe what she was seeing. If she hadn't missed that press conference to follow up on a lead, she wouldn't have been here to see the horrifying news on TV. "Mohammad Yasin!" she confirmed again.

The TV provided footage of a group of men in military uniform entering a restricted area. The newscaster was saying the man in the clip

264

was wanted for questioning in an explosion. The newsreader went on to give details of the bombing of the media bus, and killing of her colleagues. As soon as she saw the clear shot of his face, she recognised him straight away.

The man was a known high-ranking Taliban leader from the northern province of Musa Qala; he was an escaped fugitive and wanted in connection with the bombing of the World Trade Center since 2003.

What was such a high-profile Iraqi-American terrorist doing here in Kabul?

What part did he play in an explosion of a bus carrying a group of journalists? Unable to dismiss the nagging thought she was missing something, she instantly went to her laptop and pulled up her info file on Mohammad Yasin.

Within a few hours — she had some answers. It had taken years, but she now had a complete record of his activities, knowing any of which could probably seal her death warrant.

She completely ignored the warning voice in her head. She was an intelligent and strong woman; she needed to keep it that way. Plus, she had far too much riding on something else without worrying about Mohammad Yasin and his motives for being in Kabul.

An hour later, she turned on the shower water to let it warm up before removing her clothes, and stepped under the warm spray. She got out of the shower a few minutes later and dried off, slipping on a pair of black leggings and a long T-shirt, dragging back her hair and securing it in a ponytail. She made herself a sandwich and a cup of tea, unable to bring herself to finish both. Seeing Mohammad's image on the screen had upset her more than she had thought.

Sophie went back to the kitchen to take her dishes to the sink. Something wasn't right — there was an uneasy feeling of being watched which engulfed her. In the stillness, her eyes glanced around the room. A figure of a man appeared before her. She opened her mouth to scream, when the arm of a different, second man came around and covered her mouth roughly. She began to struggle as hard as she could, wriggling and throwing her weight back against him. The hand clasped harder on her face and jerked her head to the side, exposing her neck. She felt a sharp prick as the second man injected her with something. Unable to fight any longer, she felt her body go limp.

***

Kieran was still at the site of the bombing, but it was growing late, and with forensic, special forces and firefighters on the scene, there wasn't much the army could do but sit tight. A few hours of this and the men would be ready for some kip. With the thought of some sleep, it wasn't surprising something came over the radio to interrupt those thoughts.

"O'Neill, I want you to assist Afghan Special Forces," Captain Rawlins ordered.

An hour later special forces were briefing a band of ten men from the Parachute regiment chosen in a secure location, while his section men waited for word on their next move.

"A British news reporter, Haley Henderson, has been kidnapped, and it's imperative we get her back alive. She has vital information that the Taliban would torture for — and kill her if they get it."

Fucking Great! The last time Kieran was involved in an Afghan Special Forces rescue operation of a journalist, it cost a life of a British soldier and above all a great mate.

Kieran remembered at the time, Afghan police and intelligence officers had repeatedly warned the journalist that it was too dangerous to go to the area, yet he was seen interviewing Afghans near the site of the bombed city. The journalist was warned to leave the area as the Taliban were on their way. He stayed, ignoring the warning, and was taken into captivity by the Taliban.

A rescue mission was launched to get the hostages back. The remoteness of the area made it impossible for the men to spring a surprise attack without being detected. Helicopters rope-dropped a small unit of soldiers in position. Firefighting instantly broke out, and a Taliban leader was killed in the battle along with two civilians. Although the freedom of the journalist was successful, a British soldier died during the firefight. Despite that, Kieran felt the journalist acted irresponsibly ignoring numerous warnings for his safety, so Kieran was less than enthusiastic to rush in and rescue another nosey journalist putting more soldiers;' lives at risk. It wasn't the only time either.

After that, it was no secret that Kieran disliked working with journalists. From what he'd experienced, they worked by their own rule, endangering lives at no thought to others, and often took unnecessary risks at the cost of soldiers' lives who were guarding them.

Five years ago, another American TV reporter was following the men on patrol and filming it as part of a documentary. When his men became pinned down by ambush fire, the reporter was told to take cover and stay down, but jumped out from the protection of a mud wall and started filming the Taliban firing at his men. Kieran was so fucked off with him when they finally managed to rescue the reporter from an irrigation ditch at the risk of his own safety.

Angry beyond words, Kieran rammed him up against the wall and told him if he ever pulled a stunt like that again — he was on his own. No way was he about to put any soldier's life at risk to save a thrill seeker, and some body bag chaser wasn't worth taking a bullet for. Kieran had to admit — the journalist was a lot more cautious after that.

Now, it seemed he was about to risk his neck again. On top of that, the man that Kieran had spotted dressed in a military uniform after the bombing was on the UN most wanted list.

There had been no word or sighting of him until he was located that afternoon, leaving a hotel, carrying a woman unable to walk on her own. A white woman with long, dark-brown hair. The officer in charge slid a picture across his desk. "Her name is —"

"Sophie Tyson!" His face froze, and Kieran looked the officer in charge directly in the eye. "We have to get her back before he kills her."

The officer nodded. "I intend to get her back before he can get that far."

Chapter Seventeen

"Make yourself comfortable." Mohammed Yasin motioned to the chair in the house.

"I can't do that very easily now can I, considering you have my hands tied up behind my back like this?" Sophie said. She didn't appreciate his hostage humour much.

It didn't matter how luxurious the house appeared, she'd never be comfortable as long as Mohammed Yasin held her prisoner here. Especially a man she considered a dangerous killer that had grown prosperous trading in opium and trafficking people.

With a curt nod to the man beside her, with a single swish of the blade, Sophie shrank back at the sight of the long, gleaming knife. He lifted the edge up to her throat. One minute he had been talking to her and the next he had jerked her to him and pressed the knife to Sophie's throat. Sophie's eyes were wide in terror as she felt the point of the knife pinching her neck.

From behind, one of the men grabbed her shoulder and turned her to face the second bearded man at her side. He smiled at her discomfort, and at that moment she remembered where she had seen him. With a short tug, her hands were free. He replaced the knife in the sheath on his belt and concentrated on her movements.

Despite her surroundings, it felt good to have her hands free again. The return of blood flow to Sophie's hands sent pins and needles rushing into her arms, causing her to rub her wrists to massage the pain away.

Sophie was about to say something, but without a word and another nod to the two men guarding her, they led her out.

By the looks on their faces, it would have been pointless trying to refuse to go with them. Shaking her head, she remembered the pinpricks in her neck and was still fuzzy from the drugs they'd given her, but she tried to get her bearings. At one point, Sophie could have sworn they had gone below ground. One thing was sure, she wasn't in the expensive part of the house now.

As the solid wooden door opened with a creak, it became evident to her that Mohammad Yasin's hospitality was short-lived, as they pushed her inside a darkened room with no window, a concrete floor and nothing more than a dirty blanket in the corner.'

"She is going to give us trouble," said the first.

"I will deal with her."

Something about his voice sounded familiar to her. Then it was clear. She had seen him before — the Intercontinental Hotel attack — over ten years ago.

Before she realised his intention, a fist flew in her midsection.

Doubled over in pain, she heard the two men laugh as they pushed her inside. She was now terrified and she shrank back against the solid brick wall. They slammed the door on her leaving Sophie in total darkness. Darkness surrounded her and seemed to suffocate her.

Trying not to panic, she rattled her fuzzy brain to try and remember how she came to be here. Nothing. She felt nausea rush over her, and her head felt muzzy as she attempted to clear her mind to assess her situation. Nothing. It was useless. No doubt the drugs they had given her were still active in her system.

Listening to the men talking, she understood enough to know the two men spoke Urdu, which was strange considering Mohammad Yasin was Iraqi-American. All three men were dark, wearing beards with granite-like features that could be easily mistaken to be Afghan.

After what felt like hours later, the men came back, and she forgot all about the pain in her stomach. "What do you want with me?" They ignored her question and grabbed Sophie by her arms; they dragged her through the door.

Not wanting to run the risk of another punch, she went with them willingly. Trying to focus, she looked around to take in as many details of her surroundings as possible. Panic wasn't going to get her anywhere; she might as well put her mind to use.

They went down a long, dark hallway before a door opened to the outside. They went straight over a gravelled area and passed a large glass summerhouse with marble veranda, following a pebbled pathway to the entrance of a much larger house.

There was no mistaking the large guns on the rooftop guarding the premises on all sides. And this left Sophie in no mind that any thought of trying to save herself and risking escape was useless. They let her inside the house through the back door.

Inside the house, everyone she had seen was wearing an ammunition belt and carrying a firearm of sorts, walking about checking equipment and loading guns. There was no doubt about it — they were making ready for something big.

There was no mistaking that the house was beautiful, but despite the enormous white, painted marble pillars, some Grecian statues placed on the blue, mosaic marble flooring of the large entrance, and beautiful, decorative tapestries that hung from the walls — it all resembled a garish interpretation of the Parthenon.

The two men escorted her into a room that was smaller, and very formal.

Mohammad Yasin rose from his chair. "My men have brought you here to answer my questions. And the sooner you answer those questions, the better for you."

"I don't understand why you needed to kidnap me?"

He spoke in English, but his accent was thick. He continued, "You have some information for me. I want it."

"I'm sorry. I don't know what you are talking about. What information?"

"I shouldn't play stupid with me if I were you."

"What do you want from me?"

His sigh was impatient. "You have become too interested in my business. I think even you know my operation has made its money from opium for many years. But my primary source has come from transporting of people. For some time, you have been investigating my buyers, and aid workers were asking awkward questions." He laughed before adding smugly, "They can no longer answer your questions. I have ridden myself of those termites."

Sophie sucked in a breath as she now realised, he wasn't telling her this so she could be released.

Mohammad's reputation for being a brutal killer was known as well as his reputation for being ruthless. She understood just how much danger she was in.

His smile made her skin crawl. "I see you understand the situation." He stepped closer; his eyes focused on her and he touched her cheek. "I want the information you compiled on my businesses and the traitors that turned against me."

"I've spoken to many people about several stories; I don't keep all my research."

"I would think you would know better than to try and give me your journalist lies."

"I'm not lying."

He shrugged, giving an exaggerated sigh. "You know, I tried to think this wouldn't be necessary after the bus explosion. I thought I had got rid of you when I instructed that bomb. Instead, I killed everyone but you. Oh well, fewer journalists and their lies to worry about."

Sophie cringed at those words. She pulled her head away, and Yasin's eyes narrowed. "You killed all those innocent people?"

"No journalist is innocent."

"Why?"

"You — I thought I had got rid of you and all the evidence during the hotel fire ten years ago," he continued. "But the military intervening came to your rescue sadly. So this time, I thought planting an explosive would destroy you and whatever evidence you were hiding."

"I'm not hiding anything."

"I'm curious as to why you lie to me."

"Why am I here?"

"For the evidence you are hiding." He touched her cheek again. "How long you live is up to you." And shrugged.

"You were supposed to die in that bombing; I did not expect you not to be on the bus. The search of your hotel room revealed nothing."

"What more can I tell you?"

"Once I knew you were alive, I wanted my questions answered. I want names of the people who turned against me. And this time no one will find you. I had you taken to someone else's home. No one is looking for you."

"I don't have the information you want."

His backhand knocked her to the floor. The force of his hand sent her head spinning, and she could feel the intense heat of a bruise already forming on her cheek. Sophie was sure she could taste blood in her mouth.

Before she had a chance to stand, one of the guards punched her in the stomach; he laughed as she staggered back in pain. "Please don't insult my intelligence with useless lies of 'I don't have the information'. It won't help you." Almost immediately the other guard pulled her upright by her hair.

He yanked her head back; his face was inches from her own. His eyes narrowed and his voice was almost menacing as he spoke. "Let me make myself clear — I want the names of the people you spoke to. What evidence do you have?" He grabbed her jaw and squeezed it painfully. She felt tears sting her eyes. "To refuse me would be a mistake. I doubt such a small, delicate thing as you would' survive long under the interrogation I save for the more deserving." He released her face. "Being a woman will not save you," he threatened.

"I did save some research, but it's not on a computer. It's hardcopy."

Another cruel yank of her hair. "Where is it? Tell me!"

Yasin nodded at the man standing behind her holding her hair. He brought her arm behind her back in a cruel twist that had Sophie cry out in pain. "One word from me and he will break your arm, so I would think carefully before you answer if I were you."

"I'm telling you the truth."

"Did you give copies to anyone?"

"No. I promise. The only printed copy is kept in the hotel safe along with my laptop."

Mohammad looked at her for a long moment, apparently satisfied that she was telling him the truth, then shook his head at the man, who let her go and pushed her away from him. She rubbed her aching arm as she glared at him.

"I believe you. I will send someone to collect the information. I'm sure you are aware of what will happen to you if I discover you are lying to me."

Sophie shuddered, and Yasin and the two men laughed.

He ran a finger down her cheek again, and Sophie felt repulsed by his touch, and she pulled back. Instantly the humour was gone, and in response he slapped her face.

His finger trailed down her shoulder, and Sophie looked away. "I think I shall hold off on killing you — until I have what I want. No need to be in a hurry to kill you. I might have other more pleasurable uses for you."

"You mean pleasurable — like when you force young girls and boys into prostitution?"

There was no mistaking the hard rage in his face. "Difficult situations force people to make drastic decisions. I just happen to make a profit helping these people."

"By killing them or slavery?"

Sophie didn't care if he beat her again; there was no way she was giving up the details of her informants. People had risked their lives to talk with her, and she hoped her investigative story would make a difference. There was no way Sophie was going to turn against them. Besides, people had died to help her.

Sophie struggled not to throw up there and then. He turned back to his two men.

"Take her back."

It was dark outside as the two men returned her to her room. No doubt it was too late for the insurgents to get into the hotel without being detected by the army guards on the building. She was hopefully safe until morning.

"Maybe we should get the information out of her," said the first bearded guard.

Sophie choked back a sob; inevitably they wouldn't harm her without Yasin's orders. The thought of these men touching her was all too much for her to take. She was alone, hungry, thirsty, still fuzzy-headed from the drugs they'd given her, ached all over and never felt so exhausted. The first man ran a hand over her breasts as she tried to step around him. She slapped his hand away in disgust, making the other man laugh.

Her action only angered the man, and he threw her to the floor. He kicked her in the back with brute force. Sophie cried out in pain and tried to crawl away, but as much as she tried to get out of harm's way it was useless as he kicked her again. She rolled away trying to protect herself; it was useless. With one hand he grabbed the front of her T-shirt and brought her torso up to knee height. A swipe of his hand and he backhanded her face.

"When Mohammad has finished with you, and he gives you to his men, you will be praying for death," he cursed, and threw her to the ground.

And as much as she wanted not to believe him, she knew he spoke the truth. With a deep intake of breath, he struck her again, and a cloud of darkness came over her.

***

This was not how Kieran had thought he'd go into this kind of hostage situation.

But as he was the one who could ID Sophie personally, he didn't have much choice. Finding her dead was something he couldn't comprehend, and it turned his gut into knots, and thoughts of such would not help Sophie in the least. No — he needed to be professional and concentrate on the mission at hand.

Kieran and the rest of the team studied the intel that had come in about Mohammad Yasin's position, which was a large house that the insurgents had taken over forcing the owner to leave everything behind and take refuge at a neighbour's home.

Looking over the plans of the house and position of where Sophie was being held captive left minimal tactical advantage for the men to go in guns blazing. Using night cover the team would be rope-dropped, hitting the property at 2 am. It would be risky, but it was their only chance before they moved location or worse — killed Sophie.

As part of a special forces and ANA joint effort, 'Captain' knew Kieran spoke Pashto, while Rawlins spoke Dari, and that's what they were doing here. Kieran studied Rawlins. He hadn't known the man long, so he didn't know the other man spoke Dari. Kieran raised a questionable brow. "You do, Captain?"

Rawlins shrugged. "I know the important stuff," and proceeded to say something.

Kieran didn't want to explain he understood most of what he said; Kieran was sure Captain Rawlins had told him — *he was pretty and asked if he'd like to spend the night.*

Everyone laughed, and Kieran rolled his eyes at Rawlins and in return he said, "You couldn't afford me."

Despite the humour, the situation was severe, and every soldier in the group knew if they were caught, they couldn't rely on anyone coming to help them. They would deal with that if it happened. Right now, they needed to find Sophie, alive hopefully, and get her out. At least that was the plan. All they needed now was to pull it off without anyone getting injured.

***

Sophie stirred from what seemed a deepest of sleep. She moaned, unsure of what roused her, then the noise reached her ears again. Sounded like a low thud — followed by a door creaking open.

"Sophie." Someone was calling her name from afar. Fingers stroked down her cheek. Oh no, was Yasin here to question her again?

"Sophie," the voice was firmer now. The touch of the fingers on her face felt so reassuring as if nothing could hurt her ever again. She knew she was coming round because it felt like every part of her body was in pain. "Sophie." She felt the gentle brush of someone's fingers as they stroked down her cheek.

When she had opened her eyes, she licked her dry lips. Her mouth felt parched and her throat swollen. She tried to swallow a couple of times. She knew she wasn't dreaming because everything in her body ached. Her shoulder hurt as she tried to raise a hand to rub the painful area, but her head hurt so badly she was afraid to move, and her face felt like it was about to explode.

She moaned as she tried to move her head in the direction of the voice.

"That's right, Sophie, I need you to look at me." The voice sounded so soothing; she decided not to fight against it.

Kieran! Kieran had come to save her.

"You won't let him hurt me any more?"

"No. I won't let anyone hurt you ever again," he whispered, close to her ear.

But it was safer to stay in her dream with Kieran. Sophie drifted back into a deep sleep where it felt safer and pain-free.

"Sophie, please, I need you to wake up. We have to get you out of here."

Sophie didn't want to wake up. It felt so good to lie here and listen to the voice — Kieran's voice. But she wanted to stay lost in this dream with Kieran forever. "Don't leave me," she whispered to her dream.

"I won't. Never." Emotionally, Sophie had no idea how her words had got to him. Beaten and bruised, Sophie was thankfully alive.

For a brief moment, Sophie opened her eyes. "That's my girl." As she found herself looking in Kieran's brown eyes, his fingers were stroking her cheeks and, for an instant, she smiled the sweetest of smiles, but her smile faded and she didn't wake again.

A low whisper came through the headpiece that was attached to his radio. "What's the fucking hold-up?"

"Problem, she's unconscious."

"Can she be moved?"

"Yes. I will carry her if I need to. Get me some back-up cover." He cringed when he saw the bruising on her face, and picked her up. Time was of the essence. He went to the door with Sophie unconscious in his arms and spoke quietly into his radio. "We are leaving now."

The eruption of gunfire came from inside the house, cutting off his words as bullets popped at the plaster in the walls. As if a serpentine of bullets followed him, and with Sophie in his arms, Kieran made a run through the central part of the house looking for an escape route. He called over his radio. "Fuck! Under fire! Need some firepower."

Mohammad Yasin came out of the shadows and took the opportunity to gain an advantage. One of the guards grabbed Sophie. Before Kieran could do anything about it, Mohammad pressed the barrel of his handgun against her temple. "If he moves — kill her!" he growled.

Luckily, Sophie was exhausted and didn't wake. "Let her go. You know our forces are here and we will not let you leave here alive."

Dragging Sophie to the door, the men positioned her in front of Yasin. "Then I will use her as a body shield." Even the sniper gunman would have trouble getting a clear shot at him, even with night-vision goggles. "She is worthless to me."

Something made a sound on his left. Light glared straight at them.

276

A gun exploded, and with a muzzle flash, Sophie was dropped to the ground by the insurgent, and she rolled away. Kieran instantly reacted, pulling her to him, twisting so he wouldn't crush Sophie's unconscious form. He dived for cover as he heard more gunfire from in front of him as he protected Sophie with his body; that was special forces, which meant ANA had broken through Yasin's men and were close.

A bullet flew wide, over his head; the ANA men weren't close enough for accuracy yet, but hopefully it wouldn't be much longer.

Mohammad Yasin? For the first time in minutes, Kieran thought of the insurgent leader. Was he hiding inside the house? Maybe he'd been hit by one of the men, invisible in the dark.

Something or someone moved to the door opening. Yasin jerked upright. He was pointing a gun directly at Kieran's temple.

"If you move it will be a —" he whispered, as the rest of the words died on his lips. Mohammad landed on top of them. Kieran kicked out at him, pushing him away as the gun exploded. Lights lit up all around them, blinding him. Mohammad Yasin was dead — blood formed a dark pool beneath his head. A dark circle in the centre of his forehead marked a sniper's aim.

Rawlins joined him. "ANA sniper shot him. Afghan police are taking over. Time for us to get the hell out of here and get this woman to a hospital."

After a stop in Kabul to place Sophie on a medical flight back to Kandahar and then onto the UK, which she slept through the whole time, they finally landed at Brize. Even though the military doctors insisted on her being transferred to a civilian hospital, the military police believed her life could still be in danger and declared her whereabouts was kept secure until she was fit for debriefing.

Sophie woke briefly several hours later.

She had been dreaming, of course, hadn't she? The last thing she could remember was a fantastic night spent in the arms of Kieran. She certainly didn't remember feeling any pain. No, she didn't want to open her eyes, there was something or someone in a living nightmare that made her fearful of waking. She wanted to be back in Kieran's arms where she felt safe and secure. It felt so good — a blast from the past — as he rescued her, held her and protected her from harm. Now the dream was gone and so was Kieran.

Chapter Eighteen

It had been a little before dawn when Sophie opened her eyes, confused, disoriented, and unable to familiarise herself with her strange surroundings. All she knew was that her head ached. It was so painful that she was convinced the army were practising their military manoeuvres inside her head; right now — she was sure — it couldn't hurt any more than it did. Plus, she was starting to feel nauseous.

Sophie tried to clear the fog from inside her head and remember what happened, or how come she was lying in bed. Where had all her clothes gone?

Slowly, a vague realisation of the events of the previous day seemed to mingle and float through her foggy mind. Right now, she was unsure where the past ended and the present day began.

The past brought back crashing painful memories she tried to forget. But it was no use — as much as she fought the dreams — it was as though her memories had a play button that she couldn't control.

Sophie tried to relax and think of something else more pleasant. Nothing was helping. It was as if her mind was set on the most painful experience she had ever suffered, and it taunted her. Memories of the past were just images and despite being filled with such overwhelming clarity, no longer had any power over her, but the pain she felt was the real torture.

Kieran had been so angry and hurt that morning.

He'd left silently without a backward glance. How her refusal of his proposal had pained him. Sophie wanted to give him some time alone to think. She'd call him later and explain, and things would be OK again.

That was before...

The nightmare haunted her, plagued by images of the past that she couldn't shake. Now, those troubling recurring visions had taken hold of her — and weren't letting go. It was hard to distinguish between past and present.

Slipping back into the darkness, she remembered she'd walked across the hallway on her way to the lounge after a shower, still wearing her bathrobe. She'd decided she couldn't wait another minute to call Kieran, but her mobile was in the kitchen. Sophie had hated the way they had left things, and she needed to explain. Tell him she loved him above all else.

Her heart stopped as she saw Simon standing in the hallway, and his face looked cold and hard as if etched from stone.

"Simon!" She froze in the doorway, biting down hard on her lip.

"Surprise! Your little soldier boyfriend left the door unlocked," he sneered. His voice sounded strange, distant, devoid of all emotion. "That was careless of him, wasn't it?" he sneered.

Sophie didn't answer Simon's question. It was pointless having any conversation with him while he was like this.

He was dressed casually: no tie, shirt half-undone and grubby, with his shirt sleeves rolled up, and the shirt was what Sophie could only surmise as supposedly blue. His light-brown hair was disarrayed as if he hadn't slept in days. His face was flushed and the whiskers on his face revealed a few days' growth. And when he stepped towards her, she'd forgotten she'd only been wearing a cotton, towelling robe.

He stood before her, looming over her with a cold stare swaying on his feet. She knew immediately he'd been drinking. He just grabbed her arm, his fist holding her tightly and dragged her through to the kitchen.

Fear began to take hold; she had to put the panic at the back of her mind. There was no use trying to escape him, not while he was like this. Fear of him striking out and hitting her was always a possibility. Right now, her best chance was to focus on what he was doing here and how he'd found her. Try to reason with him and come up with a plan to get out of here — in one piece.

If she could only keep him talking long enough, somehow, she would find a way to call the SIB and tell them where he was. But her mobile phone was still on top of the kitchen worktop and Simon had the phone in his sights and thought nothing of trashing it underfoot. The phone was useless to her now.

Besides, SIB had given up some time ago on Simon ever reappearing again in the UK. Their last investigation revealed him living in an underdeveloped country. Judging by his appearance now — their information proved wrong.

They went down the hallway before he opened the door to the lounge. "I take it you weren't expecting me?" he muttered, his speech slurred.

"Why are you here, Simon?" she asked.

"I came back to see my wife if you must know. Had a feeling you were missing me," he said, in a dry tone. Swaying on his feet, he raised his arms in a dramatic gesture. "Got that wrong, didn't I?" Simon said in a mocking tone.

"I have a life, Simon."

"You have a life?" He fumed. "What of my life? All this time you've embarrassed me while you've run around with that boy!" His manner was accusing and resentful. Could even say jealous of her happiness.

"There is nothing wrong with wanting to be happy."

"Now it's my turn." His voice was thick and unhurried as he spoke in a quietness that made a cold shiver of fear run down her spine.

It was no use, despite her best efforts to remain calm, she had been so scared that her instincts had deserted her. She had been scared before but seeing Simon like this terrified her. She could only mutter her pleas. "Simon — don't hurt him. He's done nothing wrong. If you want to punish someone, take it out on me, not him, please."

His eyes narrowed. As he listened to Sophie's pleas, they only seemed to rile him even more. His eyes burned with anger as his hands flew out, catching her unawares; the backhander of his blow to the right side of her face sent her stumbling backwards. Not satisfied with the blow, he raised his right fist and punched her in the left eye.

"Simon — don't hurt him." He mimicked her pleas in a whining voice.

She fell onto the floor, unable to keep her balance. At that moment Sophie realised how much danger she was in. "What are you going to do to him?"

As he stood over her body looking down at her, his smile made her skin crawl. "Him — him?" He laughed, taunting her. "Right now — I would think that you should be more concerned about yourself."

"What are you going to do?"

Almost as if he couldn't stop himself, he reached down and grasped her jaw in his hand. "Oh, don't worry, I'm not going to touch him — by the time I've finished with you and your pretty face — he'll never be able to look at you again and feel anything but pity."

When she pulled her head away, his eyes rolled in disgust. Then he struck her again, even harder. Her head began to spin, and her ears rang. "You see what you make me do!" he confessed.

Despite her best instincts to remain calm and not rile him, it was not working for her. "Stop!"

Simon bent over her even further. "You are my wife! Don't forget it. Do you think some flimsy piece of paper could separate us?" He grabbed a handful of her long, damp hair and pulled it tightly, yanking her head back. Sophie cried out in pain. "Do you?" he questioned harshly, punching her in the face with such force that Sophie felt her head rock.

She dared not answer him, refusing to provoke him into a further rage.

His voice had become unyielding and remorseless. He brushed her cheek with his forefinger. "You and I," Simon began quietly, and he pointed the same accusing finger at her, bringing it down hard on her breastbone. "are going to be man and wife again — and you and I will do what normal married couples do. Got it?" His voice was cold and demanding, "You will do as I tell you. Do you hear me?"

The anger and humiliation in his demands were too much. Suddenly there seemed a hidden strength in her that Sophie didn't know she possessed. "No, do what you like with me, but I will never be yours, not now and not ever!"

"How dare you answer back to me!" He was shouting at her. It was as if she had pressed a rage button inside of him as he instantly reacted. "You speak when I allow you to!"

"No!" She screamed then before she could call out again, he struck her another backhander across her left cheek. This time Sophie tasted blood in her mouth and it trickled down her throat. She could already feel a bruise forming on her face as it tingled under the force of his strike.

Sophie fought desperately to free herself, screaming at the top of her lungs. She was frantic, and felt sick as he straddled her and succeeded in pushing large amounts of her long tresses into her mouth to halt her screams. She gagged and choked on the bulging mass of hair that was crammed into her mouth.

Simon shook his head. "No use calling out. No one will hear you," he said, and before Sophie knew what was happening, his right fist came down hard on her midsection.

Robbed instantly of her breathing, doubling over in pain, Sophie's knees came up as if to protect herself; she'd had no idea she could be in so much pain. It hurt to breathe. She tried to stifle a sob. Almost immediately, he pulled her head up with her remaining knotted hair and punched her jaw, followed quickly by the second, and the third. Each hit becoming more vicious than the last. Her head was aching so badly she could hardly move her head. Her right eye had taken so many blows that it had totally closed; her vision in her left eye blurred and her face burned in pain.

"See. No matter what happens to you no one will come." He sounded almost as if it gave him some pleasure out of mistreating her.

He grabbed her jaw again and squeezed it so tightly she felt sure he'd left bruising. Tears were beginning to flow down Sophie's face, as she took another punch to her jaw. That hit was so hard that she tasted fresh blood inside her mouth mingled with her hair, and it was hard to swallow.

Through her tears she realised to her horror what was about to happen, as Simon began to unfasten his clothes, tearing at them through his haste.

Surely he didn't intend violating her? Shaking her head violently at what she felt sure his intentions were, Sophie tried to get her thoughts together. She attempted to breathe steadily but she couldn't, and she felt sure he'd broken her ribs and her face was throbbing. Every part of her body was in agonising pain.

Sophie began shaking so hard that she had exhausted herself fighting him with blows that had landed in various parts of his body. Each was having little or no effect on his intentions.

He laughed, sneering at her feeble attempts. He gripped her wrists tightly and pinned them above her head in a cruel and iron-clasp grip that had her crying out in pain.

"Do you think after this he will want you?"

"Don't do this, Simon," she pleaded, through laboured breaths.

The cold, hard words of his voice told her he was getting pleasure out of hurting her, as he ripped the white robe off her shoulders. "You know," he laughed again. "I almost feel sorry for your soldier boy."

Breathlessly, all she could ask was, "Why?"

"Because you love him." His hatred intensified at the words he'd spoken. He pushed his fist up to her chin, applying that much pressure Sophie thought he was about to crush her jaw.

Trying to grip his wrist to loosen his hold, she fought so desperately; she clawed frantically at the back of his hands, but she no longer had the strength to resist his violent assault.

Simon sneered, laughing harshly at her weak attempts to fight him. He looked at her for the longest moment before adding, "When you have my child, do you think he'll want you then? As the saying goes — if I can't have you — I won't let him have you either."

Sophie shuddered as fear bound her as tightly and as securely as his hands around her wrists. He meant it. The look in his dilated eyes told her Simon intended to rape her!

Rigid with fright she held his hard stare. Sophie struggled hard at that moment not to vomit. The thought of Simon touching her was more than she could take.

Looking Simon in the eye, she saw that knowing, cold, steely-eyed glint that was undoubtedly visible and clear to her of his intentions. There was a look in his eyes that told her he was prepared to kill her if he had to. Filling her mind — that was his sole purpose, and she knew it.

As if he couldn't bear to look at her for another minute, he grabbed her by the towelling robe around her midsection and brought her off the ground. "Now to the bedroom for my little faithful wifey." He chuckled maliciously.

When she tried to wriggle free and protest, he gave her another punch to her midsection and threw her to the floor striking another blow to her jaw. "No matter — here will do fine." He laughed.

Although Simon hadn't hit her as hard as the other times, her breathing had become more desperate. Simon clearly felt no remorse at what he was about to do.

Her head was spinning so much that she felt sick. Sophie waited for what she knew was sure to follow — her death. With one final blow to her head, her world went black, and the darkness felt a welcome relief.

The next time she woke, Sophie found herself in a strange bed. Why was she in this bed? Where was her towelling robe? The one she'd worn after stepping out of the shower that morning?

Sophie tried to move her head, but it ached too much. Something was different.

This wasn't her home. But she couldn't remember for the life of her how she'd gotten here. She could only remember Simon; he was threatening her — the feel of his hands on her. Then the darkness. She started to shake.

Someone was holding her hand and a familiar voice was coming from far away. She heard a soft, reassuring voice filled with relief. "How are you, Sophie?"

"Jane?"

She moved slightly; her head hurt so much she could hardly move. Sophie could barely open her eyes, and squinted against the bright lights of the room. She turned her head slowly to the direction of the softly spoken voice. Jane's eyes were filled with sympathy and were roaming over her face. Sophie trembled and looked away. It felt as if every bone in her body was in agony. She ached — the pain was overwhelming and her vision blurred.

"It's all right, Sophie," she said, as she patted Sophie's limp hand and told her more reassuringly, "you're safe now."

Sophie didn't believe her.

Then more lights came on in the room. It looked like a hospital room and there was a distinct odour of disinfectant. Was she in a hospital? When she first tried to open her eyes, she hadn't been conscious enough to take in her surroundings. She licked her lips again; her throat felt so raw that she had to make a couple of attempts before she could manage to ask, "W... what... happened? H... h.... how did I get here?"

Someone was standing by her bed and it felt like a woman was touching her hair and she had a large pair of scissors in her hand. Her head ached again as she tried to move.

"Take it easy," she told her, and the woman's grip tightened on her upper arm. "I'm a nurse at the hospital, and I'm here to make you more comfortable," she said, in a matter-of-fact voice.

"Hospital!" Something was wrong. She'd been at home — Kieran had been getting ready to leave for work. She'd gone back to sleep — and then nothing.

Then she vaguely recalled Simon being in her home. She felt suddenly cold as she remembered flashes of the terror he inflicted on her. Tears began to roll down her cheeks.

Fear gripped her; she turned back to her friend. "Where's Simon?" Hysteria reeled up inside her as she sobbed with a tearful hiccup. "Where's Jane?"

Her friend's voice sounded strained, "I'm here, Sophie." Her friend patted her hand reassuringly. "Simon has gone — he tried to take his own life in an aircraft hangar. The SIB found him earlier this morning." Jane must have seen the fear in her eyes. She felt the colour drain from her face. "He's alive — just. They've taken him to a secure hospital. I'm sure SIB will be by to see you."

"No!"

Jane stroked her bruised cheek with a gentle touch of a finger. "Hush. Everything will be fine now."

"I can't, Jane. I just can't." Sophie tried to sit up, but the pain was too much. "He'll find me!"

The nurse tried to console her. "You're safe here." Her voice gentle and reassuring and comforting. "It's over now."

She didn't feel safe. "I have to leave here," Sophie whispered, "he will never let me go — never! He wants to kill me!"

Her head ached, she was shaking and she could smell blood as she touched her forehead. Was it her blood? She felt sick to her stomach. A metal dish was placed in front of her. She tried to grab the bowl but missed as her hand came into contact with something else. Bunches of hair was in her hand. It was her hair!

They had cut her hair! Why?

She wasn't shaking any longer. Sophie's eyes felt as if they rolled back in her head as massive shudders shot through her. She felt cold, so very cold. Sophie tried to sit up and winced in horrific pain.

"Sophie!" She heard a yell distantly — that voice was as familiar as her own. It was Jane. She tried to call out to her, but she couldn't speak. Sophie was vaguely aware of a woman's voice in the distance.

"She's seizing," the nurse snapped. "We need to get her stable!" She felt someone grab her arm and a prick on her skin. Her head swooned, and she felt lifeless. Sophie was tired of fighting, and the dark claimed her once more.

Hours later, next time Sophie opened her eyes, all she could hear was the sound of her breathing as she inhaled and exhaled slowly and with great difficulty. The smell of antiseptic and seeing curtains around her bed confused her for a moment and then it became clear.

She blinked a few times before she saw Jane's tear-stained gaze. Sophie tried to focus entirely on her surroundings. "You're OK, Sophie," Jane whispered.

Sophie felt anything but OK.

"We need to ask you some questions."

Sophie's head turned right at the sound of another voice that sounded vaguely familiar. She was surprised to see Detective Dent of the SIB stood beside her bed. He looked a lot paler than the last time she'd seen him.

"What happened?"

Jane glanced around the small, quiet room. "Don't move, Sophie. Listen to me. You have cracked ribs and several broken bones. Your right eye is swollen closed. They may have to operate on your jaw and left cheek. Sophie, you're lucky to be alive after what that pig did to you."

For the first time, Sophie took note of her surroundings, as she looked down at the gown in distaste. "You're in a civilian hospital, Sophie. Your bathrobe was taken away by the military police as evidence of the assault, along with samples of your hair."

"She's just come round," Jane said, through gritted teeth. "Can't this wait?"

"I'm aware of that." Detective Dent sighed. "Sophie is the only one that can tell us anything about what happened. I've had a disturbed missing airman, and I only have her to help me understand why her ex-husband did this."

Jane gave a hard, cynical shake of her head. "Because you didn't stop him."

"It's all right, Jane. Let them do their job."

"That's good." He nodded in approval. "Sophie, how did your ex-

286

husband end up being in your house?" Dent asked.

"She's just woken up, for goodness sake, and not aware of everything that's happened yet," Jane argued.

"I don't remember," Sophie whispered.

DCI Dent exhaled deeply. He didn't look like he believed her. "Then start with what you do remember. Who was at the house with you? Someone said they saw another man leaving earlier that morning."

"I don't remember... not anything."

Jane protested. "Is this necessary?"

"I only remember I was in my bed. I went for a shower." Sophie's heart raced in her chest. The machines at the side of her bed raced too. "Then I saw someone... my head hurt... then — nothing." Sophie blinked away the tears that had formed on her lashes. "I don't remember anything," she said again, forcing the words out, "I don't remember," denouncing any memory of the attack.

The machines beeped louder around her. Jane placed an arm around her shoulders and hugged her tightly. She could see Sophie was getting stressed again.

Sophie glanced up and met the eyes of DCI Dent. There were traces of concern and sadness in his gaze. "I don't remember any more." The darkness was growing in her mind. "I don't remember!"

When Sophie awoke again a few hours later, she felt a little more conscious of her whereabouts. Jane was still sitting by her bedside. Sophie smiled at her friend, feeling decidedly stronger.

"I can't stay here, Jane. I have to leave here. It's not safe for any of us while Simon is alive. But — where will I go?"

Her friend took a long, steadying breath. "Let me help you, Sophie," she pleaded with her. "Let me get you away from here. You have a family — why not go home? Go where you'll be safe, and people can protect you."

Sophie tried to laugh; it came out with a laugh and a sob. Simon would find her — he always found her. "I can't go home. It would be the first place he checked."

A moment of weakness came over her. Kieran's image flashed through her mind.

Sophie knew she needed to keep her distance from him — now more than ever. If she did go home, she would have to put this life behind her. Start a new life.

"Then we will think of something else. Any ideas?"

"I don't care where I go, Jane. Help me — please." She gripped her friend's hand tightly. She laid still; she was almost as white as the sheets on her bed. "Help me."

In the end, Sophie was kept in hospital for three months due to surgery complications and reconstruction to her jawline and cheekbone.

Each morning she woke, she refused to move any further than to a seat near an open window. She would sit for hours, day after day, staring out into space. Deep in wonder. Half-dreaming and half-remembering what brutality Simon had subjected her to.

"Well — good morning. I see you're looking better today, Mrs Campbell," her regular nurse informed her. She hadn't been able to eat properly, despite all the gentle coaxing by Jane. Sophie wanted to argue, but couldn't find the willpower or the strength.

Jane had brought her countless books and magazines; she couldn't concentrate on anything. Even television held no appeal for her. Days had passed unnoticed until one day a doctor walked into her room unannounced.

"I have some news for you, Mrs Campbell." He looked uneasy and apologetic. The young man sat on a chair opposite her anticipating her reaction. "... you're pregnant." He leaned over her and she shrank away from him.

Sophie couldn't believe her ears; she was pregnant! She laughed hysterically. How ironic — she had set Kieran free through her fear of not being able to give him children.

"No! That's not possible! He said — he would make me pay — I'll never be free of him! Oh, God!" Sophie curled herself into a tight ball.

The kindly doctor patted her hand reassuringly, trying to soothe her and calm her down. "There is no reason why you can't have a healthy baby, Sophie."

"My last period was lighter than normal. But I never thought..."

"No," Dr Mathews interrupted and smiled encouragingly. "Lighter periods can happen and be perfectly normal sometimes."

"I thought I was just run-down. I've worked myself into a nervous wreck just lately, depressed and under a lot of emotional strain regarding my ex-husband."

"What am I going to do? I can't bear it — I wish I were dead!" She began to sob uncontrollably. "I... shall... never... be able to face him. Never!"

"Who? Face who, Mrs Campbell?" The doctor sensed her hysteria.

She was becoming restless and tears were running freely down her cheeks. Her head was spinning. "You don't understand..." she called out in anger. "He won't want me now. Simon was right. He won't want me. Not now I carry another man's child inside me. Don't you see? Everything Simon threatened has come true." She sobbed.

"I think you should calm down, Mrs Campbell," the doctor urged.

"You don't understand — it's all been for nothing." Her breathing became laboured. Pain raced through her body gripping her lower stomach. She doubled over in pain.

Then the doctor spoke directly to the nurse. "I'll have to sedate her." Sophie heard him saying, "Now, try to relax — it's not going to hurt." His voice was soothing, but nothing could soothe the ache in her heart.

"But it does hurt. Don't you see — I'll never be free. Never." Tears flowed from her eyes, and her heart ached. "I will never be free from this pain." This was her punishment for being happy and loving Kieran so much.

The room began to fade as soon as the hypodermic needle left her arm. Her eyes closed in moments, gratefully, as she felt her world growing darker until she sank into oblivion.

Once again, the horror of those dreams faded into the past once more, and Sophie drifted into a deep sleep remembering the smile on Daniel's face as she hugged him the last morning before her departure.

Daniel raised his head and, with his eyes full of tears, his lashes fluttered as if to clear his tears away. "I love you, Mum."

Leaving him behind was the hardest part of her job. She had stroked his short, black hair as she held him close against her chest, her arms wrapped around him and kissed the top of his head. With his arms around her waist, he hugged her tightly. She stroked his cheek. "I love you, Daniel," she had told him.

Thinking back, it was funny how such a troubled and turbulent time in her life had turned into something different. Surviving such a traumatic experience had given her something so precious to be thankful for.

Sophie held her breath for a moment, and whispered again, "I love you too, Daniel. My precious boy," and drifted off into a deep, undisturbed sleep.

Chapter Nineteen

Sophie was now awake, and the IV was finally removed.

Little did she know Kieran had not left the hospital in three days — the entire time Sophie had been there. He hadn't been permitted to see her as the visitors were restricted to immediate family, but he'd stayed outside her room all the same.

Kieran had spoken briefly to the doctors on her admittance without giving away details of the search and rescue mission or jeopardising her safety.

The doctors paid regular visits to Sophie's bedside as she slipped in and out of consciousness. "You were fortunate. Nothing broken. Judging by your medical history and the reconstruction work — you've had some serious injuries in the past," he said, as he flipped through her chart. "But you should have no lasting problems related to the current injuries to your back. The bruising and swelling to your face should ease over the next few days," Dr Jefferies, a tall, slender man in his mid-fifties told Sophie. "I suspect you were conscious when they injected you with drugs?"

Sophie nodded.

"Results detected Ketamine in your system. Luckily, no lasting effects. Considering the amount still in your system when you arrived — you were lucky you didn't suffer cardiac arrest. It seems they didn't care how much your captors gave you. They just wanted results."

"Have I been out of it for a while?"

"In and out of consciousness — three days," he explained, "I need to keep you at least one more day. Don't worry about your safety; the military will be outside your room the entire time."

Of course, Yasin's men had taken her, resulting in their deaths. The military would want to speak with her at some stage. "I have a lot of people to thank for rescuing me. Yasin would have killed me if the forces hadn't found me and rescued me." Sophie shuddered. She tried to block it out, and tried not to think about what might have happened to her back in Afghanistan. "My family must have been worried sick."

"The military arranged for your family to be here, and they constantly have — voicing their concerns since the moment you arrived."

"Sorry about that." Sophie winced.

He merely smiled politely, ignoring the excited chatter outside her room. "Speaking of which," he paused as he heard the room door open. "Another visitor for you."

She looked away towards the door, hoping it was her mother bringing her something to wear other than a hospital gown.

"Sophie! Darling! What happened to you? I've been so worried about you. No one was allowed to see you until you were conscious."

There was no mistaking Ruby's stressed voice. "Hello, Mum-Ruby, I'm fine." Her mother-in-law, Ruby Campbell, would inevitably ask about her trip to Afghanistan.

The cover story was that Sophie, known as journalist, Haley Henderson, was abducted and freed when the newspaper paid the ransom. In any case, it was partly right. After all, she had nothing to fear or hide from Ruby.

Her parents Christine and Martin Tyson were now in their late sixties, devoted to each other, and young in their outlook on life but, still, she didn't want to give them any unnecessary concern. And just like Ruby, they doted on their only grandson, Daniel, and doted equally on their only daughter — Sophie.

Ruby, with no husband and no other children, looked upon Sophie as her own family. And Sophie adored her parents and Ruby equally, and as a family, they had always been easy-going and lovable. There was no denying, their dream was to see Sophie settled with a man who would love both her and Daniel equally. And it was true, Simon had worried his mother the most.

Her parents were always cautious about Simon's intentions, especially when Sophie's safety was at risk. There was no mistaking that Simon had convinced even his mother, who was taken in by his charms in his appeal to make amends for all he had done.

It had taken both sets of parents a long time to stop blaming themselves for the attack on Sophie. But Ruby had taken it the hardest.

A combination of guilt and loyalty at her son's treatment of Sophie weighed heavily on Ruby's mind. Because of this, Ruby had suffered from health issues for the last few years. So, any mention of her past, therefore, would be more than enough to prompt an open bombardment of questions from Ruby. And she didn't want Ruby hurt — not any more.

It was probably a strange situation looking from someone else's point of view, but she had always treated Ruby as family and to her as such she deserved that respect. "Ruby Mum, how are you? Is Daniel OK?"

"Daniel is fine. He misses you. Your parents will be popping in to see you later." Her silver hair was bobbing in the direction of the door. "Sophie, guess what? We have a surprise for you. You'll never guess." Ruby ushered herself forward, seating herself next to Sophie's bedside.

We? Something wasn't quite right; she had an awful sinking feeling inside. Sophie's heart began to slam wildly against her ribs. She said nothing, and then suddenly, she came face to face with Kieran O'Neill.

So, it hadn't been a dream!

Kieran had saved her life in Afghanistan. Not once, but twice now. Suddenly, her whole world shifted — a blast from the past, and it was as if she had stepped back in time.

There had been no warning and no sign of him coming here, and his turning up here was the last thing she had expected. She felt the colour drain from her face, probably the shock she tried to tell herself.

Kieran, however, looked thoroughly at home. Ruby was fussing over him, and he was beaming at her as if flattered by the attention. They looked so at home chatting, so Sophie assumed they had talked before. And Kieran looked every bit a British soldier hero, dressed in his desert-camo uniform and cap; he stopped at once as soon as he'd entered the room and didn't take another step forward.

"I found this young man standing guard outside your room. He tells me he is assigned to watch over you. I thought the least I could do was offer him a seat. And if he's going to keep watch over you, he might as well be comfortable."

Kieran thanked Ruby and sat down on the chair across from her bed; he appeared unfazed by the fact Sophie was watching his every move.

Taking in the sight of him, Sophie realised he hadn't changed a bit in ten years. Their eyes locked. Kieran appeared to gaze at her with a mixture of open admiration and charm, and if she wasn't mistaken, a hint of Irish humour and mischief radiated from his sparkling, dark eyes. Kieran smiled directly at her, broadly. There was the smile she had loved so much.

"Ms Haley Henderson, I presume?" he began sweetly.

Ruby interrupted him, "None of that. It's Sophie to her friends."

He nodded in Ruby's direction. "Sophie it is."

She turned to Ruby for support. And judging by Ruby's facial expression, she'd found the entire episode quite amusing, so she was not going to get any support from her. Treading carefully, not sure what information Ruby had shared with Kieran, she kept her question informal. "What is it precisely you are doing here, soldier?"

Ruby beamed at Kieran and then back to Sophie. "Sophie, where are your manners?" Ruby said, eyeing him as if he was her white knight. "Mr O'Neill —"

"Sergeant Kieran O'Neill, ma'am," Kieran interrupted.

"Sergeant O'Neill," Ruby corrected before adding, "has been so kind and understanding about the whole situation, and he explained the men guarding your room is a precaution. They have been here round the clock."

"I'm sure Sophie understands we are taking her safety seriously," he added. "And please, call me Kieran."

"You mentioned you met Sophie some time ago — when was that?"

Oh, no! He wouldn't!

"Quite some time ago, Ruby. What would you say, Sophie — roughly about 12 years ago now?" He looked directly at her, and he paused as if waiting for her to say something. "We occasionally ran into each other; our paths crossed for a few years through work and then we gradually became friends. Isn't that right, Soph?" he directed at her, forcing her to deny it if she dared.

Sophie was not disturbed so much by his mocking tone, more his choice to use that precise moment to call her by his pet name for her. For a few seconds, he stared silently at her as if wanting her to say something.

"My friend Jane introduced us," Sophie answered, feeling slightly uncomfortable on how much he intended to reveal about their past relationship.

Something like regret flooded Ruby's face. "Yes, Jane and Andrew Lister. Your friends from Brize Norton. I remember meeting them once before." She gave a deep, heartfelt sigh. "They were very good to you. It's a pity they couldn't do more to help protect you." There was no mistaking the sadness and pain in Ruby's voice, or the glistening of tears in the older woman's eyes.

"I think that's enough about the past." Sophie was starting to feel a little anxious.

"It's fine, Sophie. Don't worry. Maybe it's time to move on." Ruby shook her head in disappointment. "I loved my son. But he was also a distraught and disturbed man." Ruby's expression became nettled. "The way he hurt our poor Sophie. I could never forgive him for almost taking her away from us."

Kieran frowned. "You said almost? When was this?"

Sophie was horrified the conversation was hitting a raw nerve where her family were concerned. She needed the discussion to turn direction. "Yes, well, we don't need to talk about that right now, do we? No use in opening old wounds."

Ruby shook her bent head. "No, quite right, dear." She patted Sophie's hand. "Now, I've made up my mind. Kieran was very kind to an old lady distressed over her family, so I'm going to leave the two of you to have a nice little chat; I'm sure you two have lots to catch up on — being former acquaintances and all that." Ruby smiled at both of them in turn. There was no mistaking Ruby's intentions towards Sophie and Kieran and her matchmaking plans.

"No, we don't," Sophie was saying. Looking to Kieran for support. By the look on his face, she wasn't going to have much luck with that.

Ruby wasn't having any arguments about it. "Nonsense, I'm sure you do. And the two of you meeting like this, so suddenly, after all this time."

"Ruby, you have no idea what you're talking about," Sophie whispered, sarcastically. "Besides, I need my rest."

"Nonsense." She dismissed Sophie lightly. "I know what I'm doing."

Strange how vulnerable and alone she felt the moment Ruby left the room. She sighed heavily; Kieran O'Neill had done this to her. He had disrupted her entire world yet again.

Her self-confidence and inner strength had once saved her soul. Her life would have withered and died if it hadn't been for life inside her back then. Every day she had to live with the fact the baby that was growing inside her had not been made out of love, only the need of hate and control, and it filled her every being. That was why the baby had to know love and to feel loved above all else. She could not let Simon win.

Ruby often commented that Daniel looked so much like her, and favoured her dark eyes and hair. His eyes were a deep dark-brown than shined when he laughed. But, she thought it a blessing her son favoured nothing other from Simon than his long, lean body, and noticed how tall Daniel was getting too, and he was growing so fast these days. Oh, well, at least he was a happy child.

That last morning Sophie had hugged her son, she held her breath, blocking out the thought of them being parted. Sophie kissed his forehead for one more time and told him she loved him. He put his arms around her waist, and he told her he understood — it was vital for her to do her job and help find the bad men.

Working under a pseudonym as a reporter for the past ten years enabled her the freedom to spend quality time with her son while keeping her identity a secret. Sure, it often meant periods of hard, continuous work, and one long, hard slog. While there were other periods when things were decidedly slow, and she would have to make ends meet by taking assignments elsewhere, which meant being away from home at times.

Life had been good, but that was until the military, more specifically Captain Rawlins, found her and decided to talk her into flushing out Yasin. With a price on her head, she had very few options left open to her, Rawlins had made that perfectly clear.

Kieran was still in his chair across from her, staring at her and waiting for her to speak. Sophie didn't have to wait too long. "So — Ms Haley Henderson — What do we talk about?" His expression was filled with more questions than answers.

Sophie pushed aside the feelings of hurt; the emotion was like a rising hard ball in her throat. "Kieran, I feel so awkward about this. I didn't expect to see you."

"I guess not." He raised his eyebrow and shrugged his shoulders.

"You have no idea why I'm here do you?"

Sophie couldn't help it, as her eyes suddenly filled with tears and she reached for a pink tissue from the box on the bedside table to blot them away.

"Nothing to ask me about how you came to be here?" he paused, "Nothing at all?"

She looked up at the door, hoping someone would come through. Usually, a constant stream of people was popping in, so why not now? There was no mistaking he was leading the conversation in another direction.

She shook her head in denial.

"After the way you left — ten years is a long time — you seriously had no idea that I would want to see you?" he continued firmly, his dark eyes flashing dangerously. "Ask questions and want answers?"

"No." Sophie shook her head and blinked the tears away, refusing to turn into an emotional wreck. She looked down at her hands as they shivered slightly under his gaze.

Sophie should have known he would come seeking retribution of some kind once he found her. She should have also known, even after all this time of working up a plausible explanation ready to face him, and it was incredibly harder than she'd have imagined. But even knowing this meeting was inevitable was exceeding all her expectations emotionally.

There was no doubt about it — she couldn't hide forever. She watched as Kieran's jaw tightened; it was evident to her he was not comfortable discussing this with her.

Thinking back, over the years she had known Kieran, she came to realise one obvious thing, he'd changed so little. Sure, he's changed on the outside — those incredible boyish good looks and that beautiful physique have transformed into a man of learning and success. But the gentleness and the caring side of his nature was not visible today. Instead, his crisp intelligence was always unmistakable, and that sharp Irish wit — he had always been two steps in front of her.

Kieran sat glancing over the silver-framed picture of mother and son placed on her bedside cabinet. Sophie was cuddling her son against her chest with her face pressed against his straight, dark hair. He had laughing, dark eyes just like his mother.

"You have a nice-looking boy." He made a move across the room and sat back down on the chair next to her bedside for a closer look. "He looks like you." There was a look of sadness and regret and some other emotion she couldn't quite pinpoint flashed across Kieran's face.

"Yes, he's my life."

"Is he the reason you moved back to Lincolnshire so that he could be near both his grandparents?"

"No, not especially. For the first few years I travelled so much with my job and I wanted us to feel settled. I needed a proper home to call my own and feel safe, for my son too." She answered him tightly.

"Safe? Were you in danger?"

Sophie's face turned pale. "It doesn't matter."

He watched her hands clutch the bedclothes until her knuckles were white. "Are you thinking of leaving again?"

"No. I'm not going anywhere." The memory of her leaving that fateful day flooded her mind. There were so many times she wished she could step back in time and erase the hurt.

"You left once before." Sadness flashed across Kieran's face.

"I left for reasons of my own. I also moved to be close to my family and for personal reasons—" Her voice trailed off, as a shiver visibly went through her. "I intend to keep it that way."

Kieran swore under his breath. "Ten years! Sophie! Ten fucking years!" Kieran yelled, doing the maths from the time he remembered seeing Sophie for the last time. "You disappeared without a word of explanation. Now you're telling me that you want me to mind my own business and just forget about everything?" He lifted a questioning, dark eyebrow at her, challenging her to answer.

"In one word — yes." She smiled sweetly.

"You always were a stubborn, little thing," he said softly, "but it isn't wise to push it, Sophie. I take it your real name is Sophie, isn't it?"

Sophie stared at him numbly. "Yes, my middle name is Haley, but as a child, I hated it. Simon called me Haley on occasion because he knew I hated it. It started as a game to taunt me. But later, when we married and he first introduced me to his friends, it was as Haley Campbell. Over time, my circle of friends decreased, and somehow became his friends, so in the end, I just stopped being Sophie Tyson any more."

"And Henderson?"

Her nose crinkled in the old way when she tried to avoid revealing some truth or other about herself. "My grandmother's maiden name."

He wanted to ask about the secrecy for her name change, but instead, the question that came out of his mouth was, "Tell me one thing — when you left me and had his child — did you still love him?"

"It's not what you think," she whispered, through clenched teeth. "I needed to disappear quickly and quietly. I couldn't be Mrs Haley Campbell any more." A tremor went through her.

"Well — what else am I supposed to think?" he asked, subdued.

Her control snapped. "Do you think for one moment I could ever love such a violent and controlling man? Because if you did — you would be wrong," she fumed. "He was cruel and abusive—" She flushed and trailed off. She was trying to refrain from saying too much. As if telling him point blank — the business with her ex was none of his business.

Fighting hard to keep his expression neutral, Kieran could not let Sophie see how badly he wanted to smash her ex-husband's face in with his fist right now. He stood up and stared at her, afraid of what he might say in haste, realising he needed a moment to collect his thoughts.

"Sophie," he began. He pulled out a letter from his desert-camo inside jacket pocket, and standing directly beside her bed he turned to face her. He looked reluctant to speak at first. "Ruby approached me with this letter when you were first admitted. She received this from her son three years ago. It arrived in his personal effects after his suicide. She wants you to read it. Ruby told me to tell you it explains everything."

Confused, her brow creased as she met his gaze. "Why did Ruby give you the letter? She could have given it to me at any time." Knowing Ruby had kept it from her worried Sophie and put her on edge.

"Do you know what's in it?" Her eyes fixed on the letter he held firmly in his grasp before her.

Shaking his head, he said, "No."

Although she hadn't seen Kieran in ten years, she believed him. Sophie closed her eyes and let her head rest against her raised pillows. She felt as if her world had spun out of control; her blood seemed to drain from her body. "Take it away; I don't want it."

The sound of Kieran's voice rang out in her ears. It felt like he was calling her name from a long way off. An arm went around her. It was drawing her to him, and he was hugging her close. His strength was a solid brick wall. He felt warm to the touch; she sagged helplessly against him. With his arm wrapped around her, Kieran helped to support her while he laid her back down on the bed and covered her with a soft quilt. Sophie looked so small and fragile lying in a hospital bed covered up to her neck, almost childlike in her appearance.

"Let me help you, Sophie." Kieran placed a cool, damp cloth on her forehead, gently soothing her.

In a faint voice, she asked, "What's happening to me?"

"Side effects from the Ketamine I expect," Kieran explained calmly. The drugs were still playing havoc on her system, and she had very little control over her emotions.

Sophie lifted her head, her eyes clearing enough to see the look of concern on Kieran's face. "Take it easy, take deep breaths," he advised gently. As he sat crouching in front of her, he took her ice-cold hands in his and rubbed gently.

"I'm all right now, thank you," she said, in a croaking voice.

"No, you're not. Your hands are freezing." Kieran continued slowly. "I'm sorry for upsetting you."

Tears blurred her vision. She could say nothing.

"Don't cry, Sophie, everything will be fine. Nothing in the past can hurt you now. Believe me when I say no one will ever hurt you again, I promise." Kieran sounded so concerned and caring. And above all, she believed him.

"Thank you."

Of course, he cared; Kieran held her gaze. "Give me a chance to show you, let me help you." It was an offer, a chance to find out the truth that remained buried deep in the past. "You can trust me. I promise that you won't regret it."

She pulled her hands slowly out of his grasp and sank slowly back into the pillows on the bed. "I can't do that."

"I won't let you push me away, Sophie, not this time."

"What's that supposed to mean?"

"It means you walked out of my life — and hurt me more ways than

I could count." He stood his ground firmly, towering over her. "Don't you get it? You kept so many secrets from me. I don't plan to lose you again. I don't play to lose."

In her eyes, he captured the molten look of a challenge. Her chocolate-brown eyes were rich with dark secrets. "Your time in the army is well spent."

His smile broadened, and he nodded. "Yes, it was exciting being out on patrol in the hot desert lugging hefty backpacks plus equipment and stuff around all day."

"I see. So now, you think you're ready to settle down and become domesticated?"

He frowned. "Am I looking for a wife? Is that what you're asking me?" He leaned closer so that his chest brushed her shoulder. "What do you think?"

"I suggest you look elsewhere. You should know I'm not exactly a good recommendation for any successful relationship."

"Why not?" he enquired firmly.

"I'll tell you one day." Sophie's smile grew, though she wished that he would move back, just a little.

"Oh, this is ridiculous..." he broke off. He pushed his hands roughly through his short hair. "Stop trying to change the subject, Sophie. I know you're afraid of something from your past. What is it?" He told her firmly. His eyes filled with compassion. "I want to know, please, tell me."

She shook her head — all humour from her eyes was now gone. "I can't. The hurt goes too deep, Kieran. And talking about it — I don't think it will ever heal."

"It can — and I will help you. You have to trust me! I know what I'm talking about."

She fingered the sealed letter in her hand. A sudden realisation from the past washed over her. Tears welled up in her eyes. She pushed the letter back into the palm of his hand. "I can't. I just can't," she whispered.

"Then to hell with you!" Kieran spat out at her angrily. He stormed over to the door and held it wide. "I pity you, Sophie. Sooner or later you're going to have to trust me. But I warn you now — I'm not going anywhere, and neither are you. Not this time. I intend to know everything. I won't be satisfied until I know every last detail." He searched her pale features for some trace of emotion; there was nothing. "I'm prepared to do battle to win if that's what it takes."

For a long time, Sophie was silent. She ran the tip of her tongue over her lips in hesitation. She hadn't wanted to tell him, but he had the right to know why she'd refused to marry him.

"Before Daniel was born, I was extremely ill for a very long time. When I started to get better, the doctors told me I may never be able to have more children."

"Sophie, I'm sorry," he was saying, "I didn't know." He sounded anxious and genuinely concerned. "I wondered what you meant when you told me you were protected from us making love."

"Yes, as I said, but having Daniel felt something like a miracle."

"And now?"

"Because of this problem, there is little hope of me ever getting pregnant again." Tears were burning the back of Sophie's eyes.

"My sweet, sweet Sophie." He pulled her into his arms as he held her head cradled against his chest. "Don't you know me at all? Children aren't as important to me as you are."

"You still don't understand what I'm saying, do you? You say this now, but in years to come, you'll regret saying that. In the end, you will come to resent me just as Simon did."

"That's not the same issue here."

"It is the issue, don't you see that? Over time you would learn to hate me for not being able to give you the kind of family you crave. Do you think you will be able to look at Daniel and not resent him? Daniel deserves better than that."

He took one last look at the woman he loved — Kieran gently turned and caught sight of her as she sat up crying wholeheartedly. Her hands covered her face as she sobbed.

"OK, Sophie, I'm going to leave you to get some rest," he said, and rose from his seat, his heart heavy with sadness. "I'll check on you later." He sighed heavily and closed the door behind him in defeat. "We'll talk more then."

Kieran was leaving Sophie's room when Ruby caught sight of him. Politeness prevented him from moving from the spot. "I'm afraid Sophie refused to read the letter."

"I thought that might happen," Ruby said softly. "We will have to find another way."

"Another way for what?"

Ruby gave an audible sigh. "Sergeant O'Neill, I'm talking chemistry."

"Chemistry?" he questioned.

She smiled at him, and sat down slowly, taking the chair opposite him, and proceeded to cross her legs. "You can't deny that the two of you have a former connection. I felt it the moment I met you. The concern over Sophie for the past three days meant more to you than just doing your job, am I right?"

Kieran looked down at the floor, a trace of sadness in his reply. "I thought we cared for each other once."

She rested her hands on her lap with a grin of satisfaction. "I have something personal I wish to discuss with you," she said, in a subdued voice. "It's a matter of importance, and I feel you — Sergeant O'Neill — can help."

Kieran was intrigued, and eventually pulled himself together enough to reply. "Of course, I'll be glad to help any way I can."

Settling back into a chair in the visitor's' lounge, Kieran stared closely at Ruby Campbell. Her trim black trousers and matching jacket and cream blouse suited her slim figure, and her ageing silver hair was a style that Kieran suspected she hadn't changed in many years. He held her coat and placed it over the back of her chair before he sat next to her.

"Thank you," she replied. Relaxing her shoulders a little, as she smiled in response. "And it's Ruby," she prompted him. Kieran was instantly aware of a certain amount of tension revealed in Ruby's gaze.

"Would you like something to drink? Tea or coffee perhaps?"

"No, thank you, nothing." Ruby refused him politely. Taking a seat, she fidgeted as if nervous.

"What can I do to help you?"

"It's not what you can do to help me. That's not why I'm here. I thought it was about time you knew the truth, and it fell on someone's shoulders to talk to you and explain everything, so it falls to me. Afterwards, you can decide what to do about the rest yourself."

"Excuse me, I don't understand." A puzzled expression formed on his face.

Ruby leaned forward slightly. "You see, Kieran, I have to tell you something about my son —" She paused; there was no mistaking the raw emotion of grief as she continued, "Something vital — and what Sophie should have known before she married him. If she had, it might have prevented all this."

At the mere mention of Sophie's name his ears pricked up.

"You have to understand Simon had always been besotted with Sophie, ever since the moment he laid eyes on her. He loved her deeply; they dated for some time. Everything seemed to be taking a natural progression. Then, Simon was deployed overseas, and when he returned home on leave after his last deployment, he finally persuaded Sophie into marrying him." She licked her lips nervously. "Well, the thing is —" She hesitated again, as she shifted uncomfortably in her seat.

There was no mistaking the feeling of trepidation in her voice and tears formed on her lashes. "Whatever it is, Mrs Campbell, you can tell me."

Anxiously, she continued; her features had become drawn and pale. "Have you ever known of an undying bond between a mother and son, Kieran? I'm talking about a bond so strong that a mother would keep her son's secret even after his death."

"Why don't you relax, and try to explain a little more slowly," Kieran advised.

"It was the lies, you see; the very root of the problem. Almost from the very beginning Simon lied to Sophie — and kept lying for years. Before he married Sophie, I begged Simon not to start married life with secrets and lies. I wanted him to be honest with Sophie, but Simon thought if Sophie knew of his problem, she would never agree to marry him. He wanted that above all else."

"So he hid his secret?"

"Simon played a dangerous game; his dishonesty, manipulation and jealousy eventually proved his downfall and destroyed their relationship. My son was convinced the world was against him and he blamed Sophie more than anyone." She gently wiped away the tears on her lashes, before she continued. "The abuse had been sporadic at first. Simon would be fine for a while, and then out of the blue Sophie would be seen with a black eye or bruised face. He'd tried to get help, but in the end, he'd gone too far, and the punishment became unbearable. Their relationship became tempestuous."

"I'm afraid I don't understand what you are trying to tell me, or why."

"There is no easy way of explaining to you — I guess — Simon — he's gone now. My son took his own life three years ago. Before his death, Simon had written to me explaining everything. The way he treated Sophie was unforgivable — he was cruel and controlling, but he was so scared of losing her. But that was only the half of it."

Kieran swore. "What about Sophie?" He stared directly into Ruby's eyes. And the question he didn't want to ask. He closed his eyes. "Did he —" He struggled to form the words to ask, "was Sophie sexually assaulted by your son?"

"I have to explain. You see — Simon, my son — he couldn't father children. It was impossible."

"What!" Kieran sucked in a deep breath. "What are you saying?"

Slowly, Ruby started to explain. "During Simon's first deployment to Iraq, he and his crew were involved in locating a terrorist stronghold on an intel-seeking mission. This was a routine airstrike that went wrong and resulted in Simon giving the wrong coordinates to his crew — while flying too low, the aircraft came under direct fire. The aircraft went down, and most of the crew survived, but the stress and guilt of what had happened crippled Simon emotionally."

"Did he not get help? Talk to someone?"

"He refused point blank to talk about what happened. Then there was the stress and guilt of what happened. That's when he started drinking and taking drugs to get him through the day. Soon he was drinking a bottle of vodka a day and taking more pills than I could count just to blot it out. When he returned home, before the wedding, he continuously blamed himself for the botched mission. And at the time, you have to understand he loved Sophie and was so desperate to marry her, Simon couldn't bring himself to confide in Sophie."

"But he married her all the same."

"He thought things would improve. Instead, things got much worse. He blamed Sophie and made her life a living hell. Eventually, the toll of the overwhelming guilt and the level of alcohol he consumed left Simon incapable of fathering children. But he could never bring himself to tell Sophie, so he punished her instead. They had a very unhealthy marriage by this time."

"So he blamed Sophie?"

"Yes, but that isn't the whole story." The pain and anguish on her face were visible. "What I'm telling you, Kieran, is that it isn't possible for Daniel to belong to Simon."

"I don't understand."

"That was why I thought it was time you knew the truth. And that was why I needed to see you. I knew as soon as I met you — as you watched and worried over Sophie's condition — there was no doubt in my mind that you are Daniel's father. I didn't need to read my son's letter to see what was in front of my eyes."

Suddenly, Kieran slumped back in his chair as if he felt robbed of all his energy. "Why are you telling me this now? What about Sophie? Does she know any of this?"

Ruby ignored his question, and with caution she added, "I have to explain — I know how Simon felt before he died. He'd learnt to live with the guilt of what he'd done to Sophie over the years. When the RAF finally caught up with him, he spent a spell in Colchester military prison, which gave him time to reflect on his behaviour."

"Did he get the help he needed?"

"You see, Simon was suffering from a severe long-term problem of bipolar, brought on by a more commonly known sickness as PTSD and ubiquitous in situations such as his. Some men suffer for many years before it's detected. Simon would go into a very dark place within himself," Ruby explained. "Regret had played a huge part in his healing. I know he'd wanted so much to make amends for the trouble and heartache he'd put Sophie through. He'd always thought he'd have a chance to put things right, but he couldn't take the shame and guilt. Unable to live with so much hurt inside him — he took his own life. Help came too late for my son." Ruby's voice became raw with emotion.

"What of Sophie and the boy?"

"When Sophie finally learned of his death, she returned home to us. She was exhausted, with a young boy in tow, after hiding from my son for seven years. But there was hope in her eyes, and she was optimistic for the future."

"And you never told her any of this?"

"Please remember, Daniel is my only grandson. I wanted so desperately to hang on to a small piece of Simon, or so I believed. I have denied you the right to know your own son. Now, after meeting you, Kieran, and knowing how much you love Sophie, and how desperately she loves you—"

"Sophie loves me?" he repeated, in a dazed voice.

"Yes, didn't you know? I saw it from the very first time you walked into her room, and the way you both looked in each other's eyes. The light in her eyes as she looked at you, and especially the love you both share is visible. She needs you, Kieran, and she owes you to listen. I have no right to put my own selfish needs above a family that truly belong together."

"I don't understand. Has something happened to Sophie?"

She smiled sheepishly. "She doesn't know I'm telling you this, but she needs to hear the truth. Sophie needs to hear it from you."

"I don't understand any of this," he whispered. There was so much to take in.

"No, I grant you that." She patted both hands on her knees. "But the day I received a letter from Simon explaining everything — I didn't realise at the time it was to be his last letter to me. Simon begged me to help him make things right. He knew how much Sophie loved you. He'd always known."

"Then why continue to treat her with such contempt and brutality?"

"He'd hated himself for taking that away from her, and for what he'd become. My son was guilty of many things, but his biggest guilt of all was his love for Sophie. It was only after his death that I discovered just what he had been capable of."

Tears began to show in her eyes. She brushed them away with a clean handkerchief she took slowly out of her handbag placed at her feet. The old woman dabbed at her eyes and having taken a steadying breath said, "I have to tell you his illness had almost driven him to madness, and it took many years for him to face up to the injustice and suffering he'd forced on Sophie. And in some misguided loyalty to my son, I am as guilty."

"What you did was out of love."

"But I'd known the truth of Daniel's parentage, and I chose to keep it from Sophie. I let her believe Daniel was Simon's child. Thinking of believing such a thing kept a part of Simon with me. I know that was wrong now. I didn't want to accept it, but I knew the first moment I looked into your eyes — Daniel is your son."

"Is all this true?" He felt as though someone had gut-punched him. He and Sophie had a son.

"Yes, it's all true," Ruby confirmed, with sorrow in her voice.

"Sophie doesn't want me. What makes you think she will believe any of this when I tell her? She may not want to hear what I have to say."

Ruby made a helpless gesture. "I wouldn't know about that," she said sadly. "It was a cruel twist of fate my son dealt you both. But the fact remains — the time has come to put the past firmly behind us all. She's too proud to tell you, but she loves you."

"What convinces you Sophie still loves me?"

Ruby smiled weakly. "That's for Sophie to explain. But I for one would like to know what you are going to do about it now?"

He smiled wryly. "Now," he considered the situation. "I'm going in search of the woman I love. And this time, I'm not taking no for an answer," he said firmly.

The older woman smiled encouragingly. "That's more like it."

Chapter Twenty

Kieran opened the hospital room door and stood to watch as Sophie emptied the drawer of the bedside cabinet, fetching her clothes from the wardrobe across from her bed. She set the clothes on the bed, folding them neatly as she packed them.

Sophie was fully dressed, so it meant the doctor had released her and decided she was well enough to go home.

As Kieran stood on the threshold of her hospital room, they looked at each other. "May I come in?" Kieran asked, in a subdued voice.

Sophie eventually pulled herself together enough to invite Kieran inside. "Yes, of course."

His smile was bright, but false, as he glanced around the room. Before Kieran continued, his stare wandered lazily over her denim blue jeans and her slim-fitting T-shirt and her pale features. "You're looking better, Sophie," he observed.

She smiled, knowing his comment was far from accurate, but she accepted the compliment gracefully. "Thank you," she responded gaily. She licked her lips. "Would you like to sit down?" She directed him to the seat at her bedside.

"Thank you," he said, as he took a seat and leaned forward slightly. "Sophie, I have something I need to discuss with you — something your ex-husband kept from you. Ruby wanted to explain about the letter, details she couldn't bring herself to tell you —" He sighed heavily. "It's important."

She glanced across at Kieran. The pain and anguish on her face were visible. "I don't want to hear it."

"If you give me a moment, I'll explain everything. Don't you think I deserve a moment of your time — at least that after the way we parted ten years ago?"

He cocked an eyebrow directly at her as she remained silent. "I'm sure you'll find this information as equally fascinating as I did. But then, the Sophie I knew always ran scared from her feelings in the past. Why should I think any differently now?"

"I have not," she fumed.

"Really?" He leaned back in his chair and wearily rubbed his chin. "Forgive me, but when were my feelings ever considered when you disappeared without a trace?"

Sophie swallowed. "You mean about Simon?"

"No, I'm not talking about Simon." Kieran's eyes became dark. "Years ago, I used to think there was more between us than the risk of you not trusting me."

"Me!" Sophie gasped. "Me, not trusting you? How dare you! I never considered for one moment that Simon would try to use me to hurt you. He knew how much I loved you. He discovered you were my only weakness and used it as a weapon against me. Don't you see that?" Tears formed on her lashes. "Everything I did was done only to protect you."

"What do you mean?" He frowned and his probing, dark eyes searched her face.

There was the most prolonged pause. "We were only married a year," Sophie replied at last, deciding the safest precaution was to tell Kieran a modified version. "Our marriage was a mistake. We'd had a huge military guard-of-honour white wedding attended by all his friends. The marriage became a sham almost from the beginning, and it became harder and harder to make it work. In the end, neither of us wanted the burden of being trapped in a loveless relationship. I wanted out. That was before —" Sophie searched for the right words. "By the time I discovered about my son, an abortion was out of the question. It was too late. I didn't want that."

"Just like that, you decided?" Kieran kept his knowledge of her ex-husband to himself.

With her eyes fixed on his face, she replied steadily, "Yes, just like that."

"But you remained in your grandmother's maiden name?"

"For all the obvious reasons, but one will suffice. Simon tried to kill me and assaulted me. I wanted no part of Simon Campbell. That included his name."

Kieran frowned. "You married him, Sophie; you must have loved

310

him once?"

She looked down at her nervous hands resting in her lap. "Simon killed any love I had for him when we became afraid for my safety."

"Afraid?" He sensed her tension. Kieran pinned her with a curious stare. "In what way were you afraid?" He placed a hand lightly over hers in a reassuring hold.

"At first it was the threats. I spent years trying to keep our whereabouts and identity a secret in case Simon found us."

"You kept it a secret from your family?"

She armed herself, giving him a wary look. "Everyone I could protect." She was trying hard to mask the tremble in her voice.

"And me? Where did I fit into this equation?"

Frowning, there was no mistaking what he meant. "You don't know how much I wanted to tell you about Simon back then."

"What about Simon?" He cocked a dark, probing gaze in her direction.

Sophie felt a flush rise in her cheeks, as she squirmed a little in her seat and her chin quivered. "It happened years ago, and I for one would like to leave it there." She reached out for, and toyed with folding a T-shirt as if she needed something else to concentrate on. "What is the point of raking over dead memories, none of which will do either one of us any good."

"I disagree." Kieran refused to let Sophie easily discourage him. "We need to clear up the past. Otherwise, what hope do we have for the future?"

"You seem to be taking an awful lot for granted," Sophie said sharply.

"Maybe," Kieran nodded, smiling, then he sighed. "But will you at least hear what I've got to say?"

"I just can't see what you hope to gain by coming here and dragging up bad memories."

Kieran reached out and placed a hand on hers; she dropped the T-shirt in the bag, and her hand froze at his touch. "Please, give me a chance. If you'll listen, and then if you feel the same — I'll leave and never bother you again." It was a bit of a gamble, but he was hoping for Sophie to give him a chance. "Trust me."

Her brown eyes stared at him; unanswered questions were visible in his frown. "I've been discharged, so —"

He studied his watch, and smiling, he said, "How much time do I have?"

Sophie shrugged indifferently. "Enough. Unless you decide to concede after all and let sleeping dogs lie."

Sophie wasn't doing anything to encourage him in the least, but why should she? But that was fine by him; he knew what he wanted and why he was here in Sophie's room. And one thing was for sure, he wasn't about to let her attitude unnerve him.

It took a few minutes for him to collect himself and arrange his thoughts. He had contemplated what he had planned to say. He rubbed the back of his aching neck. Perhaps, once Sophie knew the truth, she would understand.

"You were saying?" Sophie prompted.

"Yes, let's start with Daniel." Kieran swallowed. "I'm his father?" he asked resolutely.

Sophie stared straight into his eyes, her face pale and her mouth hard. "Why would you think that?" There was a blaze of anger in her eyes. "That's a lie!"

"Is it? Think about it."

She tried to think of Daniel. His adorable, young face visible in her head, with dark hair similar to her shade of colouring. And perfect dark-brown eyes and a smile that could charm the birds out of the trees.

Kieran took a steadying breath. "Ruby came to see me. We had a long talk, and she told me about Simon's injuries and his health condition."

"What health condition?" Apart from the obvious, this was news to her.

"There is something you should know — a secret Ruby has carried for many years."

Her eyes narrowed. "I don't understand — why would she tell you and not me?"

"Ruby thought you might hate her. And she's afraid you'll take Daniel away from her if you know the truth. You and Daniel are all the family she has left."

312

She tugged and pulled her hand until it freed from under his. "I would never do that to her; she's family." She paused and caught a glimmer of something in his eyes. "There is something you're not telling me, Kieran. What is it?"

He gazed deep into her eyes. There was no easy way of telling Sophie without causing her grief. Sighing, he exhaled. "Ruby explained that Simon had found out he was medically unable to father children long before you agreed to marry him."

"If this is your idea of Irish humour, it's not funny." Sophie sat up straight. Tears pricked her eyes as she let out a humourless laugh. "Why would he do that?"

"You have to understand that Simon kept this strictly confidential. He never intended for you to know any of this. His illness had seriously convinced him that he could father children, and one day you would have his child. I don't think even his doctors understood how ill he was at the time."

"Go on," she urged. Knowing there was more to the story.

"Ruby told me you'd agreed to marry him, and after his guilt couldn't take much more, Simon became deeply depressed — he became heavily dependent on drink and other non-prescription medication. Simon had already developed a drinking problem to cope with the mental health issues that he'd tried to keep hidden from you."

"I was all too aware of his drink problems," she retorted.

"He'd become an embarrassment to the RAF. His commanding officer tried to help him, and made arrangements for you to take care of him after your divorce — right?"

"Yes, all that part is true."

Kieran's glare filled with contempt for the treatment she suffered for such a long time. He swore under his breath. "What I can't understand is why the RAF didn't do more to support him. Surely, they knew of the risk involved. He could have killed you in one of his drunken binges and not known what he'd done."

"I trusted the RAF to know they were doing the right thing for Simon."

"Maybe, at the time, they didn't know how to deal with him. Or the seriousness of his condition."

She threw her hands up. "At the time — I felt I owed Simon. I felt guilty because I'd never truly loved him as I should have, and blamed myself; he needed my support, and I divorced him. I thought I had no choice. He'd convinced me it was all my fault."

"No choice! Of course, you had a choice." His anger rose from deep within him. "And none of it was ever your fault."

"You think? What choice did I have? Back then my job involved working as a human-interest writer for the military. The forces could have cancelled my contract at any time." Anger was visible in her tone. "We needed the money. Simon's spending had dug us into a huge financial hole — he borrowed thousands and thousands. The more I earned to pay off the loans — the more he borrowed."

"That doesn't make you responsible for his bad behaviour. Some people are good at controlling others in many ways. He preyed on your sense of loyalty and kindness. You could have trusted me. I would have protected you," Kieran said.

"Do you seriously believe I would have been able to work after Simon had followed through with his threats, especially when he'd finished destroying your career too."

"He could have tried," he replied. "You forget, bullies are only as strong as you allow them to be."

"It wasn't that simple at the time."

"You mean the baby?"

"The doctor told me there were complications surrounding my pregnancy; possibly the baby wouldn't live."

"What does that mean?"

"What you probably don't know is — when I was first taken into hospital after Simon assaulted me, the doctor treating me thought it would be best if it remained uncommon knowledge, or until such a time he thought I could cope with his findings."

"Why do you think that was?"

"I could only assume the RAF doctor must have thought or assumed that I knew of Simon's other health issues—"

Kieran couldn't help himself and he interrupted, "Surely someone should have told you that Simon was medically unfit to father a child."

Sophie frowned, tears already forming on her lashes. "Why would they? Even his mother kept it quiet."

There was no denying that was true. Kieran dropped his icy gaze from her face. "I understand."

"Kieran, you have to believe me — I didn't know that Daniel was your son. I always took great care when — while I was with you. But, something must have happened."

"You never considered me?"

"It wasn't like that."

"Then tell me what it was like?" he urged.

"For months I was recovering in hospital, not knowing which way to turn. Simon was so convincing and hateful; I had no way of knowing you were Daniel's birth father. During the early stages of the pregnancy, I became ill and almost died. The hospital contacted my friends. My friend, Jane, helped me find a home, and get a new job, and she helped me with Daniel while I recovered."

"Sophie — why the fuck didn't you send for me? At least ask for me to come to you afterwards?"

Slowly, she recounted to him the events of that monstrous day. "That last day, Simon came to my house. He had seen you leaving. He went crazy; he was threatening all sorts of crazy, hateful things. But he found my one true weakness, and that was you." Sophie cringed inside.

"You must have been terrified."

"When I saw how angry he was, it was obvious he'd been drinking. His crazed jealousy had overwhelmed him. I tried to reason with him. He just kept up with his threats and saying things over — repeating offensive threats over and over. When he had finally finished abusing me, he knocked me over; while he had me pinned down, I blacked out, or fainted or something because I couldn't remember any more. When I came to, I was in a hospital. I had complications and needed reconstruction surgery on my face after his assault. I spent three months in the hospital before I was told about the pregnancy."

"So," a look of pain flickered in his eyes, and he breathed deeply before continuing, "you accepted what you thought at the time was inevitable — Daniel was Simon's son. While you had already convinced yourself that I would never want you as long as you had another man's child to care for."

315

Sophie sighed. "Yes," she said sullenly. "I want you to understand — I was ill for a very long time, and too afraid to go home to my parents at the risk of him finding me and hurting them. At one time I also had a threatened miscarriage. I — that is — unless you've known of a difficult pregnancy you couldn't possibly begin to understand the state of mind I was in, or how I felt. I didn't want to believe him but I —"

Kieran swore viciously under his breath.

Sophie rubbed the tears away from her eyes with the back of her hand. "You see I felt so guilty about the baby. At first, I didn't even want it. But, after everything that had happened, it wasn't the baby's fault."

"So you shut yourself away — assumed a new name and career to protect yourself?"

Renewed tears stung her eyes as she spoke. "It was like I was living by pure existence. The worst of my illness had passed and then a threatened miscarriage. I began to realise I needed a new life for my child. I had to protect that baby at all costs. That meant living somewhere safe and secure, away from Simon and his threats. After the shock of his death had worn off and I returned home, I made a new life for myself."

"Did he hate you that much?"

"Simon was clever at playing mind games and manipulated people. I thought I could outsmart him — but I was wrong. He found me. I would be constantly on the move, changing addresses and jobs, not daring to return home to my family. I feared for their safety. He would send hate mail — death threats against Daniel and me — and made my life a living hell. That was until his death. I decided to move back home to Lincolnshire. I wanted the chance to make a decent life for my child."

"Didn't you stop and think for one moment — think to question —?"

"For God's sake! You had your whole life ahead of you, Kieran," she interrupted.

"No, I meant, did it never occur to you that I may be the baby's father?"

"No — there was more to it than that. Simon knew he'd hit a raw nerve."

"So you kept hidden rather than face the truth?"

She answered carefully. "I'm not a mind reader, Kieran. I was heavily pregnant by the time I was well enough to travel. And I was painfully aware you had plans of your own. You told me yourself of your plans, and of your parents' hopes and dreams for your career in the army. You've achieved that. You were very young."

"So?"

"Don't you see — I could have ruined everything for you. And although I know how much I loved you — I didn't know how you would feel for instance — about me turning up pregnant, as I thought, with another man's child, at the time. Particularly, if he had a career to think of, I can tell you what was going through my mind. Your career — the army wouldn't have liked it. I can tell you now, how they would have responded — badly. Perhaps now, you can understand why —"

Kieran opened his mouth as if to interrupt her, but she waved a hand up to stop him as she continued, "Please let me finish — I don't want anything left unsaid on my part."

His eyes challenged her, and the tilt of his head was proud. "Go on," he said harshly, at last.

"You have to remember — all of Simon's life I was part of it in some form or other. He had wanted me from the beginning, by means or foul." She bit her lip and looked at Kieran closely, and closed her eyes. "Simon tried to destroy my life — but I couldn't let him destroy yours."

"Is that all?" he asked, finally. "You think you know me so well, don't you?" Kieran waited, then continued, "You never really knew me at all, did you, Sophie? You were my world." Kieran added, "Did you seriously think my love for you was so shallow that I only ever wanted to marry you for you to give me a family?"

"I can see I've achieved nothing in telling you all this."

"I could strangle you for saying that," he grated. "I wish — when I think of all the time we've wasted — not knowing my son. My son, Sophie!"

"That's not what I meant." Sophie cringed at the very force of his words. Sophie could only shiver beneath the full, savage impact of the hurt he had suffered.

He stared at her as if he genuinely would like to strangle her. But something wouldn't let her look away. His intense, dark gaze held her captive. "Then tell me."

"Throughout everything that happened — all I could think about was how much I loved you then."

Then — not now. With one word, Sophie had hurt him deeply.

"Let's face it, you used it to hide behind. You have lived your life in fear and regret. That's not love — that's being a coward."

"That's not true," she denied.

"Yes, it is, and you know it." He raised his voice in anger.

Briefly, she closed her eyes knowing he spoke the truth. She stepped over to the window and placed both hands on his back, forcing Kieran to turn with his head bent, and slowly he turned to face her. His black hair gleamed. He was leaning forward and it made their faces inches apart. She took a deep breath.

"I always wanted the very best for you. I know how much being in the army meant to you. I couldn't let Simon destroy that. And if that meant sacrificing my love for you, and that in turn gave you the happiness and successful career in the army you deserved — I would do the same thing all over again," her voice trailed off.

"And no regrets?"

His eyes narrowed, as she edged her hands across his chest. His head followed her movements. He turned his gaze back to her face, with his dark eyes trained on her face, absorbing every feature.

"I only know I loved you. You were always deep in my heart. I never forgot those sweet, precious moments we shared. Those feelings for you have never wavered."

Before he could say a word, she reached up on her toes and kissed him. She felt his surprise and resistance. Had she lost him for good?

He fought himself to resist her warm advances. Kieran shivered suddenly in response and groaned heavily; he kissed her ardently in return. As soon as she felt his mouth settle on hers, all her inhibitions and the unwelcome feelings of trepidation floated into oblivion.

She melted against him. He wrapped her protectively in his arms. It had been so many years since Sophie and Kieran had last kissed, and such a long time since they'd shared the warm comfort and tenderness of their embrace. Kieran's kisses had become hard and intense, and his hold tightened, which caused an alarming kind of excitement that began to build up inside her. As she clung to him fiercely, she could feel his heart beating frantically; his breathing became as laboured as her own.

He pulled himself free and cradled her face in his large hands. She placed feather-light kisses on the corners of his mouth. "I love you, Kieran, don't ever doubt that."

He paused as if he needed to think. "Do you?"

"I love you with my whole being," Sophie said, as she teased his mouth with the tip of her tongue. "Kieran, what are you doing?"

Sophie was practically sprawled across the bed, as Kieran was scattering pillows in all directions. He smiled wickedly, "I've missed you, Soph." When he said *Soph* in that smooth, velvety voice, it sent shivers up and down her spine. "I've wanted to make love to you on this bed since the minute I first walked in the door and saw you lying there."

"You mean when I was unconscious and hooked up to an IV?"

"Yes, even then." He smiled.

"You have? Are you kidding?" She laughed.

"No. But now you're feeling better." Kieran winked.

She was outraged by Kieran's proposal. "But if we are making out on a hospital bed, the door could open and anyone could walk in. Don't you think that suggestion is a little daring, if not naughty?" She giggled.

He lifted her hand to his mouth, placing a trail of kisses into her palm. "Afraid, Sophie? You know there is a first time for everything," he muttered softly, and his eyes twinkled mischievously.

She glanced over the large bed beneath her. "Kieran, be serious, anyone can see in." It was a plea for his sanity to return to normal. "This is madness," she added, as he moved his hand inside her T-shirt to loosen it from her jeans.

"Hell! You're wearing a bra," he said, as he caressed the lace-covered breast, squeezing it gently as he moved her closer to him. He stroked her in such a way that she swayed helplessly towards him.

"Kieran, please," she whispered huskily.

"Scared? Don't be; it will be a new experience for both of us," he promised. He stood up and gathered her into his arms. "I've waited ten years too long for you already." And he willingly kissed the next protest from her mouth with consuming passion.

"Kieran!" She placed her arms around his waist. His passion was insatiable; how could she ever fight him and win?

"What are you trying to tell me, Sophie?" He tried to coax her gently.

"Is something wrong?" He eyed her suspiciously. "Sophie, you can tell me. No more running away remember. We are a family now; whatever it is, we'll face it together — I promise you."

Absently, he stroked her hair.

"I'm sorry — not knowing about Daniel I mean. If you would like us to check his parentage and have a DNA test, I understand."

He smiled broadly. "Daniel is mine; I just know he is." Giving her a brilliant, toothy smile, he said, "Wait until I tell my folks."

"Kieran," she began apprehensively, "what do you think your parents will make of the situation?"

He shrugged, dismissing her apprehensions as unimportant. "Who cares? But I'm sure knowing my parents as I do — they are going to be thrilled at being grandparents. I think they'd given up all hope that I would find someone to marry, let alone have children."

Sophie was silent.

Kieran closed his eyes. "You will marry me, won't you?"

"Are you sure? Maybe it's a little sudden."

"I don't think a ten-year wait is a *little sudden*." He laughed. "I've been keeping the ring just in case you said yes."

Sophie laughed in response. "Yes, I'll marry you, Kieran."

Sophie threaded her fingers through his and held his hand tightly. "Does that mean we'll be living in military housing?"

A faint frown creased his forehead in concern. "Don't you want to?" he asked, adding, "I know you love living in Lincolnshire, and you have your work to consider. I've been in the army a long time and if—"

As if reading his thoughts, Sophie placed her forefinger over his lips to stop the words. "I know how much you love being a soldier. You do the job because you like helping people — I can accept that. And should you be deployed, we will be waiting for you to come home to. I don't care where we live. I can work anywhere as long as I have you and I know Daniel is happy."

"And what of you — are you happy?"

"More than that — I feel at peace. I've laid my ghosts to rest, forever." She rested her head on his broad shoulder. He held her as if he'd never let her go.

Epilogue

Sophie O'Neill went into labour one year later, on a warm summer's night where the scent of roses drifted on the breeze up the trellised walls of their Lincolnshire country garden home in Corby Glen.

It was precisely a year since the day Sophie had been laid up in a hospital room, and Kieran had re-entered her life and delivered a blow that was a blast from the past.

Just like time itself, ancient and healing, love had survived through it all.

And right now, Kieran was more nervous than Sophie, fussing and fretting as he tried to manoeuvre her, first into the BMW, and then into the nearby hospital, as if he was organising a military invasion.

Sophie tried to get him to calm down and when she insisted on not hurrying despite his panic, he tried to herd the hospital staff instead.

He ordered staff around and demanded attention in true military-style so that no one was in any doubt within a ten-mile radius that the O'Neill baby was going to be born on this very night.

Kieran held her hand throughout the labour and fretted some more. He rubbed her back when she needed him to. He breathed with her when she needed to breathe. He stroked her heated brow with a damp cloth to cool her. And when their baby was born after several hours of labour, he watched in wonder as the woman he loved delivered him a beautiful son.

Lying in the hospital bed, hot, sweaty and exhausted, he realised she'd never looked more radiant than she did right at that moment. She smiled at him; this man beaming with pride who was her husband, who had given her his heart and they had made their first child together and who was giving her another precious child.

He placed a kiss on the baby's forehead, and beaming with pride and joy, he said, "Welcome to the world, Tim, George, Ashley, Tony, Steven, Adam, Liam, Simon, Alex, Matthew, Alan, Daniel, Ben, Andrew and Jordan O'Neill."

Sophie smiled to herself. It seemed the baby's name had grown since they last discussed choosing names, she thought. "Who said anything about Tim, George, Ashley, Tony, Steven, Adam, Liam, Simon, Alex, Matthew, Alan, Daniel, Ben, Andrew and Jordan?"

"Thought the names had a nice ring to them. Don't you like it?"

"Are you kidding?" She smiled. "I love it."

He sighed with relief. "I'm so pleased you said that because I've already messaged everyone in my platoon. Jonesy and his wife, Amy, are flying back from Canada as we speak. Si and Drews are on the way from Qatar and can't wait to meet their new godson. Jacko and Ginger will drop by later with the rest of the guys."

"That's very sweet of them to drop everything to visit our family."

"Are you kidding?" he laughed. "I couldn't stop them. Jonesy asked me for the baby's name, so I gave him what we'd chosen — with few added."

Sophie had to admit she liked the idea that a particular group of men were remembered with such pride and honour. She laughed — she would leave Kieran to argue with the registrar about deciding on which name went first.

"Tim, George, Ashley, Tony, Steven, Adam, Liam, Simon, Alex, Matthew, Alan, Daniel, Ben, Andrew and Jordan, it is."

Words from the men

"Talking for the first time about my time in Afghanistan gave me a feeling of real cleansing."

"Lost mates, really good mates over there. It helped remembering the good times and the antics."

"I was in a really dark place for a long time, talking to someone has helped me a lot."

"Could not have made better friends anywhere else."

"I found a family. And brothers who always had my back."

"Respect wasn't given to us. We earned it!"

"The British Army was the making of me. It taught me a lot."

"Lost both my legs —result of an IED in Helmand. I never lost my spirit."

"Couldn't talk about what happened to me for a long time. Now I'm getting the help I need."

"Been on 3 tours, including Iraq, and I would go again. It's what we train for."

"I missed my family, we got to email and chatted a fair bit."

"My mum sent me care packages which helped a lot."

"I wrote a death letter for my parents before I was deployed. It was the hardest thing I had to do. Thankfully, it never needed posting."

"Went through hell in Helmand. Would do it all again if I needed to."

"I will never eat another Pot Noodle again!"

"Best bunch of mates I have."

"The Army means everything to me."

INFORMATION

In World War I and World War II we associated it as "Shellshock" or "Battle fatigue". ~ Present day we have a different understanding of Post-Traumatic Stress Disorder ~ more commonly known as PTSD.

PTSD ~ A neurological disorder associated with those who served or serving in combat. Shockingly, those suffering today are high, and in some cases unrelated to military service.

The symptoms of those who have PTSD can tell you that they vary enormously. Many of us know PTSD to be a psychological anxiety disorder and it usually occurs after suffering from a bad experience or witnessing a traumatic event — most common is to suffer with emotions such as feelings of guilt (what could have been done to prevent the outcome) and can have a significant impact on a daily routine, making the simplest task a challenging ordeal. For those of us that know so little about **PTSD** — or how to spot the signs — PTSD can be very traumatic, emotionally and physically — symptoms being diverse and suffering from the mildest of stress to the most severe forms of depression.

The most commonly known symptoms are from those who experience **flashbacks, nightmares, repetitive dreams** and **severe anxiety** issues such as **chest pains, heart palpitations, sickness, stomach pains, headaches, sweating, vomiting, trembling, isolating themselves** and being **withdrawn** and eventually have trouble sustaining a relationship and coping with family life. Others would have difficulty **concentrating, confusion, continually feeling on edge and irritable, sleep deprivation, mood swings and anger** issues. While others suffer from severe **depression, phobias, self-harming, and drug/alcohol abuse**.

Over a thousand veterans are reported to be struggling with alcohol or other substance abuse and depression, while around half that figure has been convicted for a violence-related crime. Thousands of veterans in prison could be as a result of mental health issues after serving in combat zones.

Figures are increasing at an alarming rate on the number of others who choose to end their mental health issues or **PTSD** misery by taking their own lives. Over 100 of our serving personnel and veterans involved in combat in Iraq and Afghanistan have taken their own lives since 2003.

Remember — **stress, depression, anxiety, PTSD** and other forms of mental health issues have many faces. **Some symptoms are unrecognisable** — we ignore them, or fail to spot the warning signs too late. There is help available for those suffering — when you accept you have a mental health issue — only then you can start fighting back. Take the first step — talk to someone.

USEFUL CONTACTS — helplines and charities:

Combat Stress (for veterans' mental health) — www.combatstress.org.uk — 24-hour helpline — 0800 138 1619

ABF The Soldiers' Charity — www.soldierscharity.org — 0207 901 8900

Care After Combat — www.careaftercombat.org — 0300 343 0258

Help for Heroes — www.helpforheroes.org.uk

Forgotten Veterans UK — www.forgottenveteransuk.com — 0300 311 0239

Minds At War — www.mindsatwar.com — 0800 031 4368

SSAFA Forcesline — www.ssafa.org.uk — 0800 731 4880

Samaritans — www.samaritans.org —116 123 (UK)

Military Mental Health (for serving personnel and families) 24/7 helpline — 0800 323 4444

Veterans' Gateway — www.veteransgateway.org.uk — 0808 802 1212

Mind — www.mind.org.uk — 0300 123 3393